Stay Hidden

Center Point
Large Print

Also by Paul Doiron and available from
Center Point Large Print:

The Bone Orchard
The Precipice
Widowmaker
Knife Creek

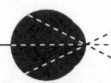

**This Large Print Book carries the
Seal of Approval of N.A.V.H.**

Stay Hidden

Paul Doiron

CENTER POINT LARGE PRINT
THORNDIKE, MAINE

This Center Point Large Print edition
is published in the year 2018 by arrangement with
St. Martin's Press.

The text of this Large Print edition is unabridged.
In other aspects, this book may vary
from the original edition.
Printed in the United States of America
on permanent paper.
Set in 16-point Times New Roman type.

ISBN: 978-1-68324-874-3

Library of Congress Cataloging-in-Publication Data

Names: Doiron, Paul, author.
Title: Stay hidden / Paul Doiron.
Description: Center Point Large Print edition. | Thorndike, Maine :
    Center Point Large Print, 2018.
Identifiers: LCCN 2018018876 | ISBN 9781683248743
    (hardcover : alk. paper)
Subjects: LCSH: Game wardens—Fiction. | Wilderness areas—
    Maine—Fiction. | Murder—Investigation—Fiction. |
    Large type books. | GSAFD: Suspense fiction. | Mystery fiction.
Classification: LCC PS3604.O37 S73 2018b | DDC 813/.6—dc23
LC record available at https://lccn.loc.gov/2018018876

For Ann Rittenberg

We are only falsehood, duplicity, contradiction; we both conceal and disguise ourselves from ourselves.

—BLAISE PASCAL, *Pensées*

1

There were two hunting deaths in Maine that day. And the deer season had barely even begun.

In the morning, a grandfather in Berwick, down on the New Hampshire state line, was out hunting with his son and grandson when he stumbled over a stone wall. His finger slipped and the bullet struck the thirteen-year-old boy in the head. Seeing what he'd done, the old man suffered a heart attack, leaving the traumatized father to run through the woods for help. The last I'd heard, the kid was in critical condition, being airlifted to Boston for emergency surgery. The grandfather had died before the first ambulance arrived.

The Maine Warden Service marshaled all the resources at its command—the Evidence Recovery Team, the Forensic Mapping Team, the Aviation Division, the K9 Team—and rushed them to the scene. Nearly every available officer was called upon to assist in the investigation. Something like thirty wardens in all.

As the newest investigator in the service, I was not one of them.

Two hours after the Bangor office had emptied, I was hunched over a computer, inputting numbers into a spreadsheet, when I received a frantic phone call. There had been another hunting-related death, this one halfway across the state from Berwick. A woman had been shot and killed on an island twenty miles off the coast of Mount Desert.

And now—because no one else was available—I was flying out to Maquoit to determine who was to blame for the shooting of Ariel Evans and whether state prosecutors should file criminal charges against the person.

The village constable who called to report the fatality described it to me as a "horrible, horrible accident," as if bad luck alone were to blame. But *accident* is not a term we use in the Maine Warden Service. Game wardens understand that even when guns misfire or bullets ricochet, when feet stumble or fingers slip, there is always a trail of causation you can follow that will lead you back to an act of culpable negligence. A human being is dead because someone—the shooter, the victim, maybe both—made a mistake that could and should have been avoided.

Wardens don't call these deaths *accidents*.

We call them *homicides*.

I had been a game warden for six years but a warden investigator for only four months. This was my first hunting homicide. The bubble of nausea rising in my stomach had nothing to do with the shuddering of the small plane. I was anxious—no, afraid—that I might mess up the most important case of my career.

It didn't help that the pilot of the windblown Cessna was my recently estranged friend, Charley Stevens. The old man had barely spoken to me since his daughter and I had ended our relationship, back in the summer. My impression was that Charley held me responsible for Stacey's rash decision to flee the state for a new life in Florida.

There is, as I said, always a trail of causation.

There is always someone to blame.

Our brusque meeting at the Hancock County–Bar Harbor Airport had made it clear that a chasm had opened between us. Charley had cordially greeted the two other passengers: my fellow warden Ronette Landry, who had been home with the flu; and a detective for the Maine State Police named Steven Klesko. But my former mentor had only shaken my hand, with pressure but not enthusiasm. There was none of our usual banter. He'd guided Klesko and Landry to their seats in the rear, explained to them that the noise from the propeller necessitated we wear headsets and speak into microphones for the duration of the flight, and offered a few words of warning on the brief but rough ride he was expecting out over the ocean to Maquoit.

"It's just a fifteen-minute frog hop," Charley had said in his backwoods Maine accent, "but

11

fifteen minutes is long enough to reacquaint you with your last meal."

Now that we were airborne, he kept his face forward—his rugged profile like that of some man-shaped rock formation you see up on a mountainside. He was chewing gum so hard the tendons in his neck flexed, as if to excuse himself from having to engage me in conversation.

Nothing else on earth could have made me sadder. Charley Stevens was the closest thing I had ever had to a real father. If I had married his daughter, as I'd long intended to do, he would have become my actual father.

Now what was he?

This day, I supposed, he was just a man flying a plane. Charley had once been the chief pilot for the Warden Service, and although he had retired years earlier, he still volunteered the use of his personal aircraft for emergencies or when the three other planes that constituted our Aviation Division were otherwise engaged. It was happenstance that had brought us together on this blustery November afternoon. The lone available investigator needed a ride to a death scene, and he was the only pilot available to take me.

It took Klesko leaning over my shoulder, his breath sharp with peppermint, to awaken me from my brooding. "Earth to Mike Bowditch."

"Sorry, Steve," I said into the microphone. "What were you saying?"

"I was asking what we know about the victim."

"Her name was Ariel Evans. She was thirty-seven years old. From Manhattan. She was shot in the backyard of the house she was renting. She was hanging laundry."

"Hanging laundry? So how could someone have mistaken her for a deer?"

"That's what the investigator is here to find out," said Charley, speaking for the first time since we'd taken off.

I found his words cheering. Acknowledging me at all seemed a crack in the wall between us. He hadn't yet explained why he'd withdrawn from my life. I assumed he was harboring a grudge against me on his daughter's behalf.

"I'm pretty sure she was a stranger to the island," I said. "And to Maine."

"Why do you say that?"

"Because the constable said she should have known better than to be outside, hanging white underwear from a clothesline on the second day of deer season."

Hunters often don't spot a white-tailed deer until it's running away. They'll see something white move suddenly and they'll take a shot at it. We get our expression *hightailing it* from the way a deer raises his tail as he bolts. The law says hunters are not permitted to fire without identifying their targets first, but it still happens. They get buck fever and start blasting.

"It sounds like the constable is blaming Ariel Evans for being the victim," Klesko said.

"That happens with every hunting homicide," I said.

Steve Klesko was the youngest detective in the Maine State Police, a year or two older than me. Some people might have called us peers; others, greenhorns. He hailed from the northernmost reaches of the state and had been a hockey star at the University of Maine before washing out of the minor leagues while his more talented teammates went on to fame and fortune in the NHL. The experience had left him with a dented nose, a dead tooth, and a fierce determination to succeed in his second-choice career as a state trooper. No one outworked Steven Klesko.

He had thick black hair that grew low on his forehead and a single unitary eyebrow. Back at the airport, he'd been dressed in a close-fitting charcoal suit that bulged whenever his biceps and deltoids contracted, but before boarding, he had switched his sharkskin jacket for a leather bomber and a pair of aviator sunglasses.

Despite the heater at my feet, I couldn't get warm inside the drafty plane. I turned my face to the vibrating window. Droplets from invisible clouds ran like tears along the Plexiglass, but it was a hell of a view. Below us, the stony summits of Acadia National Park were patches of dark gray against the deep greens, rust reds, and softer grays of the late-autumn forest. I could make out the visitors' center atop Mount Cadillac—the first place in America to see the sunrise for much of the year—with its tiny tourists scrambling over ledges and its parking lot of full Matchbox toys. November was too late for leaf-peeping along the Maine coast, but the landscape had a raw, russet beauty.

In any season, Mount Desert Island—with its barren peaks, its pristine lakes, its genteel carriage roads—was a wonder to behold.

To my right I could see a long arm of the sea inset with picture-postcard villages. Somes Sound is the only fjord on the east coast of the United States. Other Europeans probably navigated its chill waters before the French explorer Samuel de Champlain "discovered" the island in 1604. Basque fishermen almost certainly dried their netted cod along its cobblestone beaches. Archaeologists have speculated that the Vikings had even made it this far south on their epic voyages. If so, the lonely fjord must have reminded those wayfaring Northmen of their distant homeland. Maquoit Island was also rumored to have been visited by the Vikings. A promontory there was named Norse Rock for its (probably fake) runelike carvings.

Once again, Klesko was forced to drag me out of my dark labyrinth.

"Do we know what she was doing on Maquoit?"

15

Ronette Landry's stuffed-up voice came over our headsets: "Ariel Evans was a famous journalist. Her first book was a finalist for the Pulitzer, but her new one is even better. I read it in practically one sitting."

Ronette came from a big Franco-American family in the former mill town of Sanford. It was *une famille*, not unlike my late mother's. Ronette had olive skin, dark curls she seemed comfortable letting go gray, and copper-brown eyes that were always alert with curiosity. Landry was considered the best evidence analyst in the service and would normally have been considered essential to the investigation down in Berwick. I was grateful she'd dragged herself out of her sickbed to help me.

"What's her book about?" Klesko asked.

Because he was seated behind me, I couldn't see what he was doing, but I had the impression he was taking notes.

Ronette coughed into a wad of tissues. "Ariel went undercover among these neo-Nazis in Idaho, and she was imprisoned in their compound when they learned she was a reporter. They dry-fired guns at her head, threatened her with rape. The story of her escape was thrilling."

"So she was probably out on Maquoit writing another exposé," said Klesko. "It's not like November is peak tourist season."

"I can't imagine the islanders would have wel-

16

comed a reporter," Ronette said. "I've always heard the lobster wars are wicked fierce on Maquoit."

"If you dragged the bottom, I'm sure you'd find ghost traps galore," said Charley.

In the language of fishermen, a ghost trap is one that has been severed from the buoy that marks its location. Unmoored, it may bounce around on the rocky seafloor or get lost in the kelp forests that grow so thick in the Gulf of Maine. Violent storms, such as the nor'easters that lash the coast from September into April, frequently produce a bumper crop of ghost traps. So also do the equally violent feuds that occur between lobstermen. Some fisherman will take offense at his neighbor, whom he thinks is infringing on his territory. Or whom he suspects is screwing his wife. Maybe drugs are the cause of the conflict. Heroin is as easy to score as tobacco in Maine's fishing communities, where almost all financial transactions occur in cash.

We were passing over the archipelago south of Mount Desert. I have heard Maine's islands described as looking like puzzle pieces, but at that moment they resembled nothing so much as the shards of a plate shattered in a fit of rage.

Soon nothing was beneath us but frigid blue water.

I could see the shadow of our plane following us, almost furtively, along the broken surface of

17

the ocean. It seemed to be playing hide-and-seek between the whitecaps. The weak sun hung low in the south. How many hours of daylight did we have left? Not many.

Under normal circumstances a boat would be carrying a contingent of wardens to the scene, but the investigative teams were all downstate. That left Landry and me. Charley, too. My friend and mentor had been a patrol warden before the position of investigator had been created. He'd seen more than his share of fatalities in the woods. And he'd proven in courts of law that many of those deaths were not what they'd appeared to be.

"I've never been out to one of these offshore islands," said Klesko.

"Really?" Ronette Landry was as surprised by this admission as I was.

At least he doesn't pretend to know more than he does, I thought. Most of the state police detectives of my acquaintance were not humble.

"I'm a farm boy from Aroostook County," he said. "How many people live out here year-round?"

"I'd be surprised if it was more than a hundred," said Charley. "All these old fishing outposts are dying off as the groundfish disappear and the oceans warm up. Lobsters are moving north in the Gulf of Maine. Give it a few years and Maquoit will go dead in the off-season, too."

In other words, the fate of the lobster was the fate of the island.

"That's it up ahead," Charley said.

"So soon?" Klesko said.

"The flight's only fifteen minutes by air, but it's two hours by ferry."

Through the trembling windscreen I watched Maquoit grow larger as we approached. It lacked the ridge-backed mountains of Isle au Haut, to the west, and the surf-pounded cliffs of Monhegan, to the south.

What it possessed in abundance was fog. The American Meteorological Society had anointed Maquoit Island the foggiest place on the Atlantic seaboard. Whole weeks would pass without the mist lifting, and the daily mail plane would be unable to land. The constable had told me that the island had been socked in at first light, but the fog had burned off with the rising sun and the coming of an east wind.

Charley tilted the plane so the detective could catch a view of the village on the north and west sides of the island and the lighthouse at the southern tip. Ten or twelve lobsterboats floated in the one sheltered harbor. There was a vast, tweed-colored wetland at the center, dotted with duck ponds. But most of the island was cloaked in forest. The storm that had blown through Maine on Halloween had stripped leaves from the deciduous trees—the maples, beeches, and

19

apples—but the spruces still bristled with dark boughs that concealed everything beneath them from view.

Some places, when seen from the air, look wide-open and exposed. Naked even. With Maquoit it was the opposite: you noticed how much of the island was hidden.

"Are those deer on the beach?" Landry said. "What are they doing?"

There must have been a dozen lithesome animals emerging from the dunes and roaming around the cobbles.

"Eating kelp," said Charley.

"Have you ever seen that before?" I asked.

"In Alaska once. Never in Maine. Deer only eat seaweed when they can't get enough of their usual browse."

Klesko clutched the back of my seat. "Wait a minute. I just realized something. We're twenty miles from shore. How did deer get all the way out here?"

"It's a long, sad story," said the pilot.

"What happened?"

But it was too late for that. We had already started our descent.

2

Charlie brought the Cessna in from the south. From this angle, the runway appeared fore-shortened. My gaze fastened on the airplane-crushing wall of spruces at the end. Reflexively, I pushed my Bean boots against the floor as if braking a car. But Charley was the best pilot I'd ever known. We bounced off the ground, then bounced again before he finally set us down with twenty yards to spare. I heard Landry let out a gasping breath over the intercom.

"Hope no one had to upchuck," Charley said.

There were murmurs that we'd all managed to avoid vomiting.

I hadn't wanted to admit it while we were aloft, but I had never set foot on Maquoit before either. This was terra incognita for me as much as it was for Steve Klesko.

There are fifteen islands off the coast of Maine that are populated year-round. On one end of the spectrum are the floating suburbs of Casco Bay, where well-heeled islanders commute daily into the city of Portland to work and shop. On the other end is the lonely outpost of Matinicus, which is so far from land that the ferry makes only a single trip a month in the winter. Maquoit fell close to the forsaken side. That was my uninformed sense of the place anyway.

The airfield was lined with shipping containers, no doubt filled with the islanders' trash to be taken ashore, the days of dumping municipal waste being over. There was a paved helipad for medical evacuations. But the only vehicle present was a backhoe that reminded me of a dinosaur sculpture rendered in rusted steel.

"Where is everybody?" Landry asked as we taxied down the dirt strip.

"Good question," I said.

Klesko removed his headset and unbuckled his shoulder belt before we'd even come to a stop. "What did you say the constable's name was again?"

"Radcliffe," I said. "I called him before we left the mainland to say we'd be here in fifteen minutes. He said he'd meet us."

After Charley cut the engine, the only sound was the wind buffeting the fuselage. When I opened the door, I was surprised by how balmy the breeze felt. It was at least ten degrees warmer on Maquoit than it had been on the mainland. Dead leaves whipped past, and I had to raise a hand to keep the windblown dust from my eyes.

"I guess we wait," said Charley.

He was dressed in his usual "uniform" of green Dickies, green button-down shirt, and green ball cap. It was the sartorial legacy of the thirty years he'd spent as a warden.

Landry wore the real-deal uniform: military-style fatigues with an olive-green ballistic vest, blaze-orange watch cap with the Maine Warden Service logo, black boots, and a black leather belt equipped with the typical tools of the police trade, most notably her big SIG Sauer P226 chambered for .357 rounds. She'd also brought along a laptop, a hard case containing a space-age surveying device used for forensic mapping called a total station laser, and duffels filled with any and all equipment we might need to process the death scene.

Looking at Ronette, dressed like a true game warden, I felt yet again like a phony.

I had wanted so desperately to become a warden investigator, but now I couldn't pass a mirror without seeing an impostor.

I buttoned the top button of the wool peacoat I wore over my fisherman's sweater and corduroys. Most days now, I wore a jacket and tie to work, but not when I was going this far into the field. It still seemed weird not to put on a uniform in the morning, strange to run my hand through hair that was short by most standards, but longer than the buzz cut I'd worn for years. My supervisor, Captain Jock DeFord, had explained my new station this way: "As an investigator, Mike, you are for all intents and purposes a plainclothes detective. When someone looks at you, the last thing we want them to see is a game warden."

Then he'd taken away the snazzy patrol truck I'd briefly been assigned. My new ride was a nondescript, no-frills Jeep Compass.

Charley's carry-on luggage consisted of a trapper's basket made of woven strips of ash with leather shoulder straps. A Native American friend of his had made it for him.

I'd brought my own gear, as well as an emergency change of clothing, in a canvas rucksack and a battered leather carryall. Clipped to my belt was my badge and my SIG Sauer P239: a new sidearm for a new job. It was a compact version of the gun Ronette carried. I readjusted the paddle that cushioned it against my side.

"You never finished your story about the deer," Klesko said to Charley.

The old man relished nothing else so much as spinning a yarn. "They didn't swim out here, although I did see a deer cross Moosehead Lake once. Twenty miles of salty seas would've been past the limit of even that powerful buck. Back in the fifties, the State of Maine, in its wisdom, decided the poor people of Maquoit might enjoy deer hunting as much as the landlubbers. So some biologists trapped thirteen deer and ferried them out here in crates. Two died on the sea voyage. Three died their first week on the island. The rest prospered."

I chimed in, "That's putting it mildly. My

ex-girlfriend told me—" I caught myself as Charley's face began to harden. But it was too late for me to stop. "My ex-girlfriend used to be a Maine State wildlife biologist, and she said that the prime carrying capacity out here would be ten deer per square mile. The current estimate for Maquoit, based on our most recent survey, is seventy deer per square mile."

The detective spit out his peppermint gum. "No wonder they're eating seaweed."

"And most of the deer are infested with Lyme-disease-carrying ticks," added Landry. "I'd recommend you check yourself regularly, Steve."

Klesko glanced down at his shiny wool pants with concern.

Landry reached into one of her bags and found blaze-orange safety vests for us to wear. "These won't help against the ticks, but they might save us from the same fate as Ariel Evans."

I didn't know Ronette Landry well, but we had a couple of mutual friends: my former sergeant, Kathy Frost, now retired; and Dani Tate, who had transferred to the state police because of chauvinism she had encountered in the Warden Service. Their departures meant that Ronette was one of only three female game wardens in a force that numbered over 130 officers.

I removed my phone from its belt holster to call my supervisor to tell him I had arrived on

25

the island. As head of the Investigation Team, Jock DeFord was among the many wardens at the scene in Berwick. I landed in his voice mail and kept my message brief.

Just as I was finishing, two pickups came rumbling over the hilltop from the direction of town. The first was a piebald Toyota Tacoma. It had once been white but was now extensively patched with Bondo and splotched with rust. The second was a quicksilver GMC Sierra 3500 Denali that appeared to have recently rolled off the car dealer's lot.

The trucks pulled up beside each other, and the drivers got out.

Somehow I knew that the owner of the Tacoma was the island constable. Andrew Radcliffe had a reedy voice that had made me imagine him as a little fellow. He began waving vigorously as if we might have missed seeing him otherwise. "Hello there!"

"Radcliffe?"

"Are you Warden Bowditch?"

"I am."

"You don't happen to be related to the North Haven Bowditches?"

"For their sake, I hope not."

I guessed that he was in his midforties. He had wavy brown hair and long sideburns. His complexion was milk white except for two of the rosiest cheeks I'd seen on an adult. Even though he was dressed in a Sperry yachting jacket and docksiders, he reminded me of a Yorkshire farmer who'd spent the day tending his sheep on the windblown moors.

"I apologize for being late!" He had an upper-crust Boston accent that I'd assumed had died with the Kennedy brothers. "I didn't want to leave the scene without someone to watch over it. I had to wait for school to get out so that Beryl McCloud could take over. She was Ariel's friend."

We shook hands and I introduced my companions.

I had expected Radcliffe to have brought along the self-confessed shooter. On the phone, he'd left me with the firm impression that Kenneth Crowley was a teenager. I had no clue who the white-haired man with him was.

The stranger wasn't particularly tall, but he was remarkably broad across the chest and back, almost grotesquely so, with ogre arms and two of the largest hands I'd ever seen. He wore a short-brimmed Greek fisherman's cap, a T-shirt better suited for summer, canvas pants held up by clip-on suspenders, and XtraTuf boots. His jaw was square, tan, and framed by mutton-chops.

"This is Harmon Reed," said Radcliffe.

I said, "You led me to believe the hunter who shot Ariel Evans was a kid."

Reed let out a booming laugh. "I didn't shoot anybody. Nor did that whelp, Kenneth Crowley."

This surprising pronouncement left us speechless for a long time.

Then Klesko said, "Are you saying he's recanted?"

"*Recanted* is the wrong word," said Reed. "The boy never confessed."

The entire reason we'd come out to the island with so few people was because the case had been presented to me as open-and-shut. A young deer hunter had shot a woman, and he had confessed. The plan was for him to walk us through the scene while he provided us with a statement. I'd already arranged for a boat, the *Star of the Sea*, to transport the body back to the mainland and had assumed I would be taking Crowley in for booking. We were all supposed to be home by nightfall.

The spots on the constable's cheeks blossomed into red roses. "When I called you, I was under a mistaken impression. It's entirely my fault."

"Has someone else come forward?" I asked.

"I'm afraid not."

Landry stepped up. She and the constable were the same height. "It would be helpful if we could postpone these questions until after we've done an examination of the body and the scene. If this Crowley guy has recanted, we're going to need to preserve and record whatever evidence we can so the medical examiner can establish the time of death."

"We need to take two vehicles," said Radcliffe. "Gull Cottage is on the south end of the island."

"The warden can ride with you, Andy." Harmon Reed pronounced the constable's name *An-day*. "I'll take the rest of our guests in the GMC."

"And who would you be, Mr. Reed?" Charley's tone was amiable, and he had a big grin pasted on his mug. But an unmistakable challenge showed in his bright eyes.

The fisherman paused to give the pilot a close inspection. It wasn't just their advanced ages that set them apart from the rest of us. Both of these old men had spent their lives outdoors in dangerous professions. Something unsaid passed between them.

Radcliffe let out a rabbity laugh. "Harmon's the harbormaster. And the first assessor. And chair of the planning board. Gee, Harmon, what don't you do out here?"

Reed kept his gaze on Charley. "I'm not usually the taxidriver. But these are extraordinary circumstances."

"I'd like to ride with the constable as well," said Klesko.

"I only have room for one," Radcliffe said, almost with embarrassment.

For a split second, I worried the detective might try to usurp my place.

In Maine, hunting homicides are initially investigated by game wardens. But if the evidence begins to suggest that the killing was deliberate, responsibility passes to the state police. It was why both of us had been sent here.

Steve Klesko and I had only met a few months earlier. One of my charges as the new investigator in Division B was to get to know my counterparts in other law enforcement agencies: the state police, the sixteen sheriff's offices, the FBI, the DEA, the ATF, the Border Patrol, the U.S. Marshals office. Anyone with whom I might have cause to work in the future. For Klesko and me this investigation was the equivalent of a blind date.

"No problem," said the detective. "You're the primary on this, Mike. You ride with the constable." Klesko's grin exposed his gray tooth. "But take good notes!"

Radcliffe's pickup had more dents than the sole survivor of a demolition derby. As I reached for the door handle, I noticed that Charley was hanging back in the shadow of the Cessna's wing. I told the constable to wait and made my way back to the pilot.

"You're not coming?"

"Figured I'd stay with the plane."

Torn clouds cast a shadow over the flattened hilltop. "I was hoping to have your help."

"You're an investigator now, Mike. You shouldn't need my hand-holding."

The words stung, even more than he might have intended. Charley almost never used my first name. He usually called me "son" or "young feller." But that was before Stacey had bolted.

To make matters worse, he was absolutely right. I was supposed to be capable of managing a homicide investigation without the help of a seasoned warden. The state had given me the authority to do the job and expected me to do it.

"Is there a problem, gents?" Reed bellowed.

Charley scratched his lantern jaw. "Why's he in such a god-awful hurry, I wonder."

"I don't buy the concerned-citizen act."

"Nor do I."

"There's something strange going on here, Charley. First Radcliffe said that Crowley confessed. Now he says it was all a misunderstanding. Meanwhile, the island patriarch seems to be running the show. Every time Andrew Radcliffe says something, I check to see if Reed's mouth is moving."

The last bit coaxed a chuckle out of Charley. He pulled his ball cap down over his forehead as if readying himself to step out into a storm. He patted the wing of his plane the way one might a skittish horse.

Finally, he permitted himself a smile. "I guess the old girl will be all right in my absence."

31

3

When I opened the passenger door, I was startled to see that Radcliffe had brought his dog with him. The midsize animal was shaggy gray with brown patches and so old that her beard had turned snowy. She had rheumy eyes glazed with cataracts. Her heavy tail thumped a few times as I climbed onto the running board.

"This is Bella," her owner said. "She's a Spinone. Most people hear that as 'spumoni.' It's an Italian hunting breed."

The exotic dog moved down to the carpet at my feet, and I rubbed her behind the ears as I positioned my legs around her.

I have always loved dogs. It still surprised people—no one more than me—that I didn't own one. Most wardens did. Most wardens were also married with children. I'd come close to marrying Stacey. And I'd come close to adopting a wolf-dog named Shadow, before he escaped into the woods near Canada. There had been sightings of the magnificent black animal in the months since, often in the company of an honest-to-goodness she-wolf. Not a day passed when I didn't wonder how the canine pair were doing.

Every inch of the cab was coated with sawdust.

There were no seat belts and, I was guessing, no functioning air bags. On the mainland the Tacoma would have failed inspection in a millisecond, but the state seemed to take a laxer stance on the islands. My first patrol district had included Monhegan, where some of the lobstermen drove pickups that were held together by bailing wire, duct tape, and bumper stickers.

"So I guess I should explain about Kenneth Crowley." The constable seemed more relaxed outside Harmon's intimidating presence. "I apologize for the confusion. I should have gotten the full story before—"

"If you wouldn't mind, Andy, I need you to start at the beginning."

"I prefer Andrew."

"Andrew it is."

I removed my iPhone from my pocket, brought up the video recorder, and focused the camera on the constable. The days of paper notes were gone. These days, prosecutors wanted all of our interviews videoed.

Radcliffe eyed the device warily. "You understand I'm not a proper law enforcement officer? I've never been to the police academy or had any real training. I'm a wooden-boat builder by trade. Island constable is an elected office. It's only a title you get for a couple of years until the next election. We don't usually have any trouble or at least nothing that rises to the level of criminal offenses. Most problems we can handle ourselves without having to trouble the Hancock County sheriff. I don't even own a handgun."

We started off down the hill with Reed keeping his distance so as not to soil his truck with the soot from Radcliffe's tailpipe.

Andrew seemed to be in no particular rush. "But if something happens—if there is an accident or a medical emergency—I'm supposed to be the one people call. And then I get in touch with first responders on the mainland. If it's a medical emergency, I call the LifeFlight helicopter. If it's a dispute that's escalating to violence, I call the sheriff. In this case, I called the Warden Service. Maquoit is probably the last place you expected to get a call about a hunting accident."

Incident. Not *accident.*

While he'd been rambling, I'd been noticing the devastation along the road. Every edible leaf and twig had been nibbled away to a height of five feet. That was the limit a large deer could reach standing on his hind legs, and it was called the browse line. I'd never seen one so pronounced. There was still plenty of vegetation, especially of the introduced or invasive variety: barberry, knotweed, multiflora rose. Species of plants that deer either could not or would not eat.

I still couldn't understand how Radcliffe

could have gotten something as important as the identity of the shooter so significantly wrong.

"How and when did you hear that Ariel Evans had been killed?"

"Harmon called me. I wrote down the time. It was eleven a.m. Sharp."

"Reed called you?"

"Kenneth Crowley is his wife's nephew. I misunderstood what Harmon told me. I thought that Kenneth had been the hunter who'd shot Ariel when, in reality, he just happened to stumble on her lying dead in her yard."

"Why didn't Crowley contact you himself? You're the constable."

Radcliffe looked confused. "But Harmon's his uncle. Ken's just a kid, and it seems he panicked when he found the corpse and reached out to someone he trusted. You have to understand my position out here. I'm a former summer person. My mother still owns our family cottage, Clovercroft, in Marsh Harbor. We call it a cottage, but it's really a mansion. I've spent eleven winters here now, but the native islanders are never going to fully trust me."

It was the same up and down the coast of Maine. The one thing poor Mainers had over wealthy interlopers was their ability to withhold their acceptance. "Did you speak with Crowley yourself?"

"Eventually, yes. But not until after I'd called

35

your office. I drove to Harmon's, and that was when I realized my mistake."

"It didn't occur to you to bring Crowley along to meet us at the plane?"

"We didn't see the point. Maquoit's an island. It's not like Kenneth's going anywhere. We figured you'd want to examine the body first. We told him you'd be by later to take his statement."

I glanced into the dusty side mirror to study the truck behind us. "By 'we' you mean Harmon and yourself?"

He made a vaguely affirmative noise.

"When we get to this Gull Cottage, I want you to call Kenneth Crowley and tell him to get his ass on down there. I need that kid to walk me through the scene. We have limited daylight to work with, and the last thing I want is to go searching for him."

I saw the first house up ahead: an unoccupied-looking saltbox, no doubt a summer rental, with vacant flower boxes in the windows and a dead lawn strewn with wet leaves. The salt air had already begun to dissolve the paint that had been applied to the trim earlier that spring. This far offshore, fog could be as corrosive as carbolic acid.

"How can you be sure Kenneth Crowley didn't shoot Ariel Evans?"

"His rifle hadn't been fired. There was still oil in the barrel."

I fought the impulse to roll my eyes. "How do you know he didn't clean the gun after he shot her?"

"He didn't have a chance. He went straight from Ariel's cottage to Harmon's house in Marsh Harbor."

I put aside the probability that Crowley might have lied about his movements. "Harmon doesn't own a gun-cleaning kit he might have let his nephew-in-law use?"

Radcliffe reacted as if I had showed him a shocking photograph of a lady doing something unladylike. "Absolutely not! Harmon probably owns a cleaning kit. But he wouldn't have assisted Kenneth in covering up a crime. You're going to do ballistic tests, aren't you?"

"If we can locate the bullet."

When Radcliffe scratched his head, sawdust fell from his curls like dandruff. "The results will prove Kenneth's telling the truth. The young man was actually being a good citizen, reporting what he found. I'd die if I thought I'd gotten him into trouble with the law through my own stupidity."

How could Andrew Radcliffe not understand the import of his own words? If Crowley had only discovered the dead woman, it meant that someone else had killed her and was still roaming the island. I decided to tack my sails to approach the constable from a new direction.

"Tell me about Ariel Evans."

"I can't say that I knew her well enough to answer that question."

"How long had she been on the island?"

"Since the beginning of September. It's rare that people rent houses that late since so few of our buildings are winterized. She was staying at Gull Cottage, which is the last place before the Gut. That's the channel between Maquoit and Stormalong."

"Stormalong?"

"It's a small island off the southwest end of Maquoit. More like a hundred-acre rock, actually."

"Did you ever meet her yourself?"

"I ran into her a few times at Graffam's Store and the dining room of the Maquoit Inn before it closed for the season. She was quite attractive. Beautiful by island standards. Outgoing, too. She seemed fun, you know?"

"No, I don't know. How did she seem fun?"

"She used to go to the Trap House every night. We don't have any bars here. The Trap is kind of an emptied-out warehouse where the lobstermen hang out and drink. It's an ancient rule that outsiders aren't permitted there. No exceptions—until Ariel, that is."

"You said there were rumors about what she was doing."

"We knew she was a writer. And she wasn't

shy about boasting about all the books she sold and the prizes she'd won."

"Ariel never told anyone what she came here to write about?"

"Not that I ever heard. At first, we thought she was doing a follow-up on her Nazi book. There are two brothers here—the Washburns—who post a lot of filth online. But then we noticed she was spending her days over on Stormalong."

"I thought you said it was an uninhabited rock."

"I never said it was uninhabited. Someone lives over there. I guess you'd call him a hermit."

Bella whined in her sleep as if she was having a nightmare. I reached out a hand to comfort her. "A hermit?"

"His name's Blake Markman, and he's lived alone there for twenty years, give or take. He came here from Hollywood. His father was a studio boss, and Blake was a producer or something. But there was some sort of accident involving his wife. She died in a fire at his beach house. Afterward, Blake bought Stormalong and moved out there for good. To look at the guy, you'd never know he was a multi-multimillionaire. His beard is long, and he raises Icelandic sheep and dresses in sheepskins. He almost never comes to Maquoit, and he hasn't visited the mainland in decades. A writer for *Vanity Fair* tried for years to get him to talk, but it never happened."

Bella had begun to snore peacefully again at my feet. "How did Ariel succeed?"

"She charmed him, I imagine. She'd row herself over there and spend hours talking with him."

We swung a hard left along a deeply rutted trail that entered what had once been a cultivated apple orchard but had long been untended. The trees were crooked and twisted, almost human in their deformities. The branches badly needed pruning, and upstart shrubs were growing around the roots, eager to steal the sunlight away from the gnarled fruit trees.

Then I saw the deer in the road up ahead. Two does were grazing among some fallen apples the size of babies' fists. The fruit looked brown and half-rotten. The deer were so gaunt I could see their ribs articulated through their grayish winter fur.

As the Tacoma rumbled past, the gracile animals trotted into the goldenrod. They flared their white tails in annoyance. But they didn't spook the way normal deer would have. They waited patiently until both vehicles had passed, and the dust had settled, and then they returned to their beggar's banquet.

I had been a hunter since my teens, and I had never seen whitetails behave this strangely.

With deer so clueless and so abundant, Maquoit should have been the last place in Maine where a hunting homicide would occur. And with so few hunters in the woods, what were the odds that one of them would happen to shoot the only stranger on the island?

4

Eventually, we emerged from the orchard, and there was Maquoit's famous marsh stretched out before us. It was mostly sedge with tussocks of cattails scattered about, and here and there, muddy domes of rushes where muskrats had built their houses. A six-point buck raised his nose from a pool where he was drinking. His antlers seemed askew: asymmetrical in a way that suggested defects in the genome. He snorted and sprang away at our approach, but stopped to watch us from the edge of the alders, well within rifle range.

"That's a good-sized deer for this island," said Radcliffe. "In my hunting days, I would have—"

I perked up at that. "You don't hunt anymore?"

He reacted to my question as if it contained a booby trap. "Not for years. I no longer even own a rifle."

"Why'd you stop?"

He gave a sad laugh. "I happened to put a sheet under the last deer I hung from the meat pole. Within a few hours it was crawling with ticks. I burnt that sheet and never hunted again."

I couldn't blame him. "Can you give me an estimate of the number of hunters on the island?"

"Excluding poachers who'll take a deer any time of the year?"

"I'm looking to identify everyone who might own a deer rifle and take it out in the woods."

"Fifteen? Twenty? That's out of a population of eighty-nine people, last time we counted. It's hard keeping track of exactly how many folks are on the island on any given day."

"Fifteen to twenty hunters seems low."

"The deer are so skinny and sickly. There's barely any meat left on them after you do the butchering. And they're so tame. They'll eat a peanut butter sandwich out of your hand. People say it's like shooting one of your pets. The community is reaching a breaking point. Vaughn Brewster—he owns Westerly, the biggest place on the island—offered to pay two hundred thousand dollars for a professional sharpshooter to cull the herd, but the town voted against him. People said, 'We know how to peel ticks off, thank you very much.' We've had close to twenty cases of Lyme disease on Maquoit this year. That's not counting the visitors who might have gotten sick. Now there's that fatal Powassan virus to worry about. A tick bites you, and a week later you're dead of meningitis or encephalitis. Have you heard about that one?"

"I'm a game warden, Andrew. Deer are my business."

The constable gave me another of his blushing

43

smiles. "I keep forgetting that you're not a detective. It's the way you're dressed. I didn't even know warden investigators existed until I spoke with you on the phone."

I glanced at the sleeping dog so Andrew wouldn't see me scowl. In the state of Maine game wardens are fully authorized officers of the law with all the same arrest powers as state troopers. Klesko and I had both graduated from the Criminal Justice Academy. We were both police officers. We just happened to have very different beats.

"We don't get wardens out here that often," Radcliffe continued. "There's not even one assigned to the island at the moment. Hasn't been for ages."

He didn't have to tell me that. The one person who could have helped me the most would have been the district warden. But the last man to have patrolled this remote island was enjoying his retirement on a Galveston beach.

"In fact, we don't get many police officers at all." Radcliffe smiled. "And when we do, there's this sudden hush. All the ten-year-olds driving trucks immediately stop. Mostly we prefer to handle our own problems. No need to bring in outsiders."

"I'm going to need a list of those fifteen to twenty names you mentioned."

"Is that really necessary?"

"It's nonnegotiable."

Radcliffe fell into a funk.

I began to wish I'd spent more time studying a map of Maquoit. My inner compass told me that we were pointed nearly due south, taking a route parallel to the village. The Gut, which Radcliffe had mentioned, should be coming into view any second. Ariel Evans must have chosen her rental house to be as near as possible to Stormalong and its mysterious hermit.

Radcliffe confirmed my guess. "This is Gull Cottage up ahead."

A golf cart was parked in the road effectively blocking the nonexistent traffic. Somebody had spray-painted the club car with psychedelic colors. Radcliffe had mentioned leaving a woman to watch the scene and, presumably, chase off busybodies. I'd made a note of her name: Beryl McCloud. I pictured a bosomy matron with gray hair.

We pulled to a stop, and I got my first look at the rental house. The quaint saltbox had a yellow porch, a yellow door, and yellow trim, and it stood alone in a field bounded by a perfectly rectangular stone wall. Someone had constructed a small dolmen, a stack of balancing rocks, in the weeds. A sign made of a cedar shingle identified the sculpture as LE PETIT MENHIR. A bicycle was leaning against the steps, a kayak was chained to a fir tree at the edge of the property, and two cords of firewood were stacked beneath wet blue tarps. The faintest trace of smoke was rising from the chimney.

This was an occupied house. Or it had been until a few hours ago.

A young, red-headed woman emerged around the corner of the building and came striding across the grass to meet us. "Andrew! Finally!"

Despite her baggy sweater, you could tell she was a beanpole. She walked with her arms wrapped tightly around herself, like a young girl self-conscious of her new breasts. She wore patched jeans, Birkenstock sandals, and cat-eye sunglasses that seemed deliberately ironic in their nod to Hollywood glamour.

Andrew Radcliffe whispered in my ear, "Please don't say anything, but Beryl is one of the islanders with Lyme disease." Then he grinned and waved to the approaching young woman. "How are you holding up, Beryl?"

"*Not* the best day of my life."

"Thank you for staying. I know you and Ariel were close."

"We only met a month ago. But I considered her a friend, I guess. Or maybe a potential friend." Beryl's voice had a creaky vibration somewhere in the back of her throat.

"Has anyone else come by while you've been here?" I asked.

She gave me a full-body appraisal. Her skin

had an impressive tan that was rarely attainable among natural redheads. "I've been alone since Andrew left. People heard what happened and don't want anything to do with it."

Radcliffe said, "This is Mike Bowditch. He's the warden investigator assigned to find out who shot Ariel."

Beryl's nostrils flared. "That shouldn't be hard."

I wanted to ask what she meant by that, but Harmon and the others were piling out of his truck. I decided my question was best asked in private.

"Andy, what were you thinking leaving this poor girl here with her dead friend?" Harmon Reed asked in his loud baritone.

The young woman said, "He didn't leave me, Mr. Reed. I volunteered."

"Well, that was brave of you, missy. Still seems wrong to me, if you'll forgive my saying. Not a woman's job to stand watch over a dead body."

"And yet somehow I managed."

She reached under her sweater, moved a hand around her breast, and came out with a pack of American Spirits. She shook a cigarette into her palm and fumbled in her pocket for a lighter, only to discover she didn't have one. She waved the unlit smoke at us. "Can anyone here help out a lady?"

Harmon Reed produced a box of kitchen

47

matches from his pocket. With a flick of his thumbnail against the tip, he produced a flame. Then he lit her cigarette. Beryl breathed out a fragrant cloud. "I didn't want to smoke in the yard. I didn't want to foul up the scene for the police."

"We appreciate that, Ms. McCloud." Klesko produced his badge for her. "I'm Detective Steven Klesko with the Maine State Police."

The young woman removed her stylish sunglasses. Her auburn irises complimented her bronze complexion. She glanced back and forth between the detective and me with an almost flirty smile. "Wait a minute? Is this a hunting accident or a murder investigation?"

"That is to be determined," said Klesko. "In part by what you can tell us about Ms. Evans."

"I'm not feeling very well at the moment. I came here directly from school and have work to finish before I can even think of lying down."

"Beryl is our teacher as well as our librarian," said Andrew Radcliffe with almost fatherly pride.

"How long have you been on the island?" I asked.

She flicked her ashes to the ground. "I'm in the second year of my two-year contract. Before that I lived in Minneapolis. Teacher's aide-slash-barista." Beryl raised the cigarette in my direction. "I saw a job posting promising the adventure of a lifetime. And I thought I might be able to do some real good here, the kids being so isolated. Some role model I am, huh? Do you know that I stopped smoking before I came to Maquoit? I spent six months transitioning to a vape, then the patch, then the gum. Now look at me."

The breeze shifted again and carried smoke into my face. I coughed, more in annoyance than distress. "We need to get a statement from you before you go, Ms. McCloud."

She caught the hint and stepped downwind. "Andrew must have told you I have Lyme disease. Me and three of my students, and about twenty other people here. To be honest I'm having trouble even standing up at the moment. If you could swing by the school later, I'd be grateful."

The detective and I exchanged glances. I assumed we both had the same thought, which was that she should sit down in the golf cart until we were ready to question her.

Klesko shocked me with his response: "Later will be fine, Beryl."

"Thank you! I'll probably still be at the schoolhouse—or the library—so you can look for me there."

The detective was all smiles. "We do need to know if you touched anything—either in the backyard or in the house."

"No, I didn't touch a thing. I made sure to stay on the little path Andrew showed me. I never went inside."

That was good to hear. The best forensic specialists in the world can't save an investigation from a death scene that has been contaminated.

As Beryl said her goodbyes, I took a moment to reappraise my partnership with Klesko. How was it possible that I had become the bad cop in this scenario? I had never been the bad cop. But I had never been the primary on a hunting homicide investigation.

Ronette had removed a clipboard from one of her several bags. Pinned to it was the checklist we use in Major Case Investigations. The seventeen categories each had multiple action items. When she'd finished running down the list, she laughed until it turned into a coughing fit. "What do you think, Mike? The two of us should be able to handle this in three hours, don't you think?"

"No sweat."

Radcliffe beckoned us to follow him down the path that led to the hidden backyard. I noticed my bootlace had come undone and stopped to tie it. Behind me, I heard gravel crunch. I glanced up at the imposing figure of Harmon Reed.

I rose to my full height. "You need to stay here, Mr. Reed."

"And why is that?" He was half a foot shorter than I was, and forty years older, but his wide shoulders and barrel chest made him one of the most physically intimidating men I'd ever encountered.

"The scene needs to be confined to the professionals."

Harmon jerked his thumb at Charley. "What about him?"

"Mr. Stevens is a retired game warden with decades of experience investigating hunting homicides."

"Homicide!" Reed had eyes the color of pig iron. "I thought we agreed that this was an accident."

The others had already disappeared around the corner of the cottage.

"It's the legal term for what took place."

"I know something about the law." The island patriarch rose on his toes, but not enough to bring us to the same level. "Sounds to me like you're already looking to pin this on one of my people."

His people.

"Someone shot Ariel Evans. And if it wasn't your nephew, it was someone else who hasn't stepped forward to take responsibility. It's my job to find out who he or she is."

Harmon Reed snapped his suspenders with his thumbs. "I told Andy this would happen. It always does when someone from outside comes here to 'solve a problem' for us. A Maquoiter ends up getting railroaded or worse."

"Mr. Reed, I understand you feel protective—"

"Don't tell me how I feel, young man. You don't know jack shit about me or this island."

"If you want to be useful, you can call Kenneth Crowley and have him drive out here," I said, no longer making an effort to hide my impatience. "We need him to walk us through the scene. It would go a long way if he made himself available to us now. Tell him to bring his rifle."

"I suppose that's reasonable. Like I've said from the beginning, the boy only wants to cooperate."

Charley had been watching me confront the harbormaster. "How about I stay with Mr. Reed while he waits for his nephew? There isn't anything that the three of you youngsters will miss that my old eyes would have caught."

That assertion was patently untrue. But I recognized that the retired warden had a secret reason, beyond defusing a tense situation, to remain here with Harmon Reed. It didn't take a master detective to recognize that the harbormaster knew more about the circumstances surrounding Ariel Evans's death than he had yet admitted.

5

Until you see the dead body, a homicide never truly seems real.

Ariel Evans lay facedown in the grass with a basket of wet clothes spilled beside her. The clothesline ran across the back lawn from an apple tree to a mountain ash on the opposite side of the yard. A single item of clothing was pinned to the rope: a pair of white cotton panties.

She was wearing a chocolate cardigan over a white T-shirt and khakis rolled up above her ankles. I saw that she was barefoot and that her toenails were painted a deep red that, horribly, ironically, matched the gore that had soaked the grass around her head. The back of her skull had been blown completely away—the bullet must have been a hollow point—which meant she'd been facing whoever had pulled the trigger. Her hair, where it wasn't sticky with drying blood, was honey blond with a natural wave that brought to mind the antiquated word *tresses*. Physically, she was smaller than I'd expected. Petite even. I doubted whether Ariel Evans had stood much above five feet in height.

Undermanned and pressed for time, our priority was to do a 360-degree observation of the yard, the cottage, and the surrounding woods.

A phrase came to my mind, something I recalled from a text on hunting homicides: *The incident scene will speak to you.*

I closed my eyes and counted to ten. Then I opened them again. I turned in a complete circle. There was no back door to the cottage. Anyone wishing to hang laundry had to make their way around the corner of the building from the front yard. Nor were there other human trails visible. The house had three picture windows. None of them had been pierced by a bullet. With luck we would find a slug buried in one of the casements or cedar shingles, but not necessarily.

"That's odd," I said.

"What's odd?" said Klesko.

"Didn't you say it was foggy this morning, Constable?"

Radcliffe nodded like a bobble-headed toy. "Very foggy."

"Why would she have been hanging wet laundry in the fog?"

"Maybe she was planning on going somewhere for the day and needed to get it up there. The fog was supposed to burn off later, as it did."

The white underwear dangled from a single clothespin. The sheer cloth fluttered when the breeze touched it.

The most famous hunting homicide in Maine history took place in 1988. A young mother in the town of Hermon, outside Bangor, was shot to death by a hunter in her backyard. Karen Wood was a newcomer to the area; she and her family had moved to Maine from Iowa five months earlier. The shooter, a popular and well-respected man in the community, said he had mistaken her white mittens for the tail of a deer. Despite his admission of negligence, he was acquitted by a jury of his peers. The verdict—widely viewed as a small-minded act of victim blaming—sparked scathing news stories across the country. Captain DeFord told me that to this day, every time he traveled out of state to meet with his counterparts, a conservation officer would bring up the case. Karen Ann Wood had become a legend, not just in the state of Maine but among game wardens everywhere.

I said, "If you were Kenneth Crowley hunting back in those trees, and you saw what looked like an injured woman lying in the grass, what would you do?"

"Come running, I hope," said Klesko.

"But there are no prints from that direction. The only prints are along the path Ariel used to access the clothesline."

Radcliffe had fallen silent. He was standing apart from us with his hands folded over his crotch as if he was expecting to be kicked in the balls.

"Andrew," I said. "Is the owner of the cottage currently on the island?"

"No, but Jenny Pillsbury is the rental agent out here. She keeps the cottages up and handles any emergencies that might arise."

"Does she know about this emergency?"

He was as silent as a stone man.

I stepped into his personal space. "I need you to call her and have her come over with her keys. Tell her to bring whatever information she has on Ariel Evans. While you're at it, would you mind relieving Charley and sending him in to take a look? Make sure Harmon stays where he is."

"Will do."

I had little confidence that Radcliffe could stop Harmon Reed from doing anything that Harmon Reed wanted to do, but I had no other choice. I waited for the constable to move out of earshot.

"So what do you think?" Ronette asked.

"I think I need to call DeFord. But before I do, I'd like to get a better sense of what we're dealing with here. I expect you'll want to call your own supervisor, Steve."

Klesko ran a hand through his thick dark hair. "Want to call him? No. Have to call him? Unfortunately."

"I need to walk the perimeter before Crowley shows up," I said. "I've got to establish where the shooter was when he fired and also where Crowley was standing when he caught sight of the body."

Ronette Landry had already put on her disposable blue nitrile gloves. "Provided those are two different locations."

It was a good point.

"Too bad we don't have a dog," I said.

"I've been thinking that ever since we got on the plane," Landry said. "Kathy Frost and her pup could have tracked our shooter to his front door by now. But I guess there's no point dwelling on what we can't do. We need to focus on what we can do."

"Ronette," I said, "start recording as much as you can. We don't have much time to document this scene before we lose the light, and with the forecast for rain, I'm afraid of what might happen to the evidence here."

"We could hang tarps over the yard," said Ronette.

"It's too big an area."

"What can I do?" asked Klesko.

"Give Marshall a call for me and bring her up to speed."

Marshall was Danica Marshall, the assistant attorney general who had caught this case, and not my favorite person in her office. Years earlier, as a district warden, I had stumbled into a murder investigation that revealed prosecutorial malfeasance on her part. She'd received a censure, and her career had never fully recovered.

Charley appeared around the corner of the house. He had his hands in the pockets of his wool hunting jacket to keep himself from touching something he shouldn't. Even wearing emergency gloves, you can still smear fingerprints beyond recognition and contaminate evidence in innumerable ways.

I gave the old pilot a moment to take in the scene before him. I wondered how many crucial details I had overlooked.

"Any thoughts on where the shooter was when he fired the gun?" I asked at last.

The old man pursed his lips and scanned the tree line. "Hard to tell until you can determine the angle the bullet entered her body, but I'd suspect he was over in those apples."

"Why do you think so?" asked Klesko.

"It's not like on the mainland where the big bucks slink off into the woods a few days before the season opens. As hungry as the deer are here, you're likely to find a trophy anywhere. And the one thing most hunters know is that deer like apples."

I said, "I'm going to walk the perimeter, see if I can luck out and find a shell casing. Care to join me?"

Charley had lightened up since the plane ride, but he was still far from his garrulous self. He glanced at the sky, where fast-moving clouds were racing one another to be first ashore. The old pilot could probably gauge the wind speed by watching them cross the sun.

"I'd appreciate another set of eyes," I said.

"What about the body? Shouldn't someone get Walt on the phone before she starts to ripen?"

When you are at an unattended death and no medical examiner is on the scene, the protocol is to get one on the phone. I assigned Klesko to call Dr. Walter Kitteridge and have him walk us through a course of action. I had the sense the detective had done this before.

To our great surprise, the call went through on the first try.

While Ronette Landry hurriedly photographed and videotaped the area around the corpse, switching from one camera to the next, the detective explained our predicament to the medical examiner's assistant. We waited for the doctor himself to get on the phone.

The wind had shifted, and now I could smell the ocean. In November the salt air is not as intense as in June, when the green waters of the gulf are fecund with plankton. But I could still taste the brine, and it awakened in me memories of the years I had lived with my mother in a house near the sea. For the first time since we'd landed on Maquoit, I was fully conscious of being on an island.

"Dr. Kitteridge says he's ready when we are," said Klesko.

"Then let's get started," I said.

The detective began by providing a summary description of the death scene. It quickly became a strange three-sided conversation with Klesko relaying information to Kitteridge and then communicating the coroner's instructions and observations back to us.

Klesko carefully lifted one of the dead woman's wrists with his gloved hand. "Rigor is still present. Kitteridge says the cold fog would have prolonged it, and he wants to see our pictures, but he thinks she was definitely shot this morning."

"Any chance the body was moved?"

Charley chimed in, "The blood splatter seems conclusive that she died on the spot. What's that in her hand?"

Clutched in Ariel's fist was a clothespin.

"Could it have been placed there after death?" I said. "Before her hand stiffened up?"

Klesko tried to peel the fingers loose, but the dead woman was determined to hang on to her prize. "She was holding this when she was shot."

"How can you be certain?"

"Because it's cadaveric spasm," said Charley.

I had never heard of such a thing.

Klesko relayed our discovery to the medical examiner, then parroted back the coroner's words: "It's also called postmortem spasm or instantaneous rigor. It occurs during certain

60

violent deaths. The muscles stiffen suddenly around any object—a gun barrel, for instance—a person is holding when he dies."

"How do you differentiate it from rigor mortis?" I asked.

"Rigor's pretty easily broken," the detective translated. "Unless the body's frozen solid, you can open a closed fist without too much effort. Cadaveric spasm resists being undone. It was how the cops in Seattle knew that Kurt Cobain had really killed himself, that it wasn't a staged suicide. He was still clutching the shotgun he'd used to blow his head off."

I couldn't help but look at the clothesline and the pair of damp underwear. The rope was swaying, ever so slightly, in the breeze. "So she really was hanging laundry in the fog."

"It doesn't mean she was the one who hung up those panties, though," said Klesko. "Her killer could have stage-managed the scene. He could say he'd mistaken those panties for a deer's white tail. That would give him an excuse if he was ever caught."

Clearly, Klesko had been thinking of the Karen Wood case, too.

I stepped aside to share our discoveries with Captain DeFord.

6

My supervisor said, "I'd hoped to get out there this afternoon. But my ride was called away. A lady with Alzheimer's wandered off from her home in Levant. Chris Anson is doing an aerial search for her."

"It's been a hell of a day."

"You can say that again."

"For what it's worth, I think we have things in hand here."

DeFord couldn't help but laugh. "I highly doubt it, Mike. Ideally we'd have twenty wardens on the ground. But who knows. Maybe I can send you some reinforcements sooner rather than later. Keep texting me your photos and videos and stay in touch, and I'll direct you from my end."

Pride has always been one of my character defects. Fool that I was, I wanted to solve this case on my own.

I gave Radcliffe crime-scene tape to tack up from one end of Ariel's front yard to the other. It was a small thing, but the yellow cordon transformed the house from a quaint cottage to a haunted, grief-stricken place.

While Klesko assisted Landry in documenting the scene, Charley and I searched the woods in a clockwise direction, starting at the road and moving slowly, side by side, in concentric half circles. I followed the edge of the yard while he battled his way through the thicker, thornier cover. A distance of ten feet separated us. Any farther apart and we might miss a clue. The idea was that we would only stop if we came upon potential evidence: broken branches, crushed weeds, brass casings ejected from a rifle, hopefully boot prints.

As terrible as the circumstances were, it felt good to be working with my old friend again. Charley Stevens had taught me so much about the woods and waters, but he had taught me more about being a man. I had essentially grown up, both personally and professionally, under his tutelage.

If only Stacey's shadow weren't hanging over us.

We'd paced off close to a hundred feet when I heard Charley say, "There's a deer trail here."

As soon as he spoke, it was as if the formerly invisible path materialized before me. How had I missed it? I said, "I can see where the deer came out of the bushes and crossed the yard this morning. There's a clump of hair snagged on the rose thorns."

"Remember to check yourself for ticks when we finish up. I've already squished two of the little bastards I found climbing up my trouser legs."

"Deer ticks or dog ticks?" The former were the ones that carried the horrible illnesses plaguing New England.

"Deer tick nymphs."

"How did you even see them?" The arachnids were the size of a period at the end of a sentence.

"My vision's pretty decent for an old fart."

It was no boast. The old man, who had never exercised in the modern sense since basic training fifty years earlier, was a marvel of physical and mental fitness.

Five minutes later, after we'd entered the thicket of apple trees that marked the periphery of the orchard, he stopped again. "Found something here!"

"Can I come in?"

"Back up a few steps and then you should be able to crash through that shadbush pretty easy."

The shrubs caught at the fabric of my pants, and I could almost feel the ticks launching themselves onto my clothing.

Autumn is the season of rot in the Maine woods. Out of the sun and wind, under the scraggly boughs of the apple trees, the light had an almost-sepia tint. The air was still and the odor of decomposition was strong. The miasma blotted out even the smell of the sea.

Soon I found myself standing beside Charley. He poked one of his knobby fingers at the lowest limb of the tree in front of us. Three branches had been snapped off. The breaks were clean. The sapwood under the bark was as soft as human flesh. Someone had recently been here.

"The entrance wound will tell you if the angle is right. But I reckon this is the spot."

I turned toward the cottage, fifty yards away. Ronette Landry's vest showed fluorescent orange in the waning sun.

Charley had turned his attention to the fallen apple leaves and the moldering cores left behind by the deer. "This is where our 'hunter' entered from the orchard. There's a partial boot print in the mud."

I dropped a marker beside the print and recorded both it and the recently disturbed underbrush. Charley searched in vain for a telltale brass casing. There would be time later to follow the trail deeper into the orchard. For the moment, we needed to establish that there wasn't another spot along the tree line from which the shooter might have taken his fatal shot.

"Whoever he was," the old man said, "he had the presence of mind to retrieve his brass."

In other words, the shooter hadn't been so panicked that he forgot to pick up the ejected shell from the fatal round he'd fired.

We crashed along through the bushes and saplings for another five minutes before I called a halt. "I've got something."

"So do I. But you go first."

"Chewing tobacco. Someone spat out a stream of brown phlegm here. What about you?"

"I've got boot prints," Charley said from his side of the puckerbrush. "Size twelve or so, judging from my Chippewas. They come up to the bushes and stop dead. Then they turn right around and take off in the opposite direction."

"Kenneth Crowley?"

"Could be."

"And here I thought he was lying about having stumbled upon the death scene," I said.

"Stumbled I doubt. More likely he snuck in to catch a glance at the pretty stranger. Teenage boys on this island must be hard up, so to speak, to see females in the flesh."

"So there were two men here, her killer *and* a Peeping Tom?"

"Seems like Crowley paused to take a gander at the cottage, dribbled some of his chew, and then saw something that made him go limp as a noodle."

"A woman with her skull blown to bits might do that."

"I hope it would!" said the old man. "The crucial part is that young Crowley didn't hide his path, coming in or going out. And from the looks of things, he didn't set his feet to take a shot. Not to say he didn't, but it doesn't appear that way to me."

A gust of wind rattled the bony branches over our heads.

"Tell me honestly, Charley. What do you think happened here?"

"If the evidence points to murder, you're going to have to hand the case over to Detective Klesko."

"Does this point to murder?"

"A few boot prints and some tobacco juice? The attorney general would say this is just stuff and nonsense. He'll want hard evidence he can bring to a judge and jury." The old man gave me a searching look. "You're the investigator, Warden Bowditch. What do *you* think it was?"

From my first weeks in the Warden Service, I had learned how political law enforcement could be. Competing departments engaged in constant turf battles with one another. The state police were notorious for bigfooting our cases. What added to the frustration was that, in homicide cases such as this one, they were entitled to do so by law. Game wardens were not murder police.

"I'm not ready to turn this over to Klesko yet," I admitted.

The old man grinned at me like he once had, back when we'd first recognized each other as kindred rebels willing to bend the rules to the breaking point.

"You know," he said, "there's no law that says we need to share our uncorroborated suspicions."

"Uncorroborated?"

Charley had never finished high school, but every once in a while he revealed his well-kept secret: the folksy bush pilot was an autodidact.

I marked and videoed the gob of tobacco spit and the hiding place behind the shadbush. Then we continued on, finding nothing else of note, until we hit the road north of the cottage.

Pausing there on the gravel, out of sight of the building, with only the sound of the wind and the gurgling croak of a raven eyeing us from aloft, I found it easy to indulge the sensation that Charley and I were utterly alone on Maquoit.

He reached into his trapper basket and produced a thermos of coffee and a sealed bag of moose jerky. It might have been deer jerky. Or possibly bear jerky. He'd once fed me jerky he'd made from the tail of a beaver. It wasn't bad.

Behind me, I heard a laboring engine, a perforated muffler, the rustle of tires on crushed stones. A blue pickup rounded the corner. Two men were inside. The passenger was wearing an orange cap.

"I'm guessing that one's Crowley," I said.

I had no clue who the driver might be.

7

Both Radcliffe and Reed had described Kenneth Crowley as a kid. But the man who emerged from the passenger side of the newly arrived pickup was easily six-three, well muscled, and sporting a chin beard any billy goat would envy. If he was a child, then I was a senior citizen.

Crowley was wearing a black hoodie two sizes too big with the hood pulled down over his head and the brim of his hunting cap peeking out. The hat, faded from hours in the sun, was more grapefruit colored than blaze orange. Underneath his sweatshirt, he wore sweatpants tucked into the brown XtraTuf boots that seemed to be the footwear of choice for Maquoit lobstermen.

As requested, he'd brought along his hunting rifle. The Winchester 94 lever-action was almost certainly chambered for .30/30 caliber bullets. The short barrel and open sights made it ideal for hunting in dense cover. That make and model gun had probably killed more deer in the Maine woods than any other ever manufactured.

The driver of the pickup was taking his sweet time getting out.

"Kenneth." I advanced toward him. "My name is Mike Bowditch. I'm an investigator with the Maine Warden Service."

There was a bulge the size of a golf ball in his cheek. The impressive wad of chewing tobacco gave him a speech impediment of sorts. "How's it going?" came out as "How shit going?"

"Not very well or I wouldn't be here."

Crowley seemed unaware that his rifle barrel was bouncing around as he shifted his weight. It was currently aimed at my shins.

Nothing escaped Charley. "Would you mind pointing your barrel at the ground, young feller?"

"How about I take it?" I said. "I promise to give it back."

The young man flipped the sling off his shoulder and presented me with the Winchester. The safety was on, but a round was in the chamber. I cleared the action and caught the cartridge that jumped out of the breech with my gloved hand. "This was the gun you were hunting with this morning?"

"I don't know whah you hurt, but I dint shooter."

He spit a brown stream onto the gravel. Some of the juice dribbled down his goat beard. A discolored streak there suggested he hadn't yet mastered the fine art of expectoration.

I let the rifle hang by my side. "Can you do me another favor and take the wad out of your mouth. I'm having trouble understanding what you're saying."

Crowley coughed out the lump of tobacco into

70

his palm and tucked it into the pouch pocket of his hoodie. A stain began seeping through the black cotton.

Without the chew, he sounded like a normal teenager. "Check my gun if you think I shot her. You got my permission. I never even fired at nothing all morning."

"I'll do that."

"I don't see why I'm under suspicion when I was the one who found her and ran to get help."

I believed, based on what I had seen so far of Harmon Reed, that he had prepared his nephew-in-law for a police interview. Harmon had probably rehearsed with him a series of short, easy-to-remember answers to expected questions.

I let my eyes go soft, my voice go calm. "Who said you were 'under suspicion,' Kenneth?"

My response seemed to baffle him. "How come you hauled me out here if I ain't?"

"I was hoping you could show me where you were standing when you spotted her. I'd like to hear in your own words what happened. It would be a huge help to my investigation."

Finally the driver of the pickup decided to show his face.

The man looked so much like a younger version of Harmon that he had to be his son. They were of the same height, and he had the same powerful chest and back, but his hair was dark and windswept, and his muttonchops had been shaved short to resemble the feral superhero Wolverine. He wore a "denim leisure suit": blue jeans and a jean jacket. But nothing about this hard-faced lobsterman suggested he'd enjoyed a day of leisure in his life.

"Kenneth has a right against self-incrimination," he said with a slight slur. "He has a right to an attorney."

"And you would be?"

"Hiram Reed."

The Reeds seemingly had a predilection for archaic names that began with the letter *h*.

"Kenneth was going to show us where in the woods he came across Ariel Evans," I explained.

Crowley stared at his friend the way a scared puppy might at his new owner who was leaving the house.

Hiram refused to relax the sneer on his face. "I'm just saying he has constitutional rights you'd better respect. Kenneth's a minor with no one to look out for his well-being. If you try to entrap him, I will know about it, and there will be hell to pay."

"So noted," said Charley.

"After you, Kenneth," I said. "Wait here, Mr. Reed. I promise I won't entrap him until we come back."

Crowley wasn't the most graceful of woodsmen. He simply bulled his way through whatever lay in front of him—low-hanging branches, ever-green boughs, thorn bushes—with the result that I received a switch across the face as a limb snapped back behind our oblivious leader.

Five minutes later, we came upon a well-worn path leading from the abandoned orchard south past Gull Cottage.

Crowley pointed to the north. "I came from that way."

I directed my iPhone's video camera at him. "What time was it that you got here?"

"I don't own a watch."

"What about a cell phone?"

"Forgot to charge it last night. When I woke up, it was dead."

"Well, what time did you leave your house this morning?"

"I don't have a house. I have a room over the Lazy Lobster."

Out of the corner of my eyes I saw Charley suppressing a grin. "Your room then."

"Six o'clock, maybe. It was still dark, I remember."

"How long were you hunting, do you think?"

"Three or four hours."

As the sun slipped behind a cloud, the temperature took a nosedive, the way it does in the woods, in the autumn. The sky in the southeast was now the color of wet ashes. From the looks of it, I doubted if we would see the sun again.

"Can you show us where you first spotted Ariel Evans?" I asked.

Crowley plunged into the bushes. I was heartened to see that he was making for the spot behind the puckerbrush that Charley and I had identified. Sure enough, he came to a halt practically in his own boot prints.

I put an arm out to stop him. "If you can stand back a little, I'd appreciate it."

I didn't explain that Ronette Landry would soon be pouring quick-hardening dental stone into the impressions to preserve a cast of the boot print. Nor did I tell Crowley that we'd need to borrow his XtraTufs to take photographs of the soles. That so many lobstermen wore that particular make might prove to be a complication in matching the cast with Crowley's, but usually specific scuffs and marks were unique to a pair of shoes or boots.

From his silence, it was clear that Charley was going to let me conduct the interview as if he weren't present.

"What made you decide to leave the trail and bushwhack over this way?" I asked.

"I thought I heard a deer."

"You didn't come down here to get a peek at her?"

"What? No way, man."

"You might have seen her through the windows. She was a beautiful woman."

"Dude, she was *old*. Besides, it was foggy."

"So you *did* sneak down here hoping to see her walking around the house naked?"

"I ain't a pervert. And maybe I had a good reason to come this way. But you haven't even asked me the question."

"What question?"

"Whether I heard a shot or not," he said smugly. "The answer is yes. I heard a shot."

"How long was it between the time you heard the shot and the time you saw Ariel Evans lying in the yard?"

"Ten minutes max."

"You're sure?"

"Yeah, because I was up on Cider Ridge when I heard the shot. I figured one of the guys had bagged a buck, and I wanted to see how big it was. When I got here, I saw that lady with her head blown in, and I was, like, 'Holy shit, someone shot her by mistake. And what if it's the Washburns and they don't want any witnesses?'"

"Who are the Washburns?"

"Eli and Rud Washburn. They're twin brothers. They were the ones who sunk Harmon's boat. Their family has been out here longer than the Reeds. We don't go on their land, and they don't go on ours. Especially after what Harmon did to Eli."

"You're going to have to fill in the blanks for me."

Crowley reached for the tobacco ball in his pocket and stuffed it back inside his cheek. He looked like a chipmunk with a mouth full of acorns. "I thought you cops knew all this shit. Harmon shot Eli after those Nazis sunk his boat."

Charley couldn't help himself. "Nazis?"

"The Washburns buy and sell German shit on eBay. Rud said they owned one of Adolf Hitler's daggers. They've got swastika tattoos and stickers on their trucks that say 'White Pride Worldwide.' "

This new information complicated the situation. Complicated it quite a bit.

I had a dim memory of the sinking and shooting Crowley had mentioned. One Maquoit fisherman had shot another during one of their perennial lobster wars. The victim had survived the encounter, while the aggressor was put on trial in Ellsworth on attempted-murder charges. The jury had acquitted the shooter after a mere six hours of deliberation. The prosecutor had failed to paint the Nazi boat-sinker as a figure deserving of sympathy. Not that I could fault him for that.

Ariel Evans had written a bestselling exposé on neo-Nazis.

On the other hand, Harmon Reed had a vested interest in seeing his enemies incriminated or at least brought under suspicion. I had to assume

76

that he would have prompted his nephew to put me on the scent of Maquoit's white supremacists.

"Thanks, Kenneth," I said. "You've been helpful."

"Civic duty, man."

When we'd managed to bushwhack back to the road, we found that Hiram Reed had gone on to the house.

We followed his tire tracks around the bend to Gull Cottage.

Radcliffe and the Reeds were gathered together in a knot beside Harmon's gleaming truck. Whatever the topic of their conversation was, they abandoned it. The constable broke away from the others and hurried toward us.

"There you are! Detective Klesko has been asking for you. He says he found something."

We left Crowley to the care of the Reeds and made our way under the crime-scene tape and around the side of the cottage.

Klesko was standing over the corpse, still speaking into his telephone. When he spotted us, he pointed at Ariel's bare feet. "Look here."

I squatted down and began scanning the delicate white ankle.

"Between the toes," he said.

I squinted and saw the tiny red pinpricks. "Ariel Evans was a junkie?"

"Seems so," said the detective.

"That doesn't fit with her reputation," I said.

"How many investigative reporters are heroin addicts?"

Charley stroked his chin. "She might have been shooting coke."

Klesko held his hand over his phone and lowered his voice as if we were in danger of being overheard. "These wounds are recent. Definitely made since she arrived on the island. So did she bring the drugs with her, or did she acquire them here?"

More important, I thought, were they the reason someone had killed her?

8

With the medical examiner still talking him through every action, Klesko opened a body bag to one side of the corpse. Then Charley and I carefully turned the still-rigid cadaver over so that she was faceup. I use the term *faceup* loosely since the dead woman was missing much of hers.

The fatal bullet had punched a hole through the bridge of her nose, causing her eyes to tilt inward toward the wound. It made her appear almost comically cross-eyed. The corneas had dried out after the tear ducts ceased to function. Beneath the cloudy surface, the irises were a distinctly tarnished-looking shade of blue.

After death, when the heart has stopped pumping, and the lifeless body can no longer resist the relentless pull of gravity, the skin discolors where the blood begins to pool. If a corpse is face up, you will see lividity in the back, buttocks, and along the hamstrings. If a corpse is facedown, you will see the opposite. Sometimes, as with Ariel, a dead person can appear to be flushed, as if they'd died of eating ghost peppers. This process—livor mortis—is yet another means of determining time of death.

"Lividity appears to be fixed," said Klesko.

"She's definitely been dead more than six hours."

In life she must have been beautiful. Blonde hair, blue eyes, and the full lips that I have heard described as bee-stung.

"She looks younger than I'd imagined," I found myself saying. "In some of her publicity photos her skin looks weathered."

"Maybe she gave up some unhealthy habits?" offered Landry, who had paused in her documentation to look upon the face of our victim. Numbered evidence markers were arranged all over the yard. Ronette had been busy.

"And took up heroin?" I said.

"The toxicology tests for this one should prove interesting," said Klesko.

"It will make up for a total lack of ballistic evidence."

Klesko responded with a bitter laugh. "I'm sure the rifle that was used to shoot this woman has already been hurled into the sea."

"I suspect Steve is right about the firearm." Ronette paused to sneeze. "But I wouldn't give up hope yet of finding the bullet that killed her."

The procedure for investigating a hunting homicide, when there are no witnesses, is to begin by surveying the death scene to get a general sense of the circumstances.

The next step is to cordon off the site.

Establish paths into and out of the scene to prevent disturbing any additional areas that might contain evidence. For us, it was the well-worn trail that led from the front of the cottage, around the building, to the clothesline.

Then, if necessary, take action to preserve the corpse against the elements until it can be thoroughly photographed and measured.

All of this, we accomplished with a handful of officers.

But the next series of action steps made me miss the dozen or so wardens who make up the Evidence Recovery and Forensic Mapping Teams. Instead of having a platoon of specialists at my disposal, I had less than a squad. And the inside of the cottage remained to be searched. It didn't help that my phone only seemed to have a signal intermittently.

I spent ten minutes bringing Klesko up to speed. He clearly disapproved of my having spoken to our material witness without him, but the only way we were going to conquer our tasks was to divide them up, I said. As it happened, he had made good use of his time while Charley and I were beating the bushes.

"While you were gone," Klesko said, "Kitteridge had to sign off to use the bathroom."

"The prostate is a cruel master," proclaimed Charley.

"I used the interval to make some calls. I'm

afraid I'm going to have to fly back tonight. I was hoping to reschedule a court appearance, but the attorney general says he can't make it happen. I was the primary in the investigation of that Barter woman who hacked up her husband in his sleep and is now claiming self-defense."

I'd seen the headlines, but not read the articles. Only now did I make the connection. "Wanda Barter?"

"You know her?"

"Better than I wish. I knew her husband, too."

"The guy was a registered sex offender so no one's shedding tears he's gone. But the AG wants to make a statement that you can't just behead your sack-of-shit husband when he's passed out drunk and drugged."

"I'm surprised you were assigned this investigation if you need to testify tomorrow."

"We thought we had the confessed killer, remember?"

It was after three o'clock, and the sky was already darkening in the east.

"What time do you have to leave?"

"Whenever Charley says we still can."

I'd seen my friend fly in pitch-black conditions that would have intimidated an owl. If he knew the length of the runway, he could get his Cessna airborne. Whether Klesko's hair turned white in the process was an open question.

"Light's not the issue," said the pilot. "It's the rain and wind coming in tonight. But I'll get you home, Detective. Don't you worry."

Radcliffe appeared around the corner of the house. "Jenny Pillsbury's here!"

"The rental agent?" The detective checked his watch. "Took her long enough."

I asked Charley to assist Ronette while the detective and I spoke with the woman who had been Ariel's landlady during her short stay on the island.

Jenny Pillsbury was standing in the road, talking with Hiram Reed. While we'd been occupied, Harmon Reed had slipped away with Kenneth Crowley.

"Nothing suspicious about that," Klesko muttered.

The constable introduced us to Jenny Pillsbury. She was tall, almost six feet, with short dark hair and widely spaced brown eyes. She wore a flannel shirt, blue jeans, and work boots, but there was nothing mannish about her at all. From his smile, Klesko obviously found her quite attractive. He wasn't the only man among us who did.

"I'm sorry it took this long for me to get here." She presented the detective and me with business cards. The name of her rental agency was Island Accommodations. "This was my morning to work in the store. I was just saying to Hiram that it feels like he's been following me all day—or that I've been following him."

"You can't get rid of me, Jenny," he said.

"I would think you'd have had better things to do than hang out all morning with those old geezers at Graffam's. At least I was working. What's your excuse?"

"An utter lack of ambition," said Hiram Reed.

She reached into a tote. Something jangled inside. "Here are the master keys to the cottage. I'm willing to help you any way I can. I can't believe the hunter who shot Ariel would slink away like that. It's a horrible reflection on our island. Nobody's going to want to rent a house out here again."

"What can you tell us about Ariel Evans?" Klesko asked. "How did she first contact you?"

"Through my website. She made the reservation and paid the deposit online back in the winter. It was all pretty standard."

The detective removed his notebook from his pocket, reminding me to record this impromptu interview.

"So there was nothing out of the ordinary?" he asked.

"It's unusual for someone to book three months, let alone stay past Columbus Day, after the inns and restaurants close. And there was one other thing. In August Ariel warned me she would be delayed in arriving. She had an assignment overseas, she said. Then she showed up a few days later. From that phone call, I thought she wouldn't be here for weeks. But her work schedule wasn't any of my business."

"Did she ever tell you why she'd chosen Maquoit?" Klesko asked.

"Not in so many words. But the rumor going around was that she was visiting Stormalong. You've heard about our hermit?"

"We wondered if she intended to write a book about him," I said.

"I can't think what other reason she would've had for rowing over there so often. The man is disgusting."

Something about Jenny Pillsbury was discordant, I realized. She spoke at a measured pace and had unnervingly steady eyes. Yet I sensed that she was, deep down, extremely anxious.

"What were your interactions with her like?" Klesko asked.

"My interactions?"

"Was she an easy or difficult renter? What was your impression of her as a person?"

Pillsbury shuffled her feet and put a hand to her mouth. "I never had any problems with her as a renter. She liked to drink and have people over at the house, I heard. But I didn't get the sense she was destroying the place. Personally, I found her charming. Everyone on the island seemed quite taken with her. That's why I can't believe she was killed deliberately. It had to have been some sort of horrible accident. Nothing else makes sense."

9

Jenny Pillsbury jingled the keys. "I don't suppose you want me to come with you, but I can definitely let you inside."

"We're not ready to search the house," Klesko said. "We're still waiting on a warrant."

I tried not to show my surprise.

Jenny was also perplexed. "Why do you need a warrant? I'm giving you permission on behalf of the owner."

"Who is the owner, by the way?" the detective asked, readying his pen to jot the name in his notebook.

"Tom Epstein. He's a cardiologist in Philadelphia. He told me I should give you access to anything you need."

"You spoke with him?"

"Wouldn't you want to know if your tenant had been shot to death in your backyard?"

"Can I speak with you, Detective?" I asked.

We stepped to the side.

I said, "I'm the one who's supposed to file the affidavits for search warrants."

"But you didn't, and we're getting short on time. You told me we needed to divide up the tasks. I understand if you feel overwhelmed, Mike. But you need to get your head clear."

"What are you talking about?"

"Isn't it true that you had me call Danica Marshall because there's bad blood between you?"

Sometimes I forgot how small a state Maine is. It figured that Assistant Attorney General Marshall's long-standing grudge against me was common knowledge in the state police CID.

"I'm not trying to undercut you here," Klesko said when I didn't respond. "But I've done this a bunch of times before, and this is your first rodeo. We're partners, and you need to trust me."

"When the judge calls back, I want to speak with him."

"Of course."

We returned to the place where Jenny Pillsbury, Hiram Reed, and Charley Stevens were gathered. They were looking at the sky, discussing the weather. The rainstorm moving in overnight was supposed to be a doozy.

"Why do you need a warrant?" Jenny hadn't missed a beat.

I made a mental note that she was intelligent and observant: two qualities you want in a witness. The rental agent might prove useful if my investigation bogged down, as it already seemed to be doing.

"It's just a precaution," I said. "When the case goes to trial, we can't afford for there to be any weirdness. Defendants have walked free because police were told they had permission to search a piece of property and only later discovered that someone else was sharing the space, too, and had a right to privacy."

"But Ariel was renting this cottage alone. And I'm authorized to give you permission. Dr. Epstein said so."

Klesko's phone rang. It was the judge to whom the detective had submitted the affidavit for a search warrant. He handed me his mobile. The reception was much clearer than it was on mine.

"Your Honor, this is Warden Investigator Bowditch."

"What happened to Detective Klesko?"

"I'm the primary on this case. The detective submitted the application while I was interviewing a material witness."

"Yes, well. It all looks good to me. Detective Klesko's applications are always flawless. He should conduct a tutorial for his fellow officers. May I speak with him please?"

I handed the phone back to Klesko.

The door was unlocked and opened with a push of the knob. The hinges, I noticed, didn't make a sound. On an island where every metal thing rusts overnight, it's telling when someone cares enough to keep their hinges well greased.

What struck me first about the sunlit interior

of Gull Cottage was how bright it was. The sea-green floorboards had been newly painted, and the walls were as white as schooner sails. The furniture was modern, comfortable looking, and everything matched. The paintings on the walls were of ocean scenes: waves crashing against cliffs, a lighthouse beacon cutting the fog; gulls perched atop ships' masts. The Philadelphia cardiologist hadn't wanted his tenants to forget they were vacationing on a Maine island.

The second thing I noticed was the awesomeness of the mess. The hooked rugs had all been kicked out of place. Ashes had fallen from the woodstove and onto the floor beyond the protective mat. Beer cans and half-empty wineglasses occupied most of the flat surfaces. I would have bet money that the rental contract had a no-smoking clause, but the smell of stale cigarettes and marijuana blunts was pervasive.

"Looks like she threw a few parties," I said.

"That might explain why she was so popular. You're lucky you've got an evidence tech with you. I don't even know where to begin here."

While Klesko continued on into the kitchen, I peeked into the side room. It was some sort of library. The shelves were filled with well-thumbed paperbacks, the kinds of books you leave for strangers. Near the window was a trestle desk. You would have expected an author to set up her laptop there. But instead of a computer, there was an open artist's sketch box.

The house might have been chaotic, but the contents of the box—pastels, charcoal pencils, pads of drawing paper—were carefully arranged.

When I turned back toward the front room, I found myself confronted with an enormous corkboard on the wall beside the door. On it were tacked maybe twenty sketches. Some were in charcoal, others in pastel. But all were of a single person: a gray-bearded man with long hair that was sometimes loose and sometimes tied in a horse tail. His features had been scoured by the wind and burned by the sun, but he appeared well fed, physically fit, handsome even in a rough-hewn way. He was dressed in a sheepskin vest and wore a leather cord around his throat on which was strung a gold ring.

"Steve! Take a look at this."

A moment later the detective stood beside me.

"This has got to be the hermit. Don't you think?"

"I don't know who else it would be. Radcliffe said she spent days over on his rock. What was his name?"

"Blake Markman."

"Why was she sketching him?"

"Beats me. But these are really fantastic. She had a tremendous talent."

Klesko gave me a gray-toothed grin. He was still trying to make nice after our brief confrontation over the warrant. "You never struck me as the artsy type, Bowditch."

"What I mean is, none of the articles I've read about Ariel Evans said she was a visual artist as well as an author. I find it odd that there are all these drawings but no sign of her being a writer working on a book."

"I'm more intrigued by the absence of a cell phone."

"You think someone might have stolen it?"

"If they did, it meant they entered the house after they shot her." Klesko's implication—that her death was indeed a murder—hung heavily in the air. "Maybe her phone's upstairs with her computer and her notes."

I lingered behind him, spellbound by the drawings. Something about them was almost unbearably haunting. It wasn't just the hermit's pain. It was the artist's as well. Only someone who had suffered profoundly could have captured the utter brokenness of this man's spirit.

I finally caught up with Klesko upstairs in the master bedroom. He was standing with his hands on his hips and a frown on his face. The down comforter lay on the floor, at the foot of the four-poster. The sheets had been stripped from the mattress and the cases from the pillows.

"I guess this explains why she was doing laundry," he said.

The windows were open and the curtains were snapping in the breeze blowing in through the screens.

I said, "I don't see any computer or notes."

The detective made a wide circuit of the naked bed and entered the adjoining bathroom.

On the bedside table was a half-empty glass of red wine and one of those snap-open pillboxes with a variety of pills. I knew little about prescription drugs. But in general, I knew that few of them mixed well with alcohol.

A moment later I heard Klesko exclaim from the bathroom, "Bingo!"

He was bent over the overflowing wastebasket. He'd removed a pen from the inside pocket of his bomber and stuck it into the trash. When he lifted it, a torn condom wrapper was on the end.

"There are three of these in here. She must have flushed the rubbers."

Ariel didn't seem to be overly concerned about such things as clogging the landlord's plumbing. "This explains why she was washing the sheets."

"Did you notice the pillbox beside the bed?" he asked. "She had quite a pharmacy going. Ambien, Klonopin, Vicodin. But most of what was in there was lithium."

"So she was probably bipolar."

"I've never heard of anyone taking lithium

recreationally." Klesko removed a hairbrush from the gold-patterned toiletry bag beside the sink. The visible strands were long, wavy, and blond. "These mostly look like hers. I doubt the guy she was bonking bothered with a brush."

I left him to poke through Ariel's matching set of Coach luggage. I knew the bags were expensive because my late mother had favored the same brand. To my mom, there was no point to consumption that wasn't also conspicuous.

The second upstairs bedroom showed no sign of having been used at all, for sleeping or anything else. The curtains were drawn and the window was closed and locked. I doubted Ariel had ever set foot inside it.

I peeked in a couple of closets, continued on to the main bedroom.

"I can't find her computer anywhere."

"Here's her wallet at least." Klesko raised a plastic bag containing a billfold made of some exotic reptile hide: crocodile, python, maybe even Komodo dragon. "Inside is her New York driver's license, an AmEx Platinum Card, a subway card, and approximately five hundred dollars in cash."

"She traveled light."

"Look at her luggage. This wasn't a woman who traveled light. We have more of the house to search, but there's something else beside the laptop that should be here but isn't."

He didn't have to tell me what it was. "Her cell phone."

"And Mrs. Pillsbury told me that they texted this morning after Ariel discovered the dryer was broken. I tried calling the number she gave me and got an automated voice mail. I tried texting and got a notification that the message wasn't delivered. So where is the phone?"

"The better question is, who took it?"

Klesko became very still. He removed a glove and massaged the muscles in the back of his neck. I could see him searching carefully for words.

"I need you to be honest with me about something, Mike. Based on everything you've seen here, do you honestly believe this was a random hunting incident?"

I turned to the window where the curtain continued to dance in the breeze. "One of your colleagues told me not to make assumptions. She said, 'Never get ahead of your evidence.'"

Klesko picked up on the pronoun. "Was it Ellen Pomerleau who said that? Well, it's first-rate advice. An investigator starts having problems when he gets ahead of his evidence."

"Pomerleau is a first-rate detective."

"But Ellen wasn't the one who located the missing girl over in Birnam. It was you who found her."

I flicked my eyes at him. "It was more like she found me."

"From what I've heard, those freaks really put you through hell." His tone was not unkind.

I said nothing.

"After what happened," he continued in a soft, steady voice, "there were a lot of people who were shocked at your promotion. They thought you were responsible for what ended up happening in that basement. They thought you should have known better."

I tried to maintain my outward calm. "Everyone is entitled to an opinion."

"I guess the Warden Service decides things differently than we do."

I opened and closed my hands at my sides. "What do you think? Would you say I'm up to the job?"

To his credit, Klesko stared me straight in the eyes. "I wish I could say yes, Mike. But I honestly don't know yet."

10

I should have felt sorry leaving the detective to document and collect the evidence inside the cottage. But his final words had left my face stinging as if he'd slapped me.

Out in the road a sirocco of dust and leaves had formed. The detritus whirled round and round in an upward spiral. The miniature tornado was at once awesome and eerie.

Radcliffe met me in the yard. "I thought you'd want to know. The *Star of the Sea* just pulled in at Bishop's Wharf."

It was the boat I had called to ferry the body of Ariel Evans to shore.

The *Star of the Sea* was legendary along the Maine coast for all the good work it did: ministering to the spiritual needs of islanders, diagnosing and treating their health problems (babies had been born aboard the ship, and emergency surgeries had been conducted via telemedicine hookups), hosting AA and other group-therapy meetings, and generally functioning as a valued connection to a world that tended to forget these poor, isolated communities even existed.

"Thanks, Andrew."

"I'm feeling like kind of a third wheel here. Or maybe a fifth wheel would be apropos."

"You've been very helpful already. Actually there's one more thing you can do for me. Would you mind driving me down to the Gut? I'd like a look at this Stormalong place where the hermit lives."

If nothing else, those obsessive sketches had raised Blake Markman to the top of my list of people to interview.

I climbed back into Radcliffe's pickup, trying not to disturb his sleeping dog. My worries in that regard were unfounded. Bella kept snoring.

"Any breakthroughs in the case?" Radcliffe asked with forced nonchalance. "I don't suppose there's any new evidence you've found you can share with me. I promise to keep your confidence."

In the truck there was nowhere for me to hide. "It's still very early in our investigation."

"But there's nothing to suggest she was killed deliberately? It had to have been a hunting accident. Everyone on the island liked Ariel."

Not everyone, I thought. "We're pursuing multiple theories."

"But you ruled out Kenneth Crowley?"

"We're not currently looking at him as a prime suspect, but it would be wrong to say that we've ruled anyone out. Not even you, Andrew."

For a split second, Radcliffe looked absolutely panicked. "I was in my shop all morning, if that helps. My wife, Penny, and boys can attest to that."

I relaxed my face. "I don't suspect you of having shot Ariel Evans, Andrew."

He managed a nervous laugh. "That's a relief."

The drive took all of three minutes.

Radcliffe had said that Ariel had chosen to rent Gull Cottage because of its proximity to the Gut, so I shouldn't have been surprised when the evergreens parted and we emerged onto a steep bluff. The hill below us was covered with spartina grass and rosebushes, with a path descending to a pebble beach. Beyond the shore was a surging channel of seawater where hundreds of eider ducks bobbed in a great raft. On the far side of the Gut was a ridge-backed island that seemed to have been carved from a single enormous stone.

There was a similar rock off Monhegan Island, fifty miles to the southwest. It was called Manana, and it had also once been home to a sheep-keeping hermit. Perhaps that other, earlier anchorite had inspired Blake Markman to make his own unconventional life choice. But Stormalong was smaller, steeper, and less inviting than Monhegan's satellite. Except for a few grassy shelves and expanses of creeping juniper, most of the islet seemed to consist of exposed granite. If not for a rickety old dock with a dory floating beside it, one might have been forgiven for believing it was uninhabitable and uninhabited—which, no doubt, was exactly the message its sole resident wished to communicate.

"I still can't imagine that little wisp of a girl rowing back and forth over there," the constable said.

"She was a woman, not a girl."

Just looking at the current charging like white horses through the Gut produced a knot in my stomach. Whatever else Ariel Evans had been, she'd also been a fearless mariner.

I had always considered myself to be a good man in a boat. As a teenager, growing up in the seaside town of Scarborough, I had briefly been sternman on a lobsterboat out of Pine Point. A sternman is the lowly deckhand who dumps out the rotten-bait bags and refills them with slightly less decayed herring. The man I worked for was the father of a friend, an elder of his church, and a harsh taskmaster. But he had taught me to pilot his twin-engine Mako in even the fiercest of gales, and for that I was grateful. Later, I had learned to steer everything from Sunfish sailboats to small schooners. I could row a dory for miles, paddle and pole a canoe, and do Eskimo rolls in sea kayaks. If I was ever called upon, I could have lashed together a raft to float down the Mississippi.

But the Gut worried me as a boatman. Certain waters demand the utmost respect.

"Of course the tide's rising now," said

Radcliffe. "The time to go across is dead low or when it's slack. The ebb and flood are when it's the most dangerous."

Under normal circumstances I would have wanted to interview Markman immediately, but I would need to wait for the tide to turn. If it was going to be high shortly, it wouldn't be low for another six hours, which would be close to midnight. I decided that I would attempt the crossing the following day. The tide would be low around noon.

"You said that Markman rarely comes to Maquoit," I said.

"Once in a blue moon."

"He must need supplies on occasion."

"A private boat from the mainland—a gorgeous Hinckley runabout—brings him things every month without ever stopping in Marsh Harbor. Evidently, our hermit still has some of his millions left if he can get his groceries delivered way the heck out here."

Now I was more interested than ever in meeting the reclusive Markman.

"How's your cell phone reception been today?" Radcliffe asked.

"Mine's been spotty. But Klesko hasn't had any problems. He must be using a different carrier."

"You might try here. After the Coast Guard decommissioned Maquoit Island Light, my

101

mother gave the town money to install an antenna on the lighthouse. I don't understand the science, but I always get calls and texts down on Shipwreck Beach."

When I removed my mobile from my pocket, I saw that Radcliffe was right. The signal was strong, and I no longer had an excuse to put off telling DeFord about my multiplying mysteries. I was paranoid the captain would instruct me to hand the investigation over to the state police.

"You can get going, Andrew. I'll walk back to the cottage after I finish making some calls."

After the constable left, I seated myself on a driftwood log and stared at the sea. I could smell rain in the air. Leaden clouds had closed in overhead, but there was still light in the west: a pinkish-gray band that extended along the horizon. Beyond Stormalong, not a single other island was visible.

It had been a mistake to sit down. I hadn't realized how tired I was. My head was pounding. I squeezed my eyes shut, hoping for a brief rest.

At last, I dialed DeFord.

"I wondered when I'd hear from you, Mike." His voice was as clear as if he were standing beside me. "What's going on out there? I was talking to Glover over at the MSP. Klesko told him that your shooter has recanted."

"Not exactly."

In as few words as possible I did my best to explain what I had learned.

Years earlier, Jock DeFord had been an investigator himself, and he had done such a bang-up job he'd been promoted to sergeant. Not much later, he was made a lieutenant responsible for policing hundreds of miles of commercial timberland around Moosehead Lake and west of Baxter State Park. Now he was a captain on the fast track to yet another promotion. Everyone expected him to leapfrog over his immediate supervisor, the major, and become the next head of the Maine Warden Service when the acting colonel stepped aside, probably after the upcoming gubernatorial election.

In other words, Captain DeFord was too smart and too experienced to be bullshitted.

"Sounds like you have a fistful of nothing," he said.

"There's the boot prints."

"Which might or might not be from your shooter. What about the slug?"

"Give us time."

"You should plan on being there indefinitely. I hope you brought a change of Skivvies. I took the initiative and booked you a room."

"I didn't realize there were any inns open this time of year."

"It's not an inn. It's more like a housekeeping

apartment. You'll have a fridge and a microwave. The place is called the White House."

"The White House?"

"It's on the north side of the village, up near the church. I'm told you can't miss it. The woman who runs the place knows you're coming. I told her you might be late so she's putting food out for you."

Across the Gut, sheep had appeared along the hillside of Stormalong. I could make out the daubs of white against the red of the hackberry. I reached for my binoculars, then realized I'd left them back at the cottage in my rucksack.

"Has the media picked up the story yet?"

"We've withheld the name of the victim, pending notification of the next of kin, but it's bound to leak."

"So I should brace myself for reporters."

"Lucky for you the ferry only runs once a week, and the next one is early tomorrow morning. You should be safe. Hopefully, you and Klesko will have wrapped things up before the story breaks wide-open."

"You've heard Steve has court tomorrow?"

"But he'll be back afterward. Don't under-estimate Klesko as a washed-up jock. Steve might look like he took too many pucks to the head, but he's one of the best detectives in the state. Him catching the case was a lucky break for us."

"Yes, sir."

"Anything else you need?"

"Can you give me an update on the situation in Berwick?"

"The little boy is out of surgery, and the docs think he'll pull through. It'll be a long time before they know what kind of brain damage he sustained, though. In some ways, it's probably a blessing that his grandfather died at the scene. The old man was taking beta-blockers, which cause dizziness and fainting. He had no business tromping through those woods with a loaded rifle."

My concentration had been broken by what I was seeing on Stormalong. Among the sheep I could now discern a stick figure. I thought it might be a dead tree until it moved sideways. Blake Markman had emerged from his place of concealment. I had the distinct impression that he was watching me.

11

It took another two hours to process the death scene, by which time it was fully dark.

Using the laser surveying device and her expertise in forensic mapping, Ronette established the approximate location from which the fatal shot was fired. The killer had seemingly been standing behind the same bushes Charley and I had identified as the place of ambush.

By flashlight, we reenacted the shooting to prove it was possible for the shooter to have fired and hit Ariel Evans from that spot.

Charley walked the shooter's tracks back into the orchard and found decent-enough boot prints in a patch of mud that Ronette was able to make a cast of them. The bad news was that the prints had been made by someone wearing size 10 XtraTuf Legacy insulated steel-toe boots, the brand favored by Maquoit's fishermen. Size 10 is also the most common shoe size among American males.

Klesko was leaving with bags of evidence destined for the crime lab in Augusta. But he hadn't found a laptop or a cell phone in the cottage.

Finally, the five of us carried the body bag to the bed of Radcliffe's truck.

Klesko and I decided to leave yellow tape up around the property to discourage curiosity seekers, even though it was no longer an official crime scene. Then I locked the door with the key Jenny Pillsbury had given me. We were done, for the moment, with Gull Cottage.

I decided that Radcliffe would drive the body down to the wharf. Klesko would ride in the passenger seat, and Ronette volunteered to sit in the bed of the truck with Ariel. The proposed arrangement seemed to leave Charley and me without a ride.

"I'll call Joy Juno and have her pick you up," said the constable. "She runs Maquoit Trucking. You'll like her. She's a hoot."

"I'm going to need that list of deer hunters you promised me, Andrew."

"I'll have it for you first thing in the morning. Scout's honor." He actually made the Boy Scout hand sign.

"Where will I find you?"

"Graffam's Store. I'm there every morning the ferry comes in."

The decrepit Toyota belched out a cloud of oily smoke, and then they were off.

Now that Charley and I were alone again, the silence flooded back in between us like a rising tide. The old man sat down on the stone wall along the road with the trapper basket at his feet and checked his legs for ticks with a flashlight.

Watching him, I couldn't keep quiet any longer about the subject that had shadowed my thoughts all day.

"I want you and Ora to know that I'm sorry for the way things ended with Stacey," I blurted out.

Charley let his shoulders sag and his head fall. He hadn't wanted this conversation. But he seemed resigned that he could no longer avoid it.

"No need to apologize."

"To be honest, I'm not even sure they *have* ended. I feel like we're in limbo."

Purgatory might have been the better word.

He raised his large head. "You're no longer living together, though."

"But that was her choice, not mine. She told me she needed to get away from Maine for a few weeks. She said she wanted to see the Everglades before the sea swallows them up. I was distracted with my new job, but I assumed she'd come back when she ran out of money. Then the phone rang and it was her saying she'd been hired to run the Panther Protection Program."

It was a coalition of conservation organizations dedicated to safeguarding the last two hundred or so cougars in the cypress swamps of southwest Florida. She'd glimpsed one of the endangered cats in her headlights as she was speeding along the Tamiami Trail, and the sight of the magnificent predator had caused her to burst into tears. Stacey had found a new mission:

saving a beautiful creature from extinction.

Her father kicked the dirt at his feet, raised a small cloud of dust the way an idle boy might. "Stacey's always been a righteous person. Even when she was a little girl, she needed a cause to fight for. Those Florida developers are going to find out what a ferocious opponent my daughter can be."

"I never wanted her to go, Charley."

But no sooner had the words left my mouth than I recognized them as a falsehood. What I had wanted was for Stacey to be stable, at peace, and happy in our relationship. In short, I had wanted her to become a different person. I doubted whether she would—or even could— undergo that transformation. Living with me hadn't made it happen.

"It's killing me not to have you and Ora in my life anymore," I said.

The statement seemed to catch the old man off guard. "What?"

"I can't stand you being mad at me. Whatever ultimately happens between Stacey and me—"

He sprang to his feet. "We're not *mad* at you, son."

I was tongue-tied. I'd been under the impression that he and his wife blamed me for driving their daughter away. Why else hadn't Charley spoken to me in months?

"You're not?"

"We're heartbroken Stacey has run off again. We'd stopped worrying about her, knowing you were at her side. But now Ora wakes up every night in a panic. It's like we're both back in the past again."

"I'd thought you were angry with me."

He set his hand on my shoulder. "I'm the one who owes you the apology, letting you think we blamed you. Ora even said we should have you out to the lake, but I couldn't get around to extending the invitation. I was afraid that seeing you would make me feel sad about Stacey. Will you forgive me?"

"I still feel like I should be the one asking for forgiveness."

"That's because you are who you are, Mike Bowditch."

A truck engine announced itself in the distance. Half a minute later, a green Dodge Ram appeared around the bend.

Joy Juno turned out to be a big and beefy woman. She had box-dyed henna hair, a metal stud in her nose, a red bandanna knotted around her forehead, and a tattoo of Tweety Bird on one of her impressive biceps.

"Your chariot has arrived," she said in a voice that matched her appearance.

Charley removed his cap. "Much appreciated, milady."

"Ooh, you're a charmer," she cooed. "I'd better watch out for you, handsome."

He didn't blush, but I could see her compliment had left him mute. My friend had one of those polarizing faces that some women considered ugly and others thought was the epitome of rugged manliness.

The backseat was cluttered with several folded tarps, a rolled-up deer fence, an artist's easel and paint box. I also noticed an empty rifle rack mounted to the back of the cab. We ended up all scrunched together on the front bench.

She drove with the dome light on since the dash lights didn't seem to work. "Where to, gentlemen?"

"Bishop's Wharf."

Joy Juno had a car freshener dangling from her mirror that smelled vaguely of honey and was shaped like a bee with the word BEE-OTCH on it.

She wasted no time peppering us with questions. "We haven't had this much excitement on the island since Harmon's trial. So you're probably sworn to secrecy, but Sam Graffam—he runs the store in town—told me to pry what I could out of you."

"How about we trade questions?" I said. "I ask you one, then you ask me one."

"You'll just give me nonresponsive responses. I've known a few cops in my day."

"What can you tell us about Ariel Evans?"

111

"I only talked with her a few times. I brought her fancy luggage from the ferry up to the cottage when she arrived. She was dressed all in black, the way they do in cities, but the next time I saw her, she'd found some tattered jeans and a T-shirt and looked like a native islander. You could tell she really wanted to be here, which is not what you expect from people in November. Hell, even I don't like to be on Maquoit this time of year, and I've spent half my life here."

"Did she say she was writing a book?"

"It's my turn to ask a question. That's what we agreed, ace."

"Go ahead."

"So the rumor going around is that the hermit is your prime suspect."

"I can't comment on that."

She looked sideways at us. "That's your answer? Jesus, you guys are tighter than clams."

"You said you only talked with her a few times. When was the next time, and what did you talk about?"

"That's two questions, but I'll let it slide. It was at Graffam's. She was buying provisions and hired me to cart everything back to Gull Cottage. She asked if I could find a skiff for her to row over to Stormalong. I told her our hermit doesn't welcome visitors, but she laughed and said, 'He'll welcome me.' I guess she was right because, after I found a skiff, I watched her cross the Gut. That tiny, city girl knew how to row a boat! And she must have charmed old Blake. Now it's my turn to ask a question. Do you have any suspects so far and who are they?"

"Those are two questions," I said.

"I answered two of yours. Come on, man. Don't be a dick."

"We're still getting our bearings here. There's a lot about Ariel Evans that we still don't know, specifically what she did since arriving on Maquoit. Who she met, what kinds of inter-actions she had with people here—"

"So you *do* think she was murdered!"

"I didn't say that. But maybe you have some suggestions about who we should talk to."

Juno frowned. "There are people who knew her better than me."

"Like who?"

"The guys at the Trap House. They were falling over themselves to screw her, from what I heard. A girl who's single, sexy, and likes to party . . ."

"Who did she end up hooking up with?"

"I can't say."

"Can't say or won't say?"

"Both. The way I get along out here is by not making any more enemies than I have to. But let me put it this way: there aren't more than a few single men on this island, and none of them are prime catches." The truck jolted over a ridge in the road and we all bounced. "So how do you go about investigating a shooting like this? I'm picturing it's like Hercule Poirot, where you go around interviewing suspects and then gather us all together in a parlor to unmask the murderer."

"That's not how we do it in real life."

"Shit, that would have been fun."

Something moved in the headlights. The two deer we'd seen earlier eating apples in the road had been joined by another doe and four fawns. They all had the same angular faces, the same globed eyes, the same scruffy coats. They high-stepped aside, then closed in again to browse after the dust had died behind us.

I said, "I'll do interviews along with the state police detective and the constable. Hopefully, the person who shot Ariel will come forward and confess. If not, we'll try to build a case to take to the attorney general's office. It might not happen overnight. But if we do find cause to arrest someone, we'll take that person off the island as quietly as we can."

"If it's the Washburns, you'd better call in a SWAT team. No matter who it is, don't expect Andy Radcliffe to be of any help."

"Why not?" I asked but already knew the answer.

"There's basically one qualification to be the constable on Maquoit. You need to be a big, mean motherfucker. You've got to be able to break up a fight. Most of the trouble we have on-island comes when two drunks start brawling at the Trap House or down at Bishop's Wharf. Or there's some domestic shit—a guy's hitting his girl, the girl's hitting her kids. It helps if you're a good peacemaker. But basically, people have to be afraid of you. There are mice on this island scarier than Andy Radcliffe."

"How did he become the constable, then?"

"The first assessor makes the decision. And Harmon is the first assessor. You figure it out."

"How did you end up on the island, Joy?" Charley interjected.

She had a wonderful, utterly uninhibited laugh. "You guessed I'm not a native? What gave it away? My impeccable fashion sense? Nah, I grew up outside Green Bay. My dad was a papermaker for Georgia-Pacific. He'd wanted a boy, so we did manly things together. He made me play hockey until I was actually good. Took me fishing and hunting. He nearly shit himself when I told him I wanted to be a visual artist. I got my BFA at the Rhode Island School of Design and came to the island one summer to paint. The famous artists— your Rockwell Kents and Edward Hoppers—had already done Monhegan to death. But no one had really painted Maquoit."

I said, "Did Ariel ever show you her sketches of Blake Markman?"

Joy seemed genuinely taken aback. "Sketches? Ariel was a writer."

"We found drawings she had done in her cottage, portraits of Markman."

"No shit?"

"You had no idea she was a visual artist, too?" I said.

"No, but it explains some things. She came to my studio once, asking to look at my stuff, and I was surprised by how much she knew about art. She compared my work to James Fitzgerald, who's not exactly a household name. And Fitzgerald was a huge influence on me. Ariel seemed so different that day. She was soft-spoken, serious, not at all the party girl. The way she talked about art, it made me feel . . . close to her."

"She seemed like a kindred spirit?" Charley asked in his best grandfatherly tone.

"Yeah, but also—" Joy made a noise that sounded as if she were pretending to clear her throat. "I was thinking about the day I first set eyes on the island. The minute I stepped off the ferry, I knew I was home. It's the same thing I saw in Ariel's the day she arrived. Not everyone gets this place. But she did."

As we neared the village, we began passing year-round houses. The homes of the islanders all had stacks of lobster traps in their dooryards. They were boxes made of green, yellow, blue, or sometimes even purple vinyl-coated wire. A few houses still had rotting jack-o'-lanterns on their lopsided porches. But two days after Halloween, most of the pumpkins had been smashed in the road, and you could see that the deer had been at them.

After a long pause, Joy Juno spoke again. "I remember Ariel saying a strange thing in my studio. She said, 'All of my life, I have been searching for a sanctuary.' Now she's dead. Some sanctuary this place turned out to be."

12

The next house we came to belonged to a hunter. He had a dead buck hanging from a jerry-rigged meat pole in his yard. My father had hung his trophies—none of which had weighed less than two hundred pounds—to show off their impressiveness to our neighbors, most of whom already hated and feared him.

But there was nothing triumphant about this display. The hunter had hung his meat to age. He was thinking only of food.

The wind had spun this one around toward the road so we could see the bloody incision on its white belly, and the wind kept spinning it. The animal was undersize by the standards I was accustomed to. Field dressed, it might have weighed 120 pounds. Its antlers had a total of five tines. You don't often see odd-numbered antlers, but the deformity added to the grotesqueness of the already-macabre scene.

"Looks like Nat got his deer," Joy said.

"Sure is a scrawny feller," said Charley.

"On Maquoit, that stag there is a giant. Nat's a good hunter. He's a Pillsbury, the last on the island. His family was among the first settlers here, along with the Washburns and the Dennetts. The Reeds came later."

"Pillsbury as in Jenny Pillsbury?" I said.

"Nat's her husband. They have an adorable baby girl named Ava. Figures she'd be so cute, given how good-looking her parents are."

The road through the village continued. The gray houses began to crowd closer together. We passed handmade signs for the school and the library, the Maquoit Church (no denomination specified), the Olde Island Burying Ground, the Lazy Lobster restaurant, where Crowley supposedly had an upstairs room, a coin Laundromat, and a couple of bed-and-breakfasts shuttered for the winter.

People glanced at the truck as we bumped along past, displaying the full gamut of facial expressions from hostility to suspicion. A knot of fishermen emerged from Graffam's Store with styrofoam coffee cups, cans of soda, and open containers of beer. Not a single person was wearing an item of blaze-orange clothing. That told me a lot about how worried they were of being shot themselves.

It was my first view of Marsh Harbor from the ground. Powerful arc lights along the wharf illuminated the near vessels. Lobsterboats, empty of traps, bobbed at their moorings beyond, waiting for the rush that would begin when Trap Day opened Maquoit's official fishing season. A single sailing yacht was moored out past the motorboats, no doubt Radcliffe's.

119

But all eyes were on the *Star of the Sea*. The impressive seventy-five-foot ship was Maine built, with such a powerful engine and a hull so thick that it did double duty as an icebreaker. Part of me wished I could get a tour of the legendary vessel before it left port.

"Everything ready to go here?" I asked.

Klesko grinned his dead-tooth grin. "We were waiting for you slowpokes."

"You sure you don't want to take the boat back?" I asked him.

"I'd like to interview the schoolteacher at least."

From behind me Charley said, "Looks like they're going to have rough seas returning. The flight won't be silky either, but at least it'll be short."

The wind was up again, and the sky above the outer harbor was as dark as the smoke that comes from burning tires, but the air was fresh and bracing in the lungs. Gulls wheeled overhead, hopeful for whatever scraps we might discard. Small rafts of eiders were visible as white and black spots at the harbor mouth. I heard big waves crashing against the island's granite breakwater.

"I almost forgot," Klesko said. "Landry wants to talk with you. She's already aboard with Ariel."

I made my way carefully down the ridged gangplank. The apparatus could be raised and lowered to suit the weather conditions and the size of the boat trying to come alongside. Because the tide was high, the walkway was perfectly horizontal, but the choppiness of the waves made every step tenuous.

In the narrow hall, a woman, whom I took to be the mission's nurse-practitioner, given the box of prescription bottles in her hands, pressed her back against the wall for me to pass. "You're the warden investigator?"

"That's right."

"Keep going down the hall and take the first steps you see down to the galley. We had to put your shooting victim in the walk-in cooler. Excuse me, I need to run some meds up to the store before we leave."

The cook in the galley was stirring a big pot of something that smelled like chowder. He opened the cooler for me. Inside was Ronette Landry, seated on cartons of bottled water. Someone had lent her a blanket to wrap over her uniform. She had pulled her watch cap down around her ears. Her nose was reindeer red and she looked miserable. I stepped into the refrigerated air. The door closed with such force and finality that I found myself checking to make sure we hadn't been locked in.

"Thanks for coming." Her breath was visible, her nose stuffed. "I wasn't sure Steve would remember to give you my message."

"Ronette, you don't have to sit in the fridge with her."

"She shouldn't be alone."

"Did you want to compare notes before the boat pushes off?"

Either she hadn't heard my question or she had prepared a speech she was determined to give. "This is going to be a difficult case to solve, Mike. I've worked a lot of hunting homicides. The rain tonight's going to hammer the crime scene. Plus there's heavy fog moving in afterward. There will be no point in DeFord's sending over the rest of the ERT. And then there are the islanders, who are never going to turn over the man who did it. You're going to have to do this the old-fashioned way."

A shiver passed through me. I turned the collar of my peacoat up against the cold. "Maybe the autopsy will turn up something."

Again she pretended not to hear me. "There's one other thing. I didn't want to say anything before because the time wasn't right. I'm sorry about you and Stacey."

When it came to gossip, the Maine Department of Inland Fisheries and Wildlife was worse than a small-town diner.

"It's no big thing. She and I are taking a break." My heart knew this was a lie.

"She was a brilliant biologist and the toughest

woman I knew. Physically toughest. It's a real loss to the state."

My breath formed a shapeless cloud. "Thank you."

"It seems like it's been one loss after another. First Kathy Frost retiring. Then Dani choosing to become a trooper. There are only three women left in the Warden Service now. The department should declare *us* an endangered species."

Dani was former game warden Danielle Tate. She was a five-foot-four-inch blond dynamo with a black belt in Brazilian jujitsu. When we'd first met, she was straight out of Warden School, and she had struck me as a sullen, antisocial, perennially pissed-off person. To make everything worse, she'd also inexplicably developed a crush on me that had made our interactions awkward, especially after Stacey had moved in with me. But Dani had changed over the past few years, grown up, become self-confident and at ease with herself. She'd left the Warden Service because she believed she had an easier path to advancement in the state police. I was impressed with the courage that had taken.

In the weeks since Stacey had left I had occasionally found myself thinking of Dani.

I had the impression Ronette still hadn't said the thing she needed to say to me before the *Star of the Sea* left port.

"I want you to make me a promise, Mike." She removed a well-used tissue from her pocket and dabbed her nostrils. "What I'm asking is that you don't let this fall by the wayside."

"Come on, Ronette. You know we don't ever let that happen—not in the Warden Service, not in the state police."

"Not even when the female victim is unsympathetic?"

Ariel's blond beauty, not to mention her fame, would catch the interest of the news media, which would, in turn, put pressure on us to solve the case. But her image would be degraded by those who didn't care about the harm they inflicted on her friends and family. And I knew more than a few holier-than-thou cops who would claim she'd gotten what she deserved—because she was from out of state, because she should have been wearing blaze orange, because, in their eyes, she was a junkie and a slut.

"It shouldn't matter that Ariel Evans did drugs or slept around," said Ronette. "Ariel was a human being, one of God's children, and someone killed her and needs to be held accountable. That's all that matters."

"I agree completely."

Ronette Landry set her hand on the crinkly body bag beside her. "This woman is no longer with us. It's too late to save her life.

But even now she needs a champion. You need to promise me that you will be her champion because I'm not sure anyone else is up to the job."

I promised.

13

Charley and I helped the captain of the *Star of the Sea* cast off. We lifted the thick hawsers off the bronze tops of the pilings and tossed the ropes down to one of the ship's mates.

As the engine roared to life, herring gulls rose from the harbor on soft, gray wings. The screws began to churn and the water started to boil. Then the wind pushed the greasy diesel fumes toward the wharf, and I had to take a step back to keep from choking.

Ronette stood on the top deck as the ship pulled away from the island. Her face was as white as porcelain in the arc lights. She was clutching a steaming cup of coffee or tea that made me aware of my own coldness and exhaustion. In two more hours she would be in Bass Harbor, where she would meet the "coach" that would transport Ariel's body to the autopsy table. But I had no idea how long my stay on Maquoit might last.

The wind had a new sharpness, like a scythe slicing across the open water. I shivered and dug out my leather gloves.

"You gentlemen preparing to depart, too?"

It was Harmon Reed, who had come down to the ferry dock to see off the *Star of the Sea*. He had a corncob pipe clenched between his molars. The temperature had dropped as the clouds descended on the island, but the harbormaster was still dressed in short sleeves, which revealed his huge, sun-spotted forearms.

"Mr. Stevens and I will be flying back tonight," said Klesko. "But you're stuck with the warden for the time being."

"I hope you had the foresight to book a room."

"I'm staying at the White House, I think it's called."

He glanced at the hill above the village. At the top was a traditional New England church, high steepled, clapboarded, and ghost pale in the gathering darkness. "Kind of quiet up there this time of year. But at least you'll have company. Nothing warmer than a lonely widow."

With that, Harmon Reed took his leave of us. He passed through the blinding glow of the wharf lights and then was lost in the thickening shadows.

When I glanced back at the *Star of the Sea*, it had turned north past John's Point, headed for home.

Half a dozen islanders had come down to the dock to watch the ship depart, and now they began to scatter. Joy Juno sat inside her truck, tapping away on her cell phone. There was no sign of Radcliffe. He'd probably gone home to have supper with his family.

• • •

Charley said he wanted to walk up to the airstrip to get a little exercise and fill his lungs with "good sea air." He told us he'd be waiting at the plane.

Joy Juno drove Klesko and me to the schoolhouse.

"The State of Maine better be reimbursing me for taxiing you officers around," she said. "Why, I must have put on a good three miles!"

"I'm sure we can arrange something," I said.

"If you're sticking around, Warden, you might want to see about scaring up a vehicle of your own. There aren't many working trucks to be had. But probably someone has a golf cart they can loan you."

The thought of conducting suspect interviews via golf cart mortified me.

When we got to the school, we found the lights off. The small, square building was covered in white clapboards with a roof that was perfectly pyramidal. The days of the one-room schoolhouse might be long gone elsewhere in America, but the era lived on in Maine's remote island communities. Beryl's electric cart was nowhere in sight.

"She must have gotten tired of waiting," said Klesko with a hint of frustration.

"Maybe we should check the library," I said.

Juno reached her thick arm across my chest to

point down the road. "That's it there, that little brown building."

The library windows were also dark.

But I noticed something flapping on the door. "Steve, can you let me out for a second?"

What I had spotted was a note held in place by two tacks. I shined my pocket flashlight on the wind-blown paper.

I WAITED AS LONG AS I COULD. I'LL BE HERE AT 6 AM TOMORROW BEFORE CLASS IF YOU WANT TO STOP BY.

—B

When I showed the note to Klesko, he looked as if he wanted to rip it to shreds.

"Can we call her?" he asked Juno.

"We can try."

There was no answer at her landline, nor did she pick up her cell.

"She has a bad case of Lyme disease," said Joy Juno. "Sometimes it wipes her out so she can't get out of bed."

"I'll catch up with her in the morning," I told the detective.

"Where to next?" asked Joy.

"The airfield," said Klesko, his frustration audible in his voice. "The way this day has gone, it'll be a wonder if we don't crash on takeoff."

With the low cloud cover, I had begun to worry that Klesko's fears were not entirely unfounded. Charley was arguably the finest bush pilot in Maine, but you'd be hard-pressed to find an aviation expert who would recommend taking off from an unlit airstrip in pitch-black conditions, especially with twenty-knot winds buffeting the hilltop.

"How are you going to do this, Charley?" I asked.

"With Ms. Juno's kind assistance."

I should have realized that my friend had more tricks up his sleeve than a vaudeville magician.

Klesko removed his black duffel from the back of the pickup and dropped it at his feet. It landed like a bag of hammers.

"I'll aim to get back here as soon as I can tomorrow," he said. "Marshall has me scheduled as her first witness. She's putting me on the stand after opening statements. So early afternoon at the latest. I'll try to get one of our state police pilots to fly me out of Bangor to save time."

I shoved my hands into the pockets of my peacoat. "Do you mind my doing interviews without you?"

"Not as long as you record your conversations."

Charley wandered over, humming one of the folk songs he'd picked up as a child in the logging camps, "The Ballad of Roaring Bert."

"How are you going to see well enough to take off?" Klesko asked the pilot.

"Don't you worry, Steve. I've flown on nights that were as dark as two yards up a bear's behind."

I wondered if the state police detective realized that these lumber-camp expressions were part of Charley Stevens's act. My friend could turn the folksiness on or off when the situation called for it. As a warden, he had secured dozens of convictions against people who had underestimated his intelligence.

"What about those trees at the end?" I said.

"That's where Joy comes in, provided she's game for it."

The muscular woman laughed. "For a cutie like you, I'll do anything."

Charley directed her to drive along the runway and park perpendicular to the end. "Shine your headlights across the gravel if you will. Now if you all will excuse us, the investigator and I have something we need to talk about."

"Have you done this before?" I asked him when we were alone.

"Stacey did, and she lived to tell to the tale. That's good enough for me."

"Your daughter's always been a resourceful woman."

He fell silent in the darkness.

131

"Any last pieces of advice?" I asked, desperate to change the subject.

"Just because Harmon is the big cheese out here doesn't mean he knows who shot Ariel. He might have his suspicions, but he doesn't know for sure. That's why he wanted to shadow us all day."

"I thought it was to keep tabs on the investigation."

"It was that, too. But I can tell when someone's nervous. In Vietnam I used to play poker against Green Berets, and those bastards gave me a crash course in spotting bluffs. Pay attention the next time Harmon starts fiddling with his corncob pipe."

"Will do."

Charley sighed and glanced toward the cockpit of the Cessna. "Take care, young feller. The people here seem friendly enough, but never forget that someone is hiding a deadly secret. And he's already killed once. Keep your pistol under your pillow and a round in your chamber when you go to sleep tonight."

I held out my hand for him to shake as was our custom, but for the first time in my memory, he embraced me. After a moment, he let go and made his way to the plane without a backward glance.

I waited in the darkness as he went down the items on his checklist. Then the engine sputtered

132

to life, the propeller began to turn, and the aircraft started creeping forward. The next thing I knew, it was speeding and hopping along the uneven ground. Seconds before it crossed the shining, ethereal fence made by Joy Juno's headlights, I saw the wheels leave the ground.

I was marooned on Maquoit Island.

14

Joy Juno turned the truck toward the village. "Now where?"

"Is there a restaurant—?"

"Oh, sure. We have restaurants on the island. Good ones, too. If you don't mind waiting till Memorial Day for them to open."

I should have known that most businesses would be closed for the season.

"What about this famous Trap House where Ariel was said to hang out?"

"You seem like a rugged guy. But cop or no cop, you don't want to go in there without some backup. There are plenty of men on this island who have no fear of the police—or anything else. You've got to be crazy to fish in the dead of winter when your boat is caked with ice, and your fingers are too numb to even run the pot puller. Besides, the only food you're likely to find at the Trap are circus peanuts and stale popcorn."

I had no doubt she was right about the Trap House, but I had entered more rooms full of dangerous drunkards than she would ever know. Thus far, I had emerged intact except for a lone scar along my hairline: a reminder of a bad night long ago at the Dead River Inn.

"You might as well take me to the place I'm staying," I said. "It's called the White House. Is that the color or did a president sleep there?"

She nearly swerved into the bushes from laughing so hard. "It's not the White House. It's the *Wight* House! *W-I-G-H-T.* Sweet Jesus. That is the funniest thing I heard all day."

"I was beginning to wonder."

"Don't get your hopes up. It's still a shithole."

Her tires scattered pebbles like birdshot as she drove the truck up a steep hill to the north of the village. We passed a handful of old, mostly dignified dwellings, some with their date of construction on them. The oldest I spotted was 1803.

"People say the Wight House has a ghost," Joy said. "But you probably don't believe in paranormal stuff."

"I definitely know what it's like to be haunted."

"I know what you mean. The worst ghosts in my life aren't even dead."

The steeple of the church beckoned from ahead: a pale beacon in the dark.

The Wight House appeared to be a fairly typical fisherman's house. It had started as a modest Cape. Then the owner had decided to add a second story. Then another addition. Somewhere along the line, the amateur architect had decided his guests might enjoy cantilevered porches and decks and had affixed these to the exterior, along with a haphazard system of external stairways: a sop to the state fire marshal, who had, no doubt, received a complaint from a lodger who recognized what a firetrap that gray clapboard monstrosity was.

A single light flickered in the front hall. Every other window was a black mirror.

"Cheery place," I said.

"Ellen Wight is a character. She's become even more eccentric since Elmore died. He was her husband."

"I'm sure it'll be fine."

Joy lowered her voice to make it sound spooky. "That's what the last guest said."

I reached for the door handle. "Thanks for the ride."

With my rucksack on my back and carrying my computer case, I ascended the splintered, unlit porch. A weathered sign hung suspended above the door. It swung back and forth, creaking in the wind. A brass knocker was situated at eye level, but DeFord had said I could let myself in.

The hall smelled of mildew, rising from air vents, only slightly masked by oil soap recently used to clean the varnished floorboards. The décor leaned heavily in the direction of antiques that were scuffed and unloved enough to be genuine island artifacts, as opposed to tables and chairs transported from the mainland to lend the inn phony ambience.

"Hello?"

There was no answer.

I poked my head into a darkened parlor. Portraits of dead ship captains eyeballed me from the walls.

"Mrs. Wight?"

At the far end of the hall I found a small cherrywood desk with a note and a motel key on it. A desk lamp spilled light on the stationery page:

Welcome, Warden Investigator Bowdoin.

We hope you had a safe and smooth trip to our precious island. May your stay on Maquoit be a pleasure and a font of fond memories in the years to come.

Your employer has arranged payment for your accommodations and requested we provide you with provender. We have put you in "Eight Bells," one of our finest rooms. You should not want for anything, but if you find yourself in need, please use this pad to leave a note and we shall attend to it at our earliest opportunity.

The wifi is anchorchain.

Your hosts,

Elmore and Ellen Wight

The tone of the letter was beyond bizarre. The language was the same as if I'd been a tourist visiting in August. And hadn't Joy mentioned that Mrs. Wight was a widow? Had her husband's ghost coauthored the note?

Eight bells was an old maritime term that pertained to the measurement of time at sea. At noon and midnight, the ship's bell would ring eight times. Given its association with the witching hour, the term had inevitably come to be associated with death.

I expected Eight Bells to be room number eight, but instead it was number twelve. The cramped space had a twin bed, a humming dorm-size refrigerator, and a microwave with a blinking clock. The shared bathroom was down the hall. There was no telephone; nor was there a television. There was, however, a grocery bag on the counter filled with assorted canned goods: sardines, baked beans, clam chowder. A jar of dollar-store peanut butter. A loaf of Wonder bread. A box of pilot crackers. And a quart of milk in the fridge.

I hadn't detected evidence of other occupants. Aside from the usual creaks and rattles of an aging house, the building was utterly silent. I peeled back the gauzy curtains and, once my eyes adjusted to the darkness, found myself looking down into the burial ground of the adjacent church. The rows of gravestones, when glimpsed from above, reminded me of teeth. Rain began pelting the glass.

In the bathroom I peeled nine ticks off my person. Two had embedded themselves in the skin of my abdomen. One was fairly well engorged.

I didn't bother to unpack my rucksack but did hang up my peacoat in the mothball-perfumed closet, draped my pants and sweater over the frayed chair back, and set my boots in front of the door, should anyone try to enter the room while I was asleep.

I sat down on the bed with my laptop while I ate a supper of peanut butter sandwiches and milk. DeFord had copied me with the relevant files he'd unearthed in his online searches.

There were news reports from the day's other hunting fatality, but nothing about Maquoit.

Charley had texted me from the Hancock County Airport that they'd arrived safely without Klesko having had to use the "upchuck bag."

Stacey had sent me a link to an album of photos of the Everglades—manatees basked in the warm outflow of an electrical power plant, a mangrove was adorned with egrets like white flowers, a Burmese python lay coiled under a palmetto. There was no note except *WYWH*. After years together, our communication had been reduced to this: scenic pictures and abbreviations.

Unexpected was an email from the state trooper whom Ronette Landry had mentioned to me earlier. Former game warden Dani Tate and

I were not pen pals, and I couldn't remember the last time we'd spoken. This message, too, was just a photo with a short note below. The picture was of a cute-faced black cat with white paws.

Hi Mike

Thought you might recognize this pretty little lady. I stopped by the shelter and was told that no one wanted her. I broke down and adopted the poor thing. She's no longer Puddin' though! I'm calling her Xanthe after the Amazon warrior. Good luck out there on the island.

Dani

The abandoned cat had played a small but crucial part in the last case Dani and I had worked together. I'd wondered if the animal had ever found a home.

Hi Dani:

That's awesome! I remember Xanthe as a sweetheart. But I've always thought of you as a dog person, not a cat person.

Mike

The response came less than a minute later:

I go both ways.

Then before I could even laugh:

That didn't come out the way I meant!

How had Dani known I was on Maquoit? Had Ronette noticed my reaction when she'd mentioned Tate's name and taken it upon herself to text her? Something was definitely up.

I spent a solid hour and a half typing up my notes on my laptop. I hoped that the sheer volume of words would convince DeFord that I hadn't wasted my time and could be trusted to pursue the investigation to its conclusion. I attached my photos and video recordings. My finger hesitated a long time over the trackpad before I pushed send.

Next, I started reading up on the victim. Ariel Evans had been thirty-seven, Manhattan-born, attended the Dalton School, then Columbia, where she edited the daily newspaper and received a graduate degree in journalism. Her parents, Thomas and Maisey, and brother, Giacamo, had died in a car crash in Rome. She had one surviving sister, Miranda, location unknown.

In photographs, Ariel seemed to have two faces. One was fierce-eyed, wary, almost hostile. The other was strikingly open and attractive.

Make that three faces. There was also the rictus of her waxen corpse. Ariel Evans's final expression was a death mask that didn't resemble the woman it had been made to memorialize.

She'd led a life worth memorializing. In college the budding writer had spent a semester in Johannesburg, but had forsaken her studies to sneak off into the bush to record certain atrocities she'd heard about. This piece, titled "The Last Rhino," was an account of the bloody fight to save wild rhinos from extinction. What impressed me was that the twenty-year-old Evans had not only embedded herself with the South African game wardens charged with protecting the imperiled animals; she had also won the confidence of the heavily armed, khat-chewing poachers. The article had appeared in *GQ* and been nominated for a National Magazine Award.

Even exhausted as I was, I recognized how gifted and fearless a reporter she had been. Her death seemed all the more tragic for having occurred here, on an insignificant island in the North Atlantic, after a lifetime of journalistic bravery. What was Blake Markman compared to the last rhinos on earth?

15

It rained that night, and the wind wailed like all the island's banshees had risen from their graves. Occasionally, a gust would bend around the corner of the house and slam a loose shutter against the clapboards. Or a creaking in the hall would startle me upright. But after the third such occurrence, I barely batted my eyes before lapsing back into unconsciousness.

During "the season," as wardens referred to the thirty days when hunters were permitted to take deer with conventional firearms in Maine, I always awakened before dawn. Many nights I didn't sleep at all.

It was five-thirty sharp. After years of being a game warden, my biological clock was nothing if not precise.

I took a cold shower to shock myself into alertness. I hung my father's dog tags around my neck as I always did and dressed in the same clothes as the day before. I decided to forgo another peanut butter sandwich in the hope that I could find a better option at the village store.

I sat on the thin mattress and made a plan for my day. First: coffee. Then I would visit Beryl McCloud at the schoolhouse, assuming she was feeling better. Next I needed to take a run at Harmon Reed. The harbormaster almost certainly knew which islanders I should consider suspects. I would meet the ferry from Bass Harbor in case DeFord had changed his mind and sent me reinforcements. By then the tide would be right for me to row over to Stormalong and have a friendly chat with its lone resident.

Downstairs I found a note from my invisible innkeeper.

Good morning, Warden Investigator Bowdoin.

We hope you slept soundly.

You should not want for anything, but if you find yourself in need, please use this pad to leave a note and we shall attend to it at our earliest opportunity.

Your hosts,

Elmore and Ellen Wight

Maybe the footsteps I thought I'd imagined hearing had been real after all. I wasn't sure whether to laugh or shiver.

When I opened the front door, I stepped face-first into a wall of fog. I tried shining my flashlight into it, but the beam dissolved within yards. The grass was gray with dew. I focused the light on the ground to keep from stumbling over some lurking rock.

My cell phone was being willful again, and I

had to wander around the hilltop in the fog and the dark before I could find a spot with decent reception. It turned out to be the adjacent grave-yard. The rain had left coffin-shaped puddles where the caskets of the dead had sunk into the ground.

"Captain?"

"Good morning, Mike." If DeFord sounded as if he'd been awake for hours, it was because he no doubt had been. "How was your room?"

I didn't know if he would believe me if I told him. I said it was fine.

"Did that Wight woman provide you with food? She'd better have served up filet mignon, given the price she's charging us to put you up."

"No filet mignon, but the peanut butter was tasty. You actually talked with Ellen Wight?"

"Of course, why?"

I left the question unanswered. "Any news on your end?"

"Ariel made it to Augusta last night. Landry, sick as a dog, drove all the way there herself, following the coach. Kitteridge has the autopsy scheduled first thing this morning."

Ideally, I would have been present as well, along with Klesko. I had never attended an autopsy before and felt that it was a rite of passage I still needed to go through as an investigator.

"Can you tell Kitteridge to call me as soon as he's finished?"

"I will."

Off to the northwest, I could hear the clanging of the channel marker at the entrance to Maquoit Harbor. I'd only been outside for ten minutes and already my peacoat was as damp as if I'd left it hanging in the shower stall. The sea air wasn't cold by Fahrenheit, but the mist passed so easily through my clothing, I was covered in goose bumps.

"How's the weather out there?" DeFord asked.

"Fogged in."

"That's what the forecast said. Temps in the forties. Calm winds, seas two to three feet, relative humidity near one hundred percent. Conditions should persist for the next thirty-six to forty-eight hours. It's this southerly front that's moved in."

My knowledge of meteorology was more practical than academic, gained from working outdoors, day in and day out, in all seasons and all weather. But I knew enough about the science to understand what DeFord was telling me. All planes and helicopters would be grounded in the fog. And since the only ferry was scheduled to leave Mount Desert Island within hours, it meant that Steve Klesko would need to find a boat if he hoped to return to Maquoit.

It also meant that I would not be leaving the island in the near future.

• • •

When I was a rookie, my field training officer, Sergeant Kathy Frost, had told me that if you wanted to get to know a small, secretive community, you should explore the local cemetery. From the comparative sizes of the monuments to the groupings of graves, you could learn which families were prominent or had once been prominent. Long-standing grudges manifested themselves in segregated burial plots. Enemies in life were almost never interred near one another in death.

From the Olde Island Burying Ground, I learned that Maquoit's earliest settlers had been the Pillsburys and the Washburns, many of whom had died (most often in childbirth or at sea) in the first decades of the nineteenth century. The Reeds seemed to have been relative latecomers. The first marker I found with that name was a small block of granite belonging to a Harold Reed, who died in 1921. Tellingly, the sizes of the Reeds' tombstones increased over the decades. The largest of them all, a towering marble obelisk, bore the name of Horatio Reed, undoubtedly Harmon's father.

Then, in a curious reversal of this progression, came a small stone in the family plot dedicated to Heath Reed. The inscription said he'd died five years earlier at the age of twenty-eight: LOST AT SEA.

Strange that Harmon would have commissioned a monolith to mark his father's gravesite and yet barely acknowledged his son with a stone no bigger than a cinder block.

There was a wrought-iron fence around the cemetery with a gate that someone had kicked halfway off its hinges. I did my best to close it behind me, then set off down the hill, into town.

I hadn't gotten more than ten yards before I heard a crunching noise ahead of me in the fog.

"Hello?" I said.

There was no answer.

I took a step forward and raised my light. The beam caught the obsidian eyes of a deer. A spike buck, a yearling, stood before me in the gravel road. The cracking I'd heard was the deer chewing a flattened rat someone had run over. I'd never seen such a thing before: a deer driven by hunger to become carnivorous.

The roadkill dropped from the buck's mouth. Deer have no top front teeth, just a hard plate of bone to grind vegetation against. No wonder it was having trouble masticating the rat.

"Hey there, little guy," I said softly.

His white-fringed tail flagged when I spoke.

I took another step forward, and he stamped his front hoof but didn't bolt. I took another step, then another.

I was close enough now to see the pinkish translucence of his ears and to have touched

148

his mist-beaded nose. I could feel the thin heat rising from his gaunt body. Up close I could see that his bulging eyes were sunken and red around the edges. His teeth were worn and as yellowed as those of a smoker dying of emphysema. For an instant, I considered scratching his forehead, but I feared he might snap at my delicious, flesh-covered fingers.

Instead I passed him by. A moment later, I heard a scraping sound in the fog behind me. The deer was endeavoring to pick up the rat again with his stained, ineffectual teeth.

I had gone perhaps another hundred yards down the hill. I had passed a dozen more houses, most boarded up for the winter, a few showing signs of habitation, when I heard a wolf whistle. I peered through the mist and saw Joy Juno standing outside the one-room schoolhouse. Her own truck was nowhere to be seen, but a flesh-toned Datsun pickup was parked beside the swing set.

"What are you doing up this early?" I asked.

"I'm always up with the roosters. Besides, Beryl texted me this morning asking me to tell you she's home sick. She had to cancel school. That Lyme disease has really kicked her ass."

I made a mental note to check on the teacher later.

Joy was bundled up in a Carhartt work coat and was wearing a matching duck-colored cap.

I couldn't imagine worse colors to wear during deer-hunting season, but it spoke to how unafraid the islanders were of being shot, despite what had happened the day before to Ariel Evans.

"What's the deal with Mrs. Wight? She wasn't there when I checked in, but she must have come by during the night because she'd left me another note. And she signed her dead husband's name on it, too."

Joy Juno was the only person I'd met whose laugh could be accurately described as a guffaw. "Ellen is no ghost, if that's what you're worried about. The thing about signing Elmore's name, I think it's just habit. You'll run into her if you stay long enough. Any sense of how long that'll be? Oh, right. You're not allowed to tell me. But I'm allowed to guess where you're headed, aren't I? You're going down to Graffam's to talk with the breakfast club."

"No comment."

"Ha! I knew it. Well, at least you can arrive in style now." Like a game-show hostess unveiling a prize, she swept her arm toward the Datsun. "Old Mr. Blackington is back onshore getting both of his knees replaced—the poor bastard—but he said you were welcome to use this 'monster' truck of his."

"He's expecting to be reimbursed, I imagine?"

"You happen to be in luck. Mr. Blackington's a big booster of law enforcement. He was the island constable out here for ages, and his oldest boy is a state trooper in Vermont."

The ancient Datsun wasn't tan so much as speckled. It was dotted from end to end with so many rust spots it reminded me of a person with a terminal case of the measles.

"As long as it works."

"He says it does—he just put in a new tranny—but he suggests you don't go off mudding in the hayfields."

She tossed me the keys. The ring was attached to a fob shaped like an American flag. I opened the driver's door and was impressed by the pine-scented cleanliness of the cramped cab. The truck had no backseat at all, not even a place to stash a jacket. But when I turned the key in the ignition, the engine purred to life.

I cranked down the window. "You're going to need to share Mr. Blackington's address with me so I can send him a thank-you."

"He'd prefer a gallon of Allen's coffee brandy."

Now it was my turn to laugh. "So what are you up to today?"

"I'll be dealing with stuff from the ferry most of the morning. But I might be able to get in some painting later. You should stop at my studio if you have a minute. It's the second-to-last house on John's Point, right after Andy's place. There's a sign out front."

I doubted I would have time to make social

calls. But I was curious to see her art. And we were both aware that, despite our easy banter, we hadn't yet addressed her feelings about Ariel Evans. The truck driver spent her days carrying cargo around the island, talking with people, noticing who was doing what—all of which made her potentially an important witness. Sooner or later, I would need to sit down with Joy Juno for a formal interview and press her to dish her neighbors' secrets. When I did, I had a feeling she would end up liking me a lot less than she did now.

16

Daytime on Maine waterfronts always begins in the dark. It didn't surprise me to pass lit kitchen windows on my drive into the village center or to find Graffam's open for business at this ungodly hour.

Four pickups were parked in front, driven there no doubt by men who resided less than a stone's throw from the store. One of the things I knew about Maine islanders was that they drove their vehicles at every opportunity. Even if it was just a hundred yards to fetch a pack of smokes. They were even worse than their landlubbing counterparts.

Inside, five men glanced up from a picnic table. The only one I recognized was Harmon. But all of their faces were windburned and sun damaged.

"Warden Bowditch!" the harbormaster said. "The boys and I was wondering when we'd see you this morning."

"Good morning, Mr. Reed."

"How was your beauty sleep up there at the House of the Seven Gables?"

"I slept fine, thank you."

"Pour yourself a cup of coffee and order yourself some fish hash. You can squeeze in here with us. Chum, make room for the warden!"

The market was like others I had visited on working waterfronts; it was a combination grocery (stocked almost entirely with prepared foods), agency liquor store, counter-service restaurant, and ship's chandlery. The air was close and warm, and it smelled of brewing coffee and burned bacon. I felt a pang of nostalgia for that single teenage summer when I had worked on a boat and had counted myself a lobsterman.

"So have you figured out who done it yet?" said the old man Reed had addressed as Chum.

"How can he?" another man said. "He ain't even checked our alibis yet. Where was you, Chum McNulty, when the fateful shot was fired?"

"Ask your missus."

Laughter broke out as I proceeded to the counter with my coffee. The middle-aged, pot-bellied man behind the register had a shaved head but a full beard. He wore cargo shorts and a T-shirt bearing the slogan I'M NOT GAY BUT $20 IS $20.

"Coffee's on the house," he said.

"Thank you, but I can pay. I will try some of your fish hash, though."

"What are you doing, Sam?" said yet another member of the breakfast club. "Trying to bribe him with coffee? Don't you know the going price for wardens is a case of beer."

"That ain't funny, Shattuck," said Harmon Reed in his captain's voice. "You apologize now."

"Aw, I was just pulling his chain."

"Apologize."

Shattuck was the youngest of the group, and his voice became a squeak. "Jeez, all right. I'm sorry."

But Reed's mood had turned. "I told you to move your ass cheeks, Chum, and make room for our guest."

I removed my knit cap and stuffed it in my pocket. "I'd rather stand."

"So is the detective coming back on the ferry this morning?" asked Reed. "No way anyone's flying out here today in this pea soup."

Sam Graffam addressed the room from the grill where he was preparing my fish hash. "Now here's some interesting trivia!" The men at the table groaned, but it had no effect on the grocer. "I saw a show on the History Channel th'other night. About London in Victorian times and Jack the Ripper really being the Prince of Wales."

"Oh, jeez," said Shattuck with a theatrical eye roll. "Here it comes."

Graffam was undeterred. "The term *pea soup* applies to smog, you see. Not fog like we have out here. It was on account of all those coal fires burning. It turned the air thick and yellow like pea

155

soup. That's where the expression comes from."

"Pea soup is green," said Chum McNulty, as if this disproved the store owner's thesis.

"Not the French-Canadian kind," countered Graffam.

"You said the TV show was about London!"

The etymological debate might have continued to rage if Reed hadn't broken in. "What about it, Warden? Will we be seeing Detective Klesko on today's ferry or not?"

There was no point in playing coy since the ferry would arrive soon enough, and they would all know who was on board and who wasn't. They might already know if they'd gotten a call from someone at the boat-line office in Bass Harbor. Harmon struck me as the kind of man who would want advance warning if an invasion of police officers was approaching his fiefdom.

"I'm flying solo today, Mr. Reed."

The old man stroked one of his muttonchops with the back of his hand. "When you call me Mr. Reed, it reminds me of the last time I was in front of a judge. Can't say it was a pleasant experience."

"What did you do, sink someone's boat?"

The room went as silent as if someone had shattered a glass on the floor.

I wasn't sure what had made me provoke the island patriarch. Maybe I was tired of his trying to dominate every single person in sight. It had obviously been a long time since anyone had dared to challenge Harmon Reed.

His face didn't flush, his voice didn't rise. If anything his tone became quieter, more menacing for being little more than a whisper. "In actuality it was my boat that was sunk. But I expect you know that already. I expect you know all about my misadventures in the criminal justice system. Maybe you were just pulling my chain, the way Shattuck did yours."

"I meant no offense."

"I'm sure you didn't." Harmon crumpled into a ball the aluminum foil that had enfolded his breakfast sandwich. "So what's the order of business today? You'll be conducting interviews, I would assume?"

"That's right."

"And I'm at the top of your list, I expect."

"What makes you say that?"

"Because if I'm not at the top of your list, then you're a poor excuse for an investigator." He arose from his place at the table, and all the other men followed suit. "Sam, would you mind us using your office?"

The shop owner waved his spatula. "Harmon, you don't even need to ask."

I followed the harbormaster's broad back through the kitchen. The deep fryer had left a greasy film over every surface including the warped wooden floor.

Reed seated himself at Sam Graffam's cluttered desk and folded his hands over his impressive chest. He'd put on a long-sleeved chamois shirt, unbuttoned, hanging open, over his T-shirt but was otherwise dressed the same as the day before.

No other chairs were in the room. I took out my iPhone and pointed the video camera at Harmon.

The tiny machine seemed to amuse him. "That thing come with a lie detector, too?"

"That's the deluxe model."

"I was home with my wife, Martha, when the Evans girl was shot, and she'll testify to that effect. Martha, I mean. Her sister Ellie was there, too. The ladies were planning the big Thanksgiving dinner we Reeds always put on for the island. What else have you got?"

"It might save us time, Mr. Reed, if you waited for me to ask the questions before you answered them."

The old man removed his pipe from his shirt pocket and clamped the stem between his teeth while he prepared his tobacco. I stood watching him while he went about his ritual. Charley had said that Harmon Reed fiddled with his pipe when he was playing for time.

"Ask away then," he said.

"What time did your nephew appear at your house yesterday?"

"Ten oh seven."

"How can you be so precise about that?"

"Because when a scared young man knocks on your door saying he found a dead girl, you can expect that sooner or later, a police officer will ask you what time he showed up."

I have never been a smoker, not of cigarettes, not of cigars, not of marijuana. Certainly not of pipes. But Reed's tobacco had a surprisingly pleasant, woodsy aroma.

"Andrew Radcliffe claims you only called him at eleven o'clock. Why did you wait for fifty-three minutes to telephone the constable?"

"It took some time to calm the boy down."

The man lied with real confidence, I had to hand it to him. "And what did your nephew tell you at ten oh seven? Be as specific as you can, please."

"That he was hunting over near Gull Cottage and came across the Evans woman lying face-down under her clothesline. The sight of all the blood shocked him so hard he nearly pissed his britches."

"Did you have reason to believe Mr. Crowley might be lying?"

"About pissing his britches?"

"About having come across Ariel Evans after she was already dead. Did it occur to you that he might have shot her himself?"

"It occurred. That's why I asked to look over

159

his gun. I wanted to check if it had been fired. It hadn't."

"How can you be sure?"

"I was a coastie back in the sixties. I know what a firearm that's been discharged smells like."

Sam Graffam appeared at the door with my plate of fish hash. I thanked him, set it on a stack of marine supply catalogs, and closed the door. Almost immediately the room turned hazy with pipe smoke.

"Tell me about your nephew."

"Would you like his whole biography or the *Reader's Digest*?"

"You don't have much respect for authority, do you, Mr. Reed?"

"It depends on who's demanding the respect." He spoke with the pipe clenched between his molars. "You should eat your breakfast before it gets cold."

I made no attempt to do so. "Tell me about your nephew."

"Kenneth is my wife's nephew actually. He's not Ellie's boy. He's her other sister's. Mary's in the state mental hospital in Augusta. Has been for the past eight years. No one knows who Ken's sire was, not even Mary. It sure as hell wasn't an immaculate conception. That's why he's a Crowley."

"Your wife's maiden name is Crowley."

160

"A-yup. That's how we Maine lobsterman say yes. Don't you know."

By now, Harmon understood I had no intention of taking any of the bait he kept tossing in my direction. He went on, "Ken's sternman on Nat Pillsbury's boat, the *Sea Hag*. I suppose Nat knows the boy better than anyone. You might ask him for a character reference if you feel the need."

The sight of the hash provoked a grumble from my stomach. I ignored my hunger. "What else did your nephew tell you when he came to your house yesterday?"

"That he'd heard a shot in the orchard before he saw the cottage."

"Does Kenneth usually hunt down that way?"

"I don't know where he hunts. I hung up my rifle years ago. Not that I ever bothered getting a license. We don't get many visits from game wardens out here on the edge of the known world."

"Did Mr. Crowley tell you who he thought might have fired that shot?"

"I asked him that same question. Hadn't seen a soul all morning, he said."

"What did you do next?"

"Rung up the constable and told him the sad news."

"When Andrew Radcliffe called our office, he led me to believe that your nephew had confessed to shooting Ariel Evans by mistake. Do you know how the constable could have come to that conclusion?"

"You should ask him. I was clear as crystal about what the boy had told me."

"What did you do after you got off the phone?"

"Sat and finished my coffee."

"You didn't drive out to Gull Cottage to see the scene firsthand?"

"Why would I? I'm a lot of things, young man, but I'm not a ghoul. I waited for Andy to come by the house. Then he and I drove up to the airfield to meet your plane. After that, my whereabouts are fairly well established, I would expect."

"Describe Ariel Evans to me."

Harmon sucked on his pipe. "You're new at this, I take it."

"New?"

"New at interrogating people. Your questions are zooming every which way. But I'll oblige you. Miss Evans was pretty, and she enjoyed the effect her looks had on members of our sex. The Latin word for a woman like her, I believe, is *cocktease*."

"You disapproved?"

The old man laughed so hard he began coughing out smoke. "Young man, I don't know who told you I was a prude, but, no, if a sexy little thing wants to saunter around in my

162

presence, I have no objections. And if she took someone home to her bed, well, it was none of my business."

"There must have been rumors about who she was sleeping with."

"Nat Pillsbury."

"That was the rumor?"

"That was the fact. But as I said, what those two were up to was none of my business. It was definitely Jenny's business. She's Nat's wife. But it sure as shit wasn't mine."

The disclosure threw me off-balance. The rental agent who had booked Ariel Evans into Gull Cottage was the wronged wife. No wonder Jenny Pillsbury had been so dry eyed when we'd met.

"Don't think this makes me your informant out here," Harmon Reed said. "You were going to find out eventually, and frankly, I'd prefer you wrap up your inquiry sooner rather than later. Nat's the one who brought her to the Trap House. Rules are it's off-limits except to islanders, but he's the last of the Pillsbury clan, which he claims entitles him to certain rights."

Reed spoke with matter-of-factness. But only a dunce could miss how much the old man disdained the younger one.

"Was Ariel having sex with anyone else as far as you knew?"

"I will plead ignorance on that one. I can tell

you that she liked her wine. Brought three whole cases of French stuff on the boat, I heard. Must have been afraid we only drank Boone's Farm out here."

"What about drugs?"

When his eyes narrowed, his bushy white brows lowered over them. "What about them?"

"Do you know whether she used drugs?"

"No."

"She didn't use drugs, or you don't know if she used drugs?"

He removed his pipe from his mouth and licked his lips. "If she used them, I would have heard about it."

"You know everything that goes on here?"

"I've already admitted I don't. But on the subject of drugs people know not to hide secrets from me. Now, if you don't mind, I need to get ready for the ferry. It only comes once a week this time of year, you know."

"Jenny Pillsbury claimed she was working at the store at the time Ariel Evans was killed."

He returned his pipe to his mouth. "She was."

"And your son was here, too?"

"Hiram?" Harmon blew out a smoke ring. "The lazy sod didn't budge from his chair if I recall. But it seems like you're getting ahead of yourself, Inspector Clouseau."

I didn't appreciate the jab, but Harmon was right that I was having trouble staying focused.

"Two more questions."

"Oh, for—"

"Did you kill Ariel Evans?"

"I already told you I didn't. But I'll repeat myself for the record." He leaned his broad face into the camera of my iPhone. "I, Harmon J. Reed, did not kill or cause to be killed one Ariel Evans."

"Do you know who did kill her?"

"No, but I have suspicions—as does every person on this fogbound rock of ours. Will I share them with you? No, I will not. Living on an island, you learn the trouble that comes from wild speculation and unproven accusation. Besides, isn't it your job to find out the drunken fool who mistook her for a deer?"

Why *drunken?*

When the broad-backed man stood up, the room seemed to contract around him. Seated, he had seemed stout and eccentric in a grandfatherly way. On his feet, the enormous power in those huge arms became real again. I found myself stepping aside to let the squat strongman pass.

He paused in the doorway but didn't glance back. "If Nat Pillsbury asks who told you about his tomcatting, you can say it was me. If he has a problem with it, he knows where I live."

165

17

I ate my hash and drank my coffee. I expected that Radcliffe would show up eventually with the list of deer hunters I had demanded from him, but the constable never appeared. Except for a couple of old women, no one came in the store. Word must have gotten around that I was lying in wait because Sam Graffam complained he'd never seen the place so quiet on a ferry day. Eventually, to the grocer's great relief, I abandoned my stakeout and wandered down to the waterfront.

Bishop's Wharf was already loud and bustling. Every truck on the island seemed to be squeezed onto the dock. Each of them had backed in to make loading and unloading easier. Their headlights shone up the road. I could see individual water particles illuminated in the cold salt air.

The seas had calmed overnight, and now the waves were lapping gently against the blackened pilings that held up the wharf. The poles had been capped with copper and painted with creosote to prevent shipworms from turning the wood into Swiss cheese. I hung my head over the dockside to peer into the water. It was the color of pewter and so opaque I couldn't see more than a foot beneath the surface. Seaweed floated like hunks of mermaid's hair. A discarded styrofoam cup bobbed along with unsinkable buoyancy.

Out in the hidden harbor I could hear birds: the *chuck-chucking* of common eiders, the cartoonish quacking of a mallard, the distant chatter of gulls jockeying for position on some ledge newly exposed by the falling tide.

The M/V *Edmund S. Muskie* was Maquoit's lifeline to the world. It was how its people got their food, their propane tanks and wood pellets, their building materials, their Amazon packages, and, not least of all, their cases of liquor. Those who didn't own lobsterboats relied on the ferry as their sole means of transportation on and off the island.

I saw Joy Juno chewing on an apple.

Jenny Pillsbury held an infant wrapped in a cocoon of cotton and wool. I noticed she had a suitcase with her. She was leaving the island for some reason she hadn't mentioned. The timing couldn't have been worse from my perspective. I needed to talk with her again but not before I interviewed her philandering husband.

Nat Pillsbury stood beside his wife. Ariel's alleged lover cut a striking figure. He had wavy black hair and one of those rugged faces that doesn't make a mustache look affected or ridiculous. He was taller than average, lean and long, and wore an orange raincoat that was smeared with tar and duct-taped to cover rips he'd gotten hauling and stacking traps. Nat Pillsbury, in other words, didn't look like a model dressed up as a commercial fisherman for a catalog shoot; he looked like a man who worked day in and day out in the deadliest of all professions.

A voice behind me, unmistakably Harmon's, said, "Well, go wake him up! That fool knows what time the ferry comes."

At the harbormaster's command, Kenneth Crowley hurried away, but before he was lost in the fog, he cast a backward glance at me.

The squawking of a gull made me turn my head. A wild-haired, dirty-faced child had thrown a handful of gravel at the bird. It whined and flapped to the next piling down the dock.

"There you are," said Andrew Radcliffe, as rosy cheeked as ever. He was dressed in a bright yellow slicker, yellow rain pants, and a yellow sou-wester. He might have stepped off a box of fish sticks. "I've been looking all over for you."

I hated being lied to. "You found me."

"How'd you sleep? I've never stayed at the Wight House myself, but I've heard it's a quaint old manse."

"*Quaint* is one word for it. You were supposed to give me a list of the people you know who hunt deer."

"Darn it, I forgot. I apologize for that, but I promise to get right on it." His eyes darted toward the big mechanical gangway at the end of the dock where the ferry would tie up. The steel ramp could be raised and lowered depending on the height of the tide to make it easier to embark and disembark. "Do you happen to know if other officers will be arriving on the *Muskie*?"

"As far as I know, I am on my own."

His cell phone began to ring in his pocket. Radcliffe had chosen as his ringtone the klaxon of an old rotary model. He clapped a hand to one ear and shouted into the speaker, "Hello? Bethany? . . . Yes, it's Andrew. What's going on? Is the boat delayed?"

Half-listening, I scanned the crowd. I caught Jenny Pillsbury pointing me out to her husband. I could almost feel the intensity of the man's appraisal: like a hot lamp being shone on my face.

Andrew was saying, "Well, that is certainly *odd*. You're sure that's the name she used?" He paused to listen to the woman on the other end. "Is it possible it was some sort of perverse joke?"

He listened a while, then ended the call. "That was the woman at the ticket counter in Bass Harbor. The oddest thing happened there this morning. There was this passenger—"

At that moment a terrific roar brought our conversation to a skidding stop. It was the sound of racing engines and rattling chassis. Seconds

169

later, two burgundy pickups came charging out of the mist. Neither of them had their headlights on. They were going so fast and with such momentum, it seemed as if they might careen off the end of the pier.

Just as people began diving for cover, the trucks hit their brakes hard. Both of them slid to a stop mere feet from the other vehicles. Side by side now, they blocked the road. None of the other trucks could drive off the dock unless the two daredevils moved aside.

"Who is that?" I asked Radcliffe.

He let out a sigh like a slashed tire. "The Washburns."

Lobsters are cannibals. Leave them together in a tank without rubber bands around their claws, and they will dismember and devour each other in short order.

Drop a bunch of lobstermen together on an island—Maquoit, for instance, twenty miles off the Maine coast—and they begin to resemble the cold-blooded creatures they catch.

The men who emerged from the trucks seemed to be twins. They seemed to be in their late fifties, maybe early sixties, and had balding, egg-shaped heads. They were dressed in matching black anoraks and blue jeans that revealed long, powerful legs. Their rubber boots weren't the usual brown XtraTufs but the black bargain-store variety. One of them had a brush mustache.

Otherwise, they were as identical as two men could possibly be.

So these were the descendants of Maquoit's other founding family, the Reed clan's blood enemies, the violent outlaws everyone had warned me against, Eli and Rudyard Washburn.

"Which is which?" I whispered to Radcliffe.

"The one with the mustache is Rudyard. People call him Rud. The other one is Eli. He's the one whom Harmon shot."

Eli Washburn contorted his face into an expression of puzzlement.

Radcliffe said, "The boat's running a little late, Eli. That's all."

The lanky fisherman glared at him silently.

Was the man a mute?

Harmon Reed came over, and I noticed that he had several men behind him, his entourage from breakfast. The harbormaster removed his pipe from his mouth and dumped the still-smoldering embers to the dirt, where they continued to glow orange. "What's this I heard about you boys setting traps already? Someone says he spotted zebra-striped buoys two miles east of Foggy Head."

The mustached one, Rudyard, looked at his brother, and they both erupted in laughter.

Harmon, a foot shorter than either of the Washburns, but a foot wider, said, "Not sure why you find that funny. We all made a compact not to start hauling until after Trap Day. You both signed that agreement. The rest of us are abiding by it."

Eli spoke with a stammer, it turned out. "Who says . . . he saw . . . our buoys?"

"My boy Hiram."

"Must've been hallucinating. Same as . . . his brother."

"Don't you mention Heath in my presence," said Harmon.

"He was a junkie. Facts are . . . facts."

From the back of the crowd came a shout, "Shut your fucking mouth, Washburn!"

It was Hiram Reed, pushing people aside in his anger. Despite his rage, he was ghastly pale beneath his dark muttonchops. Crowley trailed after him, shoulders hunched.

"Why, it's . . . the walking dead," said Rudyard, who shared his brother's stammer along with everything else.

"Go to hell," snarled the younger Reed.

"Hasn't been . . . taking his . . . medicine," said Eli Washburn.

"Or maybe," said Rudyard. "He has."

Radcliffe, to his credit, piped up. "There's no cause for this, gentlemen."

Harmon only turned to his retainers. "What do you think, boys? It sounds like Eli and Rudyard are in need of another lesson."

"Come on . . . old man." Eli reached a hand

around his back. He might have had a handgun stuck in his pants or a knife sheathed horizontally under his jacket. The Washburns' difficulty speaking had lulled me into thinking they were somehow not dangerous. But I recognized the murderous glee in the tall man's eye.

I edged toward the confrontation.

"You think I won't shoot you again?" Harmon Reed said. "I got away with it once."

"Try it! Dare you!"

"Hey, fuckheads!" It was Nat Pillsbury. I hadn't noticed that he'd also been moving toward the action. "You Washburns might not know it—and maybe you forgot, Harmon—but there's a game warden standing right there. Maybe this isn't the best time for you guys to play Clash of the Clans."

Suddenly, everyone was looking at me as if I'd materialized out of a puff of sulfurous smoke. I made a point of opening my coat so that my badge and gun were visible on my belt. The Washburn brothers tried to stare me down.

Behind me now, in the quiet that had fallen over the dock, I could hear the rumbling of an engine. This sound was coming from the harbor. It had to be the M/V *Muskie* breaking through the haze.

The harbormaster addressed the men behind him. "Come on, boys. Let's get to work now. We've wasted enough time on this nonsense."

But as the others began pushing toward the end of the pier, Harmon grabbed his son by the shoulder, so hard it made him wince. Whatever the father whispered to his son, it definitely wasn't words of devotion. Nor did he release his grip until the young man seemed on the edge of tears.

Harmon's last words were the only ones I heard. "After the boat is gone. You understand me? We'll talk about it then."

Hiram rubbed his aching shoulder.

I heard the gangway lurching on its steel cables. Nat Pillsbury stood between me and the ferry.

"I know you need to talk to me," he said in a voice raspy from cigarettes. "All I ask is that you wait until my wife and baby daughter are on board, and the *Muskie* has left. Can you do that for me?"

"I can do that. Where are they going so sudden?"

"Ava's got an appointment to see the pediatrician in Ellsworth. She's been having ear infections. Don't make this out to be more than it is, like it's something suspicious. We've had that appointment scheduled for days."

Without another word, the brawny fisherman made his way to his wife and sick child. Jenny was trying hard not to glance at me, but it was clear that she, at least, was worried what conclusion I might be drawing from her departure.

If her husband was nervous, he hadn't showed it. What impressed me about Nat Pillsbury was that among all of the hardened men on the wharf, he alone had projected an effortless self-confidence. The Washburns were schoolyard bullies who backed down when confronted. But even the imperious Harmon Reed had shrunk under Pillsbury's reprimand.

The state ferry was large, twice the size of the *Star of the Sea*, maybe 150 feet long, and close to half a million tons. Three stories high, from the lower passenger deck to the captain's bridge. Painted bright, almost phosphorescent, white.

I slid between two pickups that were waiting to be loaded with cargo. One of them was Joy Juno's Ram. She stood in the truck bed, probably because she'd wanted a better view of the fight that hadn't materialized.

"At least you got to see one of our pissing contests," she said.

"I was worried I was going to have to step in and end it."

She smirked at me. "You wouldn't have been able to."

"Pillsbury did."

"But Nat is Nat."

She'd been gazing over my head toward the ferry when she'd uttered those words. Suddenly, the good humor left her face. Her eyes grew wide. Her smile became a grimace.

The first person to come down the ramp was a woman. She was petite with blond hair, attractive even from a distance, dressed in expensive mountaineering gear, and carrying a laptop bag.

I felt the muscles in my jaw go slack. It wasn't possible. It couldn't be.

She looked exactly like Ariel Evans.

18

The crowd parted as she stepped onto the gravel-strewn wharf. It's not every day you see a ghost.

The blond woman was observant enough to notice the curiosity and unease she provoked, but she kept her head down and moved forward with purpose. She wore a blue cap emblazoned with the insignia of the Navy SEALs. She carried a messenger bag across her lithe body. Her outfit was a mismatch of expensive outdoor brands: Arc'teryx parka, Patagonia pants, Salomon boots. Everything had been scuffed, snagged, and stained, as if from use in the field.

Nat Pillsbury had gone utterly still. It was as if he'd gazed into Medusa's face and been turned into a stone statue. His wife, clutching her baby, had an expression of pure horror.

While everyone else backed off, I started toward the dead woman's doppelgänger. A chorus of whispers rose up behind me.

"Is she the sister?"

"Must be."

"Were they twins or something?"

"How'd she get here so fast?"

It was a good question. DeFord had said he was unable to locate Ariel Evans's sister, Miranda, and to the best of my knowledge, the media still hadn't caught wind of the story. The only possible explanation, I thought, was that this poor woman had come to Maquoit to visit her sister, and now here she was, not knowing that Ariel was lying on a steel autopsy table while the state medical examiner stood over her corpse with a bone saw.

She paused, looking around as if a driver might be holding up a cardboard sign with her name on it.

"Ms. Evans?" I said.

"Yes . . ."

I noticed that her plump lips were chapped, and there were bags under her teal-blue eyes.

"I'm Mike Bowditch. I'm an investigator with the Maine Warden Service."

"What's going on here? How do all of these people know who I am?" She had a pleasant voice and enunciated her syllables with the crispness of a trained actor. "And why do they seem so freaked out?"

"I can explain, but this isn't the place for it. Do you have more bags coming off the boat?"

"A black Patagonia duffel. And a canvas tote."

"I'll grab them for you. We'll have privacy in my truck to talk about what's happened."

Now that the initial surprise had begun to wear off, she studied me through narrowed eyelids.

"Why were you waiting for me? I only got into Logan last night."

She resembled her sister, but they were by no means twins. They had the same honey-gold hair. But Ariel's was a pale, delicate, indoors kind of beauty, while her sister's features had a weathered hardness.

One of the ferry's brawny mates came out carrying a waterproof duffel in one hand, and in the other, for balance, a tote loaded with liquor bottles. I took them from him. The duffel was incredibly heavy, and the bag of booze wasn't much lighter. She had brought a whole bar, it seemed.

Despite the fog, Miranda Evans put on a pair of sunglasses as if to shield herself from the invasive stares. "Which is your vehicle?"

"The tan Datsun."

She stopped abruptly. "I'd like to see your badge and identification."

I put down her bags and produced both of the items she'd requested. She raised her sunglasses to examine the badge and compared my face to the photograph on my ID card. "Your hair looked better shorter."

"I agree."

The small woman lifted the heavy duffel using her legs and swung it into the bed of the truck. The prospect of getting mud or grease on her luggage seemed not to trouble her at all. She did, however, set the liquor tote inside the cab to keep the bottles from breaking. The laptop bag she clutched to her chest.

She made a quick survey of the vehicle as I slid behind the wheel. Her attentiveness to detail reminded me of myself, I realized. It was unusual that I met someone with situational awareness comparable to my own.

"So am I supposed to call you warden or investigator or what?" she asked in her crisp, lovely voice.

"Mike is fine." I breathed in deeply to prepare myself. "I'm afraid I have some bad news."

"Did my cottage burn down or something?" There was a strained lightness to her tone.

"Your cottage?"

"The one I'm renting. Or did my hermit die while I was stuck in Ukraine?" Her smile revealed perfectly white teeth. "Oh, I know. The Nazis learned I was coming out here. Have I gotten more death threats?"

The realization landed like a punch. *"You're* Ariel Evans."

Her laugh was musical. "Why are you surprised? You were waiting for me to get off the boat."

My tongue seemed like a dead thing in my mouth.

"Who did you think I was?" she asked, her amusement vanishing.

Someone began rapping excitedly at my truck window. It was Andrew Radcliffe. He was repeating my name, asking me to roll down the window, saying it was urgent. Now I remembered. The constable had gotten a phone call from the terminal in Bass Harbor minutes before the *Muskie* docked. The message had puzzled him.

I focused my full attention on the woman beside me.

Physically she seemed composed, but when she spoke, I could hear a fresh tremor in her voice. "What exactly is going on here, Warden?"

"Ms. Evans. Your sister, Miranda, is dead."

You would have thought I'd slapped her across the eyes. "When? Where?"

"She was shot to death yesterday morning in the backyard of the cottage you're renting. It was initially reported as a deer-hunting incident."

"Miranda was on Maquoit?"

"For the past month she's been out here, pretending she was you."

I had delivered my share of death notifications. I'd seen people laugh in disbelief, as if surely I must be delivering a bad joke. I'd watched a few go catatonic. I'd been present when knees had given way, and I'd had to catch a slumping body in my arms. Once I'd witnessed a mother whose toddler had drowned let out an animalistic wail that was the most chilling sound I'd ever heard.

What I'd never seen was Ariel's response to the news of her sister's death. She began pummeling the dashboard, not slapping it, not striking it, but punching the plastic with the ferocity one might use against a mugger. Seconds later, she leapt from the truck. She stood silently with her hands tightened into fists and her head back, glaring up at the white ceiling of fog.

As I pursued her, I felt Andrew Radcliffe tug on my arm. "I got a call from the ferry office. This woman with you—"

"I know, Andrew." I peeled his fingers off my sleeve. "I know who she is."

The constable hung back, afraid to approach the petrified woman. Not that I could blame him.

Softly I said, "Ms. Evans, I know this is a shock."

"A shock?" Her eyes had that fierceness I remembered from her less flattering photos. "It's not a shock. I've been waiting for this news most of life. I've always known it was coming. But here? Here? The Chateau Marmont or the Hotel Chelsea, I figured. But an island in Maine?" Her head tilted upward again to the heavens. "Miranda, you fucking bitch. You got me good, little sister."

"I think it would be best if we got back into the truck," I said, aware of the eyes upon us.

"Let them gawk. I'm used to it."

I presumed she was speaking of her fame. "You must have so many questions."

"My little sister was killed by a hunter on an island she couldn't have found on a map. Why would I have questions?"

Obviously, Miranda *had* found Maquoit. She'd not only located it but had come here with a fake ID and a stolen credit card with the intention of impersonating her famous sister. But to what possible end?

Before I could form another sentence, Ariel said, "I want to see her body."

"I'm afraid that's impossible. It was taken back to the mainland yesterday for an autopsy."

She rubbed her tired eyes. "I take it you don't know who killed her?"

"Why do you say that?"

"I started my career on the crime beat in Chicago. I know what cops say to the family when they've collared the perp. You said she was shot in the backyard of my cottage?"

"She was hanging laundry."

She snorted. "Really? I bet that was a first for Miranda. It was intentional, though? The shooting?"

"Why do you say that?"

"Because I know my sister, Detective. What did you say your name was again?"

"Mike Bowditch. And actually, I am a warden investigator."

"In Maine they let game wardens handle murder investigations?"

"I'm currently being assisted by a detective from the Maine State Police. He had to return to the mainland briefly. If evidence begins to point toward the killing being intentional, then he'll become the primary."

"The primary. I haven't heard that lingo since my days with the *Trib*."

After the initial excitement, the work of loading the *Muskie* had started up again, although more than a few of the islanders continued to sneak glances in the direction of my borrowed truck. Pillsbury still hadn't moved. His wife stood behind him, incandescent with rage. So she *had* known of the affair? Of course, she'd known. This was an island, as bottled up and suffocating as a killing jar.

Hiram Reed was now standing shoulder to shoulder with Nat Pillsbury. They were friends, I realized. You could see it in the way that Reed kept looking doggishly up at the taller man, waiting for cues from him. Hiram had probably been Nat's sidekick from childhood. He was still his sidekick.

"She was pretending to be me again," Ariel said almost with sadness. "That's why all these people are staring at me like I have three eyes. They thought Miranda was me. And now they know she wasn't."

"So she did it before?"

"Oh, yes. It was how she got her kicks, one of the many ways."

"Ms. Evans—"

"Call me Ariel, please. I'd like to reclaim my name."

"Ariel, I think it would be best if you got back on the ferry and returned to the mainland. I can arrange to have someone meet you in Bass Harbor, possibly the state police detective I mentioned. There's nothing for you here now."

"You don't want to question me?"

"I *do* want to question you. But the boat only runs once a week this time of year. I understand that this is your first visit to Maquoit?"

"Our parents brought Miranda and me here when we were girls. They were visiting wealthy friends who had a 'summer cottage' on the island. I still remember the name, Westerly. Like something out of a Daphne du Maurier novel."

"But you haven't visited Maquoit recently? You don't know anyone who lives out here?"

"I emailed and spoke with the woman who rented me the house. But if you're asking if I have any connections here, I don't. It was one of the things that drew me to this island. I'm one of those people who always wants to go someplace I've never been before."

"Then you really don't have any reason

to stay. And I assume there will be funeral arrangements. . . ."

Her face became hard. "You're afraid that if I stay, I'm going to get in your way?"

"I'd rather not have to worry about your safety."

"My safety? You understand that everything you're saying makes me want to stay even more?"

I caught sight of the boat captain striding around the wharf with the air of someone eager to make his exit. "Excuse me for a minute, please."

I sprinted down the dock until I reached the gangway. "Captain!"

He was a sturdy man with curly hair like the polls of a sheep. I flashed my badge and explained that I needed five minutes to persuade Ariel Evans to return with him.

"Why, of course I can hold off! That girl just found out her sis is dead? Why, she must be hysterical with grief. The poor thing isn't thinking clearly."

The old chauvinist couldn't have been further from the truth.

I let it go because I had an emergency call to make.

I was fortunate to reach DeFord, who had been on his way to meet with the commissioner. Unlike the ferry captain, he listened closely and carefully until I'd finished describing the bizarre situation.

"She's absolutely determined to stay?" he asked.

"In general she strikes me as someone who isn't easily budged."

"God, what a fiasco this thing's become. It's not your fault, Mike, but you're the only one who can clean it up."

"If she does change her mind, is there a chance Charley can bring her back when he drops off Klesko tomorrow?"

"That depends on the weather."

"What should I do with her in the meantime?"

"Take her someplace warm and safe. Go slow in questioning her. We've spent the past day learning what we could about Ariel Evans. But we don't know anything at all about her sister, Miranda."

"There's something you can do for me on your end," I said. "A woman named Jenny Pillsbury is on the ferry heading back to Bass Harbor. Could you consult with Klesko and arrange for a state police detective to meet her? Her husband was the one having an affair with Miranda Evans."

The captain paused to process this information. "Do you consider this Pillsbury woman to be a suspect?"

"She has an alibi, but I don't want her to slip

away without being interviewed. Steve will know where his colleague should focus his questioning."

"Every time I speak with you, Mike, I get the feeling that you've already concluded this was murder. If that's the case, we need to let Klesko take over. The law is clear about where our job ends."

"Give me until the end of the day. I'll know more by then."

"Until the end of the day."

As I made my way back to the truck, which was conspicuously alone now that the others had taken their deliveries off the dock, I saw that Ariel was on her phone. When she noticed me approaching, she abruptly ended her conversation. I wondered whom she had been speaking with but understood that I was in no position to pry.

I stood with the driver's door open, my head bent to peer inside the cab. "I don't suppose you've changed your mind."

"Legally, you can't make me leave."

The ferry gave a blast of its horn to signal its imminent departure. "It's too late anyway."

I slid behind the wheel. In the rearview mirror I saw the *Muskie* drifting into the mist.

"So where are we going to continue our conversation?" she asked. "Is there a police station? No, there wouldn't be. And if it's just you, it's not like you'd have a formal command post."

Truth was, I had no idea where to take her for an interview. Maquoit had no municipal office, as it was unincorporated as a township. Maybe the library had a room that Beryl would let me use?

Before I could settle on a location, Ariel said, "Take me to Gull Cottage."

"That's not a good idea."

"I want to see it. Besides, I'm the one who signed the rental agreement and paid the rent."

"I'm not sure that would be wise."

"I presume it's not an active crime scene anymore. Which means you have no grounds to keep me out of the place. If you'd like to hear my side of what happened, you'll take me to Gull Cottage."

19

The little Datsun handled the potholed roads better than I would have expected. The frame might have been disintegrating, but the new transmission had given the old engine some pep. Blackington must have replaced the shock absorbers, too.

"I'd like to begin at the beginning," I said. "I have a lot of questions about your sister and what she was doing here."

"If you don't mind, I'd prefer to wait until we get to the cottage. You're not the only one trying to process this, you know."

"Of course. I understand."

Her relative calmness, after that initial outburst, had disconcerted me. The Warden Service chaplain had once told me that grief manifests itself differently in every person. Ariel Evans seemed to be dealing with the body blow of her sister's death through self-willed nonchalance.

I expected we might make the rest of the trip in silence. But after we left the village center, we passed a moth-gray building with a mansard roof at the edge of the orchard. A sign identified the place as the Cider House B&B and said it was closed for the season.

"I think I remember that inn!" Ariel sat upright.

"Maybe I'm thinking of the John Irving novel. Or the movie with Tobey McGuire and Michael Caine."

"Never saw it."

"You're kidding."

"I'm not really into movies."

She snorted again. "Because you're a rugged outdoorsman. I've known men like you. Most of them were phonies. What about *The Great Impostor*? Tony Curtis? Did you ever see that one?"

"Afraid not."

"If I ever write a memoir about my sister, that should be my title. Not that Miranda was particularly great at anything except blowing up my life. She was an expert at setting bombs for me to trip."

"She seemed to be a talented artist."

"How did you—?" But Ariel had already arrived at the answer. "You must have found her sketch pad when you searched the cottage. Did you find her stash, too?"

"No, we didn't. How bad was her drug addiction?"

"Didn't you know? I'm the one with all the addictions. According to the tabloids, I'm the *New York Times* bestselling author with the thousand-dollar-a-day cocaine habit."

"Except it was really Miranda."

"People saw her in clubs snorting coke, and

191

the papers fabulated the rest, as they are wont to do."

I also had been on the receiving end of unfair and inaccurate news stories. I could have told her that. But I remained silent.

"Listen to me," she said after a long pause. "When did I become such a self-hating reporter? I was such an idealist in J-school and during my first years working in newsrooms. It wasn't until I became famous and found myself on the receiving end of the press that I understood what Janet Malcolm meant about journalism being morally indefensible."

"And yet you continue to write."

"I write books."

"Is there a difference?"

"I pretend there is."

Suddenly a deer appeared in my headlights. I braked, but much too late. I heard a horrific thump as the animal collided with the front grill, bounced off the hood, smashed the windshield, and was thrown into the weeds at the side of the road.

What I recall next was sitting there, stopped, the transmission somehow in park, with all the air gone from my lungs. My knuckles, where they gripped the steering wheel, were as white as bleached bones. Neither of us had been wearing seat belts since old Blackington had long ago sawed them off.

"Are you all right?" I said.

"Jesus!" Ariel was frantically feeling her body, thighs, breasts, face, as if she might be missing parts. "Jesus Christ!"

"Let me see."

She must have bumped her forehead against the dash because she had a red mark there that seemed destined to become a pretty good bruise. But neither of us was bleeding. As it was designed to do, the windshield had spider-webbed but held together instead of turning into a thousand airborne shards.

Ariel gasped. "Was that a person?"

"It was a deer." I glanced in the passenger mirror and saw a gray-brown shape in the crushed goldenrod.

"I didn't even see it! Is it dead?"

"Stay here for a minute."

I got out of the truck and staggered through the swirling exhaust fumes. My muscles had tensed at the moment of impact, and my joints had locked up.

Steam rose from the buck's mouth. His tongue was sticking out. One of his antlers had snapped off. His eyes were big black globes with long, elegantly curled lashes. I saw neither pupil nor iris. But there was still life in them—and pain.

The deer tried to rise, but his legs were limp and gory where the broken radius and tibia had pierced the skin. Blood glistened on the exposed white femur. The urinous smell of his tarsal glands tasted sour in my mouth.

In one smooth motion I pulled my pistol from its holster and fired a .357 round through his big, broken heart.

The gunshot echoed. The ejected shell casing flashed across my field of vision. The bitter smell of burnt powder filled my sinuses.

I glanced at the pickup and saw that Ariel had her door ajar. She'd been sitting with her legs swinging loose. She'd seen me euthanize the buck. Except for the rosy contusion on her forehead, she had gone totally pale.

I reholstered my SIG. "I'm sorry you had to see that."

She didn't speak, but tears began to fill her eyes. She tried blinking them back, but to no avail. Soon she began crying, quietly at first, but eventually in loud sobs that shook her from head to foot.

Should I try to console her? Emotionally stunted man that I was, I had no idea what to do.

I bent over and grabbed the dead deer by his unbroken foreleg and his unbroken rear leg. Starving as he had been, he didn't weigh much for a mature buck at the start of the rut. Less than a hundred pounds, I guessed.

I swung the deer into the bed of the pickup, where he landed with a ringing thud. His head bounced off Ariel's duffel, then settled back on it as if it were a coffin pillow. I should have put on my gloves first because blood and deer hair were stuck to my palms now. I squatted in the wet weeds to wipe them clean, but the musky odor of the deer remained.

Now that the shock was wearing off, I found myself overwhelmed by anger. The stupid, stubborn residents of Maquoit had resisted every effort my agency had made to help them with their deer overpopulation problem. The islanders didn't want the state telling them what to do, no matter if it was the right thing. Especially if it was the right thing. They loved their deer too much, they'd said.

This was what came of that love. This unnecessary suffering, this painful death, this lifeless bag of bones.

I rose with some difficulty and made a close examination of the damaged truck. Clumps of hollow hair were caught in the broken plastic of the grill. The right side of the hood had a broad deer-shaped dent from the fender to the windshield. Fortunately, the shattered glass was all on Ariel's side. I should be able to see well enough to drive, provided the truck was still drivable.

I got back behind the wheel. Ariel had pulled herself inside and closed the door, probably because she hadn't wanted me to see her bawling. I put the Datsun into first gear and we began to creep forward. I pressed the gas pedal and shifted into second. The transmission seemed unaffected by the incident—unlike the two of us.

She was using the hem of her shirt to wipe the tears sliding down her cheeks. Her nose had gone pink around the nostrils and in the divot above her mouth.

"How are you doing, Ariel?"

"How does it look like I'm doing, *Mike*."

I found a wad of paper napkins stuffed beside the seat and handed them to her. "I was driving too fast. I knew there were deer along this stretch. I should've been more careful. I'm sorry for putting you through that."

But Ariel wasn't listening to me, or she had no interest in my self-recriminations. "I can't even cry for my baby sister, but we hit a stupid deer and look what happens to me. I am such a horrible person. I'm the heartless monster Miranda always said I was."

"You're not heartless."

"How can you say that? You don't know the first thing about me."

I fell silent.

She was breathing hard, but slowly regaining some control. "What are you going to do with the deer?"

"I don't know yet."

Maybe Joy Juno could tell me who on the

island might need the meat. Of all the people I'd met so far on Maquoit, she alone inspired trust in me. I certainly didn't have confidence in Radcliffe, who kept finding inventive ways to demonstrate that he was the creature of Harmon Reed.

Ariel rubbed her tear ducts, nose, and the corners of her mouth with the napkin. "You shot it before I even knew what you were going to do."

"He was suffering. There was no point in waiting."

"That was considerate of you not to warn me. I'm not being facetious. I genuinely appreciate it." Even in extreme distress, Ariel Evans remained one of the more perceptive people I'd met in a long time. "I'm not really crying over the deer."

"I know that."

For the first time since we'd met, since we'd started together on this drive, I felt her full attention. She was studying me with newfound and genuine interest. "I was wrong about you. You're not a phony."

20

A gray shroud hung heavily over Gull Cottage. The windows were dark and hollow. The crime-scene tape sagged under the weight of accumulated water drops. I stopped the mangled truck.

Ariel said in a churchly whisper, "It looks nothing like it did on the website. And yet it looks exactly the way I imagined, if that makes any sense."

I made a vague noise that suggested that I understood. I was eager to get her inside and settled down so we could begin our formal interview. Every few seconds a new question would come pinballing through my brain.

When I opened my door, I could smell the sea and hear the foghorn moaning at Beacon Head. I noticed that Ariel avoided looking at the dead deer as she stepped clear of the vehicle. I grabbed her duffel and my rucksack and pulled them across the truck bed.

"I want to see where she was killed first," Ariel said.

"I'm not sure that's a good idea."

When she turned to me, color was again in her cheeks and the hardness had returned to her eyes. "Men have been telling women what's in our best interests since time immemorial. You don't get to do that to me even if you are some kind of cop."

She ducked under the yellow tape, following the wet path around the house as if she'd visited the place before and knew exactly where to go. I supposed it wasn't much of a mystery. The footprints pointed the way.

Miranda's laundry and laundry basket were gone, and of course her underwear had been removed from the line. All that remained was a lone clothespin. But Ariel's gaze was fixed on the flattened, glistening grass. The night's rain had washed away most of the blood, but the indentation where her sister's body had fallen was still visible. It may have been a trick of the eye, but the bent blades appeared darker than the rest of the yard.

"So the hunter who shot her was trespassing," Ariel said with more composure and detachment than I could have managed.

"Maine has something called permissive trespass. It means anyone can access any piece of land that isn't posted."

"That's ridiculous! What kind of backward, cracker-ass state is this?"

I said nothing.

Next she wanted to see the inside of the house: every room of it.

The door swung open easily. The air inside the

darkened living room smelled of lemony dusting spray. I flicked on the light to find the cottage transformed.

After we'd finished processing the crime scene, Jenny Pillsbury must have returned to pick up the wineglasses and attend to the general mess. I felt a lump in my throat that I was unable to swallow. I hadn't told her *not* to disturb the dead woman's possessions; it had never even occurred to me to issue instructions that should have been self-evident.

"The rental agent must have cleaned the place."

"Was she planning on renting it while my sister's body was still warm?"

Once again I wished that someone had told me sooner that Jenny's husband had been Miranda's lover. In law enforcement jargon that was what was known as a big fucking deal. It was difficult not to read her rush to clean the cottage as an attempt at erasing evidence, even if it wasn't. I remembered my last sight of Pillsbury staring in wide-eyed horror as Ariel came striding down the ramp. What had she been thinking in that moment? That her deceased rival had returned from the grave?

"There's something I want to show you." I gestured at the adjoining room.

Fortunately, Jenny Pillsbury had left Miranda's sketches tacked to the corkboard in the parlor.

Ariel paused, openmouthed, before a drawing of Stormalong's notorious hermit. "This is him? This is Blake Markman? How is this possible?"

"Your sister rowed a skiff across the channel to his island. The current is really strong. It took a lot of guts."

"Miranda was fearless. There's no denying that." Ariel ran her thin fingers over the sketch of the hermit the way a blind person might examine a stranger's face. "I have pictures of Markman from Hollywood, when he was younger. Pictures of him dressed in Armani with his supermodel wife on the red carpet. And then later when Andrea's family was suing him. The newspapers took photographs of him entering and exiting the courthouse."

"What did Markman do exactly?"

"There were rumors his wife was cheating on him with a famous actor. I've narrowed the list down to a few candidates. The night of the fire, Blake and Andrea had a big, public fight at a restaurant in Santa Monica. Later their Malibu beach house burned down. Blake escaped and was burned supposedly trying to save Andrea, who had passed out inside. The tox scan found a megadose of Halcion in her system, but she had no prescription for it. The cops figured Blake drugged her before he stoked his fireplace and the chimney got white-hot, starting the blaze. But they couldn't prove it was murder."

"What do you think?" I couldn't help asking.

"If he didn't murder her, why did he settle a wrongful-death civil suit with his in-laws? His lawyers advised against it. They were positive he would win. I think guilt got the better of him. I think Blake Markman is a case study in self-torture. I mean, look at his face. Twenty years later, you can still see his anguish."

I had noticed the same thing.

"Guilty or not," Ariel continued, "Miranda really connected with him."

"Why do you say that?"

"Can't you see the feeling here? My sister was talented, but she wasn't the kind of artist who could paint a stranger's portrait and capture his essence. There always needed to be a connection. This feels so intimate."

"So you think—?"

"That they had a sexual relationship? I'm not saying that. But who knows? Miranda always had a thing for older men. That artist she used to live with in North Carolina was twelve years older than she was. And Markman is still handsome if you're into Old Testament prophets. Have you spoken with him?"

"Not yet."

Her look was accusatory. "My sister dies mysteriously, and there are pictures of this odd recluse all over the house. You don't think talking to the guy should be high on your priority list?"

"I've been sidetracked this morning by your arrival. I had assumed you were dead."

"That's an insulting reply."

I tried not to sigh. "Yes, I am planning on talking with Blake Markman. But my first order of business is learning everything I can about what your sister was doing here. And interviewing you is the logical place to start. Wouldn't you agree?"

Ariel didn't respond. She made a circuit around the room, ending up eventually at her sister's wooden art box.

"When this is all over, I'd like to have these drawings."

"As next of kin, you should have them. You should have everything."

"I want to see her bedroom now. I want to look through her things. After that, I'll tell you what you want to know."

She sat on the neatly made bed with Miranda's two Coach bags open beside her.

"Did you do an inventory?" she asked, stroking a teal cashmere sweater. "Are you sure 'the maid' didn't help herself to my sister's Versace scarves?"

"We know what was here when we searched the place yesterday."

"But you don't know if the person who killed

her removed something from the house before you arrived?"

"There's no way for us to know that."

"I'm surprised you didn't box up all her stuff as evidence. It seems weird, your leaving things here."

"My evidence team took whatever seemed important. Packing up the rest—I've never had to do that before. But I'm sure the state police have a protocol they follow in situations where someone dies alone on vacation."

She folded her hands in her lap and seemed to will herself into calmness. She spent a long time looking me in the face. "How old are you?"

"I'm twenty-nine."

"Is that young for someone in your job?"

"Youngish, but not unheard of."

"You're new at it though," she pronounced.

There seemed no point in dissembling when she could find out with a few clicks of her computer. "I was promoted to the investigator position this summer."

"How many hunting accidents have you worked?"

"We prefer the term hunting *incidents*."

"Because *accident* suggests no one was at fault. It's the reason why the police now use the term car *crash*."

"I have worked many hunting homicides in my

career. But this is the first investigation where I'm the primary on the case."

She lifted her chin. "That's reassuring."

"You asked, and I thought you deserved an honest answer."

"Thank you for your candor." She zipped up the two bags and slid off the bed. "All right. I'm ready to tell you the story of my sister's life. Wait for me downstairs. I'll be down in a minute."

21

I needed to remember that Ariel Evans wasn't just a grieving sister. She was an investigative journalist with years of crime reporting on her résumé. If I wasn't careful, she would use her knowledge of police procedure on me like jujitsu.

Ariel came down the stairs. She'd changed out of her quilted vest and put on her sister's cashmere sweater. The teal color flattered her eyes. She'd also rung out her damp hair. It was longer than I had initially thought, with the same honey-gold waves as Miranda had.

"What are you going to do with me now that I'm alive?" she said.

I hesitated.

She smiled. "It's a line from an old movie."

"I don't watch a lot of movies, remember?"

"You don't know what you're missing, then." On her way into the kitchen she said, "Is the water drinkable?"

"I wouldn't drink it."

I heard the refrigerator door rattle open, bottles jostling in the door. "Never mind."

She returned to the living room a minute later with a mostly full bottle of white wine and a thin-stemmed glass.

"I don't suppose you want some of this." She sat down on the couch across the table from me. "I'm just teasing you. I know you're not allowed. Too bad, though. It's Domaine Serene. Miranda always had great taste in wine. Her drinking problem hadn't progressed to the point that she would drink whatever got her buzzed."

Ariel pulled the cork loose by expertly pinching it between her knuckles and splashed the greenish wine into her glass. She took a long sip.

I had already prepared my iPhone to start recording. As I did so, she said, "That reminds me."

From the pocket of her pants, she removed her own iPhone. She switched it on, found the voice-recording function, and hit start. We sat there with our smartphone cameras pointed at each other.

"Are you worried I'm going to misrepresent what you say here?"

"Let's just say I'm just covering my bases. Besides, I'm a journalist. I might need a record of this conversation."

I ignored the jab and directed my voice to the two recording devices, "It is nine fifty-nine a.m. on November fourth. This is Warden Investigator Michael Bowditch, and I am conducting this interview at Gull Cottage on Beacon Road on Maquoit Island. Will you state your name?"

Ariel complied.

"And will you spell your name?"

Ariel rolled her eyes elaborately—and then complied.

"So, Ms. Evans. You understand that I am here on behalf of the State of Maine to determine the circumstances of your sister Miranda Evans's death and to advise the attorney general's office whether or not I believe charges should be brought against the as-yet-unidentified person who shot her."

"They'd damn well better bring charges!"

"I am going to start by trying to establish some information about how your sister came to be on Maquoit. You're not under oath, but I hope you'll do your best to be candid with me. You might not understand at first how my questions are relevant—"

Her glass was already empty but she did not immediately refill it. "Mike, I told you I worked the crime beat in Chicago. I've probably read more police transcripts than you have. You've already tossed the standard framework out of the window by doing this interview without any advanced planning. I understand your objectives, etc. I'll stipulate you've made a yeoman effort to establish rapport. So let's get down to it, all right? You want to know who Miranda was?"

"Can you give me your sister's full name?"

"Miranda Gail Evans, named after the Shakespeare character and our aunt. My parents were theater people. I always said they should have named her Ophelia."

I felt a prickling along my scalp. "You have an aunt named Gail Evans?"

"Yeah, she's a sculptor. Kind of kooky, but not certifiably insane like my sister was. Aunt Gail actually lives in Maine over near Lake Sebago. But she may be moving to Northern California, the last I heard. She wants to commune with the redwoods."

People always said Maine was a small state, but I had met her aunt Gail. A year earlier, when I was still a patrol warden, I had responded to a call at her house of a dog chasing deer. The "dog" turned out to be a magnificent wolf hybrid. The people who owned the animal had called him Shadow, but he had escaped from my custody and was roaming the Boundary Mountains separating Maine from Quebec, as far as I knew. I often found myself wishing I could see him again.

"Why did you ask about Gail?" Ariel said, her curiosity piqued.

"The name sounded familiar. Let's get back on track here."

I asked her for Miranda's date of birth, and Ariel gave it to me. Her sister had been thirty-five years old when she died.

"I'm two years older, in case you're wondering."

"I know how old you are." I smiled. "I even now that your birthday is on Christmas. For the past twenty-four hours I've been operating under the mistaken belief that it was you who was shot. I spent last night reading articles you've written, including the piece from *Esquire* magazine that became your book about the neo-Nazis."

"I don't know whether to be impressed or creeped out by that."

"You and Miranda grew up in Manhattan, correct?"

"On the Upper East Side. Miranda also attended the Dalton School. But while I stayed in the East and went to Columbia, she went West to Pomona College. She lasted one semester before the dean called my parents to tell them she needed to take some time to 'reassess' her educational goals. The truth is she'd been busted on Sunset Boulevard trying to buy coke. She came back East and gave NYU a shot. She made it through two years there. But she wanted to be a visual artist and didn't see the point in getting a degree."

"I'd like to backtrack a little. Your parents died when you were twenty-two, is that right? So Miranda would have been twenty?"

"They were killed in a car crash in Rome. My dad grew up in Manhattan, walking, riding the subway, and taking cabs. I don't know why he thought he could drive a car in fucking *Italy*. Technically, I was her guardian for all of about a year, but I had my own troubles—my glamorous parents left us with a shitload of debt—and if Miranda wanted to drop out of NYU, I wasn't going to stop her, especially after she nearly got me kicked out of J-school."

"What happened?"

"She came uptown to Columbia, I have no idea why, and managed to talk her way into a reception for some Nobel Prize winner. She got drunk and started throwing herself at this young professor. When they were caught in a bathroom, she showed the campus cops my old driver's license. I'd forgotten I'd given it to her so she could get into bars in L.A. Except for being blond and short, we didn't look that much alike, but she knew how to do her hair and makeup to play up the resemblance. Miranda thought the whole thing was hilarious. It was the beginning of her 'impersonations,' as I called them."

"So pretending to be you became a regular game of hers?"

Ariel finally refilled her wineglass. "That came later, as her manic phases grew more intense."

"She was bipolar?"

"As the earth itself. She'd inherited the disorder from our father. Anyway, while I was off in Chicago learning my trade, she was living in a bunch of dumps downtown, hanging out with artists and musicians. I assumed that she was more interested in telling people she was a painter than actually painting. Then one day, maybe three years later, I came home from an assignment in Moscow to find a postcard in my bundle of mail. It was an announcement for a solo show of Miranda's work at a super-trendy gallery in Dumbo."

"Dumbo? The flying elephant?"

"It's a neighborhood in Brooklyn! Unfortunately, I'd been away so long I'd missed the entire exhibit. I called to apologize, but she didn't believe me. 'You can't handle me having any success of my own because you're the golden girl,' she said. We went through a period of estrangement after that. I was busy with my own career. It was probably a year later that I was talking to my aunt Gail and she told me Miranda had left New York and was living with this older artist in North Carolina, somewhere near Asheville. 'She really loves this Galen,' my aunt said. 'He's the first man in Miranda's life who really understands and appreciates her and can cope with her mood swings.'"

Ariel paused for another sip, then continued.

"She lived with Galen for seven years. What neither my aunt nor I knew was that this guy was an emotionally abusive asshole. He disparaged her work. Then she got pregnant, and he made her get an abortion.

"The next time I saw her was after my first book hit the bestseller list. I was back in the city by then, and somehow—don't ask me how she did it—she managed to find the building where I was living and talk her way past the guard in the lobby. She'd lost weight and cut off most of her hair. She told me what Galen had done to her. She was such a wreck, I took her in. Here I'd gotten this big advance, and now my book was all over the place, and it seemed wrong, given my good fortune, to throw her out in the cold.

"She stayed about three weeks and had a front-row seat to my big breakthrough. She went to Rockefeller Center with me the morning I was interviewed on the *Today* show. I started letting her answer my email because I was so overwhelmed by it all. Then one day I got a frantic call from my agent asking what the hell I was doing turning down all these requests for interviews in the most insulting manner possible. It was Miranda, of course. When I confronted her about it, she denied everything at first and stormed out of my apartment. But later she came back, drunk and totally unrepentant. I told her she had to leave. What I didn't realize was that she'd taken the opportunity of living with me to get copies made of my license and passport, both with her photos.

"I didn't learn that she'd stolen my identity until I started getting calls from collection agencies. She'd taken out credit cards in my name. I actually had to hire a private investigator to track her down in Playa del Carmen in Mexico. My attorney wanted me to press charges against her. Then I got a call from a mental hospital in Houston saying she'd been committed by a judge for attacking a cop.

"I flew down to see her. She was such a sad disaster. She couldn't stop apologizing. I arranged for her to be transferred to a facility in New Mexico, near where Gail was living back then. The best thing about that place was that she started drawing and painting again. I'd get pictures of her work that would take my breath away. By then I had money from my books, and I set up a trust for Miranda. It wasn't a lot of income, but it assuaged my guilty conscience."

"Where did she go when she got out of the mental hospital?"

"The politically correct term is *psychiatric care facility*. She lived with Gail for a bit, then bumped around, staying with friends. Occasionally she would call during one of her manic phases, and I'd ask if she was taking her meds, and she'd hang up on me."

I looked up from my note taking. "When was the last time you saw her?"

"Early August. She showed up at a book event

I was doing in the city. I barely recognized her. She looked great, was wearing designer clothes. Nice, but not *too* expensive. She said she had received a fellowship to an arts center in Provincetown for the winter. It was another lie, of course. I took her to dinner and told her about my plans to come out to Maquoit to research my next book. She asked a lot of very, very specific questions and didn't drink at all, which should have warned me she was up to something. I told her I'd rented a house on the island for September through November but would probably be delayed since I had a magazine assignment I needed to finish. It was only the next morning that I discovered she'd found a way to swipe my license and my AmEx. I canceled the credit card. I thought I'd managed to do it in the nick of time."

"Evidently not."

"Evidently not."

The wine bottle was empty. I hadn't noticed her finishing it. Ariel went into the kitchen to open another.

22

A truck rumbled past the windows. I heard the driver slow up the way someone does who's nearing a scenic vista. A minute later, I heard it return from the opposite direction, having turned around at the end of the road.

Yesterday the islanders had given Gull Cottage a wide berth, but the dead woman's return from the hereafter had transformed it into Maquoit's big tourist attraction.

Ariel reappeared with an unopened bottle of the same expensive wine and a corkscrew. "I'm afraid to look at my forehead again. Is it turning purple?"

"More like mauve."

She uncorked the new bottle with the practiced ease of a sommelier. "I'm not going to get crocked, so you can stop looking at me that way."

"How am I looking at you?"

"Like you're afraid I'm going to become a problem you have to deal with. I've always been able to hold my liquor better than most girls. It's a stupid thing, but men respect a woman who can match them drink for drink."

Her articulation was crisp. She didn't sound remotely intoxicated.

"Was that a trick you used on the Nazis? Drinking them under the table?"

She smiled. "It wasn't like I had to work hard to win their trust. An attractive, blue-eyed blonde starts showing up at their rallies eager to hear their insights about racial differences. I was basically an Aryan's wet dream."

"What were they like, the Nazis?"

"You should read my book!" She settled back on the couch, brought her knees up, and wrapped an arm around them. "Most of the guys ate a lot of paint chips when they were kids. The master-race masterminds, on the other hand, are smart enough to scare the shit out of you."

I started the recording again.

"You said you were delayed arriving on Maquoit because of an assignment overseas. Is that right?"

"I'd warned Jenny Pillsbury that it might happen, but she made me pay for the whole three months anyway. She must have been puzzled when Miranda showed up pretending to be me, but I'm sure my sister found a way to bullshit her into believing whatever lies she needed to tell."

"So aside from Jenny Pillsbury," I asked, "did you know anyone on Maquoit prior to planning your trip?"

"Not a soul."

"As far as you know, then, there was nobody here who might have wanted to hurt you?"

"I've gotten plenty of death threats since *Ghost Skins* came out. Are you thinking some neo-Nazi on the island murdered my sister thinking she was me? That's would have been quite the intriguing plot twist, but I doubt it's what happened."

I kept my head down and marched forward. "Who knew you were coming to Maquoit?"

Ariel glanced at the ceiling as she scrolled down a mental list. "My agent and my editor. Some of my girlfriends in the city. Aunt Gail because I thought I might swing by her house on my drive up. I kept it pretty quiet. I thought I had a potentially great book in Blake Markman and didn't want one of my fellow vultures to come along to steal it."

My curiosity got the better of me in that moment. "Why do you find him so compelling?"

"Hermits are currently 'hot,' first of all. And then there's the whole Hollywood aspect. Blake's dad, Bartle Markman, cofounded one of the Big Eight studios of the Golden Age. His mother was a B-movie actress. He himself produced a couple of critically acclaimed films. Blake Markman was Hollywood nobility, and then one night he burns his house to the ground with his cheating wife inside—"

"How can you be sure he murdered her?"

"I have proof."

"What kind of proof?"

Ariel must have practiced that sly expression in the mirror each morning. "You're going to have to read the book to find out. Anyway, he pays out a big settlement to his wife's family and uses his remaining funds to buy this god-forsaken rock off the most remote island on the East Coast. He starts herding sheep—this rich Jew from Bel Air—and hides himself from the world. Don't tell me you wouldn't read that book!"

"If all he wanted was to stay hidden, what made you think he'd talk to you?"

"I am not lacking in self-confidence. Besides, if Miranda managed to win his trust . . ."

"You called her a gifted con artist."

Ariel displayed her porcelain smile. "Maybe it runs in the family."

"So you don't think it's likely that someone might have come to the island to ambush you?"

"I haven't spent a lot of time on Maine islands, but my sense of them is that their residents tend to notice when a stranger shows up on the ferry carrying a rifle case."

It was an excellent point. "You received no communication from your sister while she was out here?"

"If I had, you don't think I would have—"

"What I meant was, did she send you an email or call or text where she pretended to be somewhere else?"

"I'd have to check but—" Ariel reached for the phone on the table. She ran her index finger over the screen until she found what she was looking for. Then she passed the device to me. She'd pulled up a text message, the last in a thread:

Pray for me, Ariel my angel. I'm in love with the devil. **#helltopay**

"Did you respond to this?" It didn't appear she had.

"You're not really grasping the fact that my sister was mentally ill. When she was in one of her moods and using drugs and alcohol, she sent me stuff that made 'Jabberwocky' read like an English composition textbook. It wasn't the first time I got a message from my sister telling me she wanted to have some guy's babies either. And there was the small matter of her stealing my identity *again*."

In my imagination I saw Nat Pillsbury, black haired, mustached, standing on the wharf in his Grundéns rain suit, his expression carved in granite. I heard again his commanding voice as he ordered the feuding Reeds and Washburns to back off. There had seemed nothing devilish about the man, but as the son of an alcoholic father, I knew how liquor could release a legion of demons from the jail of the human heart. And as a career law enforcement officer, I had learned that some of the most fiendish beings in existence often hide behind the faces of angels.

"The word *devil* doesn't strike you?" I said.

"*Now* it does. But it's not like she was warning me her life was in danger. At the time it sounded like Miranda being Miranda."

Through the window came the engine noise of yet another truck. In frustration, I pulled aside the curtains. I hadn't expected to see Andrew Radcliffe pull up in his rust-bitten Toyota.

I watched him open his passenger door. His grizzled dog, Bella, climbed gingerly to the ground and almost immediately squatted to relieve herself. The constable had to lift her hindquarters to return her to the truck cab.

"Who is it?" Ariel asked.

"The island constable."

I managed to get to the door before Andrew could knock. He stood on the woven mat of ropes, his hair tousled, his cheeks like two pink flowers.

"Did you hit a deer?" he asked as if he hadn't seen the dead animal in the bed of my borrowed truck.

"What's going on, Andrew?"

"Well, the whole island is talking, and I don't know what to tell people."

Ariel appeared at my side, exuding the fruity smell of wine. "Tell them I was raised from the dead."

It was the first thing she'd said that told me she was intoxicated.

"This is Ariel Evans," I said. "The woman who was killed yesterday was her sister, Miranda."

The constable cycled through a series of emotions: surprise, nervousness, confusion. "OK . . ."

"You can tell people that there was a mis-understanding that has now been cleared up," I said. "But it doesn't change the fact that we're still investigating who fired the bullet that killed *Miranda* Evans. You can help me by getting me that damned list you promised."

"I'll definitely do that." Radcliffe's jumpy eyes darted from Ariel back to me. "There is one other thing, Mike. I think you and I should probably talk about it in private."

I stepped onto the porch and pulled the door shut behind me. Then I set a hand on the smaller man's shoulder and guided him away from the windows until we were positioned beside his Tacoma, past the point where Ariel could eavesdrop.

"What is it, Andrew?"

"Two things, actually. The first is, you know how islanders like to gossip? There's a lot of hearsay on Maquoit, and yesterday I didn't want to repeat something I'd heard without any way to back it up. But Penny reminded that I had a responsibility that outweighed—"

It was rude to interrupt him, but I could feel the morning slipping away. "What have you heard?"

"The rumor is that Nat Pillsbury was the one sleeping with Ariel. I mean, what was her name again?"

"Miranda. Yes, I already know they were lovers."

"You do?"

"Pillsbury pretty much confirmed it to me this morning down on the dock."

The constable reacted by withdrawing into a trancelike state.

"What was the second thing?" I said, eager to return to my conversation with Ariel.

He blinked three or four times to break his self-hypnosis. "Detective Klesko called me."

It was no surprise. "And?"

"He said he's been trying to reach you. I explained about how hinky the cell signals out here can be, but, well, it didn't seem to satisfy him. He's still stuck at the courthouse in Bangor, and that might explain why he's so frustrated. That and the weather forecast. The fog won't be lifting until late tomorrow. He said that I should help you."

I pressed my teeth together so hard I could have cracked a walnut. Steve Klesko wanted the constable to spy on me.

"As a matter of fact, there is something you can do for me right now, Andrew."

"Whatever you need."

"Dispose of this dead deer."

The human bobblehead began doing his thing. "It's not what I expected you to say, but sure. What do you want me to do with it?"

"Give him to someone poor and hungry who needs the meat."

I opened the tailgate of the Datsun. Rigor mortis had taken hold of the buck. His broken limbs had grown so stiff that he resembled one of the plastic decoys wardens use to entice night hunters into firing illegal shots.

"Watch out for ticks," I said. "The body's still warm enough, they haven't jumped ship yet."

The blood drained from his cheeks.

"And get me that list of hunters."

My last sight of Andy Radcliffe was of him struggling to drag the stiffened, hundred-pound carcass out of my truck.

She had her stocking feet propped on the table and was squinting hard into her phone when I stepped into the dry warmth of the cottage. Without glancing from the screen, she said, "It says I have a signal, but I can't get through to my aunt. That Pillsbury woman told me this place had Wi-Fi. She didn't say I'd be unable to make phone calls or send text messages."

"That seems to be the way it is on this island. I got a strong signal down the road, not far from the turnoff to the lighthouse. It's where you first get a view of the Gut."

"The Gut is the channel between Maquoit and Stormalong?"

"It might be worth your taking a walk down there when we're done."

"Gail is going to be heartbroken when she hears what happened. She and Miranda were kindred spirits. How did you manage to keep the news out of the media, by the way?"

"We didn't want to release a statement before we understood what had happened."

"Maine doesn't have a law requiring your department of public safety to issue statements when someone dies under suspicious circumstances?"

"We were being cautious."

"Bullshit." The new intensity in her voice reminded me that, whatever her quarrels with her colleagues, she was still very much a member of the fourth estate. "You were stonewalling because you didn't want the morning ferry packed full of reporters. Not to sound egotistical or anything, but most editors would have found my violent death to be kind of newsworthy."

"I guess I'd better hurry up my investigation, then." I wrestled with my peacoat, trying to find the armholes.

She swung her feet off the table, nearly knocking over a vase of dried roses. "Where are you going? I thought we had a deal. I'd submit to your interview, and in return, you'd tell me what you've discovered so far."

"It'll have to wait. The constable says I need to phone the mainland."

Now she leapt to her feet. "Did the autopsy turn up something?"

I kept forgetting how much she knew about police procedure. "One of my calls will be to the medical examiner."

"Can I come with you?"

"It would be better if you stayed here for the time being, but I can send someone to check in on you."

"What did I tell you about men being condescending—"

"It's not that you're a woman, Ariel."

She smirked. "It's that I'm a journalist."

"No, it's because you're the sister. I know firsthand what a mistake it can be allowing the next of kin access to a homicide investigation. It's best for everybody if you don't get involved."

When my father had been accused of killing two men, one a deputy sheriff, the Warden Service had violated its own policies to include me in the manhunt. Looking back on the terrible events that followed, even I had to admit what a fiasco it had been.

"So basically you're putting me under house arrest."

"I couldn't do that even if I wanted to. Personally, I would recommend you stay close to the cottage. But there's a bicycle outside. If you do go out, wear blaze orange. I have a vest in my bag I can loan you."

"Was Miranda wearing orange when she was shot?"

"No."

"So that's going to be the defense of the person who killed her: that he thought she was a deer."

I expected the shooter's lawyer would indeed pursue that strategy, if I could ever bring the case to court. But I said nothing now.

Her eyes rounded with recognition. "She's going to be crucified in the Maine media. Rich girl from New York gets shot because she wasn't smart enough to wear orange in the woods. And your juries here have a history of excusing negligent hunters. What was that woman's name? The one with the white mittens?"

"Karen Wood. I'm surprised you heard about it."

"I read the series the *Globe* published about it in J-school."

"I promise I'll be back later this afternoon. Maybe I'll have some news."

She stood in the doorway as I took my first steps across the sodden lawn. "So that funny little man is the constable?"

"Yes, he is."

"He must have been one of the first people on the scene, then?" She was determined to interrogate me.

"That's right."

"He doesn't inspire a lot of confidence. You'd think a constable on a fishing island would be a bruiser, considering how lobstermen are always cutting each other's traplines and setting fire to each other's boats. But he's not very intimidating, is he?"

"I think that's why he was elected."

"Do you know who he reminds me of? A Jane Austen character. Those rosy cheeks and long sideburns. That wavy, flyaway hair. If only this were a Regency romance instead of a neo-Gothic nightmare."

23

The truck was totaled, and there was no question in my mind that Blackington would expect full compensation from the State of Maine for the loss of his vintage Datsun. I drove slowly back to the village, my spine rigid, my foot hovering above the brake pedal. But on this trip, I saw no deer and killed no deer.

I hadn't noticed previously, but the road passed an old structure built on piles over the water. Its shingles had once been painted red, but were now mostly a weathered gray, and it had two hinged doors large enough to admit a lobsterboat in need of repairs. This was the Trap House: Maquoit's private BYOB saloon. Miranda must have pressured Nat Pillsbury to take her inside, and Pillsbury, being the surviving son of the island's founding family and its current alpha male (however much Harmon Reed might argue otherwise), had opened those doors for his seductive guest. He must have known the scandal it would cause. He must have realized the story would get back to his wife. Yet he had gone boldly ahead anyway.

Why?

One possible answer was that he was a callous bastard: Miranda's devil.

Another possibility was that the man was genuinely lovestruck.

Whatever Pillsbury was, I needed to talk to him.

First, though, I had a few calls to make. I might have tried my phone at other locations but, in the interest of saving time, drove directly to the cemetery's lower gate. It hung open on its busted hinge. I made my way up the stepped terraces of graves until my phone buzzed, and the backlog of emails and voice mails downloaded in a rush. DeFord had emailed me once, as had Charley Stevens. There were two emails from Assistant Attorney General Danica Marshall. None from the medical examiner, Walt Kitteridge (which suggested he hadn't finished the autopsy). Detective Steve Klesko had left me three messages.

Instead of opening any of these official communications, my finger tapped on a note from Trooper Danielle Tate.

Hi Mike

Just heard through the grapevine that your vic was impersonating her own sister! I'm pretty sure that I saw that same twist on a soap opera once. Only the sisters were identical twins (same actress). It was my *mom's* soap so don't give me grief, man.

Klesko must be going nuts that he's not out there.

I know it's not my place but I spent a couple of hours last night researching Ariel Evans. At the time I thought she was dead so it seemed more interesting than alarming. But knowing she's out there with you now . . . be careful of her. She seems pretty shady even for a reporter. Don't trust her is what I am trying to say.

If you need someone to bounce ideas around with, gimme a holler.

Dani

To my surprise I felt gladness—almost a sense of buoyancy—at the thought that Dani Tate was secretly assisting me on this case.

I made my way through my other messages.

DeFord had reviewed my videos and photos, as well as the first draft of my report, and said that he saw nothing that might prove problematic at trial. (I had to read the email again to be sure it said what I thought it said.) He'd also sent along a PDF of every Maquoit resident who had obtained a hunting license over the prior ten years. Very few had. I was not surprised to read that the Warden Service had issued zero citations for fish and wildlife violations over that same time.

Assistant Attorney General Danica Marshall wanted to lecture me. She wrote that the Warden Service spokesman was going to issue a statement on the Maquoit hunting homicide shortly. It was paramount that she "consult with" me before I gave some reporter a potentially damaging quote.

Too late for that.

Finally, I was ready to tackle Klesko's trio of messages. His tone was consistently upbeat and supportive from first to last.

Like DeFord, he'd read my report, but unlike DeFord, he had some suggestions to make it "bulletproof." He'd also heard about Ariel's arrival on the island and how it upended all of our initial premises. He hoped to be done with court by early afternoon and planned to be back on Maquoit before sunset. He concluded each of his messages by requesting I update him at my earliest convenience.

I gave Klesko the call he'd repeatedly requested.

I won't lie and say I was disappointed to get his voice mail.

"I'm sorry for not being better at staying in touch, Steve. But I have things in hand here, so you don't need to worry that I'm not following proper procedures in your absence. I'll upload the interview I recorded with Ariel Evans as soon as I can. If you want to be helpful on your

232

end, put me in touch with whoever interviewed Jenny Pillsbury when she got off the boat in Bass Harbor. It turns out that Jenny's husband, Nat, was Miranda' lover. Yes, I wish we'd known that earlier. One last thing. Radcliffe told me you called him. It sure sounded like you ordered him to keep tabs on me. If I were the sort of person who's easily offended . . . Wait a minute, I *am* the sort of person who is easily offended. Don't ever pull a stunt like that on me again. I'll see you when I see you."

While I doubted Klesko would be able to find a plane to fly him to the fog-shrouded island, maybe he could get a Marine Patrol boat to bring him out. Or maybe he knew a lobsterman who could ferry him over for a price. I had a sneaking feeling I might be seeing the detective before the day was done.

All the more reason for me to take control while I still could.

I phoned the office of the medical examiner and managed to catch the man himself. Dr. Walter Kitteridge had been the state coroner since before the Stone Age. He was famous in the law enforcement community for his love of golf, his appreciation of fine cigars (his preferred bribe when you needed him to expedite something), his chummy relationship with our no-account governor, and a work ethic that had started out as dubious and had only grown more so with age.

"I finished the autopsy," he said in his smoker's rasp. "I was going to lunch at the club before I wrote up my notes."

"Glad I caught you, then."

"I am actually on my way out the door. Talk fast."

"Cause of death?"

"Gunshot wound to the head. X-rays demonstrate apparent large-caliber missile fragments in the central head region with other fragments in the forehead and smaller fragments dispersed through the midcranial. No powder residue or charring of the wound means she was shot at a distance."

"Time of death?"

"Yesterday morning between nine hundred and twelve hundred hours. Stomach contents, lividity, etcetera. Look, Warden, I really need to run."

"One last question. Those puncture marks between her toes, any chance they occurred postmortem?"

He coughed out a laugh. "What are you suggesting? That someone molested the body so we would conclude she was a user of hypodermic drugs? You need to stop watching television, Warden. She had vestigial scars indicating she'd injected herself in the past. There was some left ventricular hypertrophy unusual for a female of her age. That would be typical of a person who'd abused cocaine for an extended period."

"Any coke in her system?"

"Toxicology reports take time to come back to me. Your victim was a heavy cocaine user, but drugs didn't play a role in her death. A hollow-point bullet did. Let me give you a piece of advice since I know you are new in your job. Occam's razor nearly always obtains in these cases: the most straightforward explanation is the correct explanation. I'll send you a copy of the complete report on Ariel Evans, as soon as we have it."

Clearly no one had told the medical examiner that the body he'd dissected belonged to some-one other than the person whose name was on the toe tag. Maybe I'd call Kitteridge back later, after he'd heard the news of Ariel Evans's miraculous return to life, and I would have him tell me more about Occam's razor.

24

I relocated the home of Nat Pillsbury by watching for the dead deer Joy and I had seen hanging the night before. Orange buoys and toggles hung like Halloween decorations from tree limbs, marking the house as the home of a lobsterman.

The man himself was in his trap lot readying the hundreds of lobster traps he planned to set on the opening days of Maquoit's upcoming fishing season. His traps (not pots) looked as if they'd been tossed around the sea bottom. They were dented and dirty and not all of one color—some were blue, some were green, but most were yellow—which suggested he hadn't had the funds to replace the entire set. Nor were they weighted with newfangled ceramic blocks. When Pillsbury tossed his traps overboard, they would sink to the murky depths with the aid of good, old-fashioned bricks.

The lobsterman had removed his raincoat since I'd last seen him. He wore a long-sleeve thermal that showed off his utter lack of body fat. The secret to getting six-pack abs was evidently hauling hundreds of lobster traps in freezing weather.

Pillsbury was working with concentration,

snapping numbered and color-coded tags onto his traps so they could be identified as his property by the Marine Patrol. At first, I assumed he was alone. Then I saw Hiram Reed sitting in the shadows atop one of those enormous wooden spools that telephone companies use for their cables. He was sipping from a sixteen-ounce can of Pabst Blue Ribbon. Hiram, it seemed, was forsaking the six-pack abs in favor of the six-pack itself.

Harmon's son didn't look so hot. His face had a grayish cast beneath his whiskers. And there was something unfocused about his eyes. One of his empty cans of beer rolled onto the grass as he slid off his makeshift seat.

"What do you want?" Reed barked.

"Mr. Pillsbury and I have an appointment to talk."

"What about?" said the shorter, more pugnacious lobsterman.

I raised my face in the direction of the hanging deer carcass. "For one thing, I was going to compliment him on his buck. It looks like a monster compared to the others I've seen on the island."

"You are so full of shit."

"Yeah, I am. I'm here to talk to your friend about his relationship with Miranda Evans."

Pillsbury, who'd been listening to this back and forth without expression, paused in his trap-tagging and let his hands fall to his side. "So that was her real name. Miranda. I like it better than Ariel."

"You shouldn't talk to this guy, Natty. Not without a lawyer." Hiram Reed had assumed the role of Pillsbury's personal guard dog.

I put my hands on my hips in such a way that my holstered sidearm showed beneath the hem of my peacoat. "Why does he need a lawyer?"

Reed pitched his voice high to mimic me. " 'Why does he need a lawyer?' "

"It's OK, bud," Pillsbury told his sidekick. "I've got nothing to hide."

Reed set his beer on the table, crossed his denim-covered arms across his denim-covered chest, and leaned back against the wobbly, makeshift table. "I'm going to stay here. I'm going to be your witness in case this guy tries to twist your words. Trust me on this, Natty. I know cops better than you. They ain't ever your friends. You remember the way they tried to entrap my old man. 'Oh, yeah, Mr. Reed, it was clearly self-defense, shooting Eli Washburn. You've got nothing to worry about. There's no way the DA's going to bring charges. If you could help us out with a few quick questions, though.' Quick questions my ass."

I'd had enough of Hiram Reed. "If you're concerned about being entrapped or misquoted, I can video our conversation."

Hiram Reed would not be mollified. "Recordings can be edited, Natty."

Pillsbury placed one of his strong hands on his friend's shoulder. "I'll be OK, bud," he said in a voice that couldn't hide his sadness for Hiram's wretched condition. "You know I can take care of myself, right?"

"Yeah, but—"

"I'll catch up with you tonight at the Trap."

Reed's eyes gleamed, and when he spoke it was with great emotion. "I will always have your back, Natty. You know that. Don't you?"

"You don't even need to say it, bud."

Hiram Reed sighed hard enough for me to smell the booze on his breath from ten feet away. He collected his two unopened cans of beer and gave me a parting glare as he made his way unsteadily up the hill in the direction of the fogbound airfield.

Pillsbury didn't invite me inside his residence. Instead he directed me toward a shed of gray planks that served as his workshop. Coils of multicolored line were piled everywhere. The shelves held cans of antifouling paint for the bottom of his boat and DayGlo Filter Ray for his buoys (blaze orange was, unsurprisingly, the hunter's signature color). Hand tools such as hammers and hacksaws hung on the walls, while longer implements—including shovels, spades, and a scythe the grim reaper would have coveted—were crammed together in a rain barrel like so many umbrellas in a stand.

Steam rose from a water-filled bucket atop a potbellied stove. The air was astringent with pine-scented woodsmoke.

"Have a seat," he said over his shoulder.

There was, conspicuously, no place for either of us to sit.

Pillsbury plunged his dirty hands into the steaming bucket. He rubbed the scalding water around his long, tanned neck. He shock his head like a wet dog, and droplets flew from his hair and sizzled off the stovepipe.

"I had heard that you were the island constable once, Mr. Pillsbury."

"For four years." Nat Pillsbury smiled. He had the sharpest canine teeth I'd ever seen. "But I was never a real cop. No more than Andy Radcliffe is."

I gave Nat my standard spiel about how it was in his best interest for me to record our conversation.

He waited silently for me to ready my iPhone. Then he said, without preamble: "So I was fucking her. I admit it. What else do you want to know?"

"We're talking about Miranda Evans?"

"If that's what you say her real name was. She told me it was Ariel. I used to call her the Little Mermaid. So the chick who got off the boat this morning was her sister? And she didn't know anything about what her sister was doing here or how she died? Jesus. She must have pissed herself."

"Not exactly. Ariel Evans is tougher than she appears."

"Then they were similar in that regard. The two sisters."

On a sawhorse was a mug of old coffee with a whitish scrim along the surface. Pillsbury drank it down as if it were freshly brewed.

"How did you and Miranda meet?"

"I help out Jenny with the maintenance on her rentals. Ariel—sorry, Miranda—had problems with her hot-water heater. But it was just that the pilot had gone out when I replaced the tanks. She had knocked back half a bottle of wine by the time I got there. She offered me a beer. Twenty minutes later I had her bent over the kitchen table."

He wanted to throw me off balance. "There's no point in trying to shock me, Mr. Pillsbury."

He set the empty mug down. "I can see that."

"Not speaking ill of the dead is also a fine practice."

He crossed his arms across his chest and leaned his ass against the workbench. "She wouldn't have given a shit about what I just said. Besides, how are you going to find out what happened if you expect everyone to sugarcoat their words?

It seems to me you'd want the complete truth."

"So you would describe your relationship as purely sexual?"

Now it was his turn to bristle. "I didn't say that."

"The way you described that initial encounter—"

"Just because a woman doesn't have hang-ups doesn't make her a whore!"

True enough. "When did your wife find out that you were having sex with Miranda Evans?"

He had an easy, unforced laugh. "You think Jenny shot her? My wife has never so much as touched a gun in her life. She's terrified of them. It was how her dad died. Drunk, cleaning a fucking Luger pistol he thought was empty. Not that it matters. Jenny has about thirty alibis from yesterday. It was her morning behind the counter at Graffam's."

"You didn't answer my question about when she found out about your affair."

"Affair," he grunted. "I never thought of it that way. But whatever. If you'd asked me yesterday, I would have said Jenny didn't have a clue."

"I've heard that you and Miranda were pretty public at the Trap House. You arranged for her to drink with you there. You didn't think your wife would find out?"

He shrugged his broad shoulders. "I was letting my dick do all the thinking. I have that problem. Me and most men on the planet."

His answers came quickly, but not so fast that they seemed to have been prepared in advance. His gaze was steady and level. His body was loose and relaxed.

"What about you? What were you doing yesterday morning when Miranda Evans was shot?"

His lips curled, and he showed me those healthy canines again. "I was hunting. I thought we'd established that already."

"Hunting alone?"

"Always."

"Where?"

"East side of the island, up in the big spruces above the marsh. That's where the big bucks go before the rut. The only bucks you see in the orchard are little spikes. From your questions, it's clear that you think Miranda wasn't shot by accident. You think she was murdered."

Once again Pillsbury had me against the ropes. "I received a list from my supervisor of everyone on Maquoit who possesses a valid hunting license. Your name isn't on the list."

"Then it sounds like you should write me up for hunting without a license."

"When all of this is over, I intend to do so. What kind of gun did you use to shoot that deer?"

"My dad's thirty-aught-six."

"Do you mind showing it to me?"

He gestured toward a corner where an enormous piece of plywood rested against a tool bench. He flipped the plywood away to reveal a gun safe. I was somewhat surprised to see it. He hadn't struck me as someone who would own one.

He must have seen the question behind my eyes. "It was Jen's condition after she got pregnant. She didn't want our kid to be able to get at the guns in my armory. Besides, there are people on this island who will steal you blind when you're inshore."

"Even when you're the constable?"

Again with the wolfish grin. "Especially when you're the constable."

The safe looked heavy and expensive. It had a three-handled dial. He turned the dial right, then left, then right. I heard a mechanical click, and the heavy door swung open. Inside were two rifles, a .22 caliber Marlin Model 60 and a well-used .30-06 caliber Savage Model 99. There was a shotgun: a Mossberg Mariner 500 with the antirust barrel and the synthetic pistol grip. There were three handguns: a Smith & Wesson .45 caliber Governor Revolver, a 9mm Glock G26, and a .32 caliber Bersa Thunder.

"These are all the guns you own?"

"Yep."

"Nothing in your nightstand or your bedroom closet?"

"What caliber round was she shot with?"

"I'm not allowed to say. It's an open investigation."

"But it was a deer rifle presumably."

He handed me the Savage. The wooden stock was smooth where it had been handled over the years. The barrel smelled of bore solvent and oil. He had cleaned the gun after he'd dressed his deer. That one action told me a lot about Nat Pillsbury. I disdained gun owners who didn't respect their firearms. Strange as it might sound, I felt a certain kinship with him in that moment.

I checked the action to be sure he hadn't stored the rifle loaded. The chamber was clear.

He set the deer rifle back inside the gun safe, closed the door, and spun the dial. "You're welcome to examine any of these at the state police lab. As long as you return them to me cleaned."

Until I found a slug, there would be no point in performing ballistic tests. "When was the last time you saw Miranda Evans?"

"Three nights ago at Gull Cottage. I told her I was ready to leave Jenny and the baby for her. All she had to do was say the word, I said."

What kind of man would leave his wife and child to run away with a woman he'd just met? And how might he have reacted if she rebuffed him? Or worse, laughed at his puppy-dog proposal?

"How did Miranda react to your offer?"

"She said she wanted to have sex. She said we could talk about it after. We never did."

"You didn't see her at all the day before she died?"

"I was working on my boat in the harbor from dawn to dusk. Kenneth Crowley was with me the whole time. I came home and had supper with Jenny. I was home all night. The next morning, I went hunting alone like I said. I didn't kill Ariel—sorry—I didn't kill Miranda Evans. Do you want me to repeat that for the record?"

"No, I got it."

"I have no idea who killed her."

"You keep answering questions I'm not asking."

"I don't know about you, but my time is valuable. I hate to waste it."

"Have you spoken with your wife in the past few hours?"

"No. Why?"

"Because she was met by detectives at the terminal on Mount Desert Island when the ferry arrived."

His anger was like the explosion of a bomb I hadn't realized was in the room. One second he was calm and loose. The next, his hands had become clubs and his face was a war mask.

"What the hell for?" he all but shouted.

"Because she didn't disclose that her husband was the man sleeping with her tenant. Because you

246

were contemplating running off with Miranda. Because that gave your wife a motive to kill her."

He whipped the empty coffee mug against a wall, where it broke into shards.

"Hiram was right. You guys are assholes. If you want to continue this conversation, you'd better arrest me. If you want to search my house, you'd better come back with a warrant. In the meantime, you can get the hell off my property."

25

The FBI's recommended method for interrogating a suspect goes by the dubious acronym PEACE. The letters stand for Preparation and Planning, Engage and Explain, Account, Closure, and Evaluate. Ariel had already called me out for my lack of preparation and planning. The rest I'd made a muddle of. Now I left Pillsbury's house with plenty to evaluate.

I had failed one of the first commandments I'd been taught as a cadet at the Maine Criminal Justice Academy: never let a confrontation get personal. You do that and you surrender all of your authority as a police officer. It's not just for your sake either. The last thing society needs are thin-skinned cops patrolling the streets who are scared for their lives. Even in experienced veterans, adrenaline can become a lethal drug. Lethal for the person not wearing a badge.

I would listen to my recorded conversation again before I sent it to DeFord and Klesko. Hearing their legitimate criticisms would be easier, I hoped, if I had already identified every time I'd been knocked for a loop by one of Pillsbury's verbal punches.

On a whim I decided to go searching for Hiram Reed. As Nat's best friend, he warranted a conversation. His feral temper would likely prove an impediment. As would his double-digit blood-alcohol content. But Hiram was a weaker man than his father, and when you're splitting wood, you always aim for the crack.

The last time I'd seen the harbormaster's son, he'd been staggering uphill, away from the village. The airstrip was fogged-in and useless. So where had he been headed?

The Datsun's engine complained all the way up the incline. The exhaust coughed. Various belts squealed like piglets. I began to wonder if the truck was suffering delayed side effects from the collision with the deer.

I was about to abandon my fool's errand when I caught sight of a beer can in the roadside weeds. I continued on slowly, concerned that in the impenetrable mist I might roll over the drunken man, passed out across the road.

The fog hung suspended three feet off the ground, too heavy to rise, too light to fall. But in my low beams I could make out the weaving trail Hiram had left as he continued east toward destinations unknown. Soon I'd passed the limp orange wind sock that marked one end of the airstrip.

On the far side of the field was a tall cone of gravel that might have been the leavings of monster-movie ants. In fact, I had come upon the headquarters of the island roadworks. A yellow snowplow, soon to be reattached to someone's truck, waited for winter in the weeds beside a sand shed.

There were deep ruts between the gravel pile and the shed. Some of the tire prints had been made that morning, since they were filled with latte-colored water. Older, undisturbed puddles would have shown clear.

I paused to survey Maquoit's impressive Public Works Department. As I eased the brake down, I heard an engine start up behind the shed. I shoved the gas pedal to the floor, but by the time I had rounded the pile of gravel, all I saw was a single red taillight disappearing behind swirling gray vapors.

I called out my open window, "I know you're here, Hiram."

No response.

"This is Warden Bowditch. I am not joking around. Get your ass out here where I can see you."

Hiram Reed poked his head out from behind the sand shed. "How'd you find me?" he slurred.

"I followed your tracks from your friend's house. Some people leave a trail of bread crumbs. You left a trail of beer cans."

He emerged into the open with his hands dug into the pockets of his Levi's jacket. His thick hair had lost its considerable volume under the weight of all the dampness. His wet, wrinkled face was as white as a frog's belly.

It is my practice not to converse with intoxicated people. I don't like to subject myself to their inanities, lies, and repetitions. The only exceptions I make are potential suspects or witnesses. This mind-set must sound unethical to many civilians, but I don't know a single cop who will stop drunks from talking themselves into trouble.

"Who were you meeting up here?"

"Who said I was meeting with anyone? Besides, it's none of your business."

"I saw the truck peel out, Hiram."

He removed his left hand from his pocket but kept the other one wedged in tight. He had something hidden in there. "Why don't you just leave me alone?"

The fog was becoming a light drizzle. "You're soaked to the skin. How about I give you a lift into town?"

With one hand he tried raising his collar against the precipitation, but it kept flapping down. "Yeah, right. 'Hey, little girl, you should get out of the rain. How about a ride in this nice windowless van of mine.' Thanks, but no thanks."

"It's not every day someone compares me to a pedophile." I realized I needed to change my approach. "You were right about your friend

Nat, by the way. It would have been better for him if you'd stuck around."

His face fell. "What did he say?"

"I'm not at liberty to discuss that."

"You son of a bitch. What did he tell you? He had nothing to do with that slut's death."

I glanced into my rearview mirror and shifted into reverse. Through the open window, I said, "Whatever you say, Mr. Reed. Enjoy the walk home."

My words goaded him into action. He loped toward my vehicle, one fist still wedged in his coat, the other making a desperate grasp for the handle of the passenger door. I hit the brake to let him climb in.

"Christ!" he said, surveying the shattered windshield. "What did you do to Blackington's truck?"

"Hit a deer. You have an overpopulation problem out here."

"Gee. You think?" His breath was humid with hops and barley.

I drove with one hand on the wheel and the other recording him.

"I don't suppose you hunt?" I asked as I turned the truck toward the village.

"Used to," he said warily. "Not for a long time."

"Do you still own a deer rifle?"

He seemed to realize his mistake in admitting

252

to having been a hunter. Somewhere under those glazed pupils and frazzled nerve endings was an intelligent human being.

"I sold it."

"To who?"

"A guy over on Frenchboro."

"What kind of gun was it?"

"I don't even remember."

This was a particularly poor lie. I had never met a single gun owner who couldn't tell you what make and model firearm he owned or had owned.

"What about ammo? No boxes lying about gathering dust in your cellar?"

"Why would I have held on to bullets I couldn't use?"

"People forget things."

He snapped his head around. "I wasn't out hunting yesterday morning."

"What were you up to?"

"I was sleeping off a long night. I ain't exactly an early riser. Ask my old man."

"That must be a problem, come lobstering season."

"I manage."

"Which boat is yours?"

"The *Nennie*."

I remembered the craft because of its exceptional state of disrepair: a thirty-foot Sisu. Single engine. Canopy splattered with guano as if

Jackson Pollock painted with gull shit. Bottom slimed with algae and crusted with mussels. The season opened in less than a month, and Hiram Reed's boat didn't look remotely seaworthy.

"Are you going to be ready to go on Trap Day?"

"Why? You looking for a job as sternman?"

"I might need one after this case."

A lame joke was exactly the wrong way to get Hiram to relax his guard. "Ha. Ha. So what did Natty tell you?"

"That he was hunting alone with no alibi yesterday morning."

"Shit," Hiram breathed. "I knew he was going to talk himself into a jail cell. But he didn't have anything to do with it. I know Natty better than anyone."

"Better than his wife?"

"Oh, yeah, Natty and I are secret lovers. Haven't you heard? We've been jerking each other off since we were in school."

"I could do without the attitude."

"Natty doesn't even possess a motive. He loved that crazy bitch. He would have left Jenny and Ava for her."

My gut told me he'd said more than he'd intended.

He raised his voice suddenly. "You cops are all the same. You don't care what really happened. You're just looking for someone to hang."

"Maine abolished the death penalty in 1887."

"Fuck you, Mr. Trivial Pursuit. You can let me out here, and I'll walk the rest of the way. Sorry I got your seat all wet."

I had one last card to play before the end of our game. "I was in the churchyard this morning. It was the only good place I could get a cell signal. I saw your brother Heath's gravestone. The inscription said he was 'lost at sea.'"

I didn't expect Hiram Reed to laugh at that. "That's one way of putting it."

He made no effort to elaborate so I kept pushing. "How much older was he than you?"

"Six years."

"Do you have any siblings?"

"My sister, Holly, moved onshore after Heath died and has never been back. The next time I see her will be at my father's funeral. But I wouldn't bet on it."

We'd arrived at the town wharf. I put the transmission into park. He needed his shoulder to shove the dented door open. He didn't thank me for the lift.

"One last question," I called after him. "What have you got in your pocket?"

He straightened up with surprise. He must have thought he'd gotten through our entire conversation without me noticing he was hiding his hand.

Then a wicked grin spread across his face. "My precious," he hissed.

The last I saw of Hiram Reed, he was headed into Graffam's with the single-mindedness of a drunk in search of his next drink.

26

If Radcliffe wouldn't provide me with a list of Maquoit's deer slayers, perhaps Harmon Reed would.

The patriarch's house was impossible to miss. It was the largest of the year-round residences I'd seen on the island: a grand "cottage" with two chimneys on either end, a widow's walk in the middle, and an expansive wraparound porch overlooking the harbor. The building was clad in newly painted shingles—the color a dark, venous red—and it sat atop a massive sea wall, fifteen feet above the high-tide line. Its views, currently obscured by the white fog, were to the northwest and the outer harbor.

Harmon's yard sprawled from one stone wall to another and was large enough to have contained an Olympic volleyball court. He had a garden surrounded by an eight-foot electrical fence with only a few orange pumpkins inside left to be harvested. His apple trees, like all the others I had seen on the island, had been nibbled at by deer. Every edible branch, blossom, and leaf beneath the height of a big buck standing on his hind legs had been chewed off.

As I mounted the broad stairs, the front door swung open and an old woman appeared. She was one of those people whose skin turns faintly gray as they age, and her hair, nearly the same color, was long and hung loose around her shoulders. Even the whites of her eyes were gray. She wore dungarees, a flannel shirt, a wool vest. And she stood half a foot taller than her husband.

"You must be Martha," I said.

"And you must be the warden feller everyone's talking about. Harm and I was just sitting down to dinner."

By which she meant lunch. The evening meal in Maine is supper. "I can come back later."

"Nonsense." She waved me in.

The front hall was toasty and a relief from the fog that had soaked my clothes, pruned my skin, and chilled my blood. The air smelled of Harmon's fragrant pipe smoke, balsam pillows, and a meaty odor that might have been roasting beef. Two Scottish terriers came bounding out of a side room to yap at me.

"Who are these two?" I asked, overloud, to be heard above the dogs.

"Goofus and Gallant. You remember that old comic? Don't try to pet them, or they'll stick their teeth in you pretty good. Why don't you hand me that coat of yours, and I'll hang it over the fire."

The dogs followed at her heels as she left me alone in the unlit hallway. The walls, I observed, were decorated with surprisingly good oil paintings of the island. It was too dim for me to read the signatures, but the artist or artists had talent.

Like all fishermen, Harmon had the weather radio playing nonstop. A computerized "male" voice provided a running stream of meteorologic updates, wind-speed and barometric-pressure readings, and marine forecasts "from Eastport to the Merrimack River." It reminded me of how, in my own home, the police scanner was always on.

"How goes the investigation?" Harmon Reed had taken advantage of my distraction to sneak up on me.

"It's keeping me busy."

"Come on into the kitchen and we'll have a mug up."

These days, I rarely heard old-time Maine lingo except from stand-up comedians mocking Down East folkways, but there was nothing ironic about the Reeds' vernacular. They continued to speak the bygone language they'd learned at their parents' and grandparents' knees.

The kitchen was clean and warmer than the front room. One wall consisted of storm windows with a view across the roofed porch to the mouth of the harbor. Or that would have been the view on a clear day.

"Nice spot you've got here," I said.

"It'll do."

Two bowls of pea soup were on the table, with a loaf of home-baked bread and a dish of butter pats. Harmon grabbed a mug from a hook above the sideboard and filled it from a Mr. Coffee machine. He plopped the cup on the table so hard it sloshed onto the gingham tablecloth.

"I didn't mean to interrupt your meal," I said.

"You're awful apologetic for a lawman. Grab yourself a chair and Martha will dish you up some soup. It's got ham in it, in case you're of the Hebrew persuasion."

"I'm not Jewish."

"Muslims don't eat pigs either, I hear."

"I'm not Muslim."

His wife returned, followed by the dogs, which immediately started up again at my ankles.

"Shut it!" Harmon commanded, and the terriers dropped to their bellies, whimpering as if they expected to be kicked. He turned to his wife. "How you persuaded me to adopt these two curs, I'll never understand."

Without my coat to cover my belt, my holstered sidearm was visible, and Martha seemed unable to keep from looking at it. I took a seat at the table to hide it from her view. She gave me an anxious smile and began dipping the ladle up and down in the bubbling soup pot to stir its contents.

I had my back to the harbor, which was just as

well, since I was most interested in examining the Reeds' kitchen. There were more paintings, although these were still lifes of apples on platters and deer antlers arranged artfully on tabletops. It was all the work of the same artist. In the diffuse natural light I could finally read the signature: *Joy Juno*.

Framed photos were propped on corner shelves and arranged along the top of the sideboard. I saw Harmon and Martha on their wedding day. And on vacation somewhere tropical. I saw childhood pictures of a boy who must have been Hiram and of an unsmiling girl who must have been Holly. I saw class pictures of little girls taped to the refrigerator. Holly's kids?

What I didn't see was photographic evidence of their dead son, Heath. No baby pictures, no school pictures, no family pictures in which he was included. It was as if, after death, he'd been erased from history like one of those Soviet dissidents whose names were blotted out of textbooks.

The Reeds were waiting for me to taste the soup, I realized.

Even with the ham, it was terrifically bland. "It's good," I muttered, and reached for the salt and pepper.

Martha pushed the bread my way. "Not everyone likes pea soup."

Her husband grunted. "Sam Graffam was

yammering on about pea soup fog this morning. What a know-it-all that man is."

"People expect lobstering families to eat lobster all the time," Martha said with an air of apology.

"Why eat a bug when you can make more selling it?" Bugs were what lobstermen affectionately called lobsters.

She put her liver-spotted hand on my hand. "Because our season is in the winter, the restaurants here have to bring their lobsters over from the mainland in the summer. Of course, Harm keeps a couple of traps set for houseguests who expect it. But even then, Harm and I don't usually—"

Harmon didn't use a spoon but raised the whole bowl to his mouth to slurp. "That's enough small talk, Martha. What I want to hear from the warden is why the dead woman was out here, pretending to be her sister all that time. And don't give us some bullshit excuse about it being classified and part of an ongoing investigation. A hunting accident has nothing to do with identity theft."

"I'm still not convinced Miranda Evans's death was a negligent homicide."

He wiped his green lips with the back of his hand. "You think someone murdered her?"

"Let's say I am trying to keep an open mind. Andrew Radcliffe was supposed to give me a list of the people out here who regularly hunt for deer, but he is dragging his feet for reasons I can't explain."

"Hell, man, I can tell you that." Harmon used his thick fingers to count off the names. "There's Eli and Rud Washburn, them damn poachers. Their nephews Zachary, Elias, and Judah. Nat Pillsbury always takes a deer. My fool of a nephew, of course. Blackington, when his knees are working. Pete Shattuck. Chum McNulty's boy, Tom. Joy Juno is the only female. We call her the Huntress. Sam Graffam sometimes, but not this year. George Gordon. That bastard Corso. Ellie's two boys, Kevin and Keith, but they're off at high school in Bar Harbor. Kit Billington. Andy Radcliffe—"

I glanced up from my notebook. "Radcliffe said he stopped hunting years ago."

"That's nonsense. I saw him just the other day, headed out to Beacon Head with a rifle."

In the silence that followed I could hear gulls calling in the harbor, waves lapping against the seawall beneath the house. Andrew had told me he'd given up hunting. What did it mean that he had lied?

Then Harmon said, "So what happens next? You go searching for everyone on that list and find out where they were yesterday morning? That sounds like a shitload of work, especially when they'll all lie to you anyway."

"What makes you think they'll all lie."

"Because people act out of boneheadedness and fear. It seems stupid not to confess. Wasn't there a feller who killed a man dressed head to toe in blaze orange and he got off with barely any jail time a few years back?"

"Yes, I worked that case as a district warden."

"How'd he pull it off?"

I stirred my soup while I considered how best to reply. The blunt answer was that Maine law as it pertained to hunting homicides was a travesty. The man Harmon Reed mentioned should have gone to prison for life. Instead he did thirty days in county jail because he somehow convinced a jury he *thought* he'd been aiming at a deer.

"He didn't escape a civil suit from the victim's widow," I said.

"Yeah, but if the guy was already broke—"

"The state can garnish his wages."

"Wages?" When Harmon Reed laughed, I saw his uvula quiver in the back of his throat. "Lobstermen don't get paid wages. We're—what do you call them?—independent contractors."

"Why are you asking me these questions, Mr. Reed? You know I can't provide you with tips on how Miranda's killer can escape prosecution."

"Because I don't want you to waste your time chasing rabbits. That girl wasn't murdered. It was an accident, like we said from the get-go.

264

Your problem is you got everybody spooked. Maybe if the numbskull who shot that girl realized he wasn't going to be thrown into a hole for the rest of his life, he'd step forward and admit what he did. And you could go home where you belong."

I removed my napkin from my lap and laid it over the bowl. "Mrs. Reed, that was delicious. Would you mind giving your husband and me a few minutes? I have some questions for him that are somewhat delicate."

"Of course! You men talk as long as you need." She hurried from the kitchen with the two terriers in hot pursuit.

I waited until I heard her footsteps on the stairs to the second floor before I spoke again.

Harmon had risen and begun to clean his pipe over the kitchen wastebasket. "Delicate, huh?"

"Mr. Reed, I'm going to be candid with you. I'm not sure if you know who killed Miranda Evans. I'm not sure if you are withholding that information from me. Maybe you've been trying to talk the guilty person into confessing in return for a slap on the wrist. On the other hand, you may not know who did it. In which case, I suspect you're running your own shadow inquiry, hoping to identify the shooter before I do."

"And why would I do either of those things?"

"That's an excellent question."

He gave his pipe a final knock to free the ashes embedded in the screen, then dropped the dirty pipe cleaner into the trash. "You have this idea of me as the lord protector of Maquoit Island, but I'm just another lobsterman. Maybe I care more for my neighbors than most. Don't twist my civic pride into an indictment against me."

"I've learned a few things since last we spoke. Nothing that incriminates you."

"How could there be? But you came here for information. Ask away."

"When was the last time you saw Miranda Evans?"

He returned to his seat at the table. "Night before she died. She came in the Trap House looking for Nat, but he wasn't there, so she left."

"Did she speak with anyone?"

"How the hell would I know?" Harmon Reed was as quick to anger as Hiram. Like son, like father, I thought.

"Who else was in the bar?"

"It ain't a bar, it's a social club. It was all the usual suspects. And, no, I don't mean suspects as in criminals. Look, I didn't pay attention to who came and went."

"Except for Miranda."

"And the only reason I noticed her was because Hiram said . . ."

"Said what?"

Harmon slammed his forearms on the table.

"Hiram said he'd just spoken to Nat. He'd told him he was being a fool, stepping out on his fine wife like that. Told him to call things off with that coquette before he destroyed everything."

"And how did Nat Pillsbury respond to your son's words of warning?"

"You're a stubborn son of a bitch, ain't you?"

"I've been accused of it."

"Once you get hold of something you won't let it go. You're worse than a dog that way. I'm telling you I don't know who shot that Evans woman. But I'm sure she wasn't killed deliberately. It was a goddamned accident. The best thing you can do is let folks know that the guilty party won't be drawn and quartered if he steps forward and admits his wrong."

It hadn't passed my notice that he'd veered far away from my line of questions. "And how do you suggest I do that?"

"Come out to the Trap House tonight. Stand on a tabletop and explain how the law goes easy on hunters who make an honest mistake. I guarantee you, the guilty party will step forward."

I finished the bitter dregs in my coffee cup. "I'll consider your suggestion. But before I do any of that, I have a question. If you did know who shot Miranda Evans, would you actually tell me? Would anyone on this island?"

His chair creaked as he folded his Popeye arms across his enormous chest. "We Maquoiters don't rat each other out. Not to the clam wardens, not to the coasties, not to the staties, and not to game wardens."

"What about the Washburns? They're your worst enemies. If one of them was involved, you still wouldn't tell me?"

"If Eli and Rudyard was involved in that girl's death, I would deal with it myself."

"How has that worked for you, taking justice into your own hands?"

He smiled and brought out the bag of tobacco to refill his pipe. "I'm not in jail, am I?"

27

Mrs. Reed returned to ask if I wanted a piece of carrot cake.

I politely passed on dessert.

Harmon puffed on his pipe as I thanked them for "dinner." Martha and the dogs saw me out. No sooner had I stepped outside, onto the porch, than the Scotties slipped through the door and started up again with their vicious yapping and snapping. They worried my heels until I was safely inside the battered Datsun.

I still hadn't nailed down the last person to see Miranda alive. But at least I had a list of hunters now.

I stopped at Graffam's for yet another cup of coffee, and the room fell silent the instant my shadow darkened the door. I recognized a few of the weather-beaten faces, but when I asked their names, none of them were on the roster Harmon had provided me. Reed had suggested that I go around telling people that the person who'd shot Miranda faced no real legal jeopardy. But I wasn't going to tell an egregious lie to lure out the killer. A capable defense attorney would crucify me on the witness stand if I made such a promise.

I realized that Graffam could direct me to the

homes of the men on my list, but as I approached the counter, I found myself remembering another elusive islander. "Hey, Sam. Can you tell me where Beryl McCloud lives?"

He scratched his impressively dense beard. "I can tell you, but you won't find her there. Joy told me she gave Beryl a lift to the Spruce Point trailhead. Sounds like she was going for a hike."

So much for the schoolteacher's being incapacitated by Lyme disease. "Isn't that dangerous under the circumstances?"

The shopkeeper seemed confused.

"It's deer hunting season," I explained, "and one woman has already been killed."

"Sure, sure, but that was accidental."

"Besides, lightning doesn't strike twice," said a man at a picnic table behind me.

"Point of fact, it does, Alf," said Graffam. "I've seen pictures of the Empire State Building being struck three times at once."

"But it ain't the *exact* place."

"I'm telling you it is."

I paid for my coffee and left before I got drawn into a debate over the physics behind electrical storms.

There was no doubt in my mind now that Beryl McCloud was trying to avoid being questioned. I could have driven to the Spruce Point trailhead and followed her path in the woods. But I couldn't afford wasting that much time.

Instead I decided to return to Gull Cottage to check on Ariel.

Joy Juno must have spotted my truck because I found her examining the damage done to the hood and windshield of the Datsun. An insurance adjuster wouldn't have looked any happier.

"I hit a deer," I said.

"Oh, really? Gee, I never would have guessed."

"I'm fine in case you were worried. Sam just told me that you gave Beryl a lift to the east side of the island. She seems to have made a quick recovery from her recent bout with Lyme disease."

Joy could hear the frustration in my voice. "Don't be mad with her. She's absolutely miserable, and I can't blame her. Coming here was the worst mistake she ever made, and she may carry those damn spirochetes in her bloodstream for the rest of her life. Give her time and she'll open up."

Time was the one thing I didn't have. "What about you?"

"What about me?"

"Would you mind if I ask you a few questions?"

"You mean like a police-type interview?"

"Not really."

She pointed at the Ram pickup with the MAQUOIT TRUCKING sign. "Step into my office."

Once again I took note of the empty rifle rack mounted behind the bench seat. Her name was on Harmon's list. And she'd mentioned something about having hunted in her "tomboyhood" in Wisconsin.

I had thought we'd sit there and talk, but Joy seemed to be worried about being seen with me. As soon as I'd closed the door, she started the engine and shifted into drive. She took the first turn and pulled behind a big barn. I noticed a newly painted sign above the entrance:

MAQUOIT ISLAND V.F.D.

"Let me guess," I said. "You're the town fire chief."

She gave me a sideways look. "Now you've got me worried. How did you know that? Have you been checking up on me?"

"I just had a hunch."

"I used to be the chief, but I got tired of the politics. You think Washington is dysfunctional? Try living on a Maine island where we all hate each other." She reached for a tin of throat lozenges on the dashboard and offered me one, which I declined. "So what do you want to know?"

As soon as I got out my iPhone, she put a big hand on my wrist. "This has to be off the record or no deal."

I returned the cell to my pocket. "I didn't realize you hunted deer."

"That's what you wanted to talk with me about?"

"Partly."

"Yeah, I hunt some years. Haven't so far this season. What else do you want to know? I'm not exactly an international woman of mystery."

"That puts you in the minority, then. Most everyone I've met so far on Maquoit seems to have a cellar full of secrets."

"That's because we're all misfits. It's why we live on an island. Who have you found to be especially secretive?"

"Nat Pillsbury."

"Nat!" She laughed. "I wouldn't exactly describe him as enigmatic. But maybe you have a different definition."

"What was he like as constable?"

"He was great. He knew when to crack heads and he knew when to look the other way."

"Would you describe him as violent?"

"No more than most men. *Tough* is the word I'd use. Self-confident. He could take care of shit. I don't remember him ever feeling like he needed to call in the sheriff for backup."

"As opposed to Radcliffe?"

She grinned, showing off a gap between her front teeth. "Andy called for a deputy to come out his first week on the job. Kids were taking golf carts for joyrides, and he treated it like the crime of the century. Harmon threw a fit when the cop stepped off the ferry. It was the last time Andy brought in an outsider."

"Tell me about Nat's wife, Jenny."

"That's kind of an open-ended question."

"Give me your impression."

Her face flushed. "I don't know if I'm comfortable—"

"Just the facts, then."

"She's a Washburn. Her dad was Eli and Rudyard's little brother. Shot himself in the head when Jenny was a girl. Some say it was an accident, others it was suicide. She went to school here back when there more kids on the island. Went off-island to high school in Bar Harbor like all the kids do—except for boys like Kenneth Crowley who go right into fishing. Then she got a teaching degree at the University of Maine. She came back to be the teacher, and because she was determined to marry Nat Pillsbury."

"You make it sound like she didn't give him any choice."

"Nat does what he wants, as I'm sure you have learned already. But Jenny is the secretive one in the family. Maybe it's the Washburn genes. She can be pretty wily." Joy caught herself. "I didn't mean that the way it sounded."

I let a silence grow between us.

"Have any cops talked to Jenny yet about what happened at Gull Cottage?" she said.

"Why do you ask?"

"She's the wife of the man who was having an affair with the dead woman."

"All I know is that she has a solid alibi."

"Right," Joy said almost too quickly. "That's true."

"How long was she the teacher here?"

"Until a couple of years ago when she got pregnant. That was when Beryl was hired. I'd rather not talk about Jenny Pillsbury anymore."

Why, I wondered. "What about Heath Reed?"

"He's dead."

"I know he is. I saw his gravestone. I'm wondering how he died."

Joy had seemed antsy before, but now she seemed fearful. "I don't understand. What does that have to do with whoever shot Miranda Evans? Unless you're saying a ghost did it."

"Probably nothing, but I'm trying to connect some things. I noticed that Heath's tombstone is noticeably smaller than the monument Harmon built for his father. The inscription said he died at sea. When I asked Hiram about it, he laughed. I also found it odd that there were no pictures of Heath in his parents' house. I have a suspicion about what happened to him, and I'd like you to confirm it."

"What's your suspicion?"

"Did Heath Reed die of a drug overdose on his boat?"

"Now you're really scaring me. How in the world did you know that?"

"There are a couple of other tombstones up in the Olde Island Burying Ground of young people who died around the time Heath did. That suggested drug overdoses to me. I interpreted 'lost at sea' as a not very artful euphemism. If he'd really drowned, he would have a more significant memorial."

She crunched down on her throat lozenge. "Heroin used to be a big problem out here. Epidemic, even. It's that way wherever there are fishermen. These guys get paid in cash. They're in boats where they can smuggle stuff and make deals with no one watching. None of this is news to you, I assume?"

"No."

"Say what you want about Harmon Reed, but after Heath died, the old man laid down the law. He said he'd punish anyone he caught selling heroin on Maquoit. He'd sink their boats and set fire to their houses. He'd already been tried once for attempted murder for shooting Eli and had gotten away with it, so people took him at his word. More than a few folks left rather than take the chance."

"What about Hiram?"

"What about him?"

"He's had a problem with drugs, hasn't he?"

She seemed genuinely afraid of me now as if I'd revealed myself to be some sort of dangerous soothsayer. "You know what? I think we're going to leave things there for now. You need to remember that I live here. These are my neighbors. When all this is over, you get to go home, but I am here for the duration. Do you understand what I mean when I say that?"

I opened the door. "I appreciate your candor, Joy. And none of what you've told me is going to come back to bite you."

"Says you."

I started to walk away, but she rolled down her window. "I was sketching yesterday morning, by the way. I was out near Westerly. That's the big estate owned by the Brewsters. Come by my studio and I'll show you my studies."

I pondered the significance of her last words on my way to the Datsun. I hadn't asked Joy Juno about her whereabouts when Miranda was killed or even hinted that I suspected her. It was interesting that she'd volunteered an alibi.

I saw no deer on my trip south along the Beacon Road, but fresh deer-sign was everywhere I looked. Hoofprints in the mud. Piles of pellets the size and shape of chocolate almonds.

How long could Maquoiters live like this, watching their island become a wasteland and their family members fall sick with debilitating illnesses? Extermination was a brutal solution, but as far as I knew, the residents of Monhegan Island hadn't suffered a single case of Lyme disease since they'd taken the radical step of hiring a sharpshooter to eliminate their deer population.

It occurred to me that I was overdue for a tick check.

Gull Cottage was dark and deserted looking when I arrived. No lights were in any of the windows. I wondered if the stress of the morning, combined with all the wine, had knocked Ariel cold.

The fog seemed even heavier and colder than when I'd set out that morning. It dampened my hair and clung like tiny pearls to my peacoat. It stung my cheeks and made the joints in my fingers ache. It was as if, instead of me passing through the mist, the mist was passing through me.

Only after I had crossed the lawn did I notice the bicycle track in the sodden grass. A single line led from the house to the road. Ariel had ridden off in the direction of Beacon Head and the Gut.

I'd told her she might find a cell signal there. But in my heart I knew where the intrepid reporter was headed: Stormalong.

She had decided to visit the hermit.

28

The southern end of the island had no boat launch, just a hard-packed beach of gritty gray sand, less than fifty feet wide. Specks of smashed sea glass—blue, green, and brown— glittered even in the absence of the sun. Fright wigs of seaweed lay in random clumps above the waterline.

Ariel's borrowed bicycle leaned against a basalt outcropping.

Her boot prints showed where she'd pushed a skiff out of the spartina grass and down the strand into the water. It must have been the same rowboat Miranda had used to cross the Gut. I hadn't noticed it the day before.

The channel before me was like a rushing saltwater river. It wasn't wide—a hundred yards at most—but the current was strong and choppy. The surface was a slate gray except where greenish foam piled up along the crests of the waves. I doubted whether even the best long-distance swimmer in the world could make it from shore to shore without being swept out into the North Atlantic.

Stormalong was only half-visible in the pallid fog. I saw a steep cliff that was mostly rock with a few bushes blazing red in the mist, the hillside tumbling down to a rickety wharf that seemed likely to wash away when the next nor'easter hit. I grabbed my binoculars from my rucksack. Sure enough, a skiff was tied up to the wharf, bobbing fiercely beside the dory I'd spotted the day before.

I paced back and forth along the strand. Mermaid's purses—the brittle black egg cases of skates—crunched under my boots. Bladderwrack popped like bubble wrap. Off in the mist, the mournful foghorn at Maquoit Island Light sounded at half-minute intervals.

Was Ariel in danger from the hermit? Not having interviewed Blake Markman, I was in no position to assess his mental state or emotional stability. For all I knew the recluse might have been the one who'd shot Miranda.

I needed to find a boat.

Maybe I could call Radcliffe and persuade him to throw a dinghy in the back of his truck and drive it down here for me to use.

Then I remembered the kayak chained to a tree outside Gull Cottage.

Five minutes later I was crouched beneath the massive fir studying the mooring chain securing the boat to the trunk, wondering how to free it. The chain was old and rusted and loosely wrapped twice around the base, but the padlock appeared to be brand-new. Behind the house was a toolshed where I expected the paddle might be stowed and perhaps also the key. I was certain that if I phoned Assistant Attorney General Danica Marshall, she would say that exigent circumstances didn't apply and that I had no legal justification to break down the door and "borrow" the items I needed.

The solution to this problem was easy: I didn't call AAG Marshall.

The shed door gave way with a single kick. The wood around the latch splintered. And I was inside the dim, dusty space.

Most of the surfaces were covered with mouse shit like chocolate sprinkles. The rodents, scurrying back and forth through their own droppings, had left brown streaks. I found a paddle and personal flotation device just as I had expected. What I didn't find was a key to the padlock. Nor were there bolt cutters. I unearthed a dull-bladed ax from the clutter, but I knew that chopping with a blade through a steel chain is one of those tricks that only works in horror movies.

I was about to give up my search and call Radcliffe when I noticed the come-along in one cobwebbed corner.

I grabbed the portable winch and returned to the yard. I fastened one of the hooks to the rusted mooring chain and the other to a second link, and I started working the ratchet. The chain began to rub bark off the fir as it tightened.

One of the links yawned open, and I quickened my pace. Half a minute later I had the kayak free.

The flimsy little boat was nine feet long and made of molded plastic. It had been designed for calm waters, where a person could sit atop it without worry of being capsized. In other words it was the worst imaginable watercraft I could have found to attempt the crossing of the Gut.

When I arrived back at the beach, the fog had closed in completely over Stormalong. Gazing out upon the corrugated waves, I couldn't help but hesitate. But how would I be able to live with myself if something happened to Ariel? The woman had been half-drunk when I'd left her alone.

To have a better range of motion, I left my peacoat in the truck. I hoped the exertion would keep me warm enough to do what I needed to do before I succumbed to fog-induced hypothermia. Then I lifted the toy kayak from the pickup and carried it down to the water's edge.

The rip current was moving from my right to my left. I watched a small pale bird, a guillemot, which is a cousin of the Atlantic puffin, float past at an impressive speed. No matter how hard I paddled, the Gut would push me to the south, toward the open ocean.

I sucked in a deep breath and walked the kayak

out through the bone-chilling surf. The waves bubbled silver over my boots. Then, squatting and using the paddle to brace myself, I sat down against the plastic seat before my flimsy boat could slip away. For a moment I teetered uncertainly back and forth before I found my equilibrium. Already the riptide was turning the bow to the south. I started digging the paddle blades into the water, using every muscle in my upper body to fight the sea.

It took me a few minutes to find the right approach. I angled the bow into the current to keep from being swamped by a roller, paddled as hard as I could, paused long enough for the rushing water to swing me around. Then I turned again into the stream and began to dig hard. It wasn't unlike tacking a sailboat, only much tougher on the abdominals and trapezius muscles.

Forty-degree seawater splashed me every time I lifted a blade from the water. My forearms were soon soaked, then the tops of my legs, then my seat, where a pool began to form around my butt cheeks.

For the longest time I seemed to make no headway. Then Stormalong loomed before me like an escarpment. I had been pushed well south of where I'd hoped to land, and the muscles in my back, stomach, and arms were burning.

Then the current eased mysteriously. When I

glanced to my right, I realized that I must have passed a submerged ledge. Waves were breaking white over the drowned rocks. Now I had to make the most of this sheltered stretch of water.

I dug and dug until I was thirty feet from the island. Then twenty feet. Then ten feet. I made one last effort and ducked in behind a barnacle-crusted ledge that extended out from the basalt cliff. I grabbed hold of a clump of seaweed but found it impossible to grip the slimy stuff.

I decided my best shot of beaching the kayak was to ram the ledge head-on and hope that my momentum carried me up onto the barnacles. I swung the bow so that it was pointed at the rocks and did my best to build up a head of steam. With a hard crunch the front of the kayak caught and held fast.

But not for long, I could tell. I tossed the paddle up onto the ledge and crawled headfirst up the kayak until I had handholds on the rock. Unfortunately, my movements kicked the boat loose. Even as I clung to land, I felt the kayak slip out from under my legs until I was half-in and half-out of the icy water.

My pants were soaking from my stomach down, and my boots were full of seawater. But I had made it ashore. I watched the little red kayak be caught by the current and swept away into the stream. I would need to find another ride back from Stormalong.

• • •

I sat on the hermit's crooked dock taking stock of my situation.

Fortunately, my badge and gun were still safely attached to my belt. My waterlogged wallet was still in my pocket, as was my Gerber automatic knife. My incarcerated friend, Billy Cronk, had carried this push-buttoned blade with him through the Iraqi deserts and the Afghanistan mountains when he was a soldier. I would have been crushed to have lost my prized memento.

Relieved at my good luck, I reached for my iPhone and found that it was gone. I carried it in a protective waterproof case clipped to my belt. But somehow the cell had popped loose of its holster.

I swore out loud.

I didn't mind being soaked and freezing. My gun could be cleaned and oiled. The items in my wallet could be dried. I could reimburse the Philadelphia cardiologist for his wayward kayak. But the loss of my cell phone was a grievous blow. Fortunately I had uploaded most of the photographs and videos I had taken since arriving on the island. But I had lost my prime means of contacting my supervisor—or anyone.

I understood there was no point sitting around and beating myself up. I pulled off my boots and dumped them out, wrung as much water as I could from my wool socks, then laced everything back up.

Markman had posted a NO TRESPASSING on a sort of lintel at the end of the dock. I passed beneath it without a pause, thinking, Abandon all hope.

From the opposite shore, Stormalong had appeared to be a single humpbacked rock devoid of notable landmarks. Now that I was trekking up its spine, I saw how wrong that impression had been. There were indeed a great many individual rocks, most covered with the ocher lichen that you see so regularly on Maine's coastal cliffs. But there were hidden dells, too: small pockets where cranberry, hackberry, and bayberry bushes clustered around rainwater ponds.

Blake Markman had chosen a perfect hiding place from whatever demons had chased him out of Los Angeles.

The hike helped warm me up, but my crotch felt as if someone had applied a cold compress to it.

The sun was just a paleness in the fog above the western horizon.

Rags of mist floated across the uneven landscape. A raven rose from a wind-deformed pine, its call a gurgling croak, and flapped away on black wings before me. The crashing of the waves grew louder as I neared the southern end. Soon sheep began to appear around me, dozens of them. They were sturdy and off-white, and the lone ram I saw had magnificent curled horns. I felt as if I were wandering over a Scottish isle adrift in time and space from the modern world.

Suddenly I heard a man shout, "Put your hands up!"

I couldn't see him in the mist. Couldn't see if he was armed. But the menace in his voice was real.

I kept my hands at my side. "Markman?"

"Never mind who I am. Turn around, and get the hell off my island."

"My name is Mike Bowditch. I'm a game warden investigator with the State of Maine. I can show you my badge."

"I don't care who you are. There's no trespassing on Stormalong."

"I'm a law enforcement officer. That gives me the right to enter posted property. Can you please step forward so that I can see you?"

The hermit emerged from the fog thirty feet from where I was standing. He had a double-barreled shotgun leveled at my midsection. He wore a wool scarf knotted around his throat. He wore a poncho of tanned leather over an oilskin coat. He wore dungarees so dirty they could have stood upright on their own. Most of all, he wore the look of a man who had suffered unimaginable hardships.

All wardens practice drawing and firing their

service weapon from their holster. I was a faster shot than most, especially with my new pistol, but probably not fast enough to get off a round without taking one in return.

"Put the gun down, Blake." It was Ariel.

She materialized out of the haze behind him like her namesake sprite from *The Tempest*.

Markman remained belligerent. "He's an intruder."

"No, he's not. This is the man I've been telling you about. He's the one who's going to solve Miranda's murder."

29

Like everything else about Stormalong, the hermit's cabin was not what I'd imagined. Instead of a hovel built of driftwood planks with a thatched roof, it was an angular, tiered structure with multiple eaves. The design seemed faintly Japanese. There was a grid of solar panels arrayed nearby for the few weeks a year when the island saw the sun. The tall windmill with scimitar-shaped blades must have a been more reliable generator of electricity. A greenhouse had been built parallel to the island's southern shore to maximize its exposure to the faithless sun.

Blake Markman had been an extremely wealthy man once, and perhaps he still was. How else to explain his impressive eco-sanctuary?

I studied his back as he entered the nimbus of light surrounding the door. His grizzled hair hung about his shoulders, and his shoulders seemed stooped as if by more than age. He paused before the door to remove his metal cleats and scrape the mud off his boots. Ariel and I followed his example. When he opened the door, I felt the embrace of warm air.

"I'm not used to visitors." Markman's speaking voice was soft and gentle. It wasn't at all what

I had expected after his first threatening words. "I don't even remember the last time I had two people in here with me."

The interior was as eccentric in its design as the exterior. The floors were a mosaic of reddish wood tiles that had to have been harvested in a distant jungle. The walls had been constructed with integrated shelves that were overflowing with books and bronze and iron sculptures. At the far end of the great room was an enormous cobblestone fireplace in which flames danced.

The hermit disappeared down a hall.

"What are you doing here, Mike?" Ariel said as she removed her parka.

"I was concerned about you."

"That would be cute if it weren't insulting. Where did you find a boat to make the crossing?"

"You remember that kayak chained to the tree outside your cottage? The last time I saw it, it was bound for the Gulf Stream."

A twinkle appeared in her teal-blue eyes. "That would explain why you're dripping water all over Blake's tigerwood floor."

"How did Markman know I was on the island?" Like every warden, I prided myself on my ability to move stealthily across any landscape.

"There's a motion sensor on the dock."

No doubt plenty of others were elsewhere on the island, I now realized.

"Take off your pants," said Ariel as I stood in

a puddle of my own making. "Not here. In the bathroom."

Markman reappeared carrying a pair of shearling-lined slippers and pants made from yarn he'd probably spun himself. He offered them to me.

I undressed in the bathroom. Markman had a solar shower and used a composting toilet. His house was an environmentalist's dream. I rinsed the salt water off my pistol and magazines, knowing I'd have to oil them within the next few hours or risk the blued steel's becoming rusty.

I took the opportunity to remove three more ticks from my skin.

The pants were so short on me they wore like culottes. I returned to the great room. Markman took my sodden corduroys to dry on a rack beside the fire. My socks were already dangling there, and my boots were steaming on the hearthstones nearby.

"Stand here and get warm," he said. "I have water heating for tea."

He left us again.

The logs in the fireplace were hardwood, I realized. Where had Markman found them? No oaks or birches grew on Stormalong. Did his mysterious courier bring firewood, too? I turned to inspect my surroundings. Immediately my gaze fell upon an unframed painting of Blake Markman on an easel in a nearby nook. Even without a signature, I could recognize the work as that of Miranda Evans.

"She told him," said Ariel from across the room. "Miranda told him who she really was."

"That's not exactly true," said the hermit, returning with a steaming teakettle and tray of cups. He'd shed his sheepskins and his dirty jeans for a baggy sweater and drawstring pants similar to the ones he'd given me. "When she came over the first time, I didn't let her land. She'd introduced herself as you." He gestured at Ariel with his long hands. "I've chased off reporters before—some at gunpoint. But your sister kept trying, and one morning she slipped onto the island without me seeing. I was so impressed with her determination I let her into my world."

Not into his *house,* but into his *world.*

While I remained standing with my back to the crackling fire, Ariel and Markman sat on couches across from each other. The hermit poured us all rose-hip tea. The flavor was not to my taste, but it was hot, which was all that mattered.

"The thing that struck me about Miranda," said Markman, "was that she didn't ask me a single question about myself. She had lots of questions about the house and the greenhouse and the sheep. But she didn't ask me a thing about my past. I showed her my bedroom, and there is a picture there of my late wife. It's the only one I kept. Miranda picked it up and began to sob so hard I had to catch her before she collapsed on the floor. That was when I knew she was also an impostor."

"An impostor?" I asked.

"I spent the first part of my life pretending to be someone I wasn't. I lived in a Bel Air mansion, drove a Ferrari, partied constantly, and considered myself an artist when really I was only bankrolling men with creative vision. My self-deceit resulted in the death of my wife. It should have killed me. But I was saved to suffer. And in suffering I have found myself."

" 'Out of suffering have emerged the strongest souls; the most massive characters are seared with scars,' " said Ariel with the solemn carefulness of someone repeating a famous quotation.

Markman was evidently better read than I was. "Khalil Gibran," he said.

The unreality of the setting and the situation had caused me to lose focus. I'd forgotten my mission. I had a hundred questions for the hermit, but the only ones that mattered were those that could direct me to Miranda Evans's killer.

"Mr. Markman," I began.

"You can call me Blake."

"On the occasions when Miranda came over here to sketch you, did she mention anyone who might wish to cause her harm?"

"We didn't speak of Maquoit at all."

"What about someone from her life before she came to Maine?"

"You don't understand. We made a pact with each other that we wouldn't talk about anything except ideas. I told her I'd shaken off the rest of the world when I came to Stormalong, or as much of it as was possible. If she wanted to share my reality, she needed to do the same in my presence."

I let his pseudophilosophy slide. "Would you mind showing that shotgun to me again? Preferably with the barrel pointed somewhere besides my vital organs."

His smile was indulgent as he rose to his bare feet. "You are a single-minded man."

"That's what I'm paid to be."

"Money, I suspect, has nothing to do with it."

While he was out of the room, Ariel scowled. "You don't honestly think he killed my sister? What motive would he have had?"

I could have answered her in several ways: because Blake Markman wanted to protect his privacy and didn't trust that Miranda would be true to her promise; because Blake Markman's self-imposed solitude wasn't a quest for enlightenment but a sly maneuver to avoid facing questions about his role in his wife's death; because Blake Markman was likely mentally unbalanced.

Instead I said nothing.

After a minute, he returned with a leather case. He stood before me and opened the clasps. Inside was the now-disassembled shotgun. It was made of engraved steel and polished wood set atop a lining of bloodred velvet.

"Is this a Fabbri?" I asked, dazzled by the light reflecting off the two barrels.

"You know your shotguns."

"These cost more than most houses."

"It was my father's bequest to me."

"And you use it to chase off trespassers?"

"When I have to." He closed the case and set it on the couch. "It's the only firearm I own. Is there anything else here you'd like to see?"

"You should take the tour," Ariel said. "The island is magical."

I glanced at the nearest window and saw the fire reflected in the glass. In November, darkness descends quickly, and I didn't want to navigate the Gut half-blind.

"We should get back, Ariel."

For an instant, I thought she might tell me she wasn't coming. Having charmed Miranda, had Blake Markman now charmed her sister? Then she stretched her arms above her head and let out a yawn.

I gathered up my steaming pants, socks, and boots and returned to the bathroom.

So Markman claimed not to own a hunting

rifle. There was no way to verify his statement without tearing his home apart, which I had no justification for doing. Borrowing and losing a kayak was as much lawbreaking as I had in me for the day. Counting Blackington's totaled truck, I was running up quite a bill I would need to pay the people of Maquoit.

"Would you like me to guide you back to the dock?" asked the hermit as he opened the door for us. The twilight had thickened around the house. Condensed fog dripped steadily from the eaves.

"I can find the way," I said.

The bearded man once again showed me his smug superior smile. "There's no shame in needing a guide."

"I can find it."

Both Blake and Ariel probably assumed this was bravado on my part. But I'd made a career out of tracking people and animals in foul weather. I could see Ariel's footprints in the path as clearly as if they were illuminated by an infrared light.

Markman didn't shake hands or wish us well. He simply bowed like a Shaolin monk and closed the door.

Shadows closed in around us like a swift-rising tide.

I set off down the path. Out in the cold, I could feel the lingering dampness of my corduroys.

Several sheep watched us from a rise. The whiteness of their wool gave the silent animals a phosphorescence that bordered on ghostliness.

"Blake said those are Icelandic sheep," Ariel said. "I hope you really know where you're going."

I pretended I hadn't heard her. "What's your take on Markman? He looks like John the Baptist but lives in a state-of-the-art eco-home."

"The man *is* a shepherd, Mike."

"He isn't the crazy, unwashed hermit he wants people to think he is. He's adopted a disguise to put off visitors. He said he was living a lie in his previous life, but his current persona is also fake."

She considered this statement. "He showed me that photo in his bedroom. Miranda was a dead ringer for his late wife."

"You didn't find that creepy?"

"Of course, I did!"

We began a steep descent down the north side of the island. I heard a steady knocking that could only have been waves pushing Ariel's skiff against the dock. She had grown quiet after her revelation about Miranda's resemblance to the late Mrs. Markman.

Finally, we arrived at the teetering dock. I looked for the motion sensor and spotted it right away behind the NO TRESPASSING sign. The tide had slackened. I crouched down to loosen the rope from the cleat, then began pulling the boat close enough for us to climb aboard.

"What do you think you're doing?" she said.

"I was planning on rowing."

"I rowed myself over here without capsizing. I don't need your manly assistance."

"It's called chivalry."

"No, it's called chauvinism."

I stood aside as she settled into the bow and fitted the oars into their locks.

She was, in truth, a skilled rower.

"I've been thinking about what you said about Blake's hermit thing being an act," she said. "I don't think that's entirely fair. The man *is* living alone out there in severe conditions. Clearly, he has chosen to cut himself off from the rest of humanity."

The foghorn sounded nearby.

"Why do you think Miranda was so determined to meet him?"

"To further fuck with me. She probably wanted to mess up my chance to write a book about him. She figured to antagonize him."

"Did he seem surprised to see you when you pulled up at his dock?"

"I think Miranda must have said to expect me. It was bizarre, though. His expression didn't change at all when I told her she was dead. He didn't ask how. He just said, 'I am sorry for your loss.'"

The bow scraped a submerged rock and then wedged against the cobbles.

"Will you at least let me drag the boat up onto the beach?" I asked.

"*That* I will let you do."

I hopped out into the knee-deep water and nearly twisted an ankle on a lurking clump of Irish moss. I took the painter over my shoulder and began hauling the skiff, with Ariel aboard, up onto dryish land. She tossed the oars back into the boat, and the wooden echo seemed overly loud in the quiet between the foghorn moans.

"There's something else I've realized," she said. "Do you remember that weird text from Miranda I mentioned?"

"Yes."

"The devil she fell in love with wasn't that Pillsbury guy. The devil was Blake Markman."

30

"How do you know your sister was in love with Blake?"

"Crazy attracts crazy. But it's not only that. When I first saw him at the dock, I thought he was dirty and disgusting. But the more time I spent with him, the handsomer he got. His eyes are so dark and intense, and he has those beautiful long lashes. Then when he showed me around his amazing house, I had to remind myself that the man is bad news. Basically, Blake Markman is the kind of guy I used to fall for when I was young and stupid myself."

We walked up the darkening beach in the direction of my Datsun and her bicycle.

"It sounds like you might want to write about him after all," I said.

"Maybe in the context of my sister. I don't know. It takes me a while to find a book in a person."

"How long did it take you to decide to write about the neo-Nazis?"

"About five seconds."

We laughed together.

"Are you married, Mike?"

"No."

"I didn't think so. You're not wearing a ring,

but not all married men do. I pride myself on my ability to intuit a person's relationship status without having to ask."

"What about you?"

"Me?" She laughed again. "Never. I am the kind of girl who likes having a boy in every port."

I wasn't sure what to make of that.

"Can I borrow your phone? I need to call my captain and tell him what's been happening. My partner from the state police might be coming out here by boat tonight."

"In this fog?"

"I wouldn't put it past him."

She removed her iPhone from her pocket, tapped the passcode, and handed it to me. The illuminated screen cast a freaky glow on my wrist. "Knock yourself out. I'll meet you back at the cottage."

I watched Ariel pedal off into the fog wondering if she'd been flirting with me. Not that it mattered. When it came to involving myself with women I met through my job, I had learned my lesson through bitter experience. And my romantic life was already a mare's nest.

The thought made me open my sodden wallet to the plastic holder that contained Stacey's photograph. She'd mocked me for carrying around the snapshot: "People use phones for that purpose these days, Bowditch." But I'd lost my cell in the Gut, and her picture was only a little water stained.

I held the screen of Ariel's iPhone over the wet photograph and felt a familiar pang as I stared into those almond-shaped jade-green eyes. Ariel Evans was more conventionally good-looking than this skinny, brown-haired woman whom I still thought of as my soul mate despite all that separated us now. It was a lot more than distance.

Ariel hadn't bothered to check her cell before she gave it to me. But I saw from her notifications that she had 130 voice messages, 285 emails, and 829 texts. How were those numbers possible?

There could only be one reason: the story was out.

The world wanted to talk to the famous and controversial author who had returned from the dead.

While I'd been off the grid on Maquoit, thinking the investigation consisted only of my actions, the story had blown up back in the real world. I could only imagine the chatter at Warden Service headquarters in Augusta.

DeFord let my call go to voice mail because he didn't recognize the number but phoned back the instant he heard my message. In a tone that seemed uncharacteristically stern he asked me to summarize my activities for the day. I gave him the play-by-play while he listened in silence.

Finally he said, "What progress have you made identifying our shooter?"

The question, which I should have anticipated, put a knot in my tongue.

"Are you there, Mike?"

"I can't say I've made significant progress. I understand the island dynamics better than I did and how Miranda Evans disrupted them. But I'm no closer to ID'ing the person who fired the gun."

Now it was my turn to listen to a seemingly dead line.

"Should I send Norm Bilodeau out there to help you?" DeFord's voice had grown cold.

It was as strong a statement of disapproval as I'd ever heard from him. Bilodeau was an experienced but ethically suspect warden investigator. I'd gotten too comfortable speaking candidly with DeFord. I had forgotten that the captain had superiors of his own holding him to account.

"No, sir. That won't be necessary."

"Public safety issued a statement today about the shooting and the misidentification of the victim. You're lucky the weather forecast is as bad as it is. The media is going to start invading that island as soon as the fog lifts."

"What about Steve Klesko?"

"Detective Klesko's testimony was interrupted by a juror having a heart attack that turned out to be a panic attack. As a result, he has to return to take the stand tomorrow for cross-examination. Another stroke of good fortune for you."

"I don't see it that way."

"He'll be out tomorrow afternoon, whatever the weather. Expect a boatload of wardens and troopers. In the meantime you're the only law enforcement officer on Maquoit for the next eighteen to twenty-four hours, which means this whole thing is on you and you alone. Do you know the origin of the term *scapegoat?* It's from the Bible. The scapegoat was a goat sent off to die in the desert after the high priest ritually cursed it with the sins of the people. You can either be the hero or you can be the goat, Mike. The choice is up to you."

"Understood."

"I hope so."

The foghorn sounded again in the distance. Behind me, unseen waves broke along ledges.

I switched off the phone and set it on the hood of the truck. Then I put on my still-dry peacoat, gloves, and watch cap. The engine took thirty long seconds to turn over. The inside of the windshield began to cloud over from the dampness of my clothes. Fog within, fog without—I drove cautiously back to the cottage.

Ariel had not only started a fire in the stove but had gotten it roaring. On what assignments had she learned so many skills, so much bushcraft?

How many people, meeting this woman for the first time, underestimated the size of the heart beating inside that chest?

She stood over the woodstove sipping from a glass filled with amber-colored liquid and ice.

I handed her the phone. "I didn't mean to pry but I couldn't help but see you have a lot of messages. The story seems to be out."

"Of course, it's out. I called my editor at the *Times* this morning."

No wonder it had become such a shitstorm for DeFord.

"You might have told me," I said bitterly.

"I'm a journalist. What do you think we do?"

"But Miranda was your sister."

"Listen, I'm sorry if I've unwittingly gotten in your way. No one wants Miranda's murder solved more than I do. But I don't know you, Mike. You seem like a nice guy, but you haven't provided me with a lot of reasons why I should trust you."

Heat rose along the back of my neck. "If you want to know who I am, you can Google my name. I've been in the news enough. The only reason I attempted crossing the Gut in the first place was because I was concerned about your safety."

"My safety?"

"Blake Markman was—still is—a potential suspect. The man's a cipher. He was obviously

305

close to Miranda, maybe even as obsessed with her as she was with him, and there are still plenty of reasons to doubt his stability. You yourself believe he's a murderer. You didn't give me a chance to interview him and make an assessment before you rowed over there alone."

She rattled the cubes around the glass. "Do I really have to give you the 'I can take care of myself' speech?"

"You're interfering with a criminal investigation, Ariel."

"That's not the first time I've had some clueless cop tell me that."

"Clueless?" The heat had spread from my neck over my scalp.

Ariel spun on her heel and disappeared into the kitchen. After a moment, I gave chase. She spilled some of her Dewar's when she saw me enter the room. Her shoulders tightened as if she expected me to either smack her or kiss her.

Instead I squatted on my heels before the kitchen sink and began rummaging through the cleaning products in the cupboard until I found what I was looking for: a small can of household lubricating oil. I removed a dish towel from a drawer, laid it flat atop the counter, and fieldstripped my handgun atop the cotton square.

Ariel watched me clean my gun and magazines. "How am I supposed to interpret this?"

"As me cleaning my service weapon before

it rusts. Salt water is the enemy of every man-made thing."

When I was done, I reholstered my SIG, washed my hands with dish soap, and departed the kitchen.

She called after me, "You're not clueless, Mike. I shouldn't have said that. I'm sorry."

I paused in the front room to answer her. "Has it occurred to you that whoever shot your sister might have been gunning for the person who wrote *Ghost Skins*? If so, he didn't finish the job. If I were you, I'd stay in for the rest of the night. I'd keep away from the windows, too."

I locked the door and pulled it hard after me.

Down at Beacon Head, the foghorn continued to send out its warnings.

31

I passed no vehicles on my way back into the village but paused briefly to let a doe and fawn cross from the orchard to the marsh. The mother and child took their sweet time, like certain pedestrians in crosswalks. The blurry headlights picked out the fading spots on the tawny coat of the fawn. Those white markings had helped camouflage the young deer from nonexistent predators through the short island summer, but they were being replaced by the hollow gray bristles that would keep the fawn warm in the winter.

DeFord was right about one thing. Probably more than one thing. Instead of taking full control of my interviews, I had let the Maquoiters evade my questions and obfuscate their answers. My strategy of hanging back and letting people say more than they'd intended might have worked in the long run. But it didn't admit to the urgency of the situation.

Case in point, I had let Beryl McCloud play hide-and-seek from me all day. The school-teacher was too smart not to understand that an interview was nonnegotiable. That she'd made herself scarce told me the information she possessed was important.

It didn't surprise me in the least that the teacher didn't answer the door when I arrived at her house. Usually, people hiding in their own homes will behave predictably. They will pull the blinds and turn off lights. They will be careful to conceal the glow of their television or computer screen. There were none of those telltale attempts at concealment here.

Beryl had gone out, but where had she gone?

The obvious place for me to start looking was the school. The windows were dark, but the blinds were open. If I stood on my tiptoes and pressed my forehead to the cold glass, I could see from one interior wall to the next. No one inside.

What about the library?

As I approached the building, I saw a brief sliver of light as a heavy curtain dropped shut. I climbed the wooden steps and used the meaty part of my fist to pound on the door. The glass panes rattled so hard they seemed likely to fall out.

"Beryl? It's Warden Bowditch."

I waited a long time for the porch light to come on and the door to open. She managed to summon a smile, but the wariness in her expression was unmistakable. She was wearing a green cashmere hoodie over a white T. The sour odor of cigarettes hung about her like an invisible cloud.

"You caught me shopping," she said, affecting a cough to convince me that she was still incapacitated from her illness. "I don't have an internet connection at the house so sometimes I sneak in here to buy things. Thank heavens for eBay, Amazon, and Netflix. I don't know how people survived on this miserable island before the web."

I noted the elaborate answer to a question I hadn't asked. "Joy told me you were sick in bed."

"It was a bad morning. I have a lot of them."

"And yet you went for a hike?"

She brought out the fake cough for another spin. "I thought the sea air might do me some good."

"Where did you go?"

"I like to take the trail out to Spruce Point on the east side of the island."

"You weren't concerned about deer hunters?"

Her lip curled into an ironic smile. "No one will be hunting as long as you're on the island. That shouldn't come as a surprise. Have you been over to the east side? The trees are so tall and dense, and the needles are so thick you kind of bounce as you walk. The kids build fairy houses along the path with bark and twigs and moss. I heard a winter wren singing. Do you know they have the longest songs of any native birds, winter wrens? They go on and on."

I knew all about winter wrens. But I said nothing.

She couldn't stand the silence. "I guess I like that trail because it reminds me of when I first came to Maquoit and everything seemed so otherworldly and enchanted."

"Unlike now?"

She shrugged and gestured to the library's dimly lit interior. "Would you like a tour of the island museum? It's only a few rooms, but there's some really interesting stuff. We have a Native American harpoon used to kill minke whales, and lots of antique furniture and clothing from the nineteenth century. There are vintage photos of Maquoit when it was all clear-cut for grazing sheep and cows. There were barely any trees back then. You'd probably be interested in the taxidermy. We have scoters and harlequin ducks and even a stuffed harbor seal."

I pulled a seat out from the nearest reading table. A banker's lamp cast a pool of greenish light on the polished wood. "First I need to ask you some questions about your relationship with Miranda Evans."

She stared at the chair as if she'd never seen such a thing before and didn't understand its purpose. "We didn't have a relationship. We were friendly is all it was. Two single women on an island of macho fishermen."

I circled around the varnished table, pulled out

a chair, and settled down across from where I wanted her to sit.

She sat.

In the bright sunlight outside Gull Cottage, Beryl McCloud had had a kind of burnished glow. It wasn't just her bronzed skin. She'd looked like the kind of adventurous soul who would give up big-city life to take a teaching job on a fogbound Maine island. But her tan had seemingly faded overnight. Her eyes had developed hoods that suggested insomnia. And her fingertips were noticeably jaundiced from nicotine.

"What's her sister like? The real Ariel? I've heard there's a strong resemblance. I'd like to meet her, but, well, I guess I'm afraid to."

"Why's that?"

"It seems macabre somehow."

Without a phone, I was forced to take hand-written notes. I started with my usual back-and-forth establishing where I was and whom I was interviewing. She acquiesced.

"Where were you between nine and eleven a.m. yesterday morning?"

"Teaching school."

I didn't suspect the former barista of having fired the fatal shot, but I continued down my list to get her answers on the record. No, she hadn't killed Miranda Evans. No, she had no idea who might have committed the crime.

Finally I reached the questions I most wanted her to answer. "At any time did Miranda say anything to suggest she was using her sister's stolen identity?"

"No. Never. I didn't have a clue."

"At any time did Miranda ever use injectable drugs in front of you?"

"No, but . . ."

I paused in my writing. "Since she's dead, you won't be violating a confidence, Beryl."

"I saw the needle marks one day when she had her shoes off. She caught me looking and went into another room to put on socks."

"So you don't know where she got the drugs? Whether she brought them with her or obtained them on Maquoit?"

Her eyes drifted toward the ceiling beams. "I have absolutely no idea."

I was sure she was lying now. "Really?"

"You must have heard about what happened to Hiram's brother, Heath, and how Harmon decreed that no one is allowed to do drugs out here. Pot, obviously, is an exception. But hard drugs? Not permitted."

The banker's light began to flicker. I tapped the bulb with my pen, and it stopped. "I want to return to something you said yesterday. You said that it shouldn't be hard finding the person who shot Miranda. What did you mean by that?"

Her hand rose to her mouth. She spoke from

313

behind her yellow-tipped fingers. "I don't remember saying that! I'm not sure why I would have."

I rested my forearms on the table. "Are you frightened of someone, Beryl?"

"At the moment you're freaking me out pretty good."

"When was the last time you saw Miranda alive?"

"The day before she was killed."

"Where?"

"Her cottage. She'd returned from Stormalong, and she wanted to show me the drawings. We had a glass of wine and talked about Blake. That's the hermit's first name."

"I've met him."

Her eyes widened. "Really? I've been on this island for a year and a half and never seen him once. But you needed to interrogate him, of course."

"That's an interesting word choice."

"Aren't you interrogating me? It feels like you are." She reached into the pocket of her flannel shirt and brought out a pack of American Spirits. She set the cigarettes on the tabletop but made no attempt to light one.

"What did Miranda tell you about Blake Markman?"

"That he was intelligent, sensitive, and kind of haunted. And not grubby at all. She said

314

his house was very clean and architecturally interesting. The whole crazy-island-hermit thing was a pretense so that people would leave him alone, she said. She was fascinated by him. I think all the drawings she did make that pretty obvious. I cautioned her about falling under his spell."

"Why did you feel the need to warn her against him?"

Beryl stiffened with something like indignation. "I used to date an older guy who seemed like the perfect man—handsome, funny, this incredible musician—and then one night we had what I thought was a regular argument and he punched me in the teeth. I told Ariel—Miranda, I mean—that it was like he'd pulled off a mask and behind it was the devil."

I underlined the word in my notebook. "She didn't say anything that suggested Markman was violent?"

"No, but everyone's heard the stories about how his wife died. If he didn't murder her, why's he hiding here?"

"Maybe he wants to be alone with his grief. Or he feels guilt for not having been able to save her."

Beryl's tone turned acid. "Now you sound like Miranda. Making excuses for bad men."

"Speaking of bad men, tell me about her relationship with Nat Pillsbury."

The name caused Beryl to catch her breath. "It was just a physical thing. They were having sex. Miranda was a very sexual person. Some people give off that vibe. I'm not even into girls, but I could feel it. She used her desirability to toy with people and get what she wanted." A sudden blush started spreading up her throat. "That's just an impression I got."

"What about for Pillsbury? Did he consider it to be just a physical thing, too?"

Beryl began batting the pack of cigarettes back and forth between her hands. "Why don't you ask him?"

"What's your opinion of Nat Pillsbury? Your personal opinion?"

She gazed at me through slitted eyes. "What do you mean?"

"Do you like him? Dislike him? Did you caution Miranda against falling under his magic spell?"

"The only magical thing about Nat Pillsbury is his cock."

There it was: Beryl had had sex with him, too. "He was sleeping with you before Miranda arrived," I stated with such authority that she couldn't equivocate. "That's why you've been avoiding me, isn't it? You were afraid you'd give yourself away under questioning."

She glanced off into a shadowy corner as if someone might have been hiding there. She was

316

furiously trying to think of a retraction. But it was no use.

"There was very little sleeping involved," she finally admitted.

"Did Jenny Pillsbury know about you and Nat?"

"I'm pretty sure she had suspicions, but that was all."

I kept pressing. "To your knowledge, did Jenny know about his affair with Miranda?"

Beryl made a searching examination of the bookshelves behind me. "I don't think so."

"From what I've heard, most of the island knew or suspected. Nat was openly attentive to her at the Trap House."

"I don't go to the Trap House. I don't like to be groped."

"But Miranda went."

"Only with Nat. Nobody messes with him. Not even the Washburns."

"I heard that Jenny Pillsbury is a Washburn."

Beryl gave me that slitted look again. "Who told you that?"

"Does it matter?"

Her sly smile returned. "I wouldn't want to get on her bad side. I'll say that much."

"How did you feel when Nat threw you over for Miranda?"

"Hurt."

"That's all?"

"I mean, I couldn't blame him. She was so gorgeous and full of life. And I'm just this drab, boring person. Redheads are supposed to be fiery and passionate."

"Is it true that Jenny was the schoolteacher on Maquoit before you?"

"For eight years. Jenny started young, even younger than me. There are people on the island, Kenneth Crowley for instance. Jenny will say, 'I had him in school,' and it's hard to imagine because she seems so young and he's almost a man."

"Teenaged boys sometimes have crushes on their teachers."

Beryl shrugged off the suggestion and returned her cigarette pack to her pocket. "I've admitted that Nat and I were having sex, and I've told you why I couldn't have possibly killed Miranda Evans. Isn't that enough? You might not consider interrogation a form of torture, but I do."

"We're almost done. But I need you to answer my next questions with complete honesty."

"I've been answering your questions with complete honesty."

"How does Hiram Reed fit into all this?"

Her shoulders tightened. "I don't understand the question."

"Hiram and Nat are best friends. But how do he and Jenny get along? He's a Reed, and she's a Washburn. Their families are feuding."

"It's not the Montagues and the Capulets out here!" Beryl caught her breath again and took a moment to gather her wits. "They seem to get along fine. They both grew up here. The lobster war is a thing between the old men. Hopefully, it will die when they do."

I returned my pen and notebook to my coat pocket to give her the impression we were nearing the end of the interview. I wanted her to let her guard down. "What about you and Hiram? How do you get along?"

Her smile was altogether affectionate. "He hit on me when I first came to the island, but I wasn't into him that way. But he seems used to rejection. He hasn't had the easiest life. His brother was his father's favorite from what everyone tells me. He's had problems with drugs and alcohol, as I'm sure you know."

"I get the sense you care for him."

"Hiram used to come into the library a lot. You wouldn't guess it, but he's a big-time reader. Science fiction and fantasy mostly. Medieval history. And he was here for meetings twice a week."

"Alcoholics Anonymous meetings?"

"Oh, shit. I wasn't supposed to say that. I haven't seen as much of him lately. He's been going through a tough stretch."

"How so?"

"I wouldn't want to be Harmon's son, would you?"

In some ways, I had been.

"Is there anything you'd like to ask me?" I said by way of conclusion. "I can't promise to answer, but I'll do my best."

It was a ploy to tease out additional information from an unwilling witness. Cons who had been in and out of jail recognized the trap for what it was, but law-abiding citizens often gave themselves away by surrendering to their curiosity.

"What does all this gossip stuff matter—about Nat and Miranda—if it was all an accident? You're upsetting a lot of good people who had nothing to do with her death. Why aren't you focusing on the hunters?"

I reached for my notebook again. "If I showed you a list of deer hunters on the island, would you be able to direct me to the ones I should focus on?"

"No," she admitted.

The chair scraped across the floor as I rose to my feet. "Thank you, Beryl. You've been extremely helpful."

"I have?"

"I hope you feel better."

She eagerly escorted me to the door. Winter moths were holding an aerial dance around the globed porch light. I buttoned up my coat while Beryl shivered on the doorstep.

"I never used to hate fog until I came here," she said. "I used to think it was romantic."

"Places can change you."

Without another word, she closed the door. I heard the bolt slam shut. Then the light went out.

32

The Trap House had no sign. The long, rambling warehouse was built atop a wharf that stood on stilts above the ink-black harbor. Like its neighbors, it was armored with wet gray shingles that reminded me of scales from some prehistoric leviathan. A dozen trucks, many of which I recognized, were parked in its lot.

I could hear country music coming through the cracks in the walls. Maine lobstermen fancied themselves cowboys of the sea. They identified as hard-bitten individualists unafraid to settle their own scores. In their minds they lived by codes of rough justice that had been abandoned by a weak and civilized society. The truth was, the men who clung to these beliefs weren't outlaws. They were thugs.

But if I was going to find any of the hunters on my list, there was no better place to look.

Inside the body-warmed building, the drinkers were seated around four picnic tables, and a sort of bar was at the back of the room. What light there was came from caged incandescent bulbs hanging on hooks and strung together with heavy-duty extension cords. Drafts carried the aromas of tobacco in its various manifestations: cigarette, cigar, and pipe. The sourness of spilled beer rose from the floorboards. Above all other odors was an unmistakable fishiness that had seeped into the wood over decades of housing bait barrels.

Every face in the room turned in my direction as I entered. I counted fourteen of them. Not a single one was female. Not a single one was friendly.

Harmon Reed occupied the place of honor nearest the potbellied stove. He shared his table with some of his retainers from Graffam's store, including Chum McNulty and Pete Shattuck, as well as an underaged Kenneth Crowley, and Andrew Radcliffe. The old-money constable looked as at home in this crowd as a rabbit at a rattlesnake convention.

Crowley sprang to his feet at the sight of me. Then Harmon hissed something at him, and the young man returned to the bench. The harbormaster beckoned me to join his party.

A new song started up through the wall-mounted speakers: "Angry All the Time" by Tim McGraw. An appropriate choice for these alcohol-abusing hotheads.

"Warden Bowditch!" said Harmon. "I told the boys you'd be strolling in any minute or two."

"Have you figured me out that quickly, Mr. Reed?"

"Sit down and have a drink with us." He lifted a gallon bottle of Captain Morgan's spiced rum to show me what was on offer. Some of his hangers-on looked droopy, sweaty, if not half in the bag. But Harmon was an advertisement for moderated drinking.

"If you know me so well, you know I have to decline your offer of a drink. I'm surprised to see you here, Mr. Crowley. Tell me, which one of these adults gave you that adult beverage?"

"Not a word, Kenneth," said Reed.

I turned my attention to Radcliffe. He had a can of Moxie soda in front of him, the only nonalcoholic beverage in sight. "I didn't expect to see you either, Constable."

Harmon patted Andrew's shoulder. "Poor Andy here has been getting phone calls all afternoon. Maquoit was all over the news tonight, it seems. What's the farthest place you got a call from?"

"Sydney, Australia." Radcliffe had the defeated air of someone accustomed to being teased.

The harbormaster refused to let up. "Andy says some of those fine journalists will be coming out here tomorrow to interview us quaint and colorful islanders. Now, we were wondering, Warden, is there an open season on reporters? And if so, what's the bag limit?"

A boat engine roared to life in the harbor.

Harmon's head spun around toward the windows at the far end of the warehouse. "Who the hell is that going out in this thick of fog?"

"Sounds like Nat Pillsbury," said a hatchet-faced man seated near the window.

Reed used his powerful arms to raise himself from the table. His comrades followed him to the back wall, as did I. Fog-fuzzed lights were faintly visible moving through the harbor.

"What's Nat doing?" asked Radcliffe.

"Going to America, I'd say," said Kenneth Crowley, obviously inebriated.

It was island slang for the mainland.

The departing lobsterboat was far louder than most. I remembered having seen a forty-footer moored in the harbor the day before, seemingly the largest craft in the Maquoit fishing fleet. It had a slate-colored bow and twin engines. *Sea Hag* was the name painted on the transom.

"Serves him right if he runs into a ledge," said Chum.

"He should've told me he was going out tonight," said Reed, venting his spleen. "I'm the goddamned harbormaster."

"You know how Nat is," said Andrew Radcliffe. "He does what he does."

Reed glowered at the constable. Then, with no warning whatsoever, the old man stepped up onto the bench of the nearest picnic table and ascended to the top. It was probably the only time he had ever loomed above the heads of the men in the room.

"Shut off that damned music!"

Someone pulled a plug, and all conversation ceased with the same abruptness.

"Now everyone here knows what happened over to Gull Cottage yesterday," Reed all but shouted. "Some fool hunter shot that girl who called herself Ariel Evans. Turns out she wasn't who she pretended to be. But that's neither here nor there. The girl's still dead, and now her sister is out here stirring up trouble. From what I hear, the fake-news peddlers are on their way, too. You all remember the last time those lying sons of bitches took an interest in our private business."

Chum McNulty muttered a few words. To my ear they sounded like "When you shot Eli."

Reed must not have heard him. "Now, so far, the person who shot that girl hasn't been man enough to step forward. You all recognize the warden investigator here even if you haven't made his acquaintance yet. I assured him that the guilty party needed some time to come to his senses. I gave him *my word* that the person responsible would do the right thing because, I said, I know my people. But so far that cowardly individual hasn't seen fit to admit what he's done. That individual is making me look like a fool to Warden Bowditch. Worse than that, he's making you all look like fools, like no one on this island can be trusted."

"Why does it have to be one of us?" some brave, drunken soul asked from the back of the room. "What about Eli and Rud? Or the rest of the Washburns. Has he talked to them?"

"I am still conducting interviews," I said.

"I don't give three shits about Eli and Rudyard Washburn!" said Harmon to the crowd. "I'm talking right now to the people in this room. And here's what I'm saying: If it comes out that one of you killed the Evans girl, and you didn't say nothing when you had the chance, then so help me God, I will strike down on you with fire and fury like you've never seen. Forget being scared of what the law *might* do. You should be shitting your britches about what I *will* do!"

Just then, the door yawned open, and Ariel Evans stumbled in. She'd put on her Arc'teryx parka, zippered to the throat, and tied her hair in a long braid. The slackness of the muscles in her face told me that she was hammered. How in the world had she managed to ride her bicycle all the way to the village?

She began to clap. "Nice speech!"

Murmurs came from every darkened corner. The harbormaster hopped directly from the tabletop to the floor. Nimble, for an old coot.

I crossed the room, one step ahead of Harmon. "Ariel, you shouldn't be here."

"My sister was invited, but I'm not? What the fuck? I'm the real Ariel!"

Reed came up behind me, close enough that I could feel his body heat and smell the rum on his breath. "You have my condolences, Miss Evans, for the loss of your sister."

"You must be Harmon! That was an awesome speech. Bloody Shakespearean, as my late father might say."

"Come on, Ariel." I reached for her wrist, but she shook me off.

"No! I want to see who did it." She addressed the room again. "Don't be shy! Which one of you killed my little sister?"

"Get her out of here, Warden," Harmon huffed in my ear.

"I plan to.

"Come on, Ariel, let's get out of here. Trust me. This is not a place you want to be." I reached for her arm, but this time she punched my chest.

"I've been in a lot worse bars than this one."

Just then, Harmon Reed cocked his head like a sheepdog that has heard a wolf howl in the distance. I became aware of trucks approaching. I recognized the unique tenor of their souped-up engines.

"What's going on now?" asked Ariel.

"Please stay here." I searched for Radcliffe's face in the crowd. "Watch her for me, Andrew!"

From his expression you would have thought I'd asked him to care for my pet lioness.

I was one of the last men out the door. Two burgundy trucks were idling, side by side, with their super-bright halogen lights carving out an illuminated arena in which Harmon Reed stood, unblinking. Two shadows detached themselves from the darkness beyond the pickups. It was the Washburns.

33

The brothers advanced into the overlapping arcs made by the headlights of their vehicles. The nearly identical fishermen were dressed as they'd been the day before: in black anoraks, jeans, and heavy boots. Their nearly bald skulls were as white as condor eggs.

Harmon had his hands already balled into fists. "What are you boys doing here? You know you're banned from this establishment."

"Saw the news," stammered Eli Washburn. "Wanted to see . . ."

"The dead woman," said Rudyard.

Someone pushed into the small of my back. It was, inevitably, Ariel. I should have known Radcliffe couldn't control her. "Here I am, you fucking Nazis!"

How did she know that the Washburns were white supremacists?

Eli smirked. "Ain't she . . ."

Rudyard said, "Pretty!"

I grabbed Ariel as she surged toward them. It took a lot of strength to prevent her from attacking the Washburns.

"Let me go!"

I saw Radcliffe frozen with fear in the doorway. I called to him once again. "Constable, can you help me out here, please?"

The lights of the trucks made everyone look pale and bloodless. It sucked the life from people's faces. We had all become vampires.

"You need to leave now," I said to the brothers. "I'm a Maine game warden, and I'm telling you to leave."

"Or what?"

Unbelievable. The Washburns knew I was an armed law enforcement officer, and they were still ready to rumble. I released Ariel into Radcliffe's grasp and pushed my way down the ramp until I stood shoulder to shoulder with Harmon Reed. I made sure both my badge and sidearm were visible.

"I'm investigating a homicide. In fact, you two boys are at the top of my list. I'll be visiting you soon."

Eli said with a sneer, "We didn't . . ."

Rudyard said, "Shoot no one."

I kept my hand close to the grip of my service weapon. "I think I'm going to need more than your word on that."

Eli said, "Big bad . . ."

Rudyard said, "Game warden!"

Eli stepped close enough for me to tell by the smell of his breath that he'd eaten lobster for supper. He was two inches taller than I was, but most of his height was his legs.

"Are you reaching for my gun, Eli?" I said.

"What does it look like to you, Harmon?"

"Looks like he's reaching for your gun, Warden. Don't it, boys?"

I heard murmurs of assent behind me.

Eli blinked and stepped back.

But his brother wasn't done with the taunting. "Hey, Harmon . . . where's Hiram? Don't . . . see him."

From his aggressive stance, you wouldn't have thought Harmon Reed was rattled, but I noticed an uncharacteristic hitch in his voice. "You two stay away from my boy."

Eli had been reenergized by the rise Rudyard had gotten out of the harbormaster. "Or what?"

Harmon's voice became a growl. "I'm not going to warn you twice, Washburn."

Eli pulled up his anorak and shirt to reveal a flat belly inked with violent images. A tattooist had made a round scar into the eye of the Midgard Serpent. "You going to . . . shoot me again?"

I positioned myself to intervene, but I needed to be careful. In close-quarter combat you want to deliver rapid blows to your opponent's face and neck to disorient him and give yourself a moment to draw your weapon. You don't want to press your muzzle into his body where it might prevent the gun from firing, and you don't want to give him a chance to grab the action and restrict the slide.

"I'm videotaping this, assholes!" Ariel had her phone out and was recording the exchange. "I push a button and it uploads to *The New York Times* before you take your next breath."

The Washburns were old-fashioned law-breakers. They'd grown up on a remote island in a time before everyone carried a phone equipped with a recording device patched into a worldwide data network. This was probably their first encounter with crime prevention in the digital age, and they were clearly perplexed.

"Bitch!" shouted Eli.

"Race . . . traitor!" added Rudyard.

"Save it for the FBI," I said. "They're investigating death threats against Ms. Evans. And you boys just made their list."

Eli spat at my feet. But his bravado was gone. I kept my body sandwiched between the Washburns and Harmon Reed until the brothers had retreated to their matching trucks.

They revved their engines until the smoke billowed like dragon's breath. They wanted us to scatter, but I held my ground, and so did Reed. Finally, they shifted their transmissions into reverse and executed synchronized turns. Moments later I watched their brake lights vanish in the darkness and haze.

I was startled to turn around and see Harmon walking quietly in the direction of his house. I had expected him to stick around to gloat.

Some of the others also used the occasion to drift off, no doubt figuring the night couldn't get any more exciting. The hard-core alcoholics stumbled back into the bar.

Only Radcliffe and Ariel remained in the lot.

"Why were the Washburns asking about Hiram?" I asked the constable. "And why did it make Harmon so angry?"

"I have no idea."

The constable couldn't lie to save his own life.

But I was beginning to put together a theory about Harmon Reed's surviving son and the nature of his problems.

"I have this for you," Radcliffe said sullenly.

He handed me a sealed stationery envelope. It contained his list of hunters, I realized. I wondered if I would find his name on it. According to Harmon Reed, the constable had lied to me when he said he'd given up deer slaying.

Ariel had an air of drunken triumph about her. "You're welcome," she said.

Staring into her glassy eyes, I had a recognition. "Were you even taping that?"

"Battery's dead," she said with a loud laugh that wasn't as musical as the sober version.

"Time to go home."

Still laughing, she followed me to my pickup. I tossed her bicycle into the smeared blood where the deer had been.

. . .

Whether it was because she was sobering up or simply exhausted in body and spirit, Ariel let her head loll against the window. As we passed the spot where we'd had our crash, she asked, "What did you do with that deer?"

"Handed it over to Radcliffe to give to someone who needed the meat."

"Did you know deer's closest relatives are giraffes?"

"I did know that."

"Poor dead deer."

"It's the circle of life."

"I can still mourn it," she said with more testiness than my comment merited. She raised herself up in her seat.

"How did you know that the Washburns are neo-Nazis?"

"I'm a journalist."

"I'm serious, Ariel."

"There's this marvelous invention called the internet, you know. You should try using it. You might solve a case every once in a while."

Because she was drunk, I couldn't take offense. "Are the Washburns listed on some database of white supremacists you have access to?"

"I did a search for *Nazis* and *Maquoit*. And they popped up."

"How?"

"EBay. They buy and sell Nazi paraphernalia: coins, stamps, daggers, uniforms, flags."

"Under their own names?"

"You should read my book! These people no longer feel like they need to hide. They believe their hour's arrived to seize their country back from the Jews, the racial minorities, the feminists, the LGBTQ people, and the SJWs."

"What are SJWs?"

"Social Justice Warriors. The term's ironic."

"Is that what they call you?"

"Hell no! I'm a race traitor who exposed their secrets. I'm Public Enemy Number One."

There was no denying her courage, whatever else she was. "So I have been wondering about the title of your book. Why *Ghost Skins*?"

"It's slang for supremacists who hide their racist beliefs. Like cops who are secret members of the KKK. People in the military who are closet Aryans. Certain respectable-seeming politicians."

"I can't imagine the bravery it must have taken for you to infiltrate that compound in Idaho. I say that as someone who used to go to work every day wearing a ballistic vest."

"Someone needed to expose those assholes."

"How many death threats have you received?"

"I don't know," she said, trying to master her drunkenness for my sake. "My publisher sends the hate mail to the FBI without showing me.

But what's the expression? 'You never hear the bullet that kills you'? The special agent who's assigned to me has a way of putting it. 'Truly scary people don't make threats,' he says. 'They make plans.' "

We'd arrived at Gull Cottage. I had intended to drop her off and return to the Wight House for the night. But our ominous discussion had given me second thoughts.

Before the scene at the Trap House, I'd considered and discarded the possibility that someone on the island had murdered Miranda thinking she was the author and "race traitor" Ariel Evans. Having learned about the Washburns' sideline in Third Reich collectibles, I was no longer so confident.

"Maybe I should check out the house first," I said.

"That's so cute!"

So much for Ariel's having sobered up. "We'll go in together."

But she was already stumbling out of the truck. There was no time for me to shine my flashlight on the grass to look for fresh prints. All I could do was try to keep up.

She flipped on the lights inside the door. "Nazis! Nazis! Come out, come out, wherever you are!"

"Have a seat while I take a look around." I noticed the half-empty bottle of Scotch on the coffee table. "I wouldn't recommend having a nightcap."

"I had too much to drink already," she said, nearly tripping over a chair leg as she headed to the nearest electrical socket to plug in her dead cell phone.

I made a quick pass through the house and found no one lying in wait or any signs of the rooms having been disturbed. When I returned to the living room, I found her slumped on the couch with an almost hypnotized emptiness in her eyes.

"You'll feel better tomorrow if you sleep upstairs in a bed."

She yawned and straightened up. "Where are you going to sleep?"

"Back at my inn."

"You can stay here if you want." Her lids were heavy; her voice thick.

"That wouldn't be appropriate."

"What if the Washburns come in the night to burn a cross on the lawn and ravish me?"

"I'll stay for a while but only if you go upstairs to bed."

"My bodyguard."

I removed my peacoat and tossed it over a chair. Then I sat down on the sofa and watched her as she slowly climbed the stairs. The couch was still warm from where she'd been sitting.

34

I heard the toilet flush upstairs and then the water running in the shower. It surprised me that, drunk as she was, she had the energy to bathe.

I sat down on the sofa and tore open the envelope Radcliffe had grudgingly given me. It was just a list of typed names:

Eli Washburn
Rudyard Washburn
Elias Washburn
Judah Washburn
Zach Washburn
Blake Markman?
Tom McNulty
Pete Shattuck
Dante Corso
George Gordon
Kit Billington
Nat Pillsbury
Hiram Reed
Kenneth Crowley
Joy Juno

And I suppose I should include myself. I haven't shot a deer in years, as I said, but I've gone for walks in the woods with a rifle. I wasn't entirely honest with you about that. I still own a Sauer 202 if you'd care to see it.

It appeared to be the same roster of persons Harmon had provided me, seemingly ordered from most suspicious to least suspicious. I appreciated that Andrew had come clean about his own place on the list.

I'd spoken to many of these people already and had missed my chance to interrogate some of the others (who had no doubt been drinking at the Trap House) before the Washburns arrived. At least I had the beginnings of a plan for the coming day. I needed to seek out the hunters who had avoided me, and obviously that meant making a trip across the demilitarized zone that separated Reed land from Washburn land.

The shower stopped. I got up and went into the kitchen to raid the provisions Miranda had left behind. I doubted that Ariel would begrudge her bodyguard a late-night snack.

In the refrigerator I found wedges of artisanal cheeses, cave-aged Gruyère, Taleggio, and bleu d'Auvergne, along with an unopened Italian salami, from the fancy food shop in Ellsworth. In the breadbox was a loaf of island-baked sourdough from Graffam's. I made myself a thirty-dollar sandwich with the gourmet ingredients.

Every drink I could find in the refrigerator contained alcohol or was meant to be mixed with alcohol, so I stuck with filtered water from a jug.

I wanted to give Ariel time to fall asleep before I returned to the Wight House. Without my phone (out to sea) and my laptop (in my room), I was cut off from all communication with the outside world. For the moment I had no clue how I would summarize the events of the evening for Captain DeFord.

I brought my sandwich into the parlor with all the sketches of Blake Markman. When I sat down at the desk, Ariel's laptop flickered to life. Behind the password prompt the lock screen displayed a photograph of Ariel and Miranda as towheaded girls—seven and five years old was my best guess—dressed identically in pirate costumes. Ariel was showing off that wry, skeptical smile of hers. But Miranda's aqueous-blue eyes were what drew me into the picture. They had depths that you rarely see in a child. Even then, her thoughts were unfathomable.

Crazy attracts crazy, Ariel had said. And while she seemed unconcerned about Blake Markman, others were keen that I focus on the mysterious recluse. Beryl McCloud, for instance, had all but accused the man.

A state police detective had once told me to concentrate on means and opportunity. Motive, he said, would come later. Markman had greater opportunity than anyone else to have killed Miranda. All he had to do was slip across the Gut in his dory and slip back before the nearest neighbor could even arrive at the cottage. As for means, it was just a matter of his possessing another firearm beyond the fancy shotgun he'd shown me. He even had a motive if he feared that Miranda might expose his carefully kept secrets to the wider world.

But Ariel said that her sister had confessed her true identity to Blake Markman. If that was so, why would he have bothered killing a bipolar drug addict? Who would have believed Miranda Evans about anything?

Ultimately, I wasn't ready to follow Beryl McCloud's suspicions. I had a strong feeling that she'd pointed at the hermit as a means of distracting me from looking closely at someone else. But who?

Of everyone on the island, Jenny Pillsbury seemingly had the best reason to hate Miranda. But the shock and sadness I had seen on her face when the ferry arrived was beyond the ability of even the world's best actor to fake. The woman had been legitimately shattered. Besides which, Jenny had been working at Graffam's the morning of the shooting. Hiram had been there, too.

Had I been too quick to dismiss Kenneth

Crowley from my list? What if he had actually shot Miranda by mistake as we had all initially believed? Harmon Reed could have decided that there was no point in his nephew confessing. If they took care of the rifle and everyone stuck to their stories, the odds were good that we would never be able to prove Kenneth had fired the fatal round.

The computer screen faded to black and I was left staring into nothingness.

I had to admit to myself the possibility—even the likelihood—that I might never find answers to the many questions that were plaguing me.

After a minute, I closed the laptop and returned to the kitchen with my dirty plate.

I don't recall returning to the couch, let alone closing my eyes, but that was where I was when I heard Ariel call my name from upstairs. Her voice wasn't loud or panicked.

"Mike? Are you there?"

I arose from the sofa and crossed to the staircase. "I'm here."

The wooden steps creaked as I set one foot in front of the other. My heart made a dull, thudding noise that quickened as I neared the landing.

"Mike? Where are you?"

The hall was webbed with shadows, but her door was open and a flickering amber light came from within. I moved slowly and deliberately along the carpet runner as if I intended to surprise her.

From the edge of her room, I saw that she had lit an old-fashioned hurricane lantern. I didn't remember seeing it when Klesko and I had searched the house. The room smelled of lamp oil. The air was uncomfortably hot. Ariel lay with the blankets bunched down around her ankles and just a thin, translucent sheet pulled up to her neck. The outline of her body showed through the thin cotton. Her breasts, her navel, the shaved cleft between her legs.

"Come inside," she whispered.

I hesitated on the threshold. I needed to turn around and leave the house before I did something I would regret.

But my body wouldn't obey. My mind was unable to stop it. I crossed the floor to the bed. I stood over her in the orange glow of the oil lamp.

"Yes," she said.

I reached down, ever so slowly, for the edge of the sheet. But when I closed my fingers around the fabric, I felt a sudden resistance. Her eyes were playful and her lips were parted in a lewd smile, but she was fighting me, preventing me from tearing away the cover that barely concealed her nakedness.

Then suddenly her hands opened and the sheet came flying off.

But instead of Ariel lying in the bed, it was Dani Tate. She spoke my name and opened her arms to me.

I gasped and awoke with a start. I found myself sitting upright on the couch with an erection in my pants. My pulse was galloping.

A piece of burning wood snapped and fizzled from inside the stove.

But it wasn't the fire that had woken me. A raucous motor vehicle had arrived in the dooryard. Seconds later, I heard heavy footsteps on the porch. Then a fist pounding on the wood.

I glanced at my watch and saw that it was past midnight.

I peeled back a drape and saw a pickup I hadn't before encountered on the island: a green Ford F-150 with no muffler or tailpipe. As with all of the other vehicles on Maquoit, the chassis was engaged in a losing battle against the salt air.

With my right hand I grasped the grip of my SIG. With my left I turned the lock. I twisted the knob and took two steps backward.

Kenneth Crowley stood on the woven-rope welcome mat, panting. The skin on his face seemed bloodless, his eyes were sunken inside their sockets, crumbs were stuck in his billy-goat beard.

"It's Hiram," he said with a gasp. "He needs your help."

"What's wrong?"

"He's dying."

"How?"

"He's OD'ing."

How had Crowley known to find me here of all places?

I was no paramedic. I didn't have training as an emergency medical technician. All I had was a certificate as a wilderness first responder. In the ten-day class I'd taken with Stacey we'd learned how to treat heatstroke, set a split around a broken fibula, staunch a bleeding wound. There had been nothing in the curriculum about how to respond to a drug overdose. And while some police forces were teaching their officers how to administer rescue drugs, the Warden Service was not one of them.

Behind me, Ariel called from the staircase, "What's happening? What's wrong?"

Far from being naked as she'd been in my dream, she appeared wearing a Columbia University sweatshirt, flannel pajama bottoms, and ragg socks.

"Hiram Reed overdosed."

She continued down the steps. "Is there a doctor on the island?"

"No," I said, remembering a sign I'd seen posted on Bishop's Wharf warning all who arrived that there would no medical rescue should they fall ill or become injured. "There isn't even an EMT." I addressed Kenneth Crowley: "Does anyone on Maquoit have naloxone?"

The young man's breath was foul from the beer he'd consumed. He seemed about to burst into tears. "I don't know what that is."

"The prescription name is Narcan," I explained. "It comes as a nasal spray. You use it to rescue someone who's having an opioid overdose. Certain people can get it if they have a family member who's an addict. Do you know what Hiram took?"

Crowley's raw eyes finally began to ooze tears. "Heroin. Maybe some coke, too. He might have mixed them. The needle's still in his arm. I was afraid to take it out."

"Where is he?"

"At his house. Nat told me to check on him. I thought he was dead at first."

He might yet be, I thought. "Just take me to him."

Ariel said, "I'm going with you." Before I could protest, she added, "Have you ever had someone OD in front of you? Because I have. Go start the truck while I put on my boots."

35

We hadn't been on the road for more than five minutes before I remembered the phones. Mine was collecting barnacles at the bottom of the Gut. Ariel's was still plugged into the wall socket back at Gull Cottage.

"You left your phone," I said.

She'd put on her Gore-Tex parka over her sweatshirt and pajama bottoms. "Should we go back for it?"

"The way Crowley's driving, I'm afraid I'll lose him. And I don't know which house is Hiram's."

The young lobsterman's Ford pickup had a big V-8 under its hood in comparison to the wimpy four-cylinder engine in the Datsun. I kept losing his taillights in the fog. Every time I sped up, the road seemed to take an unexpected and mischievous twist I didn't remember having been there before. More than once I had to cut the wheel sharply to avoid a tree looming in the headlights.

"I need to call Radcliffe and have him get a LifeFlight helicopter out here," I said.

"In this fog? I was embedded with the SEALs, Mike, and I know for a fact that choppers don't fly in these conditions."

I feared that she was right. "Maybe the Coast Guard can send a Response Boat."

The sweetness of alcohol lingered on her breath, but amazingly, she seemed halfway sober. More likely, the adrenaline pumping through her bloodstream was masking the effects of the booze. "If there's no Narcan on the island, that poor guy is probably dead already. He's Harmon's only son, right?"

"His only surviving son. Hiram's older brother also died of a drug overdose. The Maine coast has been devastated by the opioid epidemic."

"The Maine coast and every rural place in America."

"When we searched Gull Cottage, we didn't find drugs," I said. "Did your sister use heroin as well as cocaine?"

"Miranda wasn't into downers of any kind. Cocaine was her poison of choice. When she was manic, she wanted to stay manic, and when she was depressed, she used the cocaine to rev herself back up. She might've given him coke, but not opiates."

"Unless he shot a speedball." It was a combination of heroin and cocaine melted into a syrup and injected into a vein.

We passed the turn off to the Cider House B&B, which meant we were on the outskirts of the village.

"Has it occurred to you that this might be a setup?" Ariel asked.

"What do you mean?"

"Like Hiram isn't really dying and Crowley was sent to lead you into a trap. And of course, I foolishly insisted on tagging along."

"Whose trap?"

"For all I know, it could be everyone on this godforsaken island. Maybe the entire population here was in on Miranda's murder. Like that old movie, *The Wicker Man*, with Christopher Lee. But you don't watch movies."

I couldn't help but smile. "Ariel, has anyone told you that you have a hyperactive imagination? You're also kind of paranoid."

"That's what makes me a good journalist. I'm always seeing conspiracies. Sometimes they turn out to be real."

Hiram Reed lived on the north shore of the village in a small blue bungalow with a screened porch and a single dormer window overlooking his junk-cluttered yard. As with the other fishermen's residences on Maquoit, it was marked not by a street number or by his name but by a buoy tied to a tree. Hiram's signature colors were blue and white.

He'd backed his truck, a blue Silverado, onto the dead grass that served as a driveway. In addition to his lobstering gear, he had an old washing machine rusting on a wooden pallet, a tower of worn tires, a soda keg, a long-dead potted ficus, and a cardboard box filled with warped and sodden paperbacks on which he had scribbled FREE FOR THE TAKING.

It had taken us nine minutes to get here from Gull Cottage. Add in however long it had taken Crowley to find me, and I didn't know whether to expect a dying man or a fresh corpse. I commanded Kenneth to wait outside because I didn't want him underfoot. I sensed that he was relieved.

Before we entered the house, I put on a pair of nitrile gloves and gave Ariel a set of her own.

The interior door was ajar, and the room beyond was black and cold. The air smelled of unwashed dishes and unlaundered sheets. I didn't bother fumbling for the light switch but followed the droning sound of a television up a set of low-ceilinged stairs.

Ariel followed close enough for me to feel her breath on my neck.

Hiram sat upright on the bed with his back braced against two sweat-stained pillows and his legs spread before him. His unshaven chin was down on his breastbone. He wore blue jeans and a sleeveless T-shirt from which black tufts of armpit hair protruded. His left arm was tied off with paracord, and as Crowley had warned us, the syringe was still stuck in the crook between the forearm and the biceps.

He'd been watching a documentary about the

Vietnam War. The *rat-tat-tat* of a machine gun exploded through the speakers.

"Don't touch anything if you can avoid it," I whispered.

"Why not?"

"Because we don't know what this is yet. And you can smear fingerprints with these gloves."

I could see congealed blood around the spot where he'd plunged in the needle. He'd also dribbled saliva down his shirt like some raving animal. At first glance, I detected no signs of respiration.

I slipped my fingers along his throat to feel for a pulse in the carotid artery. After a long agonizing moment, I was rewarded with a faint heartbeat.

"He's still alive."

"Great." Ariel breathed. "Now what?"

"Turn off that damned TV. Then go outside and tell Crowley to wake up Radcliffe. He needs to call the mainland and get medical assistance out here ASAP. Hiram's breathing is shallow. I'm not going to start CPR unless his heart stops."

Once begun, cardiopulmonary resuscitation needs to be continued until the victim can breathe regularly on his own or until help arrives.

After she'd left, I inspected Hiram more closely and saw that his lips and fingernails were blue. Doctors call the condition cyanosis, and it indicates low oxygen saturation in the blood. Because I didn't want to take the chance he might vomit and choke, I decided to leave him sitting upright.

I removed the syringe and set it atop a stack of library books on the night table. The crook of his arm was a mass of purple bruises and brown scabs. When I loosened the cord, a bright bubble of blood formed at the injection site. As I watched, it grew from the size of a bead to the size of a gumball. Then it popped and oozed down his forearm.

I removed a handkerchief from my pocket and pressed it to the wound.

He'd dropped his lighter on the sheet, where it had charred the cotton. The burned spoon lay on the floor. I didn't see the baggie or whatever he'd used to hold the drugs. Maybe it was under the bed.

It was all potential evidence that needed to be collected. But I had a feeling that the worst crime committed in this airless room had been Hiram's assault on himself. I was also pretty certain that I knew what he'd been doing lurking around the airstrip. He'd been buying smack and maybe coke from the Washburns. In addition to their other misdeeds the brothers were almost certainly running drugs.

"Wake up, Hiram." I squeezed his shoulder. "You need to wake up."

His head lolled to the side. He gasped and sputtered, then fell silent again.

"Come on, Hiram."

Ariel appeared, breathless, in the door. "The constable's on his way."

I glanced up from my patient. "You said you knew firsthand about overdoses. I've seen people who OD'd on heroin and oxycodone but never cocaine. I'm not sure what to do here."

"Miranda had a boyfriend who overdosed on coke when they were staying at my apartment. He was only twenty-five and a male model, but he had a heart attack. The guy lived, fortunately. I did a lot of research after that. With a speedball, people usually die from the heroin, especially if it's laced with fentanyl or carfentanil. After the coke leaves their systems, there's nothing to offset the depressive effect of the heroin."

"The coke may be keeping him alive, you mean."

"Ironically, yes." She paused as if listening for a soft noise. "Have you checked to make sure he still has a pulse?"

"Not since you left."

She put a gloved hand on his wishbone. Froth was caught in his chest hairs. She felt his neck for a pulse. Her eyes flashed at me. "Mike, I don't think he's breathing."

36

Ariel pulled Hiram by the legs while I removed the pillows and did my best to ease him to a supine position. I began feeling for his sternum.

"Shouldn't you do rescue breaths first?" she said.

"The doctors keep changing the CPR guidelines. Now you're supposed to start with compressions."

I placed my hands on top of each other and interlocked my fingers. After I'd done thirty compressions, I tilted his hairy head back, felt around the inside of his mouth to be sure nothing was in the way of his breathing, then pinched his nostrils shut. I placed a synthetic CPR mask over his mouth, pressed my lips around the attached tube, and blew air into his lungs until his chest rose.

"Come on, Hiram," I said. "This is all up to you, buddy. You're going to need to help us out here."

I lost track of how much time passed or how many cycles I completed.

But suddenly Ariel glanced up at me with wide-open eyes. "He's doing it! He's breathing on his own."

Through the closed windows, I became aware of motor vehicles arriving outside the house. I heard doors slam and men's voices raised in tense conversation. Heavy boot treads on the stairs.

Radcliffe poked his curly head through the half-open door. "I'm here," he announced as if it weren't obvious. "How is he?"

"Alive, but just barely," I said. "Did you call LifeFlight? The Coast Guard?"

"Not yet."

"You stupid fuck," Ariel said. "This man's going to die. He would have died if Mike hadn't given him CPR."

Radcliffe seemed confused. "But he's breathing now, you said."

I wanted to punch him. "Don't you get it, Andy? Hiram needs to be evacuated to a hospital."

"I understand. But we need to wait."

Ariel was beside herself. "What are you talking about?"

Then another loud voice echoed up the stairwell. "Get out of my way for Christ's sake! I need to see my boy."

Instead of phoning the mainland, the constable had called Harmon Reed. That was why Radcliffe had been stalling. He was under orders not to act until the patriarch of Maquoit Island arrived.

Harmon bulled his way into the room. He was

wearing his raincoat over long johns and rubber boots. He'd left his signature Greek fisherman's cap at home. It was the first time I'd seen his full head of curly white hair.

"Hiram's had an overdose," I said.

Harmon's nostrils flared. "You think I can't see that?"

"He almost died, Mr. Reed," Ariel said.

He gave her a look of utter contempt. "You should have let him."

Only Radcliffe of all people seemed capable of speech. "Now, Harmon—"

"Get out! All of you! Get out of this house and leave me alone with my boy."

"I can't do that, sir," I said.

Harmon raised his arm as if to deliver a backhand blow to my face. "How dare you."

"It's a medical emergency. And I would lower your arm, sir, if I were you."

"You shouldn't be here," Harmon snarled, turning on Ariel. "Neither of you should be here. None of this would have happened if not for your damned sister."

"Mr. Reed, you need to calm down," Ariel said with more patience than I could have managed. "You need to give us room to help Hiram. Go call the Coast Guard, please. You can still save your son's life."

"Let him die! The coward! We'd all be better off if he died."

The next voice I heard was a woman's. "Step aside, Harmon."

I hadn't noticed Martha Reed on the threshold. She was wearing a puffer vest over her night-dress. Crowley had snuck in behind her and loomed in the doorway.

"Stay out of this, Martha."

"I can't, and I won't. Not again. I'm not losing my one remaining son to your pigheaded pride."

Reed seemed incredulous that his wife had talked back to him.

The old woman approached the bed. In her hand was an odd-shaped piece of white plastic.

"Is that Narcan?" I said.

"Prop him up, will you?" She cradled his head with one hand and placed the tube part of the injector under one of her son's nostrils. "I hope I remember how the nurse said to do this."

"Where did you get that?" her husband asked shakily.

"The *Star of the Sea*. I have had it for years hoping I'd never have cause again to need it."

With her thumb, she pressed the plunger and shot a mist of medicine deep into Hiram's sinus cavity.

The effect was nearly instantaneous. His eyes shot open, and he began coughing so hard it seemed he might vomit up his internal organs. His arms thrashed and he kicked his legs, catching his father in the thigh.

Martha Reed bent over her sputtering son, her long gray hair falling like a privacy curtain around both of their faces. "Mother's here, Hiram. Mother's here. You were away from us, but you're back, and everything's going to be all right."

What little I knew about naloxone hydrochloride was that it not only counteracted an overdose, it also deactivated the opiates in a person's system. Narcan, in other words, sent an addict into immediate and painful detoxification.

Hiram Reed lurched upright. He pushed his mother away and swept his gaze over all of us in the room. The blueness was gone from his lips, but now his face shone with greasy perspiration. He looked confused, half-crazed, as if he might bite off your hand if you presented it to him. A second later he started to retch. He hung his head over the side of the bed and vomited.

Harmon was shaking his head, as if in disbelief. "You hid that drug from me."

The old woman stood her ground. "I knew you'd never allow me to keep it, Harm."

"God damn you for disobeying me, Martha. God damn you to hell."

Radcliffe gave his usual feeble refrain: "Now, Harmon—"

Reed shoved the constable against a bureau. An empty bottle of tequila overturned and rolled to the floor. "He's alive, isn't he? My son's not going to die. That's what you wanted. It means you can all leave now."

"Come on, Ariel," I said. "Radcliffe. Crowley. Let's go."

Soon all four of us were standing outside in the cold, clinging mist.

"Will he be all right?" Kenneth asked. He sounded about thirteen years old in that moment.

Ariel said, "He's not dying, but he's going to feel like he's dying. Coming down off heroin is as bad as it gets."

"But I don't need to call LifeFlight," Radcliffe said tentatively.

I'd had enough of the Maquoit constable. He wasn't wearing a toy badge, but he might as well have been. "You're a son of a bitch, Radcliffe. I just wanted to say that for the record."

He tried to win me back with a smile. "Mike, I understand why you're upset."

"I don't think you do, *Andy*. You risked Hiram's life because you were afraid of disobeying his father. If he died, it would have been your fault. I'm done with you, Radcliffe. I won't be calling on you again."

"Come on, Mike. You don't mean that."

"I'm pretty sure he does," said Ariel. "But I'll want to interview you for the book I'm writing."

"Book?"

"About my sister's murder. I'll need to address

360

how your incompetence nearly sabotaged the investigation. I expect you'll want to offer some sort of defense. I'll be in touch to set up an interview."

"You have a gift for twisting the knife," I whispered as we walked to my truck.

"It's easy when someone deserves it as much as he does."

A sudden movement over her shoulder brought me to attention. It was Kenneth Crowley, jogging toward us on those gangling moose legs.

"Hey, you two!"

I expected him to thank us for saving his friend's life. Instead he glared at Ariel. His face was pinched with childish rage. "This is all your fault."

"Excuse me."

"Everything that's happened here is because of you and your sister. You should leave now before something happens to you, too."

I got into his face. "That better not be a threat, Kenneth."

"It is what it is."

One thing I'd learned about Ariel Evans was that she would not be cowed. "I'm not leaving before I find out who killed Miranda," she said. "I don't mind if you tell people that. I want the person who killed her to know I'm coming for him."

A stray thought came into my head. "Why did

you drive to Gull Cottage looking for me tonight, Kenneth?"

"Huh? What are you talking about?"

"What made you think I'd be there and not back in my room at the Wight House?"

He practically spat out the words. "Everyone knows you two are fucking."

I wasn't sure what I found more galling. That I'd become the subject of Maquoit sexual gossip. Or how hard Ariel laughed at the absurdity of the suggestion.

37

It was about two o'clock in the morning when I dropped Ariel back at Gull Cottage. She made a joking suggestion about my coming in for a nightcap, a reference to Crowley's remark that she and I were sleeping together, but my mood had turned sour. She should have known that kind of a rumor could be toxic to my career. I told her I'd swing by in the morning after I'd checked in on Hiram Reed.

I started to drive off, then remembered something I'd meant to say and put my foot on the brake. But by then she'd already vanished into the house.

What I'd wanted to tell her was *Don't go roaming around the island again without me.*

Maybe it was for the best that I didn't get a chance to issue my patronizing command.

I had no right to insist she voluntarily confine herself to the cottage. She was an adult who had committed no crime. She was also a journalist with all the freedoms that came with being a member of the fourth estate.

I drove slowly past the marsh and into the village. I made a detour to Bishop's Wharf, where an arc light blazed all night long at the end of the dock. From a distance of twenty feet you couldn't see the pole on which it was mounted, just the detached glow. It looked like a cold star in the fog.

Pillsbury's truck was still parked in the muddy lot at the base of the hill. Wherever he'd gone that evening, he hadn't returned.

The entire village seemed to be sleeping now, even the watchdogs some of the islanders kept to warn against ill-meant visits from their own neighbors. I navigated the sharp turn up to the Wight House and the church and the graveyard beyond.

On my way up the hill, I met my phantom buck again. This time he wasn't chewing on a hunk of roadkill; he was rubbing his thin coat against a telephone pole to leave a scent warning for other males to avoid his territory. The stupid animal had already rubbed off a patch of hair he would need to survive the winter. In the headlights I could see the exposed skin below the white undercoating of fuzz. The little buck gave me the stink eye as I drove past, then returned to mortifying his own flesh.

Mrs. Wight had kindly left another of her notes under a plate of molasses cookies on the checkout desk.

Good Evening, Warden Investigator Bowdoin.
    We hope you had a restful and relaxing day exploring the island!

You seem to have forgotten to turn the do not disturb sign around to alert the maid to make up your room so we have taken the liberty of turning down your bed and providing you with fresh towels. You should not want for anything, but if you find yourself in need, please use this pad to leave a note and we shall attend to it at our earliest opportunity.

Your hosts,

Elmore and Ellen Wight

How thoughtful of my hostess to disregard my wishes about leaving my room undisturbed. Mrs. Wight's commitment to offering five-star hospitality knew no limits.

Her cookies, however, were delicious. I brought the entire plate upstairs with me. I took a long hot shower and hung my salt-crusted clothes over the air vent to dry. Then I propped myself up on the bed with my laptop resting on a pillow, closed my eyes as if preparing to enter a meditative state, then opened my email program. Messages and forwarded texts cascaded down the screen.

Many of them were from members of the media. Some bore the names of newspaper writers I'd known for years who wrote knowledgeably about the outdoors and with a modicum of respect for the unique difficulties of my job. Others had come from junior-level television reporters at the local stations; these bright-eyed young things had come to Maine to start their careers, often with no understanding at all of the state's peculiar culture. Fewest but most frightening were the messages from writers for national publications and producers for TV news programs that millions watched with their morning coffee.

What all of these journalists had in common was that they'd done an end run around the Warden Service media liaison in an attempt to score an exclusive with me. I deleted each and every request for an interview.

The other emails were familiar and expected: Commissioner Maryann Matthews writing to tell me that the governor had a "special interest" in the case; Colonel Tim Malcomb making the same point in more pointed terms; Captain DeFord issuing a "request" for an update that was really a demand; Detective Klesko reminding me that I'd sworn to be his partner in this investigation; Assistant Attorney General Danica Marshall warning me against screwing up the case for her; Chief Medical Examiner Walt Kitteridge cc'ing me on his preliminary autopsy report minus the toxicology and ballistic tests; my former sergeant Kathy Frost, who emailed whenever she'd heard I was wrestling with a tar baby; Charley Stevens offering to risk his life to fly out in the deathly fog—words that brought tears to my eyes.

Nothing more from Stacey, who must surely have heard from her parents about my latest trouble.

There was a note from Dani Tate, which this time I read last:

> Hi Mike
> I tried your line before. Then I heard your phone got dunked. Skype me when you get this. Don't worry about the time. I've got something you need to hear.
> Dani

I was a novice user of voice chat, but I had downloaded the program to stay in touch with Stacey, only to find she rarely used it herself. Now I tried Dani. She must have had her laptop beside the bed because she answered in thirty seconds.

The connection was poor, the picture was fuzzy.

Dani had dirty-blond hair that she cut herself, less to save money than because she saw no point in hiring someone to do what she could do herself, and it was now a mussed mess. Her face was flat with a snub nose and gray eyes that changed color depending on the light. It was a face you wouldn't look twice at most of the time.

367

Then she smiled and dimples appeared beneath heretofore invisible cheekbones, and you had the thrilling sensation of having witnessed something beautiful that few people were gifted with seeing.

"Sorry to wake you," I said.

"No, no. Don't be. Hang on while I adjust this thing."

She repositioned the computer, or rather, she repositioned herself, in relation to the computer. Her gymnast's shoulders were bare. Was she sleeping in the nude?

To distract myself from the image, I said, "How did you hear about my phone?"

"Good old-fashioned police work." Meaning she had pestered her friends in the Warden Service.

"Losing my iPhone didn't endear me with DeFord."

"I bet it didn't! I've heard that tomorrow he's coming out there himself, along with a team of wardens, troopers, and county cops. Has he told you yet?"

"I haven't checked his most recent message."

"I'm sorry, Mike. But Maquoit has been all over the news today. That Ariel woman has really screwed you."

A pain shot up my already aching back. "What do you mean?"

"She did an interview with NPR. The anchor

treated it like she was being patched in from Antarctica instead of a tiny Maine island. She slammed the people out there really hard. I don't even live on Maquoit, but I took offense."

I was surprised by how calmly I received this news. "Did she mention me?"

"Not by name. But the host was asking her about what the cops are doing and she said, 'They've assigned one guy to the case. He's the only cop out here with me, and he isn't even a real detective.' "

I fought the impulse to slam the laptop closed. "That's the truth, I suppose."

"Bullshit it is!"

I pretended to be distracted by something in the room so she wouldn't see my expression. "Thanks, Dani. Thanks for the heads-up."

"Wait! Are you OK, Mike? I'm having a hard time seeing you."

I kept my head turned. "I'm OK. Just tired."

"Listen, if you need to talk . . ."

"I'm sure I will—when this is over."

"It's a date, then."

"It's a date," I agreed as if the word didn't have more than one meaning.

The smart thing to do would be to begin tidying up, I thought. Answer the commissioner and the colonel. Write up my notes for DeFord to use when he assumed command of the investigation. Even respond cordially to Steve Klesko instead of burning that bridge, too. I would accept my failure with grace.

But when in my life had I ever done the smart thing?

By my reckoning I had eight or so more hours until I was relieved of my responsibilities. I made a plan to get some sleep because I couldn't keep going without rest. Then, in the morning, I'd check in on Hiram and see how he was suffering. I'd pay one last visit to Gull Cottage to confront Ariel Evans over her ill treatment of me on the radio.

I knew there was no need to set an alarm. As I lay in the dark, staring up into yet another black void, I found myself thinking of Dani. Not with desire this time, but with gratitude.

With the exceptions of my friends Kathy and Charley, everyone else who'd contacted me did so to satisfy their own needs. But Dani hadn't asked a single question about my botched investigation. It wasn't curiosity that had driven her to reach out to me. She was genuinely concerned for my welfare.

38

I awoke in darkness, but this time I knew exactly where I was and what I needed to do. My stay on Maquoit was coming to an end.

I shaved and put on clean clothes. A flannel shirt and jeans over thermal underwear. My Bean boots. My leather-trimmed peacoat. My black watch cap. There was no point in being the only one on the island dressed in blaze orange. Whatever happened today, I would not be shot by a hunter who had confused me for a deer. And if I was, what a fitting end to my absurd life that would be.

I took one last look at my messages. There were two of note.

The first was a text from Klesko:

I'm not sure how you came to see me as another of your enemies. Was it because I withheld my unconditional support that you were up to the job? Nothing you've done since then has helped you in that regard. Maybe if you actually hung out with some of your fellow officers, you'd realize we aren't all such bad guys. The lone wolf thing doesn't work, Mike. For your sake, and

Ariel's, I hope you learn that lesson sooner rather than later. If you have a problem with any of this, I'll be on the boat this morning.

The second message was an email from Stacey. The subject line was "News." I didn't dare to open it at first. Then realized I had no choice.

Dear Mike:

I've been sitting here crying—yeah, me, I know—because you're on Maquoit alone and it's your first hunting homicide and I'm three thousand miles away. It might as well be a million.

I would give anything to be with you. But I know I would only cause you more trouble than you're already dealing with. Being on my own again has made me aware that I'm not a healthy person to be around. For example, the most important thing in the world to me is that you are happy, and yet I can't bring myself to tell you to go find someone else. Somehow I want to believe that I'll get myself together and you'll be back home waiting. But what if I never get myself together?

Even this email is toxic, I realize. I should say goodbye, but I can't say goodbye. So I'm doing that yo-yo thing to you again. I wish I were better, Mike. You deserve better.

I will always love you,
Stacey

I reread the message again.

Then, because I knew that I needed a clear head for what was coming, I deleted it.

Downstairs at the checkout desk, I left an envelope with ten dollars for "the maid" (probably Mrs. Wight herself) and a note addressed to my hosts, thanking them "both" for their hospitality.

The fog had become so familiar I couldn't imagine ever seeing the sun again. I tossed my briefcase and rucksack on the passenger seat and started on my way into town.

It was 4:25. Less than two hours until sunrise. Four or five hours until the boat appeared carrying DeFord and his team of officers.

My spike buck hadn't come out to wish me a bon voyage. He was probably off dining on a dead gull.

As usual, Maquoit had awakened before dawn. Lights were on in the kitchens of the fishermen's houses, and the smell of wood-burning stoves hung so thickly in the air, it would have been easy to mistake the mist for smoke. I drove directly to Hiram Reed's decrepit house and found the windows there aglow. His blue pickup was parked as it had been the night prior, but Harmon had departed in his silver GMC.

I rapped at the screen door.

The silhouette of a woman appeared in a first-floor window, and a minute later Martha Reed stood at the door. She was dressed in her flannel nightdress, and her gray hair still hung in twisting tendrils around her face. But there was nothing haggard in her expression. Nor did her shoulders stoop. Caring for her sick son seemed to have enlivened her in ways unforeseen.

"How is he?"

"He had a bad night. His gut is hurting him wicked bad, and he sweated so much there was an actual puddle on the bed. It's the muscle spasms that are the worst—for me at least. Watching him twitch and shake like he's about to have one of them epileptic seizures."

"I noticed that Harmon left."

"He went home an hour or two ago. Harm's never been as hard a man as he lets on. He's tender under that tough skin. I'm sorry about the way he acted toward you folks last night when you were trying to help."

It wasn't for his wife to apologize. "I appreciate that. How are you holding up, Mrs. Reed?"

"I could use some tea. Hiram doesn't drink it."

"I can get you some from Graffam's if you like."

"That would be dear of you, but it don't open until five."

"It was incredibly brave what you did, concealing Narcan from your husband knowing how he felt about drugs after what happened to Heath."

"It's the nurse on the *Star of the Sea* who deserves the credit. She said to me, 'Martha, you've lost one son to this scourge. Do you really want to lose another?' I hoped I'd never have to use it. Hiram did so well for so long."

"Until Miranda Evans arrived on the island."

"I'd be lying if I said I was sorry what happened to her. Is it true that you have no leads or suspects at all?"

"Not quite true."

The muscles in her neck tensed. It was the first time I'd glimpsed any guardedness in her open face.

"There's a boat coming over from the mainland today," I said. "It's bringing more wardens and police officers to assist in the investigation. They can take Hiram to a hospital onshore."

"He won't want to go. Can they make him go?"

"It would be easier for everyone if he agreed. I'd like to talk with him if it's all right with you."

"About going to the hospital?"

"Yes."

The statement was not a lie, but it was

deceptive, and I felt a measure of guilt for using this woman's motherly concern to obtain one last interview with her sick son.

"Come in." She led me into the house and up the stairs. Halfway there, I began to smell Hiram. The odor coming from his bedroom smelled like a stew of bodily fluids.

Martha poked her head through the door. "The warden is here to see you, Hiram."

"Tell him to go away." His throat sounded raw and painful.

"There's a boat coming for you, Hiram, to take you to the hospital in Ellsworth."

"I won't go."

"They'll have medicine to make you feel better."

"I don't want to feel better! I want to die! Why won't you people let me die?"

Martha turned to me with her brow knitted in despair.

"Let me try," I said softly.

She flattened herself against the wall to let me past.

Hiram's shirt was gone, as were his pants, and he lay in dingy Fruit Of The Looms. He clapped a hand over his crotch, a gesture of surprising modesty. "Oh, for fuck's sake."

"I know what you're going through, Hiram."

"Like hell you do."

"As bad as it is now, it's going to get worse,

376

and when it does, you'll be glad to have medical care."

He winced so hard, tears flowed from the corners of his eyes. "Why are you bothering me? This is none of your business."

"The drugs I found in your possession are my business. I could arrest you now if I wanted."

Martha Reed bristled. "You didn't say you were going to arrest him!"

"Whether I do or not is up to him. I have a strong suspicion that your son knows something about what happened to Miranda Evans that he's not telling me. I think he may be protecting someone."

Hiram tried to rise up in anger, but the sudden motion caused him to roll off the bed and knock his head against the nightstand. Trapped between the mattress and the cracked drywall, he wailed like a small child.

"Oh, baby," said his mother, rushing to his side. There wasn't space enough for me to help him back onto the bed. Nor would my assistance have been welcomed. Her eyes blazed at me as she helped him up. "You should be ashamed of yourself. I want you to leave this house and not come back."

Most cops won't admit it, but almost all police work is premised on the shaky concept of the ends justifying the means. "Whatever it takes" is the motto of many of the officers I have known.

This mind-set secures prosecutions against very bad people who would otherwise continue to victimize the most defenseless members of society. But that same line of thinking is also responsible for the worst abuses committed by those individuals who disgrace my profession.

Which is to say I was ashamed and not ashamed.

I paused when I reached the bottom of the steps to scan the room, not having had a chance to do so the night before. The entire house seemed to be one multichambered man cave. The sofa and armchairs were made of leather, scratched by the claws of a big dog no longer in residence. Over the open fireplace was mounted an honest-to-goodness trophy deer head.

Lots of older mounts have eyes that are so fake looking they look like black marbles. This deer had the newfangled glass models that aren't one color but have depth to them, concentric circles of ever-darkening brown all the way to the obsidian pupils. I had paid extra myself for a similar pair of realistic eyes for the twelve-point buck I had shot just the year before.

A man's deep voice startled me. "What are you doing here?"

I hadn't heard Nat Pillsbury's truck, but there he was, standing in the doorway. Despite the chill in the wet air, he wore no jacket, just his usual Henley, tight jeans, and XtraTuf boots.

His unshaven chin showed white hairs not yet in evidence in his black mustache. I had expected him to look more tired, but he seemed alert and energized—wired, almost.

"Checking on Hiram," I said.

"I heard you and Ariel helped save his life. I guess I should thank you for that."

Technically that was not an expression of gratitude, but I let it go. "Where did you disappear to last night?"

"I went ashore to pick up my wife. Your buddies in the state police worked her over pretty hard. They were lucky I wasn't there at the time."

"I'm sure it wasn't exactly the third degree."

His brow lowered. "Are you calling Jenny a liar?"

I ignored the schoolyard provocation. "You don't have a problem taking your boat out at night in the fog?"

"I'm a Maquoit native" was the extent of his answer.

"So Jenny and your baby are home safe and sound?"

"As if you care."

"It's interesting how protective you are of a woman you were preparing to leave a few days ago."

"Fuck you, man. I don't care if you are law enforcement. You don't have the right to trash-talk my family."

"Actually, I was trash-talking you."

I half expected Pillsbury to fly across the room at me with both fists. Somehow he mastered his violent impulses. "What were you talking to Hiram about?"

If this was my last morning on Maquoit, there was no point in hiding my cards. Time to play them.

"All I'm prepared to say is he provided me with a missing puzzle piece."

"What puzzle piece?"

I pretended to check my watch. "I have somewhere I need to be. Do you mind stepping aside?"

The muscle-bound lobsterman held his ground.

"Really?" I said. "That's the way you want this to go?"

He moved about a foot to his left. It didn't afford me much room to pass, and he made sure to bump my shoulder.

I heard him call, "Hiram Reed is a better man than you'll ever be."

39

The windows of Graffam's Store were all steamed up from the number of people packed into that already cramped space. Half the island, it seemed, had gotten up early to gossip about Hiram Reed's overdose.

The conversation stopped dead as soon as I stepped through the door. The breakfast club occupied its usual table, minus Harmon. It surprised me that the harbormaster wasn't going about his normal routine. He seemed like the kind of tough guy who would pretend nothing had happened, if only to prevent his neighbors from whispering behind his back.

Just as surprising was the sight of Jenny Pillsbury behind the cash register. It was my understanding that she worked only one morning a week. After a late-night crossing, her presence was unexpected and therefore noteworthy.

Sam Graffam and Andy Radcliffe were huddled near the range top while the store owner fried his eggs, fish, and potatoes for breakfast orders.

"Heard what happened to Hiram last night," said Chum McNulty. "Is he going to pull through?"

"I suspect he is."

"Can't say I'm surprised it happened," the old

381

salt said. "He's been lurching around like a zombie lately. Hasn't been in here for coffee in ages."

I made my way to the counter, where Jenny Pillsbury fought back a yawn. On the floor behind her was a baby car seat with her infant, Ava, sleeping under a mound of blankets.

"Thank you for what you did for Hiram," the tall woman said. Unlike her husband, she appeared exhausted. "He's a sweet man. I know you don't believe that. If he had died last night, a lot of us would have been heartbroken."

"He has a long recovery ahead of him—if he even wants it."

She paused to process my words, then said, "Would you like some breakfast? It's on me for what you did."

"I'll have the fish hash. But I'm required to pay for myself. Thank you for the offer though."

She passed the order to Graffam, who was dressed as he had been the day before except that his new T-shirt said MAY CONTAIN ALCOHOL. Sam seemed to be one of those perpetually over-heated men who wear cargo shorts all year long.

Radcliffe sneered at me as if I had tracked dog shit into the store. In his mind he was the aggrieved party. I ignored him.

"You had a long night, too," I said to Jenny. "What time did you get back here?"

"Three a.m."

"Nat told me the state police detectives were pretty rough with their questioning."

"When did he tell you that?" she asked, but smart woman that she was, she had already figured it out. "You must have run into him at Hiram's just now. Those cops were just doing their jobs. Besides, I have nothing to hide."

"Beryl told me that when you were the teacher here, you had Kenneth Crowley as a student."

"Why are you asking me about that?"

"It's not unusual for teenage boys to have crushes on their pretty teachers."

"You think, Kenneth—?" Her mouth snapped open and then closed like a sprung trap.

"Has he been in this morning?"

"No. Why?"

"Crowley blew up at Ariel Evans last night, blamed her for her sister's death. I was there."

Sam Graffam brought over a paper plate with my hash and a plastic spork. "That boy's always had a hair-trigger temper."

Andy Radcliffe couldn't help himself now. "What's that you're saying about Kenneth Crowley?"

"I was telling Mrs. Pillsbury here about an excited utterance he made last night outside Hiram Reed's house. It may have qualified as a spontaneous confession."

"A confession to what?" the constable said.

"Having shot Miranda Evans."

"That's been settled. The boy found her body. You already cleared him!"

"I haven't *cleared* anyone." I put my money on the counter and turned to leave. "Tell Kenneth I'm looking for him."

I wolfed down my greasy breakfast sitting behind the wheel of the Datsun.

Three minutes passed. Then Andrew Radcliffe came hurrying out of the store with his dog, Bella, trotting behind him, lame, barely able to keep up. He strode with purpose in the direction of Harmon Reed's house.

I decided to give the constable a five-minute head start before I showed up at the harbormaster's door.

I was still sitting there, drinking my coffee, self-satisfied in my mischief making, when Ariel Evans rode up on her bicycle. She propped the bike against the side of the moldering building and removed her laptop bag from the basket. I pushed open the door of my truck and sprinted down the road, calling her name.

She peered into the mist, unable to see who it was at first. When she recognized me, her face broke into a grin.

"What are you doing here?"

"I thought the time had come to begin meeting the islanders. I heard that this was the center of activity first thing in the morning."

"You're here to interview them?"

She heard the serrated edge in my tone. "No, I'm here to *talk* to them."

"But you're here for your story or your book or whatever you plan on writing. So you'll actually be interviewing them."

"That's not how I do things, Mike. The people I interview know when they're being interviewed. I consider myself a professional. I have certain standards. What's with the hostility this morning? Are you still upset about that stupid rumor going around about us being—"

"I need to talk with you about something important. My truck's over there."

"I don't make it a habit to get into vehicles with agitated men."

I cocked my head. "Really?"

"That was a joke, or at least I thought it was. The truth is, you're acting kind of strange."

"Give me five minutes."

She followed me to my truck.

When we were both inside, out of the weather, she said, "I need to find someone willing to rent me a golf cart. This island was definitely not made for biking, especially when you're drunk or hungover."

I pivoted toward her and rested my left forearm on the steering wheel. "You didn't tell me you did an interview yesterday with NPR."

"Is that why you're so upset?"

"Partly."

"I'm a journalist who happens to be at the center of the one of the weirdest stories in years. What did you expect me to do?"

"I heard that you described me as 'not even a real detective.' "

She scrunched up her face. "Oh."

"Thanks for that."

"I knew it wasn't coming out the way I intended. I was trying to explain that you're not a homicide investigator. I was a little buzzed."

"I was sent to Maquoit to investigate your sister's homicide."

"When it was thought to be a hunting accident."

"*Incident.* Not *accident.*"

"I only meant that your job doesn't include solving murders. And that's the truth, isn't it?" Her embarrassment had begun to crumble behind the weight of her self-righteousness. "If a case you're investigating begins to look like it was a murder, you're supposed to hand it over to the state police. That's what you told me."

I said nothing.

"I'm sorry, OK? I didn't mean to put you in a bad light. But I won't apologize for doing my job. You're the only law enforcement officer on the island, but I'm the only journalist."

Again I said nothing.

My silence seemed to be causing her physical discomfort. "Why aren't you saying anything?"

"Because you belittled me in a national interview. You're smart enough to know that would damage me inside my department."

Her face flushed. "You can accept my apology or not. That's entirely up to you."

"Mostly I'm disappointed, Ariel. I expected better of you."

"You seem to be operating under the mistaken idea that we're friends. You seem to be a good man, Mike. I've enjoyed hanging out with you. But if you're not capable of finding my sister's killer, then what good are you to me?"

Before I could recover from the body blow, she had gotten out of the truck.

Through the cracked windshield I watched her disappear into the store.

As I set off toward Harmon's house, I tried to push Ariel out of my mind. But the thought of her was as stubborn as the woman herself.

She had wronged me. Every time I started feeling sorry for myself, I would only have to remember how she had betrayed my confidence. I would carry around that grievance like a polished stone in my pocket.

Technically, it was just past dawn. The sun had risen, but the only sign of its appearance was a change in the color of the fog. From deep charcoal it had become slate gray. As I passed the Trap House, the sky changed again, this time to the color of wet cement.

I nearly ran over Andy Radcliffe jogging toward me down the middle of the road. His hair was wild, his face was aglow.

"Harmon is gone!" he bleated through my window.

"What do you mean, he's gone?"

"His truck isn't at his house, and it wasn't down at the waterfront either."

The cause of Radcliffe's panic confused me until I remembered how furious the old man had been the night before. If he wasn't at Graffam's and he wasn't at his son's bedside . . .

He'd gone after the Washburns, of course.

Harmon blamed Eli and Rudyard for selling his son the drugs that had nearly killed him. But this insult was only the latest in a series of blows their families had traded over the years. On this tiny, claustrophobic island there was only ever one conflict, and that was the feud between the Reeds and the Washburns.

"Get in," I told Radcliffe.

I swung the pickup around, nearly toppling a split-rail fence that ran along the edge of some summer person's yard, backed up until we were pointed east, and hit the gas.

"Which way do I go?"

"There's only the one road out to Dennettsville. Drive back to the airstrip, cross the helipad, and keep going."

"What do you think Harmon is planning to do?"

Radcliffe seemed dismayed by our sudden velocity. "I can't imagine."

"Try."

"Sink their boats, burn their houses."

"Or he might just kill them."

"Or he might just kill them," the constable agreed.

40

This was my first visit to the eastern side of the island, and the change in the topography became apparent within five minutes of crossing the airfield. Through the gaps in the fog, I caught a glimpse of hayfields rolling down to the marsh. Seconds later we were climbing a hill lined with mud-splashed alders that the deer had ravaged and thorny barberries that had resisted their desperate attempts at eating.

Suddenly, we were in a forest.

Tall spruces surrounded us and blocked even the faint light filtering through the dripping boughs. The trees were so densely crowded, and there were so many deadfalls and blowdowns, that even the creeping mist had trouble penetrating the understory. It was as if the earth had spun backward into night.

I flipped on my high beams in time to catch a doe slinking off between the spruces. The brighter light revealed a forest floor that was rust orange with fallen needles or green with luxuriant carpets of moss. Then we passed over a ridge and the road dropped as fast as it had climbed.

The fog thickened again as the trees fell away, and I had a sense, from the tang in the air, that we were again nearing the sea.

"I haven't heard gunshots," Radcliffe said. "That seems like a good sign."

"Unless they've already murdered each other."

From the mortified look on his face, it was clear that the constable didn't appreciate my gallows humor.

Better to approach with caution, I decided. I cut the lights and shifted into neutral. Gravity pulled us softly down the incline.

"How far away are we from their houses?"

"Two hundred yards maybe. Eli and Rudyard live side by side along the cove."

"Who else lives here?"

"Their nephews have places farther down the Reach. In Dennettsville itself there's kind of a flophouse for their sternmen and the foreign workers who staff their summer businesses. The Washburns have a take-out stand and souvenir shop they open when the tourists are here. The trailhead out to Norse Rock abuts their property. There's always lots of curiosity seekers who come out this way to see the Viking runes."

"So Dennettsville isn't even a real village?"

"It used to be until Eli and Rud's grandfather drove the last of the Dennetts from the island."

Even from inside the truck, I spotted fresh tire prints in the mud. Wardens make a professional study of identifying tracks of all sorts, and I recognized the jagged diamond pattern as belonging to Goodyear Wranglers. The make and

391

model came as an option with the newer GMC Sierra Denalis.

Harmon Reed had driven into Dennettsville, but there was no sign of him having driven out.

"Can you grab my flashlight from the rucksack at your feet? It's in the side pocket. . . . No, the other side."

As quietly as possible, I opened and closed my door, but Radcliffe had to use his shoulder to get his dented door open. The loudness of the noise set my teeth on edge.

"I don't suppose you're armed?"

He tried to make a joke of it. "I've got my Leatherman."

"What about a phone?"

"Yeah, but the reception here is always sketchy until you climb up to Norse Rock or Foggy Head and find a sight line to the tower." He checked the signal, then held up the luminous screen for me to see that we were, once again, disconnected from the rest of the world. "When Harmon was road commissioner, he once said he was going to 'accidentally' knock down the telephone poles along here with his snowplow so Eli and Rudyard couldn't use their landlines."

I gave Radcliffe the keys to the Datsun, which he accepted as happily as if I'd dropped a wolf spider onto his hand. "Here's what we're going to do," I said. "I'm going ahead. I need you to count to thirty and then start following me. Not too fast, though. Keep counting as you go and when you hit thirty again, pause and wait thirty seconds. Repeat that until you catch up with me or until you hear something that sounds like trouble."

"What does trouble sound like?"

"Gunshots. Screaming." I focused my full attention on those big, ingenuous eyes of his. "If it sounds like a pitched battle, you need to get the hell out of here, Andrew. Drive to the first place you get a signal and call the state police and tell them an officer is taking fire. They won't be able to do anything to save me, but at least they'll have an easier time solving my murder after my corpse 'disappears.' If I am wounded, I'll try to signal by firing three shots spaced five seconds apart."

"I could round up some folks and come back with a posse, so to speak."

"Better to leave it to the professionals. There's a boatload of cops headed out here this morning."

"Really? I hadn't heard."

"I expect that was deliberate, Andrew. Do I have to tell you why?"

He bowed his curly head.

"You wouldn't happen to know what kind of firearm Harmon might be carrying?"

"A revolver. I think it's a .38 Special."

"And the Washburns?"

"Oh, they've got a whole armory, from what

I hear. The Washburns buy and sell all sorts of World War Two stuff."

I glanced in the direction of the cove. "We've already wasted too much time here. Do you remember my instructions? I'm trusting you, Constable. This is your chance to make some things right."

His Adam's apple bobbed up and down as he nodded his understanding.

I removed my SIG from its holster and set off into the fog. The grass was patchworked with spiderwebs that held the dew like jeweled veils.

I came upon Harmon's silver truck parked at the trailhead to Norse Rock. He had backed into the space as if he expected to make a fast getaway. I touched the hood and found it cold. I glanced inside the cab but saw nothing of note. Then I circled around to the back of the pickup and noticed a diesel smell wafting up from the bedliner.

So Harmon was planning arson.

I headed down the hill. The first building I passed was the former Dennettsville Volunteer Fire Barn. The roof of the derelict structure was one good snowstorm away from collapsing.

From a distance the sea made a sound like breathing. Somewhere out in the cove a long-tailed duck began to yodel.

I came upon the take-out stand Radcliffe had

mentioned, shuttered now for the season. It was an old hamburger cart the Washburns had hauled over from the mainland and repurposed to sell seafood. The name of the business was the Chowdah House. The faded menu advertised deep-fried lobster as a specialty, which struck me as an abomination.

I made a point of listening for Radcliffe since I feared he would have trouble obeying my instructions.

Soon I stood atop the old seawall. It had been built to protect the road around the cove. Cigarette butts and rubber bands used to bind the crushing claws of lobsters floated in the froth. During full and new moons, the waves must have regularly spilled over the top of the barrier and washed out the road.

I spent half a minute surveying the cove, or what I could see of it in the fog. I saw the silhouettes of the ducks paddling in zigzag patterns out in the deeper water. I picked out a big white ball that marked the mooring for someone's lobsterboat. A dinghy was tied up to the giant buoy.

The next building was the flophouse where the Washburns housed their employees. No one seemed to be in residence at the moment.

Past the seawall were the remains of vanished wharfs in the form of pilings rising like a submerged forest from the surface of the sea. Farther to the northeast were docks still standing. The stench of rotten fish hung on the air. I passed a rope shed. I passed a row of rusted barrels, some empty and collecting rainwater, others containing fermenting pogies to be used as lobster bait.

Off in the water another mooring ball bobbed on the waves, this one with a canoe tied up.

Two big houses stood side by side. Both had barren yards that stretched to the water's edge. Both had private docks. Both had burgundy trucks labeled with racist and anti-Semitic symbols.

I was so intent upon the Washburns' homes that it took me a minute to notice the shadow at the end of the nearest dock. I froze as soon as I realized it was Harmon. He was sitting on a piling, his muscled back to me, staring out at the fogbound cove. On the rough wood beside him were two big plastic containers, and I had no doubt they held enough gasoline to incinerate Eli's and Rudyard's houses.

I didn't level my gun at him. Not yet. My footsteps were soundless until I stepped on a loose board that knocked hard against its neighbor. The echo caused Reed to flinch, but he didn't turn around.

"What are you doing, Harmon?"

The old man refused to face me. "Who is that? The warden?"

"Yeah, it's me. Investigator Bowditch."

"I am exploring my options," he said wistfully. "I just missed them, you see. Heard their engines as they rounded the Daggers. They won't be back till nightfall."

"They went out fishing?"

"Season don't start until December, but those bastards couldn't give two shits about any agreement they made. They're already hauling and probably have some accessory who comes out, maybe from Swan's or Frenchboro, to pick up their catch. Could be the same piece of dung who's been providing them with drugs. God only knows who else they've been selling to here besides Hiram. But it won't be long until the overdoses start up again."

"So you've been sitting here, planning your revenge?"

"That would be an accurate summary."

"What have you been waiting for?"

"Can't decide what to burn."

"Not the houses?"

"They've got those overinsured, I'm pretty certain. They'd probably welcome the chance to rebuild. Torching their boats would have hurt them the worst. But that's not happening. I've been contemplating incinerating their vehicles, but it doesn't seem . . . proportionate. Is that a real word?"

"It is."

"I haven't met a lot of fish and game wardens. Are they all as book-smart as you?"

"I'm an outlier."

"Thought so." He shifted his rear end on the piling. "You're going to try to stop me from taking my revenge, ain't you?"

"You know I have to."

"There's something I need to tell you."

A board knocked and I realized Radcliffe had tiptoed up behind me. I kept my focus on Reed.

"Who's that with you?" the harbormaster snapped.

"It's Andrew, Harmon." The tremor in the constable's voice was more pronounced than usual. "I have been worried about you."

"Have I ever told you what a horse's ass you are, Radcliffe?"

I did my best to keep my tone calm. "What is it you need to tell me, Harmon?"

"I've got a gun in my lap here."

"Maybe you should set it down beside you."

"And if I don't, what do you plan on doing?"

"I'm exploring my options."

He slapped his knee as if in actual good humor. "That's a good one. You got me there."

"I don't know you very well, Harmon. But I don't think you're a murderer."

"Eli might hold a different opinion."

"There's a difference between shooting a man

who's threatened your family and shooting a law enforcement officer."

"Maybe I want to go out in a blaze of glory."

"You don't strike me as the suicidal type."

"Why not? I'm the last of my line. My daughter won't speak to me or let me see my grandkids. And even if Hiram recovers, he's only going to do it again. I raised a weak boy, Warden. I raised two weak boys. My old man would have been ashamed of me."

"He'd be even more ashamed of you if you killed yourself."

"Good thing the old bastard's dead, then."

"Put down the revolver, Hiram. If not for your own sake, for Martha's. What's life going to be like for her with you gone?"

"She'll be pleased as punch. She can move back to America and be with her daughter and grandkids."

"I doubt that's what she wants."

"With due respect, Warden, you don't know jack shit about her or me."

I could feel my palm grow slippery around the grip of my pistol. "Please don't make me do this, Harmon."

Radcliffe piped up, "If I could say one thing here—"

Harmon and I spoke the exact same word at the exact same moment: "No!"

What happened next shocked me. Harmon

Reed began to chuckle. First it was soft, but it quickly became a loud belly laugh. I wasn't sure what to make of his response until he tossed his heavy gun onto the wharf beside him.

Radcliffe had been wrong about the caliber. It wasn't a .38 Special. It was a .44 Magnum capable of taking down a charging bull moose. The barrel of the Ruger Redhawk was longer than a porn star's penis.

Harmon, laughing, swung around on the piling. His horny hands clutched his kneecaps. His bushy eyebrows bounced beneath the brim of his hat.

"What's so funny?" Radcliffe asked as if he had reason to fear the answer.

"You are, Andy. If I shot myself in front of you, I know for a fact that you'd dissolve into a puddle of jelly. It would be a miraculous transformation of man into marmalade. But I wouldn't be around to see it! Now, how could I miss a sight like that?"

41

I tried to persuade Harmon to let me keep his gun for him—just until the present crisis had passed—but the old man refused to yield.

He fastened the long-barreled Redhawk into a shoulder holster beneath his raincoat. "Don't press your luck, Warden. Besides, you'll be leaving this island sooner or later, and things will return to the way they've always been. I expect I'll be needing this *pistola* before too long."

"You could expedite my departure by coming clean about what really happened after Crowley appeared on your doorstep the other morning."

He lowered those expressive brows. "Are you accusing me of lying, sir?"

"If you prefer, we can call it obfuscating the truth."

His pipe-stained teeth made a surprise reappearance when he smiled. "Well, in that case! The boy was panicked. He said he hadn't shot the Evans girl and he showed me his rifle. The bore was all dirty. I suggested we clean the thing to be on the safe side. I asked him if he'd seen anybody else while he'd been hunting and he said no. Truth be told, I had a sense Kenneth was hiding something. So I decided to call Andy with the news and ask him a question: If

Kenneth really had shot that woman by mistake, what would the legal consequences be? I wanted to know if I could protect the youth from being tyrannized by the state as I had been."

Radcliffe hadn't fully recovered from Reed's threat to blow out his own brains, but now he spoke up in his own defense. "You can see how I misunderstood what Harmon was telling me. I thought he was saying that Kenneth really had shot Ms. Evans."

The harbormaster shook his big square head. "Andy, I've met twelve-year-old girls less excitable than you."

"Harmon, I'm sick and tired of being the butt of your jokes."

"If you don't want to be the butt, then stop being an ass!"

By this time I had decided to take another run at Crowley. His tantrum the previous night, coupled with this new information, warranted another conversation with the gangling goat boy.

The clock was ticking on my investigation.

"If you won't let me watch your gun for you," I told Harmon, "how about I take those cans of gas back to town with me in my truck."

"Warden Bowditch, you are a stitch. I will let you follow me into town if it will ease your troubled mind. But I'll be returning these spare jerricans to my boat where they belong. Last thing I need is to be out fishing someday and run out of diesel because I'd given my spares to my game-warden babysitter."

Radcliffe rode with Reed on the return into town. It was not my choice. While I tended to believe their latest version of what had happened in the hours following Miranda's murder, I hated giving the coconspirators another chance to reconcile their accounts. But I had no standing to insist the constable ride shotgun with me again.

Harmon managed the drive back through the fairy-tale forest without ever dropping below fifty miles per hour. I lost sight of his taillights well before I arrived in the village.

Up ahead I saw Joy Juno approaching in her monster truck. The road was narrow, hemmed in by knotweed and barberry, so I pulled over to let her pass. I cranked down the window, expecting she would stop to exchange a few words, but she didn't so much as acknowledge me. As she rumbled past, I spotted Beryl McCloud slunk down in the passenger seat. The teacher had the same complexion as a cadaver.

Harmon must have driven straight back to his house in Marsh Harbor because there was no sign of his GMC on Bishop's Wharf or anywhere else along the waterfront. I noticed Crowley's green Ford backed into an alley that led out to one of the wharfs on the east side of the harbor. But before I took another charge at Kenneth, I thought it might be prudent to check in on Ariel to be sure the villagers hadn't ridden her out of town on a rail.

Her bicycle was still leaning against the side of the store where I'd last seen it.

The crowd inside Graffam's had thinned out as it always did after the lobstermen had finished their gabbing.

There was no sign of Ariel.

Jenny Pillsbury and her baby were gone, too. The store owner himself now manned the cash register. I filled a coffee cup and approached the counter. "Hi, Sam. I don't suppose you know where Ariel Evans went?"

"Can't say I do."

"What about the time she left?"

"Ten, fifteen minutes ago."

"Did she leave with somebody."

"I was cleaning the grill and emptying the fry oil into the barrel out back."

"Come on, Sam. Don't pretend you don't watch what's going on here even when you're busy."

He scratched his impressively dense beard. "She went off on her own."

"Who had she been talking to?"

"She *tried* to talk to quite a few folks. Can't say she had much luck. Think she spoke to Alfie Lunt. Chum McNulty. Jenny, of course."

"Jenny Pillsbury?" I wasn't sure why I was

hearing a buzzing in my skull, but I had learned long ago not to disregard these random warnings. "Could Ariel have gone with her?"

"It's possible, I guess."

"Thanks, Sam."

The storekeeper called after me, "Are you going to pay for that coffee?"

I slapped some bills on the counter.

Outside, I turned right and I turned left. I saw no sign of Nat Pillsbury's truck. Was it possible Ariel had cajoled the wronged wife into taking her back to the house for a confidential interview?

Across the street, Chum McNulty ambled out between two rattrap buildings. He began unloading marine gear from the bed of the pickup. I guessed he was bringing supplies out to his lobsterboat.

"Hey, Chum!"

The old man spun slowly around until he located the source of the interruption. "Hey, Warden. Ch'up ta?"

"Have you seen Ariel Evans this morning?"

"Sure did. Not ten minutes ago. She was headed out with Kenneth."

"What?"

"He'd pulled the *Sea Hag* up to the dock for her to board. Didn't hear what they was saying. I'm deafer than a haddock, you know. Figured he was giving her a tour around the island. Not

405

that there's much to see yet. Fog's burning off, though. Marine forecast is for partly sunny weather into the weekend. I ain't complaining."

"I don't suppose there's a motorboat tied up somewhere I can use?"

"I've got a Beacon dinghy down the end of the dock. Outboard's kind of temperamental, but there's a pair of oars if the engine conks out, which it most likely will."

"I'll take it."

As I slid along the side of his truck, I spotted a personal flotation device, or PFD, sitting atop the pile of random gear in the bed. I grabbed it. Then noticed an orange ditty bag underneath. It was the kind of sack into which you might stuff a sleeping bag. "Is that an immersion suit?"

"You mean survival suit? Yeah, it's a Mustang I picked up at West Marine. Sam makes fun of me for bringing it along. He says if the *Siren* ever goes down, I won't have time to put it on anyhow."

"Mind if I borrow it?"

"You planning on going for a polar-bear dip? Water's forty degrees last I checked."

I made my way down the alley between the two sad-faced buildings and along the wharf where Ariel had boarded Pillsbury's boat only minutes before. An aluminum ramp descended to a second floating dock, where a small boat was tied up. My hollow footsteps rang out across the harbor as I made my way down to the waterline.

Chum's dinghy was about eight feet long and made of white fiberglass with an emerald-green underside where it had acquired a coating of algae. The engine was an antique Yamaha two-stroke. The oars lay across the molded seat. I tossed the PFD and the ditty bag with the survival suit into the rainwater pooled in the bottom. Then I unfastened the line from the cleat. The dinghy tipped back and forth until I found my balance. The old man gawked at me from the wharf. I hoped to God I wouldn't have to take this shallow, unstable craft into heavy seas.

As I drifted clear of the dock, Chum McNulty called after me, "Do you have a plan or are you just frigging around?"

It was a damn good question.

42

It was like boating through a cloud. There was no wind and little current, and the surface, at first, was as smooth as a black pearl.

I jogged past several lobsterboats floating silently on their moorings. A V-shaped wake trailed from my sputtering engine. It caused the unattended boats to rock like cradles. I have always found something forbidding about ships and boats with no one aboard.

I couldn't explain the panic that had seized hold of me. I had never viewed Kenneth Crowley as the most likely suspect in Miranda's murder. But something about his having invited Ariel onto a boat alone was worrisome, especially after how he'd blown up at her the night before. I couldn't imagine why she'd gone with him unless it was to prove she wasn't afraid. She was as foolhardy as I was in that respect.

The *Sea Hag* could be anywhere. It could be miles from the island. How far would I get in an eight-foot motorboat?

I came upon a raftlike float called a lobster car. In a month the island lobstermen would tie up crates to it containing their daily catch. But for now it waited. A cormorant surfaced from beneath the raft and confronted me with red eyes. Clamped in its cruel bill was a writhing pollack, which the bird swallowed whole.

As I rounded the Marsh Harbor Breakwater—a wall of boulders extending a hundred feet into the bay—I encountered a faint chop that bounced the dinghy up and down. Already I could hear the booming of distant breakers as they ran headlong into the outer ledges. Rip currents began slowing my forward progress. I throttled the engine until I was safely away from the breakwater. I couldn't smell anything except the gasoline fumes coming from the outboard.

Somewhere off to my right must have been John's Point. I had read that a monument there commemorated Captain John Smith's "discovery" of Maquoit in 1614. The explorer, of Pocahontas fame, had previously planted King James's flag on nearby Monhegan Island. Both Andrew Radcliffe and Joy Juno lived on John's Point.

The seas grew rough. The dinghy hadn't been designed to face big water. The only consolation was that the fog seemed to be breaking. I opened up the throttle and received heavy spray in my face as the price of speed. My lips tasted of salt.

The engine had made me deaf to all other sounds. I decided to take a breather to clear the fumes from my lungs. I switched off the motor and found that I could hear the chattering of gulls and the cawing of crows maybe a hundred yards to the northwest. There must have been an island or ledge there where the birds gathered. Rocking back and forth on the churning seas, I listened.

In the distance a woman was laughing. The faint sound seemed to be coming from the same direction as the cries of the birds. Who else could it be but Ariel?

I decided to creep up on the *Sea Hag*. I pulled the motor's skeg and propeller up and fitted the oars into the oarlocks. I tried to keep the racket to a minimum. The birds were raucous enough to cover whatever rowing sounds I made.

As I neared the lobsterboat, bits and pieces of dialogue drifted toward me across the water.

> Crowley: "That seal that went under— that was a harbor seal. You can tell from the shape of the muzzle. It's sort of puppy-dog-like. The gray seals have these big horse heads."
>
> Ariel: "Will we see gray seals, too?"
>
> Crowley: "Maybe. They're a lot more common than when I was a kid."
>
> Ariel: "When you were a kid, huh?"
>
> Crowley: "The grays have brought back the sharks, though."
>
> Ariel: "Do you ever see sharks out here?"
>
> Crowley: "Heck, yeah! Lots of them. I've

seen blues, mostly, and basking sharks. Those are sizable sons of bitches. I've seen mako sharks jump ten feet in the air. We even had a great white come into the harbor once. Don't think anyone went swimming for a full year after."

What is this, a nature tour?
If the kid had malicious intentions toward Ariel, there was no hint of it in their casual conversation. My face and hair were soaked from the spray that my oars had whipped from the tops of the waves. Cold water ran down the handles and into my shirtsleeves when I feathered the blades.

"Kenneth, is that a man in a boat?" Ariel had spotted me.

"Whoever he is, he's in Chum's dinghy." Crowley's voice rose. "Ahoy there!"

I pulled on the left oar to bring myself around in a circle so that I was facing them.

Ariel leaned over the gunwale. She was wearing her parka and a shapeless wool hat I hadn't seen before. "Mike?"

I put on a smile. "Hello!"

"What are you doing out here? We must be a mile from shore."

Crowley ducked out from under the standing shelter. He stared at me with the focused intensity of a predatory animal that has isolated its prey from the herd.

"You get lost in the fog, Warden?"

"Wouldn't be the first time."

I didn't know why I was joking around. If my attempt was to put the lobsterman at his ease, it was not succeeding. He'd moved close enough to Ariel to push her overboard with one touch of his strong hand.

"Seriously, Mike?" Ariel said. "What's going on?"

"Chum McNulty told me you two were out here. I found something outside the cottage that you need to see, Ariel. It's important."

Her face tightened. "What is it?"

I dug the oars in, this time using a reverse stroke to approach the lobsterboat's stern at a perpendicular angle. "I'll come up to your transom, Captain. And Ariel can step into the dinghy."

My little boat bumped the *Sea Hag*. Crowley grabbed hold of the gaff he used to snag the toggles of traps. He brought the cruel hook down hard on the gunwale of the dinghy, holding me fast against his stern.

"You sure you don't want to come up?" he said. "Nat's got a pint of peach schnapps stashed somewhere."

"It's tempting, Kenneth, but I need to get Ariel back. I'm afraid it can't wait."

The gulls on the ledge kept up their maniacal

jeering. Wisps of cottony fog began closing in around our boats.

"It seems like he don't want you out here with me or something," said Crowley with an insulted tone.

"That's ridiculous, Kenneth."

"Maybe I should go with him," said Ariel. I saw alarm flicker in her eyes. She had finally stopped seeing Crowley as a hapless teenager.

"This is stupid!" The iron hook in his hands was an intimidating weapon. "You're not afraid of me, are you, Ariel?"

"Not at all, Kenneth. I just need to go with the warden."

He pulled the gaff loose, and the two boats began floating apart. I backed oars until I knocked the transom again. I had to keep rowing to hold the little boat in place.

"I'm sorry I said what I said about your sister. I was kind of a little drunk."

She put a hand lightly on his forearm. "Kenneth, I'm the one who should apologize. Miranda ruined a lot of people's lives out here. She had a habit of doing that."

Now his face darkened again. "Chum's shitty engine's gonna die on you before you get half-way to the breakwater."

"We'll take our chances," I said.

"What's wrong with you people? I told you I'd take you in! Why are you afraid of me?"

This time, Ariel herself reached for the dinghy and held it while she stepped over the transom.

"Keep your center of gravity low," I cautioned.

She sat down on the molded seat in the stern so that her back was to the *Sea Hag*. Her eyes were wide and full of questions. I tried to keep my own expression blank.

Crowley gave the dinghy such a forceful shove that we wobbled. Ariel reached out to steady herself against the gunwales. I hurried to drop the oar blades in the water.

He shouted after us, "If you capsize or get swept out into the gulf, don't expect me to come looking for you!"

He removed his chewing tobacco from his pocket, shoved a wad inside his cheek, and watched us until we could no longer see him through the opaque curtain of fog.

"Didn't you learn anything from your last attempt at 'rescuing' me?" Ariel said in a harsh whisper. "Are you going to tell me what the hell is going on?"

I kept my voice low as I rowed. "In a minute."

"For God's sake, Mike."

I pulled the oars in and gave the outboard motor a yank. It didn't catch. I tried again and it didn't catch. I fiddled with the choke. The third time was the charm. Black smoke billowed around us.

Off in the fog, the *Sea Hag* roared to life.

I knew that we couldn't outrun the powerful lobsterboat. But I had formulated a plan if things took a bad turn.

"What are you doing?" Ariel shouted at me over the outboard. "You're taking us out to sea."

"Just around the back side of the ledge."

She straightened up suddenly. "Oh, shit. I left my messenger bag on the boat. I knew I was forgetting something. We've got to go back for it."

"We can't."

"Why the hell not?"

"I don't trust Crowley. I think he's dangerous."

Her expression was one of strained disbelief. "He's just a strange, mixed-up kid. You need to turn around. My phone is in that bag—and all my notes. I'm not kidding, Mike. We've got to go back for it."

The *Sea Hag* was moving off in the direction of the harbor. I cut the engine again. Suddenly we could hear the gulls once more. I prayed that Crowley hadn't glimpsed me pilot the dinghy around the back side of the ledge. With the fog breaking up, we couldn't afford to be seen.

"What's this all about?" Ariel demanded.

"It has to do with Nat Pillsbury. A week ago, by all accounts, he was head over heels in love with your sister. But ever since she died, he's been acting like a devoted, protective husband. He made a midnight crossing in dangerous conditions last night just to pick up his wife and daughter and bring them back to Maquoit. It wasn't because the state police brutalized her. So why did he do it?"

"Because he felt guilty for the way he'd treated Jenny?"

"Maybe. But I just don't get the impression from him that he came to his senses. When people said Nat wanted to run off with Miranda, I took it as an exaggeration. But what if he had been serious about it? What if he really had intended to leave his family for a new life with your sister?"

Ariel laughed at the absurdity of the suggestion. "Miranda would have told him he was dreaming. If anything, she probably wanted to shack up with the hermit, tend sheep, and burn incense."

"Maybe she told Nat that."

"Told him what?"

"That she didn't love him. That she was just using him for sex. Maybe it made him furious."

"I wouldn't have put it past her. Miranda prided herself on being brutally honest, with the emphasis on *brutally*."

"Then there's Jenny Pillsbury. When I saw her this morning at the store, she was almost too friendly. She even offered to buy my breakfast. What was she even doing working after the night she'd had?"

"At least she was friendly to you. She could barely bring herself to look at me, and when she did, it was with hatred. But I thought you said she had an alibi for the morning of the shooting. Wasn't she at the store?"

"She was at Graffam's at the time Miranda died. She and Hiram Reed."

"But what does any of this have to do with Crowley?"

"He's Nat's sternman. Whose idea was it to go out on the *Sea Hag*?"

She paused before answering. "It was Kenneth's idea. I asked if he had time to talk about Miranda, and he said Nat had asked him to test out the engines. He said I was welcome to come with him out to Calderwood Ledge to look for seals."

The sound of the lobsterboat engines had grown so faint they were hard to hear.

Now the dark shape of the ledge began to take shape. The seabirds, with their superior vision, reacted to our encroachment with a chorus of screeches. The rocks on the windward side of the island were sheer and steep. When the waves broke against them, brilliant splashes exploded high and white into the air. The lower reaches were enrobed with a thick, ocher coat of bladder wrack.

Most of the birds grouped along the ridge were herring gulls, with a few great black-backed gulls among them. On a separate outcropping the cormorants were drying their outstretched wings. They perched, menacing and cruciform, atop the rocks. From a distance, a mariner might have mistaken them for stone crosses marking the watery graves of the island's lost fishermen.

"Mike?"

"Sorry, I am still trying to put this all together."

"No. Listen."

Watching the birds, I had been so lost in thought that I hadn't noticed the growl of the *Sea Hag* returning.

43

Crowley must have searched the outer harbor, and when he didn't find us, he must have realized that I'd snuck in behind the ledge. There would have been no other place I could have hidden the dinghy in such a short time.

I tried the engine, but it wouldn't catch. The gremlin inside must have been waiting until I absolutely needed the spark plugs to fire.

I reached for the orange ditty bag at my feet. "I need you to put this on. It's an immersion suit. You'll float in it, and it will protect you from the cold water. I'll help secure it. You won't need to do a thing."

"What about you?"

I lifted the sopped personal flotation device from the boat bottom. "I have this."

"Mike, the water must be fifty degrees."

"Forty degrees according to Chum McNulty."

"It won't matter if you have a life jacket. You'll die of hypothermia in twenty minutes. Didn't you see *Titanic*?"

I pulled the orange neoprene suit from the bag. "What did I tell you about movies?"

"That you don't watch them."

This standard one-piece Mustang survival suit had a center zipper, hood, and inflatable head pillow. At my instruction, she slipped her feet—shoes and all—into the bootees and wiggled the suit up her legs, past her hips to her chest. I guided her arms into the sleeves as if we were a couple on a date, and I were a gentlemen helping her put on her coat. The arms ended in gloves that were too big for her tiny hands. But otherwise, the fit was passable.

When we were done, she stared nervously at me from beneath her orange cowl and mumbled through the flap that covered the lower half of her face, "What do I do now?"

"You wait." I pulled the personal flotation device over my head and cinched the side straps. The bulky, blocky thing had been orange before the sun faded the fabric to a dull persimmon. "You'll float automatically if you go into the water so there's no need to freak out. But you'll want to blow into the tube beside your mouth to inflate the pillow behind your head. It's designed to keep your face abovewater."

"You don't really think that kid intends to kill us?"

"I don't know what he intends to do, but I want to be prepared for the worst-case scenario."

With those words, I removed my pistol from its holster and tucked it into the vest above my wishbone. The PFD came with two exterior pockets. I placed my spare magazines in one pocket and my Gerber push-button automatic knife in the other. After a moment's consideration, I added my badge to the items I was unwilling to lose.

Through the wispy fog we saw the *Sea Hag* round the north end of the ledge. Once Crowley was well clear of the rocks, he cut the engine and let the lobsterboat drift forward on its own momentum.

"What is he doing?"

"I assume Nat keeps binoculars on the counter. All fishermen have a pair on their boats. He's watching us now."

I tried the engine again. This time I got it sputtering. I turned the tiller toward the ledges.

"You're going to crash us!" Ariel said through her mouthpiece.

"Hopefully not. I can't outrun him, but if I can get us close enough to the rocks, he won't be able to plot a collision course without risking his own boat."

It took a moment for Crowley to recognize my stratagem for what it was. He restarted the dual engines and pushed the throttle down. Most fishing boats are built to plow through the water, but the *Sea Hag* was so powerful, with its twin inboards, it seemed to skim along the whitecaps.

Too late, I saw the flaw in my plan. Instead of smashing us head-on with his bow, Crowley turned aside at the last second, creating a horrific wave that lifted the dinghy, spun it around, and pushed it toward the looming ledge.

Ariel flopped against me. "He really is trying to kill us!"

"Brace yourself!"

We came in hard, and the fiberglass made a painful crunching noise. Worse, the lobsterboat had created a wave that crashed over the gunwale, flooding the bottom of the dinghy, and extinguishing the outboard.

The gulls had erupted into the hazy air, screaming so loudly we could hardly hear each other over their shrill voices.

Meanwhile Crowley had come around and was once more facing us as we collided again and again against the low cliff.

"He's hoping the waves will swamp us," I said.

"Should we try climbing that seaweed? Maybe we can get on top of it."

"We won't be able to get a grip on that bladder wrack. Or the basalt above. Take the oar. Use it as a paddle as best you can to keep us clear of the ledge."

"What are you going to do?"

"I'm going to defend us. Promise me you're going to survive this, Ariel. I'm going to need your testimony when I go in front of the attorney general."

I wrapped my hands around the grip of my service weapon and leveled it at the figure behind the windscreen. Before he could react, I squeezed off a shot. The white-hot shell bounced off my shoulder as it was ejected from the chamber.

I saw a single hole in the plastic close to where Crowley had been standing. The jostling of the waves had caused me to fire wide and to the left. Now the lobsterman ducked down so that I couldn't obtain a target. He pulled back the throttle so that the screws turned counterclockwise and the boat backed off.

"There's a marine shotgun onboard," Ariel said. "He said Nat uses it on gulls sometimes when they mob his boat."

I remembered the Mossberg pump Pillsbury had shown me. He must have brought the gun to the *Sea Hag* after our conversation. "He's not going to shoot us."

"Why not?"

"He wants it to look like our boat got swamped and we drowned or froze. Our deaths have to appear accidental." The water in the bottom of the dinghy was above the tops of my Bean boots and oozing down my socks. I had no clue how much more it would take for the fiberglass hull to start sinking. "Right now his plan is to wait us out."

The *Sea Hag* rose suddenly on a wave, then dropped just as fast.

"Hang on! Here comes a big one!"

The white-ridged crest rose nearly to the gunwale, and we found ourselves hurtling again toward the rocks. Ariel tried using the oar to brace us, but she lost her grip, and it was carried away by the current. Seconds later we were slammed against the basalt with such force I heard the fiberglass crack.

It was all I could do to hang on to my handgun as ice-cold water covered me from head to toe. The shock went through me like a surge of electricity. My heart clenched. My lungs gasped out the air they'd been holding. I was left so disoriented I didn't notice that Ariel had fallen into the sea.

"Mike!"

I rubbed away the mucus flushed from my burning sinuses. "Inflate the head pillow! You're going to float. Kick your feet to get clear of the rocks."

The dinghy was swamped now. It would be dragged to the bottom soon, weighed down by the engine.

I glanced back at the *Sea Hag*, but Crowley refused to show himself. I raised the gun above my head and fired once into the air. Then I counted to five. Again I fired. Counted once more to five. And fired.

Three shots: the universal signal for a person in distress.

But would anyone back on Maquoit be able

to hear them? Would anyone recognize their meaning?

Crowley lifted his head. Maybe he hadn't counted on my firing distress signals. Maybe he'd caught sight of Ariel floating off in a survival suit and was forming an idea how to finish us off.

I squared my pistol sights and squeezed the trigger as the dinghy fell suddenly away.

It was as if the sea had reached up and pulled me underwater by the legs. For a split second I had no idea what had happened. Everything had gone green. My sinuses felt as if I'd snorted Drano. Worst of all was the full-body shock that came from being immersed in gelid water. When my head popped up, buoyed by the life jacket, my vision was out of focus, and my lungs were flooded.

I have seen corpses brought up by warden divers from beneath the ice with expressions of horror frozen on their faces. I felt a piercing pain in my forehead as if someone had driven a marlinspike through my skull. Don't let anyone tell you that drowning is a peaceful way to die.

Even though the life jacket was keeping my head above the waves, I found myself breathing short, shivering breaths. I kicked my legs and swung myself around in time to see the *Sea Hag* bearing down on me again. Crowley, dumb kid that he was, had decided to try the same play. He would veer off at the last second, counting on the wash from his screws to engulf me and perhaps smash my skull like a pumpkin against the rocks.

This time he would be turning to starboard. The wheel he used to steer the craft was on the port side. He would be exposed as he came around.

Crowley spun the wheel. I saw his tanned face and his goat beard poking out from beneath his black hood. I raised my weapon from beneath the froth and fired.

Did I hit him? At the moment, I had no idea.

Later, the medical examiner would state he could find no bullet wounds on the corpse.

Traveling at a speed of approximately forty knots, the Coast Guard said in its own report, the *Sea Hag* had failed to negotiate its turn. The port side of the keel collided with a basalt outcropping five feet below the waterline. The impact not only carved a gash along the hull from stem to stern. It also ejected the boat's pilot from beneath the standing shelter. He struck his temple, most likely on the metal hauler he used to raise his traps, and was knocked unconscious. Having fallen senseless into the sea, Kenneth Crowley drowned in the waters off Calderwood Ledge.

"Death by misadventure" was the conclusion

426

jointly reached by the US Coast Guard and the State of Maine.

At the time, I knew nothing of this. I was being tossed like a rag doll by the waves. I heard a horrible crash and thought I smelled smoke. I definitely smelled petroleum. Overhead, a great black-backed gull—the largest gull in the world—hovered like some pelagic carrion bird. Would it even wait for me to expire before it plucked out my eyes?

I felt a sudden tug and flopped my neck in that direction. It was Ariel. She floated on her back in the survival suit, her head sustained by an air-filled pillow. But she was smiling. She looked as friendly as a sea otter.

"Hang in there, Mike."

I could barely utter the words. "What happened?"

"Crowley crashed his boat. It's halfway up a rock. I think I can scramble onto it. I'll try to pull you up after me. Can you kick your legs?"

They were stiff, but I willed them to move. I doubt it helped much, but we made progress.

"Where is he?"

"He fell into the water when the boat hit. His body looked limp. I don't know if he was unconscious or dead."

I remember lifting my right arm and finding to my surprise that I was still clutching my service weapon.

"How did you manage to hang on to that?" Ariel asked in amazement.

I tried to mumble out a joke: "Cadaveric spasm."

It must have sounded to her like gibberish.

44

Nat Pillsbury's lobsterboat had come to rest on its side, balanced on one of the submerged rocks it had struck. It pitched violently beneath us every time a wave crashed against the now-vertical deck. We were stretched out along the slick hull of the boat, a few feet above the water.

I was shivering and shaking so violently you might have thought I was being electrocuted.

"Should I take off the suit and put it on you?" Ariel asked.

My first attempt at speech turned into a coughing jag. "You need it."

"Being a hero is only going to get you killed."

The gun slipped from my hand and began to slide along the hull. I swatted at it with my frozen paw. Ariel trapped the pistol with her foot.

"You need to fire three shots," I said through chattering teeth. "Like I did. Before."

"Three?"

"It's a signal. People will recognize. Five seconds."

"What?"

"Between shots."

"I don't know if I can do it in these gloves." As she tried to force her thick neoprene-covered finger into the trigger guard, she unintentionally fired a round that ricocheted off the ledge fifty yards away. She dropped the gun as if it had scalded her. "Christ!"

"Get it!"

Once again she scrambled after my pistol.

"Again. This time . . ."

"I know, point away from the rocks."

"Five."

"Five seconds, I get it."

When she had finished, I patted one of the pockets of my life vest. "Put it here. Careful!"

Ariel rubbed my arms and legs as if her intention was to chafe off the skin beneath my soaked clothes. What she didn't understand about hypothermia was that my core temperature had fallen. Forcing rewarmed blood from the extremities back into a half-frozen heart can bring on cardiac arrest.

"Stop."

"Mike, you're not thinking clearly."

"You don't understand."

The sea spray raining down upon us tasted of diesel fuel. I let my head loll in the direction of the ocean. The petroleum that had spilled from the engines had created a purplish-green slick around the boat.

The flotsam and jetsam of the *Sea Hag* included a faded Red Sox baseball cap; an unopened bag of salt-and-vinegar potato chips; another PFD,

430

too far away to be of use; cigarette butts; empty aluminum cans of Pabst Blue Ribbon. Nothing that would improve our situation. The marine radio was underwater and had almost certainly short-circuited.

I tucked my numb hands into the chest pockets of my peacoat. The wool was soaked, but it would keep me warm. My socks were made of wool, too. I tried flexing my toes with small success. It was my legs, clad in wet denim, that felt like frozen shanks of beef.

It had been years since I'd been plunged into cold water, and now it had happened twice in two days.

"How do you feel?" Ariel asked me.

"Better."

"Don't lie to me."

After three failed attempts, I managed to prop myself up on my elbow. The fog was continuing to break apart. Low clouds drifted above the waves, but overhead were uneven patches of blue sky. Suddenly the light began to change. I craned my neck and watched the sun emerge from the mist. Its rays touched our upraised faces.

After a minute of basking in the warmth, Ariel said, "Is that a sailboat?"

I opened my eyes to see light sparkling off waves. The fog was retreating before the relentless advance of the sun.

"Where?"

She began waving her orange arms. Then she climbed to her feet. The flooded boat wobbled, but she kept her balance. "Hey! Over here! Help!"

A ketch was making its way toward us, its sails luffing and snapping in the breeze.

"Who is it?" Ariel asked. "Do you know?"

"Radcliffe."

The constable had remembered what I'd taught him about three shots being a distress signal.

In that moment I forgave the son of a bitch everything.

Radcliffe's boat was a beauty: mahogany on oak, bronze fastened, with a fresh coat of varnish. Its flapping sails were clean, crisp, and white. But the most beautiful thing about the *Lucky Penny* was that it had arrived in time to save us.

The constable lowered his sails and engaged his motor to maneuver the ketch as close as he dared to the ledge. He tossed down an inflatable raft on a line, but it was too far away for Ariel to reach, and she was forced to swim out to it. She towed the raft over to the wreck of the *Sea Hag*. It took everything I had to belly flop into the bouncy rubber oval. I rolled over and lay on my back staring up at a sky of lapis lazuli as Andrew pulled the raft along the choppy tops of the waves.

In no time I was beside the boat, looking up into his anxious face. "What happened? Where's Kenneth?"

"I don't know."

"Is he dead?"

"I don't know."

Once Andrew had pulled me aboard, I sat down on the side deck and began fumbling with the straps of the PFD while the constable hauled up Ariel. "Crowley tried to kill us," she explained.

"I don't believe it. Why?"

Ariel unzipped the survival suit and began shaking herself out of it. "We have no idea."

This wasn't true. But I wasn't prepared to take Radcliffe into my confidence yet, especially when I could barely form a sentence.

The constable glanced around in the water where litter from the wrecked lobsterboat continued to float merrily along. There was no sign at all of Crowley. My buddies in the dive team had told me that a corpse will sink as soon as the residual air leaks from its lungs. It will stay submerged until it starts to decompose and its gut swells with gases.

It would be a while before anyone saw Kenneth Crowley again.

"He swamped the dinghy I was rowing," I said.

"I don't believe it."

"It's the truth," Ariel said, standing with the orange suit around her ankles like a newly shed skin. She was remarkably dry. But you could see the stark contrast between her sea-pruned face and her tan hands. "He would have rammed us if we hadn't taken refuge against the rocks."

Radcliffe ran a hand through his dark curls. "But how did he crash the boat?"

I bent over and pulled my handgun from the pocket of the life vest. When I straightened up, I was nearly overcome by dizziness. "I distracted him."

"You wouldn't have a blanket or some hot coffee would you?" Ariel said.

"Of course. Sorry!"

He ducked down the stairs to the cabin. Ariel sat beside me and took hold of my free hand.

"Careful," I said. "My fingers are starting to burn. But that's a good thing."

Andrew returned with two expensive-looking wool blankets woven in a Southwestern motif. He handed one to Ariel, who, instead of taking it for herself, wrapped it around my shoulders. She tousled my damp hair and gave Radcliffe the side-eye. "What about a towel?"

"Right!"

Less than a minute later he returned with towels and a thermos. It contained tea, he said. All I cared about was that it was hot.

The constable tried asking a couple more times what had precipitated Crowley's attack on us, but Ariel was unable to offer him a satisfying answer.

"Thank God you heard our signal," she said, trying to move him off the subject.

His chest swelled visibly now that she'd given him the chance to recount his heroism. "Yes, well. I was at home—we live out on John's Point, my family and I—and I heard sort of a sharp crack, and I said to Penny, 'Gee, that sounds like a gunshot. Doesn't it? I wonder if someone is out at Calderwood Ledge shooting gulls. Or maybe they're hunting sea ducks.' It wasn't much later that I heard Mike's signal. I knew it was you because you'd just taught it to me. Plus I'd been looking for you earlier because . . .'"

His cheeks flushed apple red again.

I blew on the steaming cup of tea. "Because what?"

"Here, I thought you'd missed all the excitement today. The hermit came to town!"

"Blake Markman rowed over to Maquoit?" Ariel said.

"I know! It was a real shock. I'd glimpsed him over on Stormalong with his sheep, of course, and he'd always looked like a deranged character. So I was surprised that he was dressed in normal clothes and clean and well-spoken. He still had that rat's nest of a beard but—"

"Andrew," I said, urging him to the point.

"He was looking for Ariel. He said he'd

been waiting all morning at her house. He had something he wanted to give her, he said."

"What was it?"

"He wouldn't tell us. Anyway, I thought you should know, Mike, so I asked if anyone had seen you since you came back from Dennettsville, and Sam Graffam said you'd come in the store. Chum was there, and he said you seemed agitated when he told you Ariel had gone out with Kenneth in the *Sea Hag*. Long story short—"

"Too late for that," I breathed into my mug.

"Long story short, when I heard the signal, I put it all together—or partly together—and decided I should take the *Penny* out here ASAP. I'm glad now I hadn't put it up for the winter like I'd been planning."

"We're glad, too," said Ariel. "We owe you our lives, Andrew."

He blushed again. "Gee."

I unlaced my Bean boots and dumped out the water, then wrung out my woolen socks. After I'd put my damp footwear back on, I made a show of dropping the blanket and rising to my feet.

Ariel glowered at me. "Mike, you need to sit down."

"I'm fine."

"What is it about men needing to prove how tough they are?"

I borrowed Radcliffe's binoculars to scan the

surface of the ocean, but there was no sign of Crowley, alive or dead.

Radcliffe raised a hand to an ear. "Do you hear that?"

I became aware of a distant hum.

"It sounds like a big boat," said Radcliffe. "Not the ferry. Not the *Star of the Sea* either. It could be the Coast Guard."

Ariel said, "It's getting louder."

"I know who it is," I said. "It's reinforcements."

45

Once we had gotten clear of the ledge, Radcliffe raised his sails. Ariel assisted him. My only goal was to warm up and conserve energy. The slow rising of my core temperature had brought on all sorts of aches and pains, and my thoughts were as dull as butter knives.

Using Andrew's binoculars, I saw that one of the Maine Marine Patrol's high-speed *Protector*s had docked at the end of the wharf where the ferry and the *Star of the Sea* usually tied up. I spotted two marine wardens, a man and a woman, in their green coats, khaki shirts and olive pants, hanging out on the boat. The other officers who had come with them must have hurried off into town.

"We need to radio them," I said. "We need to let them know about the *Sea Hag*."

"Crowley can't possibly be alive," said Ariel.

"We can't presume anything."

Andrew handed me his radio. I hailed the *Protector* and got its captain on the horn.

Her name was Jankowski, and we had worked a few cases together when we'd both been stationed on the Midcoast. Her rank, marine patrol specialist, was an odd designation for the commanding officer of the vessel, in my opinion.

"Fancy sailboat, Bowditch! Were you out on a Maquoit Island sunrise cruise?"

"I wish. Do you see that ledge out there in the outer harbor?"

"Calderwood? What about it?"

"There's a lobsterboat wrecked against the west side. It's the *Sea Hag*."

"Nat Pillsbury's boat?"

"Nat wasn't on board. His sternman, Kenneth Crowley, was at the helm. He misjudged his position relative to the rocks. We saw him go into the water without a PFD. We searched for him, but his body never resurfaced."

"Fuck."

I trained the binoculars on the dock as Jankowski started her boat's twin 225-horsepower engines. Even from a distance, I could feel the roar inside the ribbed vault of my chest. It took less than a minute for the wardens to swing the craft around and accelerate off across the harbor, leaving a wake that had us all staggering like drunks when it hit the side of the *Lucky Penny*.

The sailboat passed the breakwater and entered the inner harbor.

As we got near enough to the wharf to see the starfish stuck to the pilings, Andrew engaged his cruising motor. He brought the *Lucky Penny* alongside one of the slips that visiting boats used to tie up at the dock.

A plane came buzzing in overhead from the southwest. "Is that your friend?" Ariel asked.

I squinted up at the gleaming white underbelly. "That's a Beechcraft. Charley Stevens flies a Cessna."

She peered at the airplane from beneath her flattened palm. "Looks like they're coming around for a landing. Who do you think it is?"

"Your competitors. It looks you're not the only journalist on Maquoit anymore."

"And you're not the only law enforcement officer."

I had to use the handrail to drag my sorry self up to the main wharf. No pickups or utility vehicles were parked on the wooden boards or in the gravel lot. I wondered whom DeFord had recruited to provide transportation.

I would need to pass along the drugs and drug paraphernalia I'd found in Hiram's house to Klesko, presuming the detective was on the island. But I doubted that the state police would recommend the DA prosecute Reed for possession. The district attorney would be better off pursuing the Washburns, who had dealt Hiram the dose that nearly killed him—perhaps had been intended to kill him.

Ariel's previously waterlogged face had regained its usual healthy glow. "Now what?"

We were both without phones. I could have borrowed Andrew's, but I had wanted to delay my moment of reckoning with Captain DeFord as long as I could.

I said, "The whole island is going to hear the *Sea Hag* was wrecked over the VHF radio. People are going to want to help out with the search."

"I mean what do *we* do?"

"I could use some dry clothes and a gallon of coffee."

"I was thinking brandy."

"The only brandy you're going to find on this island is Allen's coffee brandy."

"I've never tried it."

I took her arm, as much for physical support as out of friendliness. "We'll need to remedy that. You won't understand Maine until you've given it a taste."

I stopped at the Datsun to grab a change of clothing. I had to remove everything from my pockets. My wet wallet. My knife. And a flimsy piece of paper that took me a moment to recognize as the list Radcliffe had given me.

The constable tagged along behind us in full puppy-dog mode all the way to the store. I believe he was torn between wanting to remain at the dock in case the *Protector* returned with Crowley's drowned body and thinking he should call his wife to boast of his heroics. In the end curiosity got the best of him and he followed us to Graffam's.

Sam was sitting at the picnic table with a can of Moxie, talking with the store's perennial fixture Chum McNulty. They hadn't heard the news about the *Sea Hag* yet. I decided not to tell them.

Graffam rose from the bench. "There you are! Your colleagues are looking high and low for you, Warden."

"I'm sure they are."

"They seemed none too happy that you weren't at the dock to meet them."

"Where's my dinghy?" the old man asked.

"I'll reimburse you for that boat, Chum. Can I use your office to change my clothes, Sam?"

His smile mingled friendliness and mild ridicule. "Did you fall into the drink?"

"You could say that." I crossed to the coffee machine and filled two twenty-ounce cups. "Any idea where my colleagues went?"

"Gull Cottage, I heard," said Graffam.

Ariel frowned. She didn't seem to relish the idea of law enforcement officers ransacking her rented house. "Did Jenny Pillsbury go with them?"

"She and Nat went over to Hiram's," said Graffam.

Chum said again, "What happened to my dinghy?"

Ariel was leaning on the counter, examining the shelves of liquor bottles behind the register.

"How much for one of these pints of Allen's coffee brandy?"

Graffam rose to make the sale. "Six forty-nine."

Chum McNulty roused himself from thoughts of his dinghy. "In my day we called it 'liquid panty remover'!"

"Ignore that fossil," Graffam said.

The VHF radio crackled in the back room just after I'd changed into my dry clothing. It was my cue to leave.

Radcliffe remained inside the store while Ariel and I stepped outside to enjoy the warmth of the sun. I downed one entire cup of coffee in five gulps and tossed the cup into the waste barrel beside the door.

"Do you want to drive down to the cottage?" asked Ariel.

"I should go give the death notification to Martha. She and her sister are Crowley's closest next of kin on the island. I would guess she's still at Hiram's house."

Ariel let out a groan. "I can't deal with Jenny Pillsbury again. Or her husband." Ariel took a nip from the liquor bottle. "God, this is disgusting."

Nevertheless she took another drink.

I remembered the wet piece of paper in my pocket. Carefully, because I feared it would shred, I unfolded the list of hunters that Radcliffe had given me. I had thought the names matched those Harmon had provided, but now I spotted one significant discrepancy.

"How did I not see it?"

"What?"

"I just realized who killed Miranda, and I think I even know why."

She waited for me to say more, but not for long. "Are you going to tell me?"

"I need a confession. There's not enough evidence to convict without one. I'm going to need to find a phone first. Maybe I can borrow Radcliffe's."

"A confession from *who?*" Her voice was sharp with anger and frustration.

"Someone with an ironclad alibi."

46

Jenny Pillsbury answered the door. The tall, dark-eyed woman flinched visibly when she saw me standing alone on Hiram Reed's porch. She had changed out of the ill-fitting clothes she had been wearing behind the counter of the store that morning. She was now dressed in a silver turtleneck under a gray denim jacket and tight jeans that showed off the length of her legs.

"Are you here about Kenneth?" she said with genuine alarm. "We heard about the *Sea Hag* over the VHF. Nat ran off to join the search. Do you know what happened? We heard Kenneth was taking that Evans woman out in the *Hag* with him. What did that bitch make him do?"

I kept my tone level. "Is Martha here?"

"I sent her home to get some sleep. Why are you asking for her?" She kept her arm locked like a gate across the doorway. "You didn't answer my question about Kenneth."

Withholding the news violated just about every principle I stood for. Yet keeping Jenny in the dark until I'd talked with Hiram was my only chance to hear the truth spoken out loud. Stacey had warned me that the job would compromise me in ways I wouldn't like.

"I need to speak to Hiram, Jenny. It's important."

"Why won't you tell me what you know about Kenneth? He's dead, isn't he?"

"I'm going upstairs." I moved forward thinking she would remove her arm.

But the gate remained locked. "Like hell you are! Hiram's in no shape to answer your questions. Why are you even bothering him when Kenneth is missing?"

"Here's the thing. We both know that this isn't your house and you have no right to keep me out."

She'd closed her mouth so tight I couldn't see her lips. Then she said, "I'm going to call Harmon."

"This house isn't his either. It belongs to his son. As the homeowner, Hiram can tell me to leave. But that would require us talking."

Her obstructive arm didn't budge.

I tried again, "An assistant attorney general arrived on the island this morning, and I'm pretty sure she can help me obtain a warrant to search this place for more drugs, if that's the route you prefer we pursue. If we find more than six grams of heroin, we can charge him with trafficking. That's a Class A crime punishable by up to thirty years in prison."

Jenny Pillsbury flashed some of the hatred she'd shown Ariel. "You are such an asshole."

I stepped past her into the cluttered first floor of Hiram's house.

Someone had been busy cleaning up since my last visit. The dishes had been washed and set to dry in a rack. The open windows had aired out some of the stench. But once again, it was the impressive deer mount that drew my attention.

"Please don't say anything about Kenneth or the *Hag* to Hiram," she said. "I'm worried he'll slash his wrists."

Exhausted and sore, I trudged up the stairs.

Jenny followed close behind. "You smell like you took a swim in your clothes."

In the hallway, she slipped past me. This time, she used her whole body to keep me from entering the bedroom.

"Hiram, that warden is here to see you. I told him you were sleeping—"

"I wish I could sleep."

"Do you want me to tell him to come back later? I said you're really not up to seeing visitors."

I raised my voice to be heard in the next room. "I saved your life, Reed. You owe me an audience."

"Jesus Christ!"

"It won't take long," I said loudly. "I'm leaving the island in a few hours."

"Let him in, Jenny."

She pressed her back to the cracked drywall to

allow me passage. The bedroom had that familiar odor of vomit and urine. Hiram's caretakers had changed his bedclothes and gotten him into a pair of sweatpants and a T-shirt.

His complexion was sallow beneath his whiskers. His muscle tone had seemingly vanished overnight. He looked less like a wolverine now than a luckless ape that some mad scientist had used to test electroshock therapy.

Jenny took up a protective position beside the bed. "You can't make me leave unless Hiram says so."

"Why would I want you to leave? What I have to say concerns the both of you."

I pulled out the wooden chair his mother had used and had a seat. I rested my left hand on my knee. I kept my right hand hidden in my coat pocket and pressed record on Radcliffe's smartphone. Assistant Attorney General Marshall would need to be satisfied with a voice recording for the confession.

"This has been a hell of a few days," I began.

Reed scratched his hairy knuckles. "You think?"

"Miranda Evans really set this island on its head when she arrived. It's amazing to think one woman could cause so much chaos, but she seemed to have a rare gift for upsetting the lives of others."

"My husband told me he was fucking her," said

448

Jenny, crossing her arms. "I've forgiven him."

"Thank you for that, Jenny, but I'm talking to Hiram at the moment."

The poor man closed his eyes as if in extreme pain. "Can you say whatever you need to say and leave me alone?"

"I need to establish a few facts first. Correct me if I am wrong. Miranda Evans showed up on Maquoit, pretending to be her rich and famous sister, Ariel, and she started throwing wild parties at her rental cottage. She had cases of expensive wine. Maybe she had something even more exotic. Cocaine by the bagful."

"When I found out about the coke, I was going to evict her from the cottage," said Jenny.

"But you didn't evict her. Maybe your husband dissuaded you."

"My marriage is none of your business."

"In this case it is. And the death of Miranda Evans is definitely my business. I came to Maquoit because I got a call from your constable that Miranda was shot by a hunter who mistook her for a deer. Radcliffe called it a 'horrible, horrible accident.' Is that what you'd call it, Hiram—an accident?"

"I suppose."

"You don't think someone shot her deliberately?"

"How would I know? Why are you asking me?"

"I wanted to give you the chance to state what happened for the record."

"I was in town all morning. Ask Jenny. She saw me. Lots of folks did."

"That's right," added Jenny Pillsbury. "Hiram and I both have alibis."

"But your husband doesn't."

"Nat didn't kill that bitch! He says he fucking loved her. The idiot thought she wanted to run away with him."

I'd had the hardest time getting Ariel to go back to her cottage. I could only imagine what she would have given to be one of the many flies buzzing about the room. In time the recording would become public, and the journalist could hear it all for herself.

"Miranda Evans was the one who supplied you with cocaine, Hiram. Isn't that correct?"

"So what if she did?"

"Because you'd been sober for years, ever since your brother overdosed. Beryl McCloud told me that. She didn't mean to violate your anonymity, so don't be mad at her. For a long time you've been afraid that if you started using *anything* again—alcohol, pot, pills—you'd be back to heroin in no time."

He struggled to lift himself from the sweat-stained pillows. "Are you saying I killed the girl who was giving me free drugs?"

"That's exactly what I'm saying."

"Why?"

"He couldn't have done it," Jenny said. "Hiram was in town when that woman was killed. Ask anyone."

I leaned back in the chair. "You two have known each other since you were kids. You went to school together."

"What does that have to do with anything?" she said.

"It's a fucking one-room schoolhouse," he said.

"Beryl said something else I found interesting," I said calmly. "We were talking about the feud between the Reeds and the Washburns, and she said, 'It's not like the Montagues and the Capulets.' And I thought, 'Why would she mention *Romeo and Juliet*?' But that's who you two were when you were teenagers, I think. You were star-crossed lovers whose families were fighting and who could never be together."

"She's married to my best friend!" Hiram protested.

But Jenny was smarter than he was. "He's trying to trap you, Hiram. Don't say anything more."

I was counting on Reed's belligerence to assist me, and he didn't disappoint. "If what you're saying is true, then why the fuck would I want Miranda Evans dead?"

Jenny reached for his hand but he wouldn't give it to her. "Hiram, please . . ."

"If Nat had run off with Miranda, then Jenny and I could have—"

Her voice broke. "Please don't say anything else! Not without a lawyer."

Hiram managed a smug grin. "When Miranda died, it guaranteed that Nat would stay here with Jenny and Ava."

"Exactly," I said.

A tear slid down her cheek.

I leaned forward again. "I suspect you weren't entirely in your right mind when you did it, Hiram. You were probably drunk and coked up. Still, it was a romantic gesture—if you can call murdering a woman in cold blood a romantic gesture."

A vehicle pulled up outside. Was it Klesko? DeFord? Both?

"You sacrificed your own happiness to save the woman you loved from losing the man *she* loved. Because you do love him, don't you, Jenny? You love Nat with all your heart and soul, and you were terrified that he was going to abandon you and your baby."

Her eyes had begun to twitch. She was desperately trying to think her way out of this predicament.

Hiram tried to swing his legs off the bed to come to her defense, but he was too weak to stand. "Leave her alone! She had nothing to do with it!"

"Stop," she said with a whimper. "Please stop."

"I believe you, Hiram. I believe that Jenny had no idea that you'd shot Miranda Evans, not until you rolled onto the scene outside Gull Cottage and she saw your face. It was then she realized what you'd done for her. And to protect you, she gave you an alibi. She volunteered that you'd been in the village at the time Miranda was shot. She swore up and down to it until other people began questioning their recollections. 'Maybe Hiram had been at Graffam's after all.'"

"You have no proof," Jenny said, "you have no proof of any of this."

"No, but I can always interview the breakfast club and everyone else who was at the store that morning. I can ask them specifics about what time Hiram came in. Chum McNulty already mentioned that he hadn't seen Hiram there for ages. I don't expect your alibi will hold up very long."

Hiram collapsed against the pillows.

"The thing is," I said, "I think you could have gotten away with this if you'd just pretended you'd shot Miranda while you were hunting. That it was an act of negligence. You might have paid a fine and done time in jail. Maybe you would have confessed if Crowley hadn't confused everything."

"Don't say a word, Hiram!"

"Nat, Jenny, and Kenneth have been protecting

you since I got to the island. Your father, too, although I don't think he knew at first. He had his suspicions, but he wasn't sure. Not until you overdosed. And now that stupid kid is dead because your family and friends tried to protect you."

"What are you talking about?" said Hiram. "Jenny, what's he saying?"

She hissed at me, "You fucking asshole. You son of a bitch."

Hiram pressed his hands flat against his temples as if his skull had begun to shrink. "I don't understand what's going on here."

"Not another word, Hiram. If you ever cared for me, not another word."

"I think you should go outside now, Jenny," I said. "There are some men out there waiting to take your statement. For the sake of your family, I would recommend being honest this time. And I would tell Nat to come clean, too."

"Is this another of your tricks?"

"Look out the window."

She stormed past me and yanked aside one of the dusty curtains. "Why won't people leave us alone out here?"

"Because you're part of the world," I said.

"I don't even know what that means."

But I had finally managed to instill fear in her hardened heart. Fear of losing her husband. Fear of losing her freedom. Fear of losing her child.

And I despised myself for having had to do it. Her footsteps on the stairs were hammer blows driving nails into my flesh.

Hiram began to blink rapidly. "Did something bad happen to Kenneth?"

"He's dead, Hiram. He died trying to kill Ariel Evans and me. He crashed Nat's boat against Calderwood Ledge and drowned."

"How? Why?"

"Crowley thought it was the only way to protect you. It was desperate and childish. He didn't really have a plan when he took Ariel out. Maybe he thought he could push her overboard and somehow explain it away as an accident. He hadn't thought ahead to how he was going to get rid of me."

Hiram sobbed into his hands. "What have I done?"

"You know what you did, Hiram. But you have to admit it."

He kept sobbing.

"Confessing is the only way you can protect Nat and Jenny now."

He raised his hairy face. "OK."

I removed Radcliffe's phone from my pocket. Then I took a card from my wallet and read the sentences on it word for word, apprising him of his rights. I spoke into the microphone, establishing the time, date, who I was, where I was, and who I was interviewing.

Finally, I asked, "Hiram Reed, did you shoot Miranda Evans on the morning of November second outside Gull Cottage?"

"Yes."

"Did you shoot Miranda Evans with the intent to kill her?"

"Yes."

I felt empty inside. There was no sense of completion. No relief. I paused to take a breath while Hiram Reed, sobbing uncontrollably, was set upon by flesh-tearing harpies only he could see.

47

Half an hour later, we were standing on Hiram's porch, Captain DeFord, Assistant Attorney General Marshall, and me. I had just played them the recording of Reed's confession—for the third time.

"Well?"

"His defense attorney is going to say you coerced him," said the prosecutor, cutting me with her blue eyes. "He's going to say Reed's statement was made under duress."

"Because he was going through withdrawal?"

"I'd cite the Fifth Amendment if I were defending him." As a young woman, Danica Marshall had been crowned Miss Maine, and she was still striking in her forties, but she had exercised herself to gauntness since last I'd seen her.

"You should've had a veteran officer in there with you," said DeFord.

If you could see that Marshall had been a teenage beauty queen, you could also see that John DeFord had been a high school athlete who excelled at every sport. He had a handsome, unwrinkled face, and the flat stomach I hoped to have when I hit my fifties. Not for nothing was he nicknamed Jock.

"Hiram is going to sign a statement," I said. "The only thing that matters to him now is protecting Jenny and Nat."

The prosecutor remained unappeased. "Even if he does sign, you most likely lost me any chance of bringing an indictment against the woman or her husband."

"Klesko said she confessed to him," said DeFord.

The news caught Marshall off guard. "When?"

"He called me a few minutes ago from her house. He said she confessed to having obstructed the investigation. Mike seems to have put the fear of God into her."

Marshall refused to show any satisfaction. She seemed more interested in seeing me stumble than in seeing her case come together. She'd been unhappy for as long as I'd known her.

"Any word from the Marine Patrol?" I asked.

"They haven't recovered the body yet," said DeFord. "But they've got another vessel on the way. The Coast Guard is sending a Response Boat down from Southwest Harbor and another one over from Rockland. Nat Pillsbury and nearly all of the island fishermen have gone out looking, as well. Kenneth Crowley was well liked. It's a good thing you're leaving, Mike. I don't think the locals believe your version of what happened. Islanders may hate one another, but it's always them against the world when outsiders show up."

"What about Ariel Evans?" asked AAG Marshall. "Is she going back with us, too? I don't want to have to deal with another hunting homicide tomorrow."

"Unfortunately, we can't make her leave," said the captain.

This time, I was the one caught off guard. "You mean she's staying?"

DeFord shrugged. "She says that if she could handle neo-Nazis, she can handle a few pissed-off Maine lobstermen."

"She's never dealt with lobstermen before." I reached into my pocket for the keys to the Datsun. "I'm going to talk with her."

"Try not to run over any reporters," Marshall said. "The island is teeming with them."

DeFord called after me, "Tomorrow in my office, Mike. We have a lot to discuss about the quality of your decision making over the past few days. And your 'issues' with procedure and communication."

I paused in midstride. "Won't we be riding back together to the mainland?"

"You're getting a private flight. Charley Stevens is flying out here to pick you up. I told him there was no need, but you know how incorrigible that old man is."

"Yes, I do."

It was the best news I'd gotten on this other-wise horrible day.

The last time I saw Harmon Reed, he was sitting behind the wheel of his fifty-thousand-dollar truck with his windows rolled up. He had parked down the street from Hiram's house to watch the troopers bring his son in chains to the boat. I didn't get the best look at the old man, but he seemed to have aged ten years in a single morning.

One son dead, the other headed to prison. His only daughter estranged. Reed was like one of those monarchs who lives too long and spends his final days watching his dynasty dribble away like sand through his grasping fingers.

I drove the banged-up Datsun for the last time through the village. Bishop's Wharf seemed to be the center of the action. Trucks were parked in the lot, with clusters of islanders talking among themselves, dogs running around.

I spotted a woman taking photographs with a camera that had a lens longer than my forearm. A man dressed as if for an arctic expedition, taking notes. A television reporter interviewing Graffam outside his store while a cameraman recorded the conversation.

Sam must have run back to his house to put on his Sunday best: new cargo shorts and a T-shirt with the slogan HUG DEALER. As I drove past,

Graffam scowled at me, causing the camera guy to spin around to film the source of the shop-keeper's displeasure.

I won't be sorry to leave Maquoit.

Then a squadron of hooded mergansers took off from one of the unseen ponds in the marsh, their wings catching the afternoon light. I had spent three days on the island and seen almost none of it, not the trails along the east-side cliffs, not the shipwrecks on the southern beaches, not even the grand summer cottages of Marsh Harbor. The human violence that had occurred on Maquoit had obscured the natural beauty of the place as much as the fog had. I felt as if I were seeing the island now for the first time.

Despite it being the first sunny day since Ariel had arrived on Maquoit, she had closed all her curtains. She had also posted a sign on the door:

I AM GRIEVING FOR MY SISTER
PLEASE GIVE ME THE PRIVACY TO DO SO

The words struck me as disingenuous. Miranda's murder had been a real blow to Ariel, but I also knew that it was a death foretold. How many years had the older sister waited for a call from some hospital saying her sister had overdosed or crashed her car or been strangled by one of the dangerous men she had loved?

This plea for sympathy was no more than the DO NOT DISTURB sign you hang outside your hotel room.

I rapped at the door. "Ariel? It's Mike!"

She peeled back a curtain and then released the lock and let me in. I had caught her in the middle of a conversation on her cell phone. She held up a finger to indicate that I needed to give her a minute.

Her luggage was packed and waiting. I wondered if she had reconsidered her decision to remain on Maquoit.

"I don't want it to be a conventional memoir," she told the person on the other end. "Obviously my relationship with Miranda will be the through line. But I need to work in the island, too. Blake Markman will play a major role—he says he's ready for his story to be told—and it plays so well off Miranda's own compulsion for concealment. These islands are where people come who wish to hide from humanity. It's like some tragic retreat for those who can't handle the modern world."

She pretended to listen to the man droning on the other end.

She had showered and washed and dried her hair and put on makeup and clothes I hadn't seen before—a silk shirt in ivory, black pants, and flats—that made her look less like a field correspondent and more like a bestselling author from Manhattan.

"The focus will definitely be on Miranda and me," she broke in. "Don't worry about that. Someone tried to kill me this morning. I'm not going to leave that part out. I haven't had a chance to sit down yet and begin mapping out the structure, but you can pitch it as 'a story written in heart's blood.' "

She paused to listen to the drone again.

"Great! I think we're both on the same page, then. I'll work up some notes and send them to you. . . . No, I have email here. There's even this hunky game-warden investigator who plays a role in the story. . . . No, he's not my love interest! Believe me, Miranda had sex enough for the two of us. Listen, someone's at the door. I'll send you my notes and we can talk later."

She ended the call with a roll of her eyes. "My agent."

"You plan on writing about me?"

"How could I not? You saved my life out there this morning."

"My work requires that I don't seek out the spotlight, Ariel. As it is, I doubt I'll ever be able to go undercover in the state of Maine. Too many bad guys have heard of me."

"Maybe you should learn to enjoy the fame. The stuff I found online about your life—"

"I'm still going to pass."

"I'm going to have to include you, though. There's no avoiding it. I'd prefer to do it with your cooperation."

"You're a brilliant writer. You'll find a work-around." Every muscle in my body was sore from shivering so hard earlier. "I'm here to tell you that Hiram Reed confessed to killing Miranda. I got it all on tape."

"How? Why?"

"Maybe you should have a seat."

"I don't need to have a seat," she snapped. "Tell me what happened."

"Well, I'm going to have a seat because I'm exhausted and probably still a little hypo-thermic." I collapsed in the armchair. "I noticed your luggage is packed. Does that mean you're going home?"

She perched herself on the couch. "Just trading spaces. Jenny Pillsbury doesn't want me here so I've taken a room at the Wight House. How is that place?"

"Quiet."

"Enough stalling. Tell me everything."

Ariel interrupted me constantly as I told her about Hiram and Jenny. Midway through my story, she went to fetch the Scotch bottle from the kitchen, but I refused her offer of a drink. Eventually, I couldn't take any more questions. I used the armchair to climb to my feet. Every joint in my body had ossified.

"Where are you going? We're not done here."

"A plane is coming to pick me up. I'm glad to see that you're holding up all right, Ariel. I worry about you."

Her eyes hardened. "I've reported from combat zones. I've been interrogated by Aryan extremists. I've been in tougher spots."

"I just meant that I care how you're doing."

"I'm sorry. I'm so used to men patronizing me and depreciating my accomplishments. You never did that. I hope your girlfriend appreciates how lucky she is. You're a keeper, Mike Bowditch."

I let that one go. "What did Blake Markman come all the way over here to give you? It must have been something big if he was willing to set foot on Maquoit for the first time in ages."

She laughed that musical laugh. "So it was insatiable curiosity that really brought you here to see me! I should have known. Hang on a minute, and I'll go get it."

A moment later she returned with a leather-bound journal and the ghost of a smile. "The hermit's diary. Miranda asked to read it, but she never got the chance."

"I was hoping it was going to be your sister's missing phone. Maybe Hiram threw it into the sea along with his hunting rifle. It could be we'll never know what happened to it."

She opened a bookmarked page to show me

a drawing that Miranda had done of Markman in the journal, an exquisite portrait. With a few pencil strokes, she had captured not just the man's likeness but something of his soul. In its brilliance it reminded me of sketches I'd seen by Rembrandt in the Museum of Fine Arts in Boston when my college girlfriend had dragged me there.

"Mike, this is more than an account of Blake Markman's life on Stormalong," Ariel said in a hushed voice. "It's his confession. He really was criminally responsible for the death of his wife."

"Why did he choose to entrust this with you?"

"He confused me for my sister, I think. He doesn't realize how much more mercenary and self-promoting I am than Miranda ever was. She always had the kinder, more generous spirit. In a way, it's fitting that people still can't recognize the differences between us."

48

Joy Juno wanted to punch me in the face. "Go fuck yourself."

I had met her in Blackington's yard to return the totaled Datsun. The muscular woman stood with her legs braced and her fists clenched. I had nabbed some badass poachers in my career— dangerous men who had done time in prison— but few of them had projected such an attitude of outright hostility toward me.

"The state will pay to replace Mr. Blackington's truck," I said in the same voice I might have used to soothe a vicious dog. "I'll make sure he gets top dollar. He's going to come out of this ahead."

I held out the keys to the Datsun.

She slapped them to the ground. "I don't give a shit about the truck. You killed Kenneth Crowley."

"That's not technically true. He died trying to kill Ariel and me."

"So you say, but I'm hearing different things."

Joy's own truck was parked along the road, and Beryl McCloud was again in the passenger seat. The schoolteacher hadn't come out to speak with me. Through the grimy windshield her face appeared wan, her eyes vacant, her hair limp. She looked like a person whose spirit had been shattered, and I remembered that she had considered Hiram Reed a friend.

"Are you OK, Beryl?" I asked.

"She's grieving, asshole," Joy said. "And so am I. We were in AA together, Hiram and me. Do you even know how many lives you've destroyed out here? Jenny and Nat. Harmon and Martha. Not to mention everyone who cared for Kenneth. Meanwhile the Washburns are laughing their asses off. In a week those fascists are going to be running this island. You wait and see."

"You could try standing up to them, all of you together."

She rolled her eyes halfway into her skull. "I can't believe I ever thought you were a cool guy."

"Well, I'm leaving now, and the only way I'll be back is if something happens to Ariel Evans. You don't want to see what happens if I get word that she's been hurt—or worse."

Joy raised a fist to the ready position. "Are you threatening me?"

"I'm not singling you out, Joy. I'm threatening everyone on Maquoit."

"I hope your plane crashes."

She stormed over to her truck, got in, and slammed the door. She began declaiming to Beryl. The sound was muffled but most police officers are experts at reading lips, especially with regard to certain single-syllable Anglo-Saxon words.

After a minute, I hitched my rucksack over my shoulder and continued on toward the airstrip. Dead leaves were caught in the thorns of the barberry bushes along the road. I passed a boarded-up cottage. In their hunger, the deer had devoured an ornamental rhododendron in its front yard. The plant wouldn't kill the animals, but nor would it nourish them. It was like a person trying to subsist on a diet of copy paper.

A blue pickup came barreling up the road behind me. I didn't recognize it at first, Then I realized it was Hiram Reed's truck. Steve Klesko was behind the wheel.

"I was afraid I missed you," he said through the open window. His face seemed friendly, but he was wearing sunglasses so I couldn't be entirely certain of his intentions.

"Did you commandeer this?"

"More like borrowed. Hiram won't miss it, I figured. Not in his current condition and circumstances. Do you want a lift up to the airfield?"

With a laugh, I threw my gear into the truck bed and climbed in beside him.

"You did good, Mike." Klesko shifted into first gear. "The brass will give you shit because you didn't follow all the procedures, but you got a confession. Marshall's worried it won't stand up, but my gut tells me Hiram is done fighting. I wouldn't recommend you do any of this again, though."

"No lone wolves, right?"

"No lone wolves."

"Listen, Steve, something's been weighing on me. I owe you an apology. You were right that I should have trusted you from the start. You were a good partner, but I was so afraid of screwing up the case that I wouldn't let you help me. I'm sorry about that."

He lifted his sunglasses so that they rested on the top of his thick dark hair. He stared hard into my eyes. "Apologies are just words."

"True."

"When we're both back in Bangor, I need you to do something if you want to make this right."

"OK?"

"Buy me a beer at Paddy Murphy's."

"It's a deal."

He stopped the pickup at the edge of the airstrip and let the engine idle. We shook hands, then I watched the truck disappear down the hill. It had been a long time since I'd made a friend.

Two planes were parked along the gravel runway. One was the Beechcraft I had seen earlier. The second was an elegant little Cirrus. The two charter pilots were hanging out in the windbreak of the Beechcraft's fuselage. They glanced at me as if unsure whether I was one of their passengers. Then they decided they didn't recognize me and returned to their conversation. I checked my watch and saw that it was 3:57 p.m. Charley Stevens was never late.

Exactly three minutes later, I noticed the charter pilots glancing skyward. I peered to the north and saw a speck that I might have mistaken for a seabird until the whine of the engine distinguished itself above the breeze.

As always, Charley landed the Cessna into the wind. He engaged his flaps to assist in braking. The single propeller chopped the air as he turned the red-and-white aircraft around so that it could take off into the wind as well.

The pilot's door popped open and the old man swung like a gibbon from the strut. He advanced toward me with his strong hand outstretched. After we shook, he clapped me hard between the shoulder blades.

"I heard you nearly drowned, young feller."

"I just got a little wet is all."

He laughed at that. "So I just got off the horn with the colonel. Congratulations on a job well done."

"I don't think Captain DeFord agrees that I did so well."

"You caught the killer, didn't you?"

"It would have been better if Crowley hadn't died. He was a stupid kid, trying to protect his friend."

"You can't blame yourself for another man's boneheadedness."

"Tell that to the islanders. All I know is I'm ready to leave Maquoit. I hope I never come back here."

Charley chuckled deep in his throat as if recalling a favorite joke.

"What's so funny?"

"The only people worse at predicting the future than the elderly are the young."

The takeoff was so smooth I couldn't identify the exact instant we left the ground. Above the treetops the northeast wind began fighting us, but Charley seemed to know how to deal with every atmospheric condition. The summits of Mount Desert Island glowed in the distance as if cast in gold.

I spoke through my headset, "Would you mind taking me around the island quickly?"

"I thought you disdained this place."

Charley banked the plane so that we began circling Maquoit clockwise. We passed first over the long harbor that ended in Dennettsville. But the Washburns were still out in their lobsterboats hauling their unauthorized traps or maybe even smuggling their illegal drugs. I remembered what Joy Juno had said about those outlaws taking over the island now that Harmon had become a shell of himself. Maybe it would happen, maybe it wouldn't. But I knew that men such as Eli and Rudyard lacked the willpower to restrain themselves. Their day of reckoning would come because it always did.

The Cessna paralleled the black cliffs along the eastern shore of the island. In the warm months, gulls and cormorants nested in the safety of the high crevices, and every outcropping was marbled white with their guano.

Lost in thought, I missed seeing Shipwreck Beach or the famous lighthouse, but I did catch a view of Stormalong and the hermit's sanctuary. Sheep scattered at the whine of our engine. What would become of Blake Markman now? Ariel said he'd confessed to having killed his wife, but how long would his newfound contrition last? Probably until two detectives from Los Angeles showed up to extradite him back home for trial. He would never see the inside of a jail cell, I predicted.

We turned to the northwest, and I had my first glimpse of the splendid Marsh Harbor mansions for which the island was famed.

The outer harbor was as full of boats as if a regatta were under way. Coast Guard Response Boats and the two Marine Patrol *Protector*s and a dozen lobsterboats were plumbing the depths for the island's lost son. I saw Andrew Radcliffe's ketch, the *Lucky Penny*, gliding among them.

Once more we were over the sea. Lines of

whitecaps angled out of the northeast in evenly spaced ridges that had an almost agricultural aspect. I shivered as I gazed upon the water for I knew that it was even colder than it appeared.

I had desired this last look of Maquoit from above because I knew that I would never set eyes on the island again and because I am prone to bouts of nostalgia so acute they are almost painful. I wanted to preserve this sight forever in my memory, knowing that time would inevitably blur the details. I wanted to hang on to what this place had been in my life: the site of my first hunting homicide investigation.

And I had solved it.

Although I had never met the Wights, I realized with a smile.

"About Stacey," Charley began.

My smile was short-lived. "I got an email from her the other night," I said over the intercom.

"Yes, I know. She called her mother after she sent it. They were both in tears."

"It was never what I wanted, Charley. I hope you know that."

"I do, son."

"You told me something a long time ago, when we first met. I think about it a lot. You said, 'If you live in the past, you just miss out on the present.'"

"That sounds like one of my pearls of wisdom."

Now it was his turn to go quiet. We didn't

speak again for the remainder of the short flight.

Only as we were coming in for a landing did he mutter, "Looks like you're not the only one with an investigative bent."

"What is it?"

"It's not a what. It's a who. I'm going to have to take my own medicine about not living in the past."

His body was blocking my view. The Hancock County–Bar Harbor Airport was small, and the runway was close to the road. The small terminal and the parking lot were within shouting distance of the place the Cessna finally came to a stop.

"I'll grab those bags of yours," my friend said with an air of sad resignation. "You go say hello."

Somehow he managed a smile that was altogether kind and genuine.

Mystified, I removed my headset and climbed out of the aircraft. I made a wide circuit of the still-rotating propeller. A powder-blue Ford Interceptor SUV was parked near the terminal. A short woman in a trooper's uniform stood beside the police vehicle. The mountains of Acadia National Park loomed behind her. Dani Tate had driven halfway across the state to meet my plane.

"Welcome back!" she shouted across the tarmac.

"It's good to be back!"

I caught sight of my shadowy reflection in the gleaming fuselage of the plane. How many days had I been on Maquoit? It seemed like weeks, even months. Long enough to recognize myself again.

AUTHOR'S NOTE

In writing this book I was helped by Richard Nelson's *Heart and Blood: Living with Deer in America*, a book that grows more topical every year. I also relied on *Blood on the Leaves: Real Hunting Accident Investigations—and Lessons in Hunter Safety* by Rod Slings, Mike Van Durme, and B. Keith Byers.

No book, of course, can substitute for first-hand experience. For that reason and for so many others, I am deeply grateful to Troy and Jeri Ripley for welcoming me into their home and sharing with a stranger the meaningful life and untimely death of their daughter Megan who was killed by a hunter in December of 2006. I continue to find inspiration in the Ripleys' courage, compassion, and commitment to toughening Maine's still inadequate laws pertaining to hunting homicides.

Lieutenant Dan Scott and Corporal John MacDonald, both of the Maine Warden Service, filled in many gaps in my knowledge. I hope they will forgive the great liberties I took in describing how a hunting homicide investigation is handled in Maine.

Also at the Maine Department of Inland Fisheries and Wildlife, thanks to biologists Judy

Camuso and Keel Kemper for sharing their stories of hapless islands dealing (or more often, not dealing) with too many deer.

Maquoit Island has little in common with its famous cousin, Monhegan, where over the course of twenty years and dozens of visits, I have learned a great deal about the secret lives of offshore communities. I won't violate any confidences by naming the people who told me their stories—with one exception. Thank you Matt Weber, lobsterman, craft brewer, and Monhegan constable: Matt, you are no Andrew Radcliffe.

Bruce Coffin, Portland police sergeant (retired), friend, and fellow crime writer, I appreciate your walking me through a figurative death scene.

Mapmaker Jane Crosen and designer Barbara Tedesco, thank you for helping to bring Maquoit to life.

To all the folks at Minotaur Books—especially Charlie Spicer, Andy Martin, Sarah Melnyk, Paul Hochman, and April Osborn—you have my deepest thanks.

Last but far from least, I want to thank my family: specifically Erin and Sander Van Otterloo for "Niceness," David Henderson for proofreading, and my wife, Kristen, who inspires and sustains me.

Center Point Large Print
600 Brooks Road / PO Box 1
Thorndike, ME 04986-0001 USA

(207) 568-3717

US & Canada:
1 800 929-9108
www.centerpointlargeprint.com